THE
SHADOW CABINET

DON'T MISS THE FIRST TWO BOOKS
IN THE SHADES OF LONDON SERIES:

The Name of the Star
The Madness Underneath

ALSO BY MAUREEN JOHNSON

13 Little Blue Envelopes
The Last Little Blue Envelope
Suite Scarlett
Scarlett Fever
Girl at Sea
Devilish
The Bermudez Triangle
The Key to the Golden Firebird

Vacations from Hell with Libba Bray, Cassandra Clare,
Claudia Gray and Sarah Mlynowski

Let It Snow with John Green and Lauren Myracle

THE

SHADOW
CABINET

THE SHADES OF LONDON,
BOOK THREE

maureen johnson

G. P. Putnam's Sons
An Imprint of Penguin Group (USA)

G. P. Putnam's Sons
Published by the Penguin Group
Penguin Group (USA) LLC
375 Hudson Street
New York, NY 10014

USA | Canada | UK | Ireland | Australia
New Zealand | India | South Africa | China
penguin.com
A Penguin Random House Company

Library of Congress Cataloging-in-Publication Data
Johnson, Maureen, 1973–
The shadow cabinet / Maureen Johnson.
pages cm—(Shades of London ; book 3)
Summary: "Rory, Callum and Boo are still reeling from a series of tragic
events, while new dangers lurk around the city from Jane and her nefarious
organization"—Provided by publisher.
[1. Boarding schools—Fiction. 2. Schools—Fiction. 3. Murder—Fiction. 4. Ghosts—
Fiction. 5. London (England)—Fiction. 6. England—Fiction.] I. Title.
PZ7.J634145Sh 2015 [Fic]—dc23 2014031153

Printed in the United States of America.
ISBN 978-0-399-25662-2
3 5 7 9 10 8 6 4 2

Design by Annie Ericsson and Marikka Tamura.
Text set in ITC New Baskerville Std.
The publisher does not have any control over and does not assume
any responsibility for third-party websites or their content.

For Zelda

DECEMBER 22, 1973
WEST LONDON

THE CURTAINS AT 16 HYSSOP CLOSE HADN'T BEEN OPENED all day. The neighbors all agreed—something wasn't right about the place anymore, not since the Smithfield-Wyatts had died and their twins now ruled the roost. The *people* that went in and out, for a start. Rock musicians. Actors. Old, bearded men in cloaks who the more suspicious locals thought might be poets. Worst of all were the gaggle of young people—all rough-looking, with long hair and ragged, garish clothing. It was the same group every time, coming in and out at all hours, laughing and chatting and flicking their cigarettes into everyone else's rosebushes. (*Were* they cigarettes?) And that girl who lived there—the one with her hair cut short and dyed the color of a London bus, the one who wore men's suits—who was *she?* Aside from up to no good.

The thing was, the twins were always so polite, and they never made any noise, really, so there was no cause to call the police. It wasn't a crime to have strange-looking characters come in and out all day long or not to open the curtains. But things went wrong on Hyssop Close now. There were power cuts that could never be explained and didn't affect neighboring streets. Windows cracked, and cats ran away.

Maybe it was a commune. Maybe it was a meeting place for student revolutionaries—those were springing up all over. Why, in New York, these kinds of student groups were taking up residence in the better neighborhoods and building bombs. One of them managed to blow up a house! It had been in the papers. Maybe number sixteen was full of bomb builders.

Whatever the case, something was wrong with that house, and the neighbors watched it closely, waiting for the curtains to move, trying to get a glimpse of what was inside . . .

Inside, the girl with the short hair dyed the color of a London bus was lighting candles in the main reception room. Her name was Jane Quaint. The group of kids who made the neighbors so wary were sitting on all the sofas and on the thick shag carpets. Jane made her way around the room with her lighter. Sid and Sadie insisted on candlelight, and lots of it. The candlelight was especially effective in this room because so much of the furniture was mirrored, cutting sharp traces of light through the velvety darkness. Blinding light or deepest shadow—this was a room of extremes in a house of extremes. One popular wag had described it as looking like a Victorian brothel on Mars.

As she made her way around, Jane examined the visitors' faces in the various reflections and pools of light: Michael, Domino, Prudence, Dinah, Johnny, Mick, Aileen, Badge, George, and Ruth. Jane knew them all so well. They were good kids, all special. Maybe not the brightest, generally, but she was fond of them.

"Where are Sid and Sadie?" Dinah asked.

Dinah was the youngest—only fifteen. Unlike Jane's, her red hair was natural, and her face was flecked all over with freckles.

"Coming," Jane said.

"What's going on tonight?"

The person asking was Mick—Mick of the beautiful long black hair and a face to match. Everyone was in love with Mick, and he knew it. This easy and widely available love made him presumptuous. He had the air of someone expecting to be told at any moment that he had royal blood and was in line for some minor crown in a far-off but green land.

"When Sid and Sadie are ready, they'll be down. When they want you to know what's going on, they'll tell you. Remember, you're lucky to be here."

Mick smiled and dared Jane with a flutter of his long eyelashes.

"We've been waiting *ages*."

"You've been waiting an hour. Be quiet and have a smoke or something."

"And what's all this for?"

He indicated an arrangement of red glass goblets on the mirrored table.

"You know better than to ask," Jane said. "When you need to know, you'll know."

"Sod that. Give us a drink."

"Did you all do as you were told?" Jane asked, ignoring this.

Murmurs of assent from around the room. Jane looked to each person to make sure.

"Did it matter how long we went in?" Aileen asked. "Only, the pigs come when you get in the river, even down by the beach. I just got in for a minute, but I washed my face and hands like you said."

"That should be fine," Jane said.

"We'll probably get dysentery," Mick added, half pushing himself from his spot on the rug. "All the blessed children will have naughty tummies from bathing in the Thames. Give us a *drink*, Jane."

"You'll keep your fast until they come down."

"I'm going to go up, see what's keeping them."

"You're going to see the back of my hand," Jane said.

The others watched this tiny dispute with wide-eyed amusement. These breaches of conduct didn't usually happen. Something about tonight was different, and everyone could feel it. Sid and Sadie had summoned the group, and a summons from them brought excitement. Jane understood this better than anyone.

Jane's life had been nothing before Sid and Sadie. She was a nobody, stuck in a northern town, working in a shop. Then one night the local menace had followed her across a moonlit field, attacked her, left her for dead. But Jane did not die. She survived the night and gained the gift. From then on, she could see them—the ones on the other side. Her old life was over. She got on a bus and went to London. That she had no money wasn't important to her. She lived in squats and ate thrown-away food from garbage bins and hung out at occult bookstores and read. Then, one summer's day, *they* walked into the bookshop Jane was in. Sid wore a silver suit with a red tie and had a hat cocked over his eye. Sadie was like a wood nymph in a flowing green silk dress and soft leather slippers. They looked like creatures from another, more perfect world. They smelled of night jasmine and patchouli and fine cigarettes. They looked at Jane on the floor, dressed in her filthy, stolen dress, reading Aleister Crowley.

Sadie walked right up to her, looked down, and said, "Why do I feel like you might be one of us? Sid, you see it, don't you?"

Sid tipped back his hat and considered Jane.

"I think so, dear sister. I think so. Your eyes are opened, aren't they, love?"

How they knew, Jane could never tell. She would soon learn that Sid and Sadie Smithfield-Wyatt were not like anyone else. They knew things other people did not. If you had the gift, Sid and Sadie considered you family and you became one of *theirs*—one of that group of strange young people that followed them about. But Jane had always been different, right from the start. Her level of ability was exactly the same as the others—what made her stand out was her toughness. The others had come into their sight in a series of minor accidents or illnesses, then fallen into this lifestyle. Jane had fought for her life on that dark moor. It must have been there, in the set of her jaw, in the look in her eyes. The others were lovely moonchildren—Jane had fought against death and won.

Sid and Sadie knew it just by looking at her. They saw all.

"Oh, yes," Sid had said, reaching down a hand to help Jane off the floor. "She's special."

"I like her, Sid. She belongs with us."

"I agree completely, dear sister. It's decided, then. You're coming with us. We have far better books."

He dismissed the bookstore and everyone in it with a flick

of the wrist. Everything about them was right and sure, and so Jane took Sid's hand and went outside with them. She got into their yellow Jaguar, and together they rode off to Chelsea. A week later, she moved into their house with them and became their second in command. That was five years ago.

In many ways, everything had been building to this night.

Mick was about to start mouthing off again when, as if on cue, the door to the living room opened. Sid and Sadie filled the space. They were twins—not identical, of course, but their resemblance was remarkable. They were both tall, both blond and pale. They wore similar makeup—a silvery dusting on the cheeks and white above the eyes, an effect that seemed to erase their eyebrows and give their blue eyes a spectral appearance. In defiance of the cold and the dark, they were dressed completely in white—Sid in a light white suit, Sadie in a filmy, almost transparent gown that brushed and clung to the heavy carpet. Around their necks they wore identical silver lockets in the shape of a crescent moon.

"Well, well," Sid said. "Who's being impatient?"

"The usual suspect," Jane said, pointing at Mick.

Mick was still smiling, but he dug his fingertips into the carpet sheepishly.

"That will never do," Sid said, leaning down to look at Mick. "It will never do."

"Sorry, Sid," Mick mumbled. All of his bravado slipped away.

"All is forgiven. You know we can't help but love you." Sid patted Mick's head, and he and his sister continued into the room, the group leaning and moving to clear whatever path they chose to take.

"What's happening tonight?" asked Dinah. "You said it was something special."

"Oh, it is," Sid said, coming around and taking a seat.

"Wonderful things are happening," Sadie added, smiling at Jane across the room. "Tonight, we celebrate the most sacred mystery in our faith. Jane, will do you the honors?"

Jane picked up the red crystal decanter from the sideboard and filled the glasses on the table.

"The kykeon," Sadie said. "The sacred drink of the mysteries. We have prepared it exactly as it should be prepared. The sacred barley, the mint, the honey."

"We're performing the mysteries tonight?" Dinah said.

"We are indeed, darling," Sid said, handing her a glass.

A wave of excited shock seemed to pass around the room. Jane had been waiting for this. It was no small thing to perform the mysteries.

"You didn't tell us," Domino said.

"It's best to come to these things with a fresh and open mind," Sadie said. "There is nothing better than a surprise."

"Have you all done as instructed?" Sid asked. "Have you washed in the sacred river and kept your fast?"

Again, murmurs of assent, but louder this time, and Mick was among them. Sid and Sadie passed out the glasses, touching each person on the head gently, whispering a friendly word to each. Jane poured three last glasses, for herself and Sid and Sadie. Once they had their glasses, Sid and Sadie took their positions at the other end of the room.

"Tonight," Sadie said, "as you know, is the solstice. As a family, we dismiss the dark. As a family, we know there is no day, there is no night, there is no life without death and no death without life. We are a circle, without end. And tonight, I ask you to lift your glasses. Tonight, something wonderful will be revealed. Lift, and drink."

Thirteen glasses were lifted. Ten drank.

"Oh," Dinah said, taking the glass from her lips. "It tastes . . ."

She was the first to twitch. She was the smallest, after all. Within moments, the ten on the floor all began to cough and grab at their throats. Jane saw that flicker of confusion—the realization that the drink had more to it than a bitter taste.

"It will be quick," Sid said. "Don't fight it, my loves."

Jane had expected it to be a little less dramatic—that they would just nod off and sleep. She wasn't expecting them to gag and cry and claw at the air and the carpet. There was a smell of almond mixing with the incense and candle smoke—then a bit of vomit. George started crawling to the door, but Sadie set her foot on his back and he dropped to the floor. The noise was the worst part, so Sid went to the console and put the needle on a record and turned up the volume. Soon, the room was flooded with the sound of David Bowie's latest.

It took about five minutes, long enough for a song to play out. Mick was the last to go, and he was the one Jane had to watch. She saw that beautiful face, so cheerfully smug, turn ashen. She saw the panic in his eyes. She saw this proud, lovely creature realize he was about to die—and even though he said he didn't believe in death, his expression told a different story. She wanted to reach out to him, to go to him and cradle him and reassure him. It would be all right. It was worth it. But she found that she couldn't move, except when Mick made one final, brave lunge for where she was standing by the back door. Jane jumped aside in terror. Mick didn't quite make it to the door when he was overcome. He landed by her feet and stopped moving.

There was no more music. Sid had chosen a track near the end of the side, so there was the whispery hiss of the record as it played out the silent bit where the grooves stopped. Jane heard the tiny sound of the arm of the record player lifting and going back to its resting position. There was no more movement from the people scattered around the room.

"Well, that's a relief," Sid said. "It went on a bit longer than expected, but the best things often do. We should press on."

Sadie went to the table and opened the large box, revealing three knives with curved blades.

"I have taken from the kiste," she said, removing two and passing one to her brother. She held out the third for Jane. Jane found herself unable to leave her spot by the wall. She had known there would be ten bodies, but she had never envisioned them like this, contorted, twisted in pain. Some had grabbed hold of others, forming a horrid knot. She hadn't imagined having to step over and around them—these *things* that had been people seconds before.

"Jane . . ." Sadie prompted.

"Sorry," Jane said. "Yes. Of course."

Jane shook her head, took a deep breath, and stepped over Mick. His lovely black hair covered most of his face, but not all of it. His eyes were bloodshot and wide, his mouth open, gasping, the lips blue. She took the third knife.

It was short work to make a small cut in each body. As the

blood drained out, a bit from each person was put into a clean wineglass that the three of them passed around, until all ten bodies had been sampled.

"This carpet will have to go," Sid said sadly, looking at his feet. "But come, now. No time to waste."

The three ascended the darkened stairs together, to the room at the top of the house. This room faced the street. This was the library—quiet and padded with overlapping Persian carpets and tapestries. The incense and smoke had woven into every fiber and every page. Every surface aside from the shelves had a patina of candle wax and ash. And the books—the precious books that Sid and Sadie had so carefully gathered from every corner of the earth, these were stored lovingly. They were fragile, many hand-copied, and most had no duplicate anywhere.

Sadie went to the window and pulled open the curtains, releasing a visible cloud of dust and filling the room with a delicate moonlit glow.

"Must you, darling?" Sid asked. He stood at the round table in the middle of the room that held a bottle and a metal goblet.

"We need moonlight," Sadie said. "It's proper, if not strictly necessary."

"I suppose, but those nosy old dears from across the way will probably look in. You know what they're like."

"Let them."

Sid held up the wineglass of blood and examined it in the moonlight.

"The blood in the light," he said.

Sadie smiled and came over to join him.

"Blessed Demeter," she said, picking up the bottle.

"Fab, fab, fab Demeter."

"Oh, Sid. Show a *little* respect."

"She knows I love her."

At the same time, they poured the contents of their respective containers into the goblet—the blood flowing more slowly than the barley liquid. When the cup was full, Sadie picked up a curved blade, similar to the ones from downstairs, and gently stirred the substances together. When this was done, she wiped the blade carefully with a white cloth and set them both down. They had never looked more wonderful to Jane than they did at that moment in the moonlight, over that cup. They were like an image off a tarot card.

"Well?" Sadie asked.

"Well indeed, dear sister."

"Do you feel ready?" she asked.

"I always feel ready. The worst we can be is wrong."

"We're not wrong," Sadie said. But there was a touch of a question in her voice. Sadie was wavering. Jane was transfixed. She'd never seen either of them hesitate before.

"It hardly matters at this point," Sid replied calmly. "There's no going back now, is there?"

"I suppose not."

"And if we're right, which we are, it's worth the risk. You don't get everything without risking something. We're not meant to grow old, dear sister. We're not meant to die."

He ran his finger along the side of his sister's face, tipping up her chin. She broke into a smile.

"You're right," she said. "Of course."

The touch of nerves passed away, as quick as that. They turned to Jane.

"Thank you, Jane," Sadie said. "We will see you soon."

"Very soon," Sid said.

"I know," said Jane.

Sid and Sadie faced each other again. They were alone, lost in their own company, smiling. They reached for their necklaces and opened the lockets. Each contained a small, dirty bit of diamond.

"We have performed the work," Sadie said.

"And we have, in our own inimitable fashion, replaced the kalathos," Sid replied.

They both put a hand on the goblet.

"Do I look good?" Sid asked. "I want to look good."

"You look wonderful," Sadie replied.

"Well," Sid said, "as Oscar Wilde said, 'Either the wallpaper goes, or I do.'"

"Oh, Sid. *Really.*"

"Those are fine last words. Can you improve upon them?"

"I can," Sadie said. "Here are mine: *surprise me.*"

Sadie drank first, with Sid supporting the goblet when she spasmed and fell back. He put it to his own lips. A few seconds later, the cup fell free and struck the table, spilling the dark red liquid before bouncing to the floor. The dose of poison they had taken was much more concentrated than the one from downstairs. It would go faster.

It wasn't fast enough for Jane's liking.

She had to watch. It was her duty. She would keep watching for as long as it took to work.

THREE MISSING

The night is darkening round me
The wild winds coldly blow
But a tyrant spell has bound me
And I cannot, cannot go

> —*Emily Brontë,*
> *"Spellbound"*

1

THE ROOM WAS FULL OF A SOFT DECEMBER-MORNING LIGHT, a kind of gentle dove-gray color. Stephen was on the bed. Glasses off. Peaceful. Outside, London rumbled by as it always did and presumably always would.

"Rory, are you sure?" Thorpe said. "Are you sure it worked?"

It was just me, Boo, and Thorpe now. Thorpe was our overseer from MI5, someone I knew very little about except that he was young with white hair. Stephen had always been the one to deal with Thorpe, and Thorpe would make things happen. Security systems would be shut down, records altered, CCTV footage obtained, door opened. But Thorpe did not have our ability, our sight, and there was nothing he could do about what was happening now, in this hospital room.

Callum was gone—he had stormed out when he realized what I had done. Or, what I thought I'd done. It wasn't like I'd made a choice. There had simply been no time to think of what it all meant.

Stephen had been dead for four minutes.

"I know he's here," Boo was saying. "We need to start looking. We do the hospital. We do the flat, both the old one and the new one. And if that fails, we come back here and we do it again. Yeah?"

I'd grabbed Stephen's hand and hadn't let go. I was a terminus, and if my theory was right, I had the power to pull him back—not to stop him from dying, but to make him a ghost.

"I mean . . ." Boo paced the side of the bed by the door, unable to remain still. "When Jo woke up, she woke up where she died. Most of them, we find them where they died. Not all of them, but most of them. A lot of them, anyway. Maybe we need to stay here. Or at least look around the hospital. But here? He'd probably come here? I mean, I think it can take a while sometimes?"

No one was listening to Boo.

"Do you know anything?" she asked me, her voice pitching high. "Did you feel something, or . . ."

It took me a moment to shake myself out of my haze and realize I was supposed to answer.

"I don't know," I said.

"Rory, try. *Try.*"

"Is that a thing?" Thorpe asked. "Can you . . . feel them?"

"*Rory,*" Boo said.

She had broken the seal on my calm, and I felt a surge run through me. I saw it coming, like a big, flat wave off the shoreline, a wall of water about to crash down and take me away forever. I was not going to let that happen.

"Shut *up!*" I yelled across the bed. "Let me *think.*"

I had no idea what I was doing. I tried to remember what it was like in those last moments, when they'd told me he was dying, when I'd closed my eyes like this and taken his hand. So I did that. I grabbed his hand, which was warm, but not as warm as it should have been. It was Stephen's hand, the one I had felt on my face last night, on the space under my shirt, along my belly where my scar was.

When we had kissed. My eyes were closed then too.

No muscle movement. His hand was an inanimate object. I squeezed harder. I tightened my eyes until starbursts appeared behind them.

Stephen. Where are you? Where are you? Where are you?

He had sighed into my mouth when we kissed.

Where are you where are you where are you . . .

There was no answer, no clear echo in my head, no hand gripping mine. I went harder, pushing into my own mind, recalling the very moments before, when it had all happened and his life support had been turned off. There was the whiteness, the rushing feeling, a pushing and a pulling, and a feeling of falling—

Suddenly, in my mind, I was back in Louisiana, standing in my uncle Bick's bird shop, A Bird in Hand. I was imagining this, of course, but my mind had landed there quite naturally. Uncle Bick was behind the counter in his Tulane baseball cap, sorting a bunch of bird toys. I could smell birdseed.

The birds were allowed to fly free in the shop (he had a series of three doors you came through to make sure they were safe), so there was always a chance that a bird would land on your head. Or, more likely, bird poop would land on your head.

I was always a little nervous in there. It never fazed Uncle Bick. Birds almost never pooped on him.

"Here's the thing," said the Uncle Bick in my head, "they actually want to be found. They're not designed for the wild."

He was talking about parakeets. Uncle Bick had a passion for finding the ones that were lost or released by callous college students, who regarded them as a school-year pet. They sat in the local trees, deeply confused by their situation. My uncle Bick drove around in his truck and rescued them (and got labeled a possible predator by the university security department for lingering by dorm room windows).

Except of course this wasn't about parakeets. My brain was filtering information, and this was the format it had chosen.

"So how do I find him?" I asked Imaginary Uncle Bick. He pushed the box aside and adjusted his baseball cap.

"Parakeets never go far," he said. "They're not used to long flights or heights. They stick close to home. They never meant to leave."

"I'm honestly not sure if I should be talking to you," I said to my imaginary uncle. "I'm trying to find Stephen."

"And I'm not your uncle," said my imaginary uncle. "I'm your own head, telling you what you already know."

"What does that mean? *I don't know anything.*"

"Oh," said my own brain, "you do."

Someone was shaking me. I opened my eyes to find Boo next to me, pointing wildly. The lights on Stephen's machine all came on at once. The pulse monitor flashed to triple zeros and then started flicking through random digits, going up and down wildly before becoming a blur. The line that had flattened when Stephen had—well, that line was now a frantic mountain range, jagging and peaking and speeding itself into nonsense. The machine was alive.

Thorpe seemed to fly across the room. He grabbed Stephen's other hand and put his fingers on the pulse point in the wrist.

"I don't feel . . ."

The machine began to emit a loud hum, then the lights in the ceiling dimmed to a brownish glow, then to a high, uncomfortable brightness. Then the bulb shorted out and the room went dark, including the machine. There was a yell from out in the hall. Then another. Then a chorus of panicked calls. Thorpe opened the door to reveal that the entire hall had gone dark. Things were being knocked over; nurses and doctors ran past with bags and tubes.

"Rory . . ." Thorpe looked past me. I heard a tinkling sound and turned to watch the window of the room frost over—at least, it looked like frost creeping up from the bottom of the pane. What it was actually, we realized a moment later, was a spidery, spreading fracture. It climbed and climbed, and when it hit the top of the frame, the window whited out and burst in a cloud of glass dust, some of it blowing back in on the cold December wind.

The power flooded back on. The machine flashed and went quiet. The yelling continued in the hall.

"I don't know if that is the backup generator," Thorpe said. "I don't know anything at this point except that you are leaving this building. Now."

He didn't grab me, exactly, but he approached me with intent. He would move me if he had to.

"I'll look for Stephen," Boo said. "I'll meet you. Go."

I gave Stephen one final look before leaving the room with Thorpe. His dark hair stood out against the pale blue hospital pillow and the white and blue gown they'd dressed him in. His mouth had eased into a soft smile, and his face lost some of its angular sharpness. I reminded myself that this look wouldn't be my last. This was a temporary good-bye, that was all.

In the hall, there was a residual air of alarm, even though the power in general seemed to be back on. People were saying they'd lost coverage on their cell phones. Security waved us away from the elevators. Thorpe smoothly ushered me down the hall. None of this was real. Stephen would appear at any time. He would be there, in his uniform and looking mildly perturbed by the turn of events. I glanced into the open rooms we passed, expecting to see his tall figure in every doorway.

I almost walked into the nurse. She was standing directly in the middle of the hallway, unmoved by the quickly flowing foot traffic around her. She wasn't wearing scrubs—instead, she had on a long blue dress and a white apron with a large red cross over the chest. On her head was something that looked like a nun's veil, white, spreading to either side of her head like wings. She was older; her hair was gray, what I could see of it.

Some ghosts were like an image being poorly projected at a wall. Not the nurse. She seemed to be made of light and color, the blue of her dress bleeding into the air of the hallway, the white like a halo around her head, the cross throbbing on her chest. I skidded to a halt, making Thorpe stumble a bit. He tried to move me on, but when I froze, he followed my lead. It must have been very confusing to him. He couldn't see what I did.

"You look lost," the nurse said. "The stairs are that way."

She pointed in the direction we had been moving.

"My friend," I said. "He . . . he was down the hall. He"—I was not ready to say the word, but this was no time to look for another way to phrase it—"died. Just a few minutes ago. But I think he's here."

She folded her hands by her waist and said nothing.

"Did you hear me?" I said. "My friend. His name is Stephen. He's tall, he's got dark brown hair, he's . . ."

Someone stopped for a second to watch me talk to an empty space in the middle of the hall. Thorpe wheeled around a bit and ended up standing next to the nurse. Someone else bumped us and told us to move to the side.

"My friend," I said again. "Did you see him?"

"The stairs are this way." She indicated the direction once again.

I was in no mood to deal with this ghost. Not now. I put my hand in front of her face.

"Listen to me. This . . ." I pointed to the ceiling to indicate the general chaos. "I did this. If I touch you, you go away. *Now, tell me if you saw my friend.*"

Thorpe's brow wrinkled, but the nurse didn't change expression. She didn't so much as glance at my hand.

"I am here for the dying," she said. "You don't belong here. You will go."

"I'll leave when you tell me . . ."

"You'll leave now," she said. "*You do not belong here.*"

Everything about her went kind of blurry—like I was seeing her through a fuzzy lens. She was color and an expanding area of light, something terrible and strong. I backed up quickly, and Thorpe took a few steps toward me to try to follow this strange dance. I didn't know if I had anything to fear from her. I didn't know if I could destroy her, but I had no intention of doing that. This was her hospital, and she seemed to understand something about me that I didn't know. I dropped my hand and felt all will ebbing away from me.

I was scared. I wanted to go home. I wanted Stephen back. It was too much to cry about, so I didn't.

Thorpe, sensing the encounter had to end, scooped me under the armpits and started moving down the hall again.

"I wouldn't have hurt her," I said, partially to Thorpe, maybe to her, maybe to myself.

"Stop talking," he said.

We walked out of the hospital, which faced Paddington station. There was a post-rush-hour crush of people still pouring out onto the streets. I got a heavy lungful of London air, which was flecked with damp crystals that felt like glass when you breathed them in. The streetlamps were on, even though it was day. We waited at the crowded intersection for the traffic light to change.

"Where are we going?" I asked Thorpe.

"My car is in the car park across the road."

"But . . ."

"Just walk," Thorpe said.

There was anger in his voice. Maybe he thought this was my fault. Maybe he was right. Somehow, this madness, the crash, and the events of this morning had all started with me getting expelled. Somehow, this had happened because I couldn't manage all of this bullshit and "further maths." I'd been chased by the Ripper ghost and stabbed and turned into a terminus, but oh, no. In the end, math. Math*s*. That was the butterfly that caused the earthquake on the other side of the world.

Thorpe's car was a sedate black Mercedes. He unlocked it and told me to get in. As I did, he got behind the wheel. He didn't put the key into the ignition. We sat there in silence and shivered in our respective seats for a few moments. I looked over at him once or twice, at his youngish face and unexpectedly pure-white hair. Thorpe had that kind of greyhound profile of someone who did marathons and actually cared about soluble fiber and stuff like that. Not in a vain way—more in the way of someone who had to be professionally fit and functional. There was something in his expression and posture that suggested huge calculations were going on inside his mind.

"I need to understand what is happening," he finally said. "No details left out. You'll tell me everything. The basics, as I understand them, are as follows. About thirty-six hours ago, you left Wexford after being told you were expelled."

I was pretty sure my heartbeat was audible. I considered fainting. That would at least make everything go away.

"Yes," I said.

"And you then proceeded to Jane Quaint's house? Your therapist? And you spent the night there."

"Yes."

"The next morning, there was a death near Wexford. A woman named Dawn Somner who worked as a psychic fell out of a window. The squad reported because of the proximity and because of the nature of her job. You attended this scene as well, which is when Stephen discovered you had run off. Stephen instructed you to return to Wexford, but you didn't do so."

It was like something squeezed my heart. If I'd gone back like he asked . . .

"Rory, answer." Thorpe had no patience for my silences. "Where did you go then?"

"Back to Jane's."

"For what purpose?"

"She told me she could help me," I said. "She's one of us. She has the sight."

"Help you how?"

"She's in some kind of cult or something. A whole bunch of kids with the sight live with her, and they said they could help me. It seemed good when she first explained it. She said they were the only people who really understood and that I needed to be around people who were like me. I didn't know what else to do, so . . . I was going to go with them."

"Go where?"

"All they said was that it was a house in the country."

It sounded ridiculous now. At the time, Jane had been so amazing. I'd been able to talk to her, to really explain everything. I couldn't tell my other therapist that I'd been stabbed *by a ghost*. Jane, though. She understood. She helped. She was so nice. She fed me and let me stay. And then—

"Charlotte," he said. "At some point that same morning, your classmate Charlotte was seen leaving Wexford before her scheduled Latin exam. We know she went to Jane's house on her own. How were Charlotte and Jane connected?"

"Jane was Charlotte's therapist too. That's how I met Jane. Charlotte kept telling me I had to go and see her, how amazing she was. But on that last day I realized Jane was just getting us stoned."

"How?"

"She put something in the food. She'd always make us eat something—brownies, cookies, things like that. Then I'd get really relaxed and talk a lot."

"So she was drugging you."

"I'm pretty sure," I said. "I put it all together too late."

"Did you see Charlotte at Jane's that day?"

"No," I said. "Just her blazer. I was in the kitchen with Jane and these people Devina and Jack."

"Devina and Jack?"

"Devina lived there. I don't know about Jack. He showed up that morning, and he was kind of freaky. I got up to go to the bathroom and went through the front hall. I saw Charlotte's blazer on a hook. It was damp. I asked them about her, and they said she was gone. I knew . . . like, that second, that something was wrong. I ran, but Jack jumped on me in the hall. They said they had her and that I had to come with them. If I didn't do what they wanted, Charlotte would get hurt, and they'd get my parents too. They said they'd *hurt* people. They were threatening everyone. So I got in the car with them."

Thorpe eased his expression a bit.

"They coerced you into the car," he said. "Did they give any indication where they were taking you?"

"All they would say was the country. They were talking about Greek myths and how they were going to *defeat death,* and I was going to help. Something about mysteries—Greek mysteries. Rituals. These people—they're nuts. And they have Charlotte."

"How did the accident happen?"

"It just did," I said. In my mind, this event was all in gray scale. "We were driving and a car pulled in front of us and we hit it. It wasn't that big of a crash. And then Stephen got out of the car with Boo and Callum behind him. Stephen threatened them and told them to let me out. Boo and Callum—one of them—smashed the window with a tire iron or something. I got out, and we left the three of them there. I think someone took their keys. Stephen had a cut on his head," I said. I pointed to the spot on the temple where I'd seen blood.

"How did Stephen find you?"

"He put his phone in my pocket that morning," I said. "He guessed I wouldn't go back to Wexford, so he used it to track me. And I guess he thought the only way to stop them was to crash? Why didn't he—"

"He was trying to get you out of there as quickly as possible," Thorpe said. "And I assume he was trying to prevent a full police response. It was, for the most part, a controlled crash. We recovered the cars."

"A controlled crash?" I asked.

I think he realized how this sounded.

"You went to his parents' flat in Maida Vale," he went on.

"He was fine last night," I said.

Stephen *had* been fine the night before. More than fine.

There was a lot I could have said here, like that he'd been changing his shirt because there was blood on the one he was wearing. He had his shirt off, and then we were sitting next to each other on the edge of the bed, and then we were suddenly very close to each other, and then we were *really* close to each other.

Thorpe didn't need to know about the kissing. He didn't need to know that everything changed last night. Last night, I think I knew what love was—love and a few other things. And this morning, it was all gone.

I saw Boo in the side-view mirror, jogging up to us. She got into the backseat, bringing with her a cloud of fresh air and cold.

"Nothing," she said. "I looked everywhere I could get into. Obviously not the whole hospital, but the rooms along the corridor. I think the power cut was just the one floor. I think? If he was there? I think he would have . . . yeah, I don't know, I don't think he's there."

"Neither do I," I said.

"Why not?" Thorpe asked.

Because my imaginary uncle told me a story about birds in my head, Thorpe. That's why.

"I don't know," I said.

I could feel frustration coming off him like a smell, and I saw Boo slump in the back and put her hands over her eyes.

"I have to phone Callum," she said. "I'll get him to come back. I can look again."

Thorpe turned on the engine.

"We're leaving?" she asked.

"Rory's been missing for over twenty-four hours," he said, craning his head to back the car up. He did this with surprising speed, hooking the tail of the car around like a whip. "Combined with the fact that Charlotte also went missing, and the fact that you are both known Ripper victims—this is already getting attention."

"If you send me to my parents," I said, "we will be on a plane to Louisiana in an hour, and I will never get back here again.

Stephen is here *now*. Charlotte is missing *now*, and I'm the only person who really knows anything about the people who took her. I need to be here. I'm not *just some runaway*."

"She's right," Boo said, leaning between the two front seats.

"I'm aware of this," he said. "Now, get down in the seat where you can't be seen. We're going to my flat."

2

THERE ARE SOME PEOPLE YOU MEET WHOM YOU CAN'T
picture having a normal life. In your mind, they don't have a
house or a bed or eat food. They don't watch television or use
a pen to get a weird itch in the middle of their back. They seem
to exist in some permanent state of other. Thorpe was one of
these people.

I mean, first of all, he was called Thorpe. That was his last
name. I didn't know his first name. He worked for some secret
service, probably MI5. He was young but had white hair. If he
did shower or sleep, I could only assume he did so in a suit.
So the fact that I was going to where Thorpe lived was strange
enough. But then I turned to see that his eyes were red.

Thorpe had *feelings*. Feelings about Stephen. I think this
alone was enough to keep me in my suspended state of non-
reality. Stephen couldn't be dead, because Thorpe didn't cry
and he didn't live anywhere. Wrong again.

Thorpe lived in some very modern apartment building on the Thames, as it happened, in the City of London area—not all that far from Wexford, and very close to Tower Bridge. The building seemed to be all windows and glass balconies, endless glass through which to see the gray sky and the river. He told me to scooch down in the seat as we pulled into the underground parking lot and to keep my face tipped down as we entered the lobby and rode up on the elevator.

I opened my mouth to speak, but Thorpe cut me off.

"We talk inside the flat," he said.

I watched the red LED lights flick along until they hit twelve and we were ushered out by a creepily smooth automated female voice that said this was the top floor. The halls of this place had a sterile feel and smelled strongly of new carpeting. There was black-and-white framed photography on the walls, and you could tell it was the expensive kind, and not the kind they sold in places like Which Craft? where all of Bénouville bought its scrapbooking supplies and requisite framed pictures of kittens and watermelons and flowers.

Thorpe's inner sanctum was chilly and perfectly neat. He was the first person I'd ever met who really seemed to live in one of those rooms you see in fancy furniture catalogs. Everything was leather or stainless steel or emotionless but dignified gray. The living room and kitchen were all one big space, separated by a kitchen bar. He motioned me to sit there, on a high chair.

"When was the last time you ate?" he asked.

"I don't know . . . yesterday? I'm not hungry."

He opened the refrigerator and produced a prepackaged sandwich and a bottle of water, which he set in front of me.

"It doesn't matter if you're hungry. You've been in an accident, and you've had a number of shocks. It's a matter of keeping your blood sugar level. Eat this."

I dutifully opened the sandwich and put it in my mouth. He made me a cup of very sugary and milky instant coffee.

"Now what?" Boo asked.

"Triage," he said. "We have three missing people, but not in the traditional sense. Rory is missing, but obviously we know where she is. Stephen is missing, but his case is . . . complicated. Charlotte, however, is missing in the most immediate and obvious sense. Charlotte is actively in danger and needs to be found. The Met is in charge of that, but there are problems. As far as the police know, Charlotte left Wexford of her own accord, which is true. The next piece of evidence is that you, Rory, found her school blazer, damp, in the hall of Jane's house that same morning. And then Jane told you that she had taken Charlotte away to the country. None of your statements can go into the report. Many aspects of this entire affair connect directly to the existence of the squad, which is covered by the Official Secrets Act. So that lead cannot be reported—at least, not as it really happened. I've already put in a call to one of my contacts and had him pose as a witness and say he saw Charlotte going into the house. It's the best I could do, and at least it points the investigation in the right direction. Right now, Rory's disappearance and Charlotte's are being conflated into one event, which will disrupt and confuse the search. So, the first thing we are going to do is remove you from that search."

"How?" I asked.

"You are going to call your parents. You'll tell them that you are fine, that you left school of your own accord. At the very least, the search will then focus on one missing girl, not two. If they ask about Charlotte, be truthful and say you don't know where she is. The conversation will be short."

I wasn't ready for this particular instruction.

"I can't."

"Then I turn you in, right now. You'll be with your parents within the hour."

Thorpe walked around the bar and into the living room space, to a desk by a window. He opened a box on one of the top shelves and produced a cell phone, which he placed in my hand.

"This will trace back to a public telephone," he said. "When they ask where you are, and they will, you say you're somewhere safe. Then you tell them you'll be in touch, that they shouldn't worry, whatever you like, and then you hang up. Keep it brief."

I turned to Boo, as if she could help me with this, but she looked down and traced one of her long green nails along the granite.

"The number . . . I can't remember."

"I have the number." He took out his own phone and flicked through a few screens, then dialed the phone for me, handing it back. All I had to do was hit Call.

"I realize this has not been a good day," he said. "This isn't easy. You still need to do it if you intend to remain and find Stephen, and if you want to help Charlotte get to safety. This is not about your feelings. This is about what needs to happen."

I guess I pressed Call? It was like I twitched and the phone was ringing, and my father answered just as the first ring had gone. So fast. Everything happened so fast.

"Hello? Who is this?"

His accent, like mine, was thick and warm and Southern.

"Hello?" he said again.

"It's me, Dad," I said. My voice was nothing—a broken little noise, born of nowhere.

A pause.

"Rory? *Rory?* Is that you? Rory?"

I didn't want to hear him say my name so many times.

I thought about Stephen on the bed, eyes closed. The lights bursting and windows breaking.

"Yes," I said.

"Where are you? Are you okay?" I heard his voice wavering and my mom in the background saying, "Is it her? Is it her?"

"I'm fine," I said. Now there was some strength in my voice, but I was openly crying and turned to the wall, away from Boo and Thorpe. My dad was crying, and my mom had the phone, and I kept saying I was fine. They asked again where I was, and I said something about being safe. They just wanted to know where—where? Where? They would be wherever it was now. They'd come. Where where where . . .

I said I was safe. I said I didn't know where Charlotte was. I said I wasn't with her. I said to tell the police that. I said I needed time. I tried to tell them I loved them, but that was too hard. I hung up in the middle of them saying where, where, where . . .

I set the phone back on the granite bar and grabbed a paper towel to dry my face. I took a long sip of the water bottle and crinkled it in my grip. The silence that settled on all of us after that noise was one of the most deeply unsettling that I'd ever felt.

"There are some things we need to do," Thorpe said. "An

attempt was made to kidnap you, and you generally need to stay under the radar for a bit. Your parents won't immediately stop looking. Basic precautions need to be taken."

He went over to his bookcase and pulled down a heavy German-to-English dictionary. Under the cover was a stack of twenty- and fifty-pound notes. He counted off a few of these and handed them to Boo.

"There's a Boots two streets north of here. We need hair dye. Not green."

Boo always had a different color in her hair. Red or pink streaks, purple edges. At the moment, the bottom third of her bobbed hair was green.

"Something more natural," he said. "A contrast. Rory has dark hair. We'll need to change it. There's a Marks and Spencer across the road from the Boots. Get Rory a full set of clothes—trousers, a jumper, some shoes and socks. Don't go for fashionable. As basic as possible. Whatever's in the front window. Make the shoes practical—a pair of trainers is best. She'll need a coat as well, and hat, gloves, and scarf. Black, if possible, or any solid color. Nothing with a distinctive pattern or decoration."

As Boo left, Thorpe went to the kitchen and got out some scissors and a trash bag.

"Your hair," he said. "You need to cut it. Take everything you wore when you arrived here and put it in this bag. All the clothes. Shoes. The lot. There's a dressing gown on the back of the toilet door you can put on until Boo brings your new clothes. The toilet is the first door on the left."

It was unsentimental and sudden, but it was action. I needed something to do. I walked in and shut the door and took in my first fully private moment in some time. My parents' voices were still ringing in my ears. I grabbed a handful of hair on one side and cut. I'd grabbed too much, because the scissors couldn't get through it, and I had to hack at it a few times, dropping clumps into the sink with every labored snip. Suddenly, my neck and jawline were exposed, curtained by an uneven jag of what remained of that side of my hair. I stood there and looked at myself, mid transition, this lopsided freak and partial stranger.

My face was very round.

The girl in the mirror had started to cry. No time for that. I wiped my face on one of Thorpe's steel-gray hand towels and started in on the other side, going much more slowly. This was a better effort than the first, but it still leaned in the wrong direction, and I had to work at it again to try to make the two sides match. Within twenty minutes, I had what appeared from the front to be a reasonably passable haircut. Or at least I told myself I did. It was not, I told myself firmly, reminiscent of an upside-down pear. I tried to reach around to the back, but I knew I'd mess that up immediately and decided to leave it for Boo.

I stripped down, taking off the clothes from Jane's house and putting them in the trash bag. It felt a bit weird changing into what had to be Thorpe's robe, which was a heavy blue terry-cloth thing, much too large for me. Still, it was pleasantly soft and very warm. It even had a hood. I tied the belt as tight as I could and came out into the hall with my bag of clothes and my strange new hair.

"That looks . . . very different," Thorpe said. "I think you should let Boo work on it a bit."

"Now what?" I asked.

"Now you focus on what you remember. If you want to help Charlotte, that's the most important thing to do. Write down anything at all that comes to you. Anything. You can start now while I make some calls."

There were paper and pen waiting for me on the coffee table. Thorpe went into the bedroom and shut the door. He spoke so low, or the doors were so thick, that I could hear nothing. I took the cap off the pen and let the tip hover over the page. What else had happened, aside from everything? I started to write.

> Her blazer hanging in the hall. It was wet.
> They talked about some kind of ancient Greek mystery.
> Ell—

I couldn't quite remember the word, and I don't think I could have spelled it if I had.

> They said they were going to defeat death, whatever the hell that meant.

It wasn't much of a list. I set the pen and paper down on the coffee table and sat there, my hands on my lap, until Boo came back in with several plastic bags. She examined the chop job I'd done on my head.

"Yeah, I need to work on this," she said. "Come on."

Boo dragged one of the kitchen bar chairs into the bathroom and set to work fixing the damage I'd done. In a relatively short time, I had a bob, one that wasn't crooked.

"Your hair is a bit thick," she said, examining her work, "but it looks right. We'll have to keep it trimmed. Now . . ."

She got the plastic bag from the floor that contained the dyes.

"We'll need to bleach you out first before we add the color. I got red. It's nice."

She held a box of hair color in front of my face, and I looked at the model smiling back at me with her head of thick and luscious auburn hair.

"It won't look like that on me," I said.

"It will. Now . . ."

The next part of the hour was all plastic gloves, tubes of gunk, and crap being squished into my head. In the end, my hair was in an uncomfortable stage between yellow and orange and terrible, terrible mistake. Boo turned me around and put the red goop on. Again, we waited and rinsed. The result was supposed to be "natural copper" but it came out "nuclear-accident strawberry blond."

"I told you," I said.

She held up a finger and produced another dye kit from the bag, a brown one. The process was repeated, and this time, my hair turned out in a color known to nature—a bright brown-red, sort of the color of a well-used penny.

My hair smelled like cat food and felt like massaged steel wool, but it didn't look too bad.

"I got some makeup," she said, digging out more packages from the bag and picking off the cellophane wrappers. There were makeup sponges and liquid foundation, which was applied all over my face. It made me look tan—the kind of tan my gran has when she comes back from her annual booze cruise down the Mississippi, when she's been out on the deck too long with her mai tais. This was the first time I'd ever really seen my resemblance to Granny Deveaux, and it was a little scary. I mean, I love her, but she doesn't have a look I've ever wanted to emulate. This is a woman who gets discount Botox shots from her dog groomer because he found a hookup who sells them illegally. My parents have repeatedly tried to explain that Botox is a poison and probably shouldn't be put into the human body under the best of circumstances, but definitely not by a dog groomer—but whenever they do that, she starts talking about getting a discount chin lift and tummy tuck package, and everyone shuts up.

I was going to turn into Granny Deveaux. It was getting worse with every second, as Boo plucked at my eyebrows. Gran had made me a standing offer to pay if I'd get my eyebrows waxed. She'd been encouraging me to do it since I was twelve, and she never understood why I didn't want hot wax near my eyes and wire-thin eyebrows like hers. I imagined myself turning into my gran—my gran, with all her over-sixty friends hanging off the rail of the *Miss A Drinky* as it paddled into the sunset toward New Orleans and oblivion . . .

That life was over.

I looked into Boo's eyes as she worked on my face. They were bloodshot. She'd been crying again. Her eyeliner was smudged. It looked like she'd tried to clean it up a bit, but there were traces under her eyes.

"Okay," she said, stepping back.

I was not myself anymore. My eyebrows had been plucked until they were almost gone, then darkened and arched. My fake tan almost matched my new, copper penny-red hair.

"Clothes," she said, picking up the larger bag from the floor. "Just basic stuff. Jeans. Hoodie. Trainers."

She left, and I dressed. The clothes had the feeling of plastic. My transformation was complete. It had taken a few hours to disassemble my appearance. It had taken only a few minutes for Stephen to die. Nothing in life was as stable as I'd been led to believe.

3

WHEN I EMERGED, THORPE HAD HOOKED HIS LAPTOP UP to the television. He'd taken off his suit jacket and pushed up his sleeves to the elbow, which, for Thorpe, was almost like he'd taken his shirt off entirely. He finished furiously spooning some yogurt into his mouth and set the container down on the edge of a bookshelf.

"Sit," he said. "Boo, close the blinds."

The yogurt container tipped to the side under the weight of the spoon. Thorpe didn't set it upright, or even seem to notice. All of this combined—being in Thorpe's house, the pushed-back sleeves, the yogurt, and the air of urgency and secrecy—it made my internal engine start running faster again. There was the rapid heartbeat. There was the rush of blood to the face, the zing down the arms.

"No one knows I'm here?" I asked.

"Officially, you're not. Unofficially, though, you are now a member of this team. This means you take orders from me.

You do not have the training the others have, but you have an ability, and you have information. You were also the subject of a kidnap attempt, the perpetrators of which are still at large. So keeping you secure is going to be a priority."

Boo finished with the blinds and perched on the edge of the sofa, knees flexed, as if at any second she was ready to spring up and run ten miles. That's what competent secret ghost police looked like. I, on the other hand, was slouched, absently touching the bristle-stiff ends of my new, smelly hair.

Thorpe returned to the fake German dictionary and took out some more bills. He handed these to me.

"The key to remaining undetected is to keep it simple and not return to any places you are known. You'll use cash for everything. You do not, under any circumstances, contact anyone else. You don't go online, because you'll only be tempted to reach out. You don't reach out. You never go out without one of us. Boo and Callum are both extremely able. On that point, we need Callum here."

"I've been trying his phone," Boo said.

"Well, he'll be hearing from me, and he had better respond. For now, though, I'm going to share with you what was found when we pulled the files on Jane Quaint that were requested last night, along with some information we gathered after the accident. I asked for CCTV footage from the area in Barnes where the accident occurred. That particular lane is not well serviced by CCTV, so there's no direct image of the cars involved, which is probably for the best. We don't want an actual record of the accident."

It was also good because there was no way I was going to watch that.

"We do have footage from other streets." He clicked on a folder and brought up some low-quality video of three people making their way down a street. I'd have known those figures anywhere. Jane, with her wild red hair. Jack with his slicked-back blond hair. Devina, so waiflike, walking a bit unsteadily.

"That's Jane, we know. Are these the Devina and Jack you mentioned earlier?"

"That's them," I said.

"Last names?"

"No."

"We'll see what we can do in terms of fingerprints or materials we find in the house. The three abandoned the car and left via Barnes Common. The common isn't well covered, so we found no record of their exit. We lose them in Barnes. So we went back and pulled CCTV from London to try to trace Charlotte."

He clicked a few more times and brought up some footage taken from a vantage point somewhere on Jane's street.

"We began on Hyssop Close," he said. "This is Jane's house here. We have footage of Charlotte walking in, completely on her own, at ten thirty-seven."

I saw a blob of red hair and a blurry image of a person connected to it making her way down the sidewalk and turning toward the house, disappearing behind the wall that fronted Jane's garden.

"At eleven fifteen, this red car appears at the house and pulls into the drive, then pulls out again twenty minutes later. There's no further sign of Charlotte coming out of this house, so it is a reasonable assumption that she was removed in this car. We traced the car down the connecting streets. It drives west on the Fulham Road and north toward Earl's Court, where it turns onto a road that isn't covered, and we lose it. Everything from the surrounding roads was checked. Whatever path they took at this point, it wasn't covered by CCTV. The car is registered to a Laura Falley of West Wickham, who died in August. The car was left, along with a few other belongings, to a niece who now lives in America. As far as anyone knew, the car was sitting in a garage next to the empty house while the affairs were being settled from abroad. An excellent car to steal, if someone knew where to look. So, stolen car, untraceable route. A well-planned affair."

"How would they have planned it?" I said. "I ran away. And why take Charlotte?"

"It's an excellent question," he said. "There are a number of possibilities. One, the plan was originally intended for you, and for some reason, they decided they had to take Charlotte as well. Charlotte may have heard or seen something that she shouldn't have. Or perhaps they wanted Charlotte all along, for reasons that are currently unknown to us. When we looked into Jane Quaint, things became more oblique. She was born Jane Anderson in Danby, which is a small town in the moors outside of York. She is a licensed psychologist. Very little history on the books of her seeing patients, but what information is there is straightforward. That's the only part of Jane's life that makes any sense on paper. But when we looked back at her personal and financial records, things got very strange indeed. All records of her being in Danby end in 1968. The next we see of her is in London in 1970, when she registered at a local surgery. She listed her address as 16 Hyssop Close. 16 Hyssop Close belonged to a Sarah and Sidney Smithfield-Wyatt, known to friends and acquaintances as Sid and Sadie. And this, perhaps, is where we start looking, because this is where the story starts to come into the rather unusual territory that we currently occupy. This is Sarah and Sidney Smithfield-Wyatt."

He pulled up a picture of two very tall, very blond, very pale people. They were almost exactly alike in stature, in face, and even in expression. Their gold-blond hair was of different lengths. The one I assumed was Sid had it cut short and slicked over, almost exactly like Jack's. Sadie's was longer, brushing her shoulders, winged back lightly from her face. Their eyebrows and eyelashes were seemingly nonexistent, so their faces were nearly bald. Both wore slashes of duck-egg-blue eye shadow and had silver disks painted on their foreheads. He wore a wide-lapel white suit and a gold lamé tie; she wore a modified kimono in a green silky material. This kimono opened low at the neck and came up high and wide in a revealing slit in the front. It would have fallen open if not for a thick brown leather belt marked with the image of a triangle. Both wore matching high platform boots of the same bright gold as Sid's tie.

So, not casual dressers.

"Fraternal twins," Thorpe said. "But verging on identical in appearance."

"They look like aliens," Boo said.

"It was the fashion of the time, I gather," he said. "They were the sole heirs to a large fortune. Their parents died in an automobile accident, in which they were also involved, when they were fifteen years old."

"Near death when they were fifteen?" I said. "Jane said she was part of a group with the sight."

"A fair assumption, given what we know. For three years,

the family estate was managed by lawyers. At eighteen, Sid and Sadie gained access to some accounts, and at twenty-one inherited it all. They had quite the reputation. Most references to them appear in the footnotes of rock musician biographies—they were known for the parties at their house on Hyssop Close. Several sources claim that they were involved in what is only referred to as 'the occult.' They had no arrest records, but the police kept a bit of an eye on the property because the neighbors were alarmed by the people they saw going in and out—not unusual for that period either. On the twenty-eighth of December, 1973, the police were called to the house by Jane Quaint. She had legally changed her name by that time. She said she had been away for the holiday, and when she returned, she found a note in the upstairs study."

He pulled up an image of a handwritten note, scrawled in green ink on a piece of yellowing paper:

Dearest Jane,

Our curiosity has gotten the better of us. We are children of blessed Demeter and blessed Hecate, living in the doorway, always wondering what's inside. We're bored, and we must know what comes next. They'll never find us, dearest. What we have planned is simply too wonderful for that. It would never do just to die and rot on the floor like pensioners.

Don't mourn us—you know how silly that is. Take care of our lovely things.

You will see us soon.

With love,
Sid and Sadie

"The investigators at the time were deeply suspicious," he said. "Two rich young people, everything left to the care of another young person, and a questionable suicide note that indicates the bodies won't be found. They searched the house. The investigation notes make for interesting reading. The police clearly had very little idea what to make of what they found there: incense-covered altars, statues of three-headed dogs, strange plants that they thought were cannabis but turned out to be perfectly legal, if unusual, herbs. There were drugs found on the property—none in Jane's quarters, but plenty in Sid and Sadie's bedrooms, in boxes in the living areas, in the kitchen in containers marked for tea and coffee and sugar. Jane was briefly detained for this, but the house wasn't hers, and therefore, neither were the drugs."

He flicked through a few black-and-white photos taken of the inside of the house. It looked like it was dirtier. Some of the electronics and appliances were different. The television was some kind of massive cabinet. The refrigerator and stove were smaller. Aside from those things, though, it hadn't actually changed much since 1973. Jane really had kept most of the decor exactly as it was. There were lots of close-up photos, with pointing fingers indicating what the police found suspicious— tea canisters loaded with what must have been pot, boxes with glass hypodermic needles and rolled bits of tinfoil, leather books that were all about magic and the occult practices, curved knives, goblets.

"Jane," he went on, "according to the record, was nothing more than a housekeeper and assistant. Furthermore, the police concluded that no effort had been made to clean up the house before they were called, which added veracity to Jane's account. She said that Sid and Sadie had an interest in the occult, which was obvious from the books and objects in the house, and dabbled in what she called 'death magic.' The neighbors confirmed that there were unusual goings-on. The notes indicate that the police believed Jane. Still, the twins' accounts were frozen for several years. Jane continued maintaining the house. She went to university. Finally, in 1980, she asked for a small amount of money to be unfrozen so she could repair a bit of the roof that had developed a leak. Since seven years had elapsed and everything seemed to be in order, Sid and Sadie were declared dead and the assets unfrozen. Jane's activities were monitored for a short time, but she didn't remove any large sums or change her lifestyle. She seemed to have no interest in profiting from their death. Any investigation into the matter was closed in the mid-eighties."

"So she murdered them and got away with it?" Boo asked.

"We don't know that. It's just a possibility. What matters more right now are the property records. We've run checks on any additional properties that might be owned by the Smithfield-Wyatts. There were some, but they were sold off in the late 1960s and early 1970s, further adding to the massive cash reserves the pair had. The only house they kept, that we can find, is the one in London. We checked the bank accounts. There have been no significant lump sums removed, but in the mid-nineties, smaller amounts were moved around and withdrawn over a few years, about one hundred thousand pounds in all. This is not a large amount, considering the wealth here, but that was certainly enough for a small house somewhere. There's nothing in Jane's name, so it's likely in someone else's. We're running Jane's relatives and known associates."

"How does Charlotte get found?" I asked. "If you can't find this house?"

"There's an alert at all airports, train stations, and ports. Her photo has been released to all police stations around the country and is already on the BBC website and will be on the news. Given everything we've heard and that we know, she's likely still in the country."

"What about that thing they say about the first forty-eight hours being important? Is it true? It's already been a day."

I was hoping he would tell me that's just something they say on TV, but he didn't.

"We need to get moving," he said. "I've managed to keep the news about Stephen quiet, but that won't last. Once it's out, I don't know what will happen to this team. If they decide to close us down, they'll send a team to his flat and take everything. We need to get there first and preserve any records Stephen kept."

"We can check to see if Stephen is there," Boo said, nodding. "It's as good a place as any to start looking."

"Is the flat secure?" Thorpe said. "Did either of you tell anyone where it was?"

I was about to say no, and then I remembered something else about that last day.

"One of them," I said. "Devina . . . she drove me to Stephen and Callum's place. Well, not all the way there. I didn't want her to have the address, because no one was supposed to know about the flat. I had her drop me at Waterloo station. I don't think she followed me."

"How sure are you of that?"

"Pretty sure?"

"I don't like *pretty sure*," he said. "But I think this Devina has gone to ground with Jane, and our time to get into that flat may be limited. We'll be fast and careful. Put your coat on."

He handed me the plain brown coat Boo had purchased for me.

"You do what I say," he said, "when I say it. You have a habit of not following instructions. I'm not Stephen. Remember that."

This statement fixed me firmly back in reality. Despite the fact that he had taken me into his house, Thorpe had no intention of coddling me. I wasn't going to be curled up on his couch or sharing cups of tea and personal stories, like I had been with Stephen. Thorpe was the suited, white-haired enigma again. I may have been with other people, but I was very much on my own.

4

WHEN I FIRST MET STEPHEN AND CALLUM AND BOO, Stephen and Callum lived together in a flat off Charing Cross Road, in an alley so narrow you could stretch out your arms and touch the houses on either side. The front of it looked like it was a storefront from a Dickens novel—a large window cut into a dozen or more little panes, shiny black paint, lights that I think were supposed to look old-fashioned. They'd gotten the place on a good deal because it appeared to be haunted and people didn't like staying there. Then they dehaunted it, it became a more pleasant place to live, and the rent went up. They found another, more basic place on the streets behind Waterloo station. This one was a grungy walk-up with a malfunctioning hall light and weird stairway carpet and everyone's old mail all over the floor by the door.

This was the flat we waited by now, tucked inside Thorpe's car. We didn't park right in front of it. At first, Thorpe wouldn't stop at all—he drove around the block slowly, scanning all the

cars. Then he parked a few streets away and instructed someone to send a CCTV feed to his phone. He studied this for
another ten minutes or so. He told Boo to walk to the street
the flat was on, go past it, buy something from the shop on the
corner past the house, and come back again. I was instructed
to keep down, so I lay on the backseat and stared up through
the rain-dotted window at the gray sky. Boo came back after ten
minutes or so and reported that the curtains were open and
the lights were off.

On the way over, Thorpe had run through what we'd be doing inside. We'd check the flat for Stephen. If he wasn't there,
Thorpe and Boo would immediately begin removing any of
Stephen's notes and files, as well as his computer and tablet.
I was to go to his room and look around quickly for anything
that seemed important—a second phone, notepads, anything
of significance that had to do with his work or life. We'd been
given reusable shopping bags for these purposes. We were to
fill them and be out the door within five minutes.

We waited some more. Thorpe continued to study his
phone, the street. He told Boo to take his place behind the
wheel and to drive off if anyone got anywhere near the car.
He then did the same errand he'd sent Boo on. Boo sat in the
front, I remained lying down in the back, and we both listened
to the rain hitting the roof of the car.

"How did we get here?" I asked.

"Dunno," she said. She sounded exhausted. I had never
known Boo to seem even remotely tired. When I'd lived with
her at Wexford for a few weeks, she seemed to be powered by
taurine and enriched uranium.

"I know he came back," Boo said. "I saw how you reacted

when he . . . I mean, when you were holding his hand. You didn't just fall—you were thrown, like you'd had a shock. I know he's out there, and it's *good* that he is. And we *will* find him. Jo told me that sometimes they get confused. They don't know what's happened to them. It's like . . . amnesia or something. They're in shock."

Jo had been Boo's best friend. She was a ghost, a soldier from World War II who'd been killed during a bombing raid on London. Jo patrolled the streets of East London for over seventy years. When Boo had the car accident that gave her the sight, it was Jo who helped get her out of the wreck before the car caught fire. Jo had come to my aid when the Ripper, Alexander Newman, cornered me and stabbed me in the downstairs bathroom in my house at Wexford. Jo took the terminus and used it on Newman, taking him out and taking herself out in the process. The resulting explosion was so powerful that it shattered all the glass in the room, cracked the floor, and made me what I was. Boo never got over Jo's loss. She didn't mention her name much anymore, but I could tell Jo was never far from her thoughts.

"We need to think of places," she went on.

"What about his sister?" I asked. "He might try to find her."

"He already did that," Boo said. "He told me. First thing he did when he joined the squad and got access to the police database. He went looking for her where she died, and he said she wasn't there."

"He told you that?"

For some reason, it bothered me that Stephen would share something as personal as that with Boo. It shouldn't have, but it did.

"When I joined," she said. "He told me not to go looking for the dead."

We let that remark go.

"Last night," she said, turning around for a moment to look at me. "Something weird was going on. What were you two talking about in the bedroom?"

"We . . . were kissing."

Boo wheeled around and widened her eyes so suddenly and so extremely that I thought they might come out of their sockets. Because that can happen. I mean, I know it happens to dogs. One of our neighbors at home had a pug whose eyes used to come out every once in a while, and they'd put them back in. They called him Popeye. Swear to God.

I hoped Boo's eyes wouldn't fall out.

"I *knew* it," she said. "I *knew* it. I knew it was going to happen. I knew it."

"Callum saw," I said. "But he said something about a bet."

Boo shook her head, then turned back around.

"It's good," she said. "You two—that was coming for ages. It's good he had that. He needed that. He was always so . . ."

"Is," I corrected her.

"We're all going to be all right, yeah?" she said, though it sounded more like she was reassuring herself. "We're going to find him. We're all going to be fine, yeah? *All* of us."

She pulled out her phone and checked it. From her expression, I could tell she didn't see what she wanted to see.

"Callum hasn't called?" I asked.

"He will," she said, pocketing the phone.

Thorpe came back to the car a few minutes later and got

into the passenger side and told Boo to pull the car around to the front of the flat.

"It's clear," he said. "We'll walk over, slowly. Drive over and park by the door."

Everything about Stephen came flooding down on me as soon as we stepped into the dark threshold of the foyer. Funny, I'd only been in these flats a handful of times, and yet they formed some of my most important memories of my time in London. This counted school, and seeing the Ripper, and all of the messed-up things I'd been through. Nothing was quite as vivid as the memory of sitting around with Stephen at the crappy old kitchen table they had, drinking tea out of chipped, mismatched mugs, smelling old curry takeaway containers in the garbage. His surroundings were a sharp contrast to his actual person, which was always perfectly neat, perfectly composed.

We went quietly up the stairs. Thorpe went first, and we followed.

I never expected to see Stephen standing there waiting for us. He'd only been in this flat for a few weeks. It wasn't the place I think he would call home—if he called anywhere home. Still, as we opened the door, my heart skipped a bit.

There was nothing. It was a dark, cold flat, all the lights off, the usual takeout containers and dirty tea mugs strewn about. There was a sofa, with a sweater thrown over the back and a book resting on the arm, like the sofa itself was a huge bookmark. Thorpe looked to us to see if we saw anything or anyone, and we shook our heads at the same time. He walked around quietly, testing the doors, looking into the rooms. It was soon clear that we were alone.

"All right," he said. "Go."

Both he and Boo made for Stephen's work area at once. Thorpe bagged the computer and papers. Boo started pulling down notes that were pinned to the corkboard and taped to the wall. I headed to Stephen's bedroom, swallowing hard.

He really did live like a monk. A messy monk. Nothing on the walls. An unmade bed with a plain green wool blanket and another ugly clay-red blanket tucked at the foot. There were a lot of books piled along the walls, a bit of laundry, poorly folded in a broken basket. Instead of a bedside stand, there was a plastic crate of books and a lamp with a crooked shade. On top, resting on a small pile of novels, was a spare pair of glasses.

A wave hit me—an agony so profound it was exquisite. It stopped my heart and took my air and made the floor feel like it was falling away. Nope. Nope, nope, nope. Feelings denied. I had to be fine for him, and therefore I would be fine. This was an order.

I went to the bureau. Top drawer was filled with underwear. Boxers, to be specific. This was exactly the kind of moment when he might turn up, with me peering into the depths of the underwear drawer.

When I looked over my shoulder, he wasn't there.

I turned back to the drawer and took a moment to acknowledge the weirdness of this activity, and another to note that he had nice boxers that were surprisingly colorful and even patterned. Under the uniform, he'd been sporting some purples and pinks and snazzy stripes. I shut the drawer maybe a little too firmly and loudly and moved on to the next and the next and the next. What I wanted to find was some kind of personal journal entitled *All My Thoughts and Emotions Explained*,

Especially the Parts about Rory. What I found were T-shirts and sweat clothes and socks. I moved to the closet.

This was sparsely packed, but here I saw signs of quality, the evidence of money in his past. Four dress shirts, two blue, one gray, one pink. They had those long, open-fold cuffs that didn't have buttons because they were designed for cuff links. One suit, which, when I looked at the label, was from a Savile Row tailor. The label indicated that it was bespoke. There were several plain white shirts of a kind of hardy polyester-cotton—police shirts. Police sweater. Police pants and jacket.

At the bottom of the closet, along with the uniform shoes and one pair of dress shoes, there were sneakers and cleated sneakers and yet some other, entirely different kind of sneaker. A small pile of mystifying sports gear—pads, things like that. At the back of the closet—a painted oar that clearly came from Eton. Also, one closed cardboard box marked with a sticker that read: PERSONAL. This was promising.

"Rory."

Thorpe was at the door.

"Time to go."

I grabbed the box.

5

THORPE DIDN'T TELL US MUCH ABOUT THE NEXT STOP ON this trip, except that it was "a property we use for various things." His tone suggested that we didn't really want to delve too deeply into what that actually meant. I couldn't see where we were going, because I was still under orders to remain flat in the backseat, now largely covered in bags of Stephen's paperwork. It was turning dark, although it probably wasn't even four o'clock yet. I watched the top halves of buses roll past and sometimes saw up the sides of tall buildings. Then there were no tall buildings and fewer buses, and then we stopped on a street that sounded quite quiet.

"Get up," he said to me. "We're here."

The street was lined with brick houses. In London, the houses I'd seen that were like this tended to be joined up and tall, with long windows—more social. The particular house he walked us to was the least social of any on the street. It stood alone at the end of the row. It was dark, with no other decoration in the front garden but two bins, for trash and recycling, each labeled in marker with the house number. While the doorway looked like the others, Thorpe pushed a ceramic house number plate aside to reveal a keypad. He punched in a few numbers, then unlocked the door and ushered us in.

"Close the curtains," he said, as soon as we got inside.

The house was furnished in a basic and tidy fashion using what looked like the greatest hits of the IKEA catalog—at least the hits that had no personality. There were no pictures on the walls, no rugs on the floors. The sofa and chairs were tan, and all the tables and everything else were plain pine. There were white plastic lamps with those energy-efficient bulbs that emit a faintly greenish light. The curtains were the only thing that passed as any kind of decoration at all. They were thick and serious, proper blackout curtains that would have held back the light even if the sun expanded and hovered outside the window.

"Right," he said. "Boo, bring in everything from the car. Put it here, on the floor."

Boo jogged out and started the unloading.

"What happens now?" I asked.

"Now I have to go back to my office and attend to a few things. You'll stay here with Boo."

"We need to be *looking*."

"Looking where? You have no plan. For now, your job is to keep safe. There are some basic provisions in the kitchen—tea and . . . possibly nothing else. Pot noodle, perhaps. If you're tired, there's a bed in the front bedroom."

Boo brought in everything in a half-dozen sprints. When

she was done and slightly out of breath, Thorpe handed her his car keys.

"Keep these in case you need them," he said. "I'll use Tube and taxis to get back. Set the alarm when I leave. The code is 3762. If it goes off, Boo, you take Rory and you get her out of here. I'll be back in a few hours. Bhuvana, a word outside, please."

The two of them stepped out, and Boo returned a moment later, looking solemn.

"We're just going to sit here?" I said.

She took off her jacket and set it on the back of one of the chairs. Her eyes were flicking back and forth, looking over the bags of paperwork, over to the windows, to the wall.

"I have to stay with you," she said.

"We'll *both* go."

"No," she said. "Thorpe's right. Jane and them, yeah? They're out there."

"So let them come find me. If they find me, you find them, you get Charlotte. We could do that—I could—stand some-where and we could—"

Boo ignored my ridiculous nonplan.

"Leave me," I said. "If you won't go with me, then I'll stay here. There's an alarm."

"Go with you where?" she said. And that was the essential problem. Thorpe was correct. We had no plan.

"I've texted Callum ten times," she said. "We need him here. If he's here, I can go look."

Callum had left the hospital in a really emotional state as soon as he realized what I'd done. It was another terrible ele-ment in an already terrible series of events. I'd lost track of him in the blur of it all. But Boo was in love with Callum. Nothing had ever happened between them, as far as I knew. I wasn't even sure if Callum knew.

It was funny—all these important life events had happened to me, and they'd been there, and I really knew very little about either of them. I knew Boo had family in Mumbai, but she was from East London. She still lived with her parents. She was out of school and, as far as they knew, working. She had some kind of cover story for what she did. She had gotten her sight in a car accident, and her friend Jo had saved her life. Her attitude was always ghost-positive. Callum's mother was from Kingston, Jamaica, and he had been in training to be a professional football player until the accident that gave him the sight. It was a ghost that caused the accident, which involved a live wire in some standing groundwater. Callum had hated ghosts from the start. He was in the squad to destroy them.

Which is why this was going to be so hard. I had made Stephen into the thing that Callum despised.

Boo's phone buzzed. She had been gripping it in her hand the entire time.

"Callum," she said. "Finally. Thorpe must have rung him. He's on his way here. I think I'm going to meet him outside first, yeah?"

"I get it," I said.

When Boo left, the house settled around me. I sat on the cold, bare floor, under the faintly greenish light, Stephen's work things around me in bags, the box from the closet sitting over by the staircase. Any other day, I would have been in that box like a rabbit down a hole, but now it sat there like some kind of silent threat.

I crouched down next to it and pulled open the folded flaps. This was wrong—going from learning about his life in tiny spoonfuls to total access to everything because he could do nothing to stop it. The dead had no rights to privacy. Everything Stephen held dear was out there for everyone else to see and pick through.

The box was packed to the brim. On the top were a bunch of notebooks marked with labels that read *Latin, Classics, History (English pre-1600)*. School stuff from Eton. I gave these a quick page through to see his handwriting, to see what kinds of things he had learned. Mostly they were handouts, all dense and serious, like something you'd get when you were in college. Beneath these were some pieces of what I guessed was the Eton uniform—a tie, a vest with silver buttons. A few books— six novels and a book of Shakespeare's poetry. An orange train ticket from six years before. Near the bottom, there were two photographs. One was of a dog with curly red fur. The second photo was of Stephen. There was a girl with him, her arm wrapped over his shoulders. They were kneeling in the sand, and he was crouching a bit to be level with her.

His sister. There was something about the eyes, and they had the same dark brown hair. She was physically much smaller, her smile much wider, much bolder. She wore a two-piece bathing suit, and there were bracelets down her arm. She tipped her head against his. He was clearly younger in this photo—his face smoother and thinner. His eyes and brow still had that worried look, like something was coming in the immediate future. But he was also smiling. I'd very rarely seen him smile.

A photo of two dead people.

I don't know how long I sat there holding that picture,

looking at it as if I could magic myself into its world, fall inside its boundaries, and turn up on a beach in the past. Feelings kept spilling over me, confusing waves—jealousy of his sister, for making him so happy. Happiness that I'd found the photo, then giddiness, then a sharp hysteria, and then . . .

Just crying. Heavy-duty, no air, no light, nothing but the sound of heaving crying. Crying until my body was dry and there was nothing left and it heaved in vain. When that was done, I was still sitting there in the empty room, holding a picture. I set it down gingerly and pushed myself to my feet. I stumbled back, my eyes still blurry, in the direction of what I believed to be the kitchen. There were blinds in this room, not curtains, and they had been drawn. Little lines of light came through and partially illuminated the sink. I put my head under the faucet and ran the tap water right into my mouth until I gagged and coughed. Then I leaned against the sink for a moment and waited until the gagging stopped. Now that I had let that all out, my thoughts were a little clearer. I lifted two slats of the blinds with my fingers and looked out at a view that consisted entirely of darkness, albeit darkness contained by what looked like some pretty high brick garden walls.

I heard the front door open and Boo call my name. I splashed my face, dried it on my hoodie, and went back into the living room. Boo was there, looking a bit strained. Behind her, Callum had his hands rooted into the pockets of his coat.

"Hey," I said.

Callum said nothing. A quiet Callum was an intimidating sight. He was—as much as I hate this word, I have to use it— built. Built like a thing that has been built by poets and people who love building things. And when I say intimidating, I don't mean I thought Callum would hurt me. He never would. The pain, the rage at what happened, those things were evident. He was a mass of potential energy.

Boo tapped his arm.

"Listen," she said, "we have to stick together, yeah? There's work to be done. And we're a team. We have to keep it together. We need to talk."

Nothing. He might as well have been a statue.

"So," Boo said, bravely carrying on, "we need to make a plan. Together. All of us."

"A plan for what?" Callum said.

"Finding him," she said.

"Don't say that," Callum said.

"Callum—"

"I didn't come here for that."

"Callum—"

"He's not—"

"He is," I said.

The great statue that was Callum tipped its head toward me.

"I know what I saw," he said, and there was something terrible and raw in his voice. "I saw my best friend *die*."

"Callum . . ." Boo said again.

"I've been walking around, yeah?" he said. "I walked all day. I walked because I thought I'd go mental if I stopped walking. I know what I saw. He died."

"You know that doesn't mean anything," Boo said. "Look at what we *do*."

"It means *everything*. Dead is dead. If you actually did bring him back, then you did the worst possible thing you could do to him. You got him into that accident. You should have let him go. I have to think he's gone. He was *my friend.* You barely knew him."

"That's it!" Boo said. Her hand went up, and her finger hovered in front of his face. "That's enough, yeah? That's *enough.* Rory did not kill Stephen. He drove that car himself. Rory did something in that room, and if it brought him back, he's back. He's still Stephen, and he's still your friend. He's still one of us, and *nothing* is different. Is *this* how you're going to treat him? Like he's a monster? So if you're his friend, you get your head together and help us find him, and you do it now. Or else sling your hook."

Boo was shaking as she said these words. Callum drew into himself, his muscles straining against the fabric of his coat. He walked to the wall and back. The air between us felt like it was twitching.

"*If* this happened, yeah?" Callum's London accent had never seemed so gruff, so foreign to my ears. "*If* this happened—if you did this to him—then we have to find him. But if he was really here, wouldn't he have come to us?"

"It happened," I said.

"You didn't stay for what happened next," Boo added. "The lights in the hospital went out. The window in his room shattered and broke."

This didn't seem to do much to endear me to Callum.

"But he wasn't there," Callum said.

"That's not always how it works," Boo said.

"We usually find them where they die."

"*Usually,*" Boo said. "But this isn't usual. We were thinking about places he lived. We checked the flat."

"So did I," Callum said. "Both of them."

Callum had checked some places. He was sort of on our side.

"Then we'll check other places he lived. Eton. Do you know where his parents live?"

"Somewhere in Kent."

"It's probably in here somewhere," Boo said, looking around at the bags on the floor. "Some record or something from school."

"He wouldn't go to his parents. He hated them. Eton too."

"Might not be a choice," Boo said. "We have to look. He got the sight at Eton, yeah?"

"When he—" Callum cut himself off.

"He told me," I said, "he almost killed himself. Because of what happened to his sister. It was in a boathouse or something?"

"It's somewhere to look." Boo pulled out her phone and checked something.

"Eton is near Windsor. If we take Thorpe's car, we can be there in an hour. Let's find the other address."

She dove into the bags of paperwork alone and dug around for a few minutes before giving up.

"We'll get it from Thorpe," she said. "We'll start at Eton. Rory, are you okay, being here?"

So she had changed her mind on that one. I didn't want to hold them back, and I didn't want to be alone. Alone was the end of the world.

"Go," I said.

Callum turned to the door and left. Boo came over to me and took me by the shoulders and looked me in the eye.

"We'll sort it," she said. "It'll be okay, yeah?"

"Callum hates me."

"He doesn't. He's upset, that's all. I'll talk to him. I'll sort it."

I didn't know if Boo believed these things could all be fixed or was talking herself into it.

Then it was just me and the box again, and I wasn't going back in there. I curled up on the sofa and turned on the television for some company. I needed noise, light, something to fill the vacuum. I would use this time. I would think about this problem. Where would Stephen be? Not Eton, not his parents'. Those didn't feel right to me. There had to be an answer.

Or there was no answer at all. That was the other possibility.

I closed my eyes like I had at the hospital and tried to return to Imaginary Uncle Bick and the bird store. I could see the store in my mind, hear the birds tweeting and bickering overhead, feel the little feathers fluttering down and landing on my face. I could see my uncle's beardy face, hear his broad Southern accent saying my name, see the A Bird in Hand logo on his baseball cap—but he had no wisdom to impart to me. He was sweetly silent, and the birds flew around. As I found myself drifting, I felt like there might be someone lingering in the aisles of the store, over by the birdseed bells and tiny mirrors, and I wanted to say something about this to Uncle Bick, but he shook his head and said, "They're sleeping."

Then I was too.

6

THE NEXT THING I KNEW, THORPE WAS SITTING ACROSS from me in different clothes. I sat up with a jolt.

"What time is it?"

"Just after nine."

"Nine?"

"In the morning," he said.

The curtains were still closed, so the room was dark.

"I slept?" I said, rubbing my head.

"Shock," he said. "It's what happens. Boo and Callum went to Eton last night. They didn't find anything. They're driving to Kent now, to where Stephen's family is."

"I don't think they're going to find anything there," I said.

"Why's that?"

"I don't know."

"Normally," he said, standing up, "I wouldn't be able to work with that. But this isn't normal, is it?"

He blinked, and I wondered if he had slept. It was possible he'd been sitting in that chair all night, looking at me. He had a massive paper coffee cup sitting on the floor and another in his hand.

"That's a lot of coffee," I said.

"I need to go out as well," he said. "Something to attend to. I didn't want to leave until I spoke to you. You're secure in here. Boo left you last night, which was against instruction, but as long as the alarm is on and you don't . . ."

He fumbled around with his coat. No, no sleep for Thorpe. This was not happening. I was going to be left in this stupid empty house again while Stephen and Charlotte were out there. Not that I had any more of a plan than last night.

"I should be doing something," I said.

"You should be staying here, at least until we have Jane and the others in custody. Set the alarm behind me. Boo and Callum will be back in a few hours."

"But . . ."

"I have to attend to the body," he said. He wasn't mean about it, just direct. The body. In this impossible new reality, Stephen was "the body." Which made me think of something that should have occurred to me sooner—I mean, I knew it on some level, but there is knowing something in the back of your mind, and knowing it in the front of your mind, where you see how it's relevant to your actual life. That body, now separated from Stephen, was the same one I had seen some parts of and touched some parts of the night before. And now, just when everything was good, that body was gone. However Stephen came back to us, I could not touch him. I was actively dangerous to him.

I looked at my hands, as if this were their fault.

"I'll be back as soon as I can," he said. "You *can* do something. You can go through these bags. There might be something in there that's useful."

This was Thorpe's way of throwing me a bone. Those bags contained notes, documents—stuff relating to the squad that I guessed very few people would ever be allowed to see.

"Make yourself some tea," he said. "I brought some fruit and packets of cereal. Eat."

"Yeah," I said.

"I mean it. If you don't eat, you don't function. If you want to be useful, eat, then go through the documents."

When he left, I did as he said—I made a cup of tea, and I ate some honey nut flakes dry, out of the box. In the living room, I opened the curtains to let in some light. I was going to sit on the floor, so it wasn't like anyone was going to be able to see me, and I couldn't read all these papers under the sick glow of the cheap lamps.

Also, I was tired of being in the dark.

There were nine bags in total, all stuffed and thick with papers, folders, and notebooks. This prospect was less imposing than the box. These were Stephen's professional thoughts, and somewhere in here there might be an answer. In the light of day, tea in body, something to do—I started to feel almost normal.

The first bag was useless. Lots of police stuff, lots of the forms that Stephen had tried to implement to bring some order to what they did. Boo and Callum had made fun of him for these, and I could see why. Nothing direct was mentioned on the forms. They didn't have boxes marked, "List how many ghosts you blew up today." There were places for an address, a time, a few coded things. All they told me was where a ghost had been found and if a *T* had happened. *T*, I soon figured, meant *terminus* or *terminate*, which was the same thing. Boo's rarely had *T*s. Callum's almost always did. Stephen's was half and half. In with these there was a *London A–Z*, which was a standard-issue book of maps they sold everywhere in the city. It was all of London, in detail, with an index in the back so you could look up any street and go right to that page. He had marked this one up with dots and Post-its stuck to the pages, dozens of them.

12 December

Called to Tower Hill after unexplained power cut. Subject (female, date unknown) seen walking on track surface. Coaxed to platform. Subject had fallen in front of the train. T, 18:45.

16 December

Subject at Dead Man's Hole, female, recent (within last ten years). Left to remain. Possible contact.

18 December

Family of six (date unknown but looked to be late 19th or early 20th), two parents, three children, one infant, found in Catharine Wheel Alley. On questioning responded that there had been a fire in the night. T group, 20:35.

28 December

*Subject (male, date unknown) spotted on
Embankment. Subject had jumped into river. This
subject seemed aware of passing time. T, 22:00.*

These notes weren't on every page—London is massive—but there were a lot of them. Maybe a hundred, maybe two hundred. What it looked like he was doing was taking the information from the forms and making a map of the ghosts of London—who they were, what they were generally up to.

I dug into the next bag. This was full of loose paperwork. Most of it looked boring or irrelevant—details of police training at Hendon. Handouts about police procedures, paperwork, uniforms, standards of conduct. There were copies of signed forms signifying the completion of different units of training—defensive driving, evidence processing, what forms to fill out. So much of this was about filling out forms. There were several sets of photocopies from what looked like academic works on magic and myth and ritual. I glanced through these very quickly before setting them into their own pile.

At the bottom of one of the bags was a small black hardback notebook bound shut with an elastic band. I snapped this off. Inside, I was greeted with what looked like pure gibberish:

LXXIKTZIHVHZ
NCXWTUGVGTA
QXQDYPWNY

There were a few pages of this, broken usually into blocks of one or two lines. I flipped through the entire book, but nothing else was written in it. I stared at this for a while. This was clearly something very different from the rest of the materials. I set this aside. This would need coming back to.

I continued going through the bags quickly, trying to get a sense of what was here. What I found in the next two was more police paperwork and forms. The forms were *endless*. I nearly went into a trance sifting through these and was about to push the bag aside, when one piece of paper caught my eye. It was thicker, better quality. There was a raised official seal in the corner that read FOR HOME OFFICE USE ONLY. And then I saw— it was Stephen's whole past on a page.

INTAKE FORM

Surname: Dene

Given name: Stephen Dorian

Place of birth: Canterbury, Kent

Parents: Edward and Diana Dene (banker/wedding planner)

Siblings: Regina Claudette Dene (deceased aged 17, recreational opiate overdose, ruled accidental)

Education:

Winchester House School, Brackley, Northamptonshire

Eton College

Honours: House Captain, Godolphin House; Oppidan Scholar; Sixth Form Select

Sport: Rowing

Admitted to Trinity College, Cambridge, department of Natural Sciences (Chemistry) [did not attend]

Languages known: French, Latin, some Italian

Recruited: via hospital

Notes on first interview: Dene presents as highly intelligent, competent. Does not appear to have many outside interests outside of reading and some sport. Does not appear to have wide social circle. Speaks of Eton and parents with flat affect. When asked about sister, will not reply beyond fact that she is deceased. **Recommendation:** Exceptional intelligence and sterling academic record make him natural candidate. Recommended for stage two at Hendon immediately following discharge.

There was an addendum at the bottom of the page:

Instructors at Hendon note that Dene is highly competent and progressing well. However, in standard risk-assessment simulations, Dene either fails to notice or discounts certain dangers. He seems to have a certain lack of regard for personal safety. Despite some reservations, recommended for stage three. Continue monitoring.

Which told me exactly one thing—they knew. They knew that Stephen was exactly the kind of person who would throw himself into the line of fire. He'd done it *twice* with me, the second time being the one that really counted.

Someone had known he was like this and had let things go on anyway.

This is when the rage began. It came down on me like thunder—like a big Southern summer storm, taking over everything, cracking through the sky. Thorpe, and whoever else Thorpe worked with, they let this happen. Thorpe, who was matter-of-factly dealing with the body. The *body*.

Last night's tears were this morning's current of electricity. I was leaving this house. I would look all over London. I would burn London down if I had to.

But I *still* didn't have a plan.

I stood, hands on hips, heart pounding, staring down at the piles I had created around the room. I grabbed the *A–Z* and flipped through the book. I turned to where I thought we were now, Highgate. There were a few notes on this page, but the one that caught my eye was this:

> *4 April*
> *Found in Highgate Cemetery/tree, subject*
> *"Resurrection Man." Mid 19th c. Clearly well*
> *informed. Left to remain. Possible contact.*

A possible informant, around where I was currently staying. Resurrection Man was a weird name, but one that sounded promising. This was enough for me.

7

CONVENIENTLY, THERE WAS VERY LITTLE WAY OF MISSING Highgate Cemetery. All I had to do, according to the map, was walk up a street called Swain's Lane, and I would be in the middle of it. This street was very quiet, and the tree count went up considerably. On my right, there was a low wall with a fence of black spikes, and tombstones were clearly visible. The road eventually led to a gatehouse that looked like the entry to a Gothic church. It cost a few pounds to get in, and I paid a little bit more for a map. There was a warning at the bottom explaining that the cemetery was huge and in some places unstable, so there were areas no one was supposed to enter. This was quickly explained when I saw what the place was like inside. It was wild, so broken. There were so many gravestones, rarely two of them alike. There were the standard slab ones you expected to find if someone was drawing a cartoon of a graveyard. Along with those, there were Celtic crosses, plain crosses, pillars, columns, urns, human figures. They were pressed together, with barely any space between. Many had been pushed up or had sunk over time, and most were at least a bit crooked. Many of the shorter ones had ivy clumped on top of them like mad, ill-fitting toupees. There were trees everywhere, shooting up from clusters of graves, all bare of leaves. Some of the roots had snaked out of the ground and clutched at the monuments, hugging them with long, thick tendrils. It reminded me of a show I once watched about what the world would look like if humans stopped taking care of things, and electricity turned off, and water was shut off, and no one maintained anything. Apparently, it wouldn't take long at all for the plants to come and run the place, knocking everything to the side and generally getting some long-awaited horticultural revenge.

This was going to make finding "tree" difficult.

The paths varied between paved and well maintained to places in the undergrowth that had been sufficiently tramped down by human feet to become bald. A few of the hardier London birds screamed in the trees, and the wind ripped through them. Highgate, I soon realized, got the name from being really high up. From some points, you could look down over London.

I passed a few other people—cold, faintly miserable tourists clutching guidebooks in a smattering of different languages. All seemed to be wondering why they had come to a cemetery in England in December, when even the best day was a bit gloomy and spitting rain. They dutifully took pictures of the more interesting stones, and I pulled up my hood and walked past with my head turned the other way. Not that these people would have any idea who I was. It was Thorpe's instruction, and I was feeling twitchy. The sky above looked like it planned to let loose at any moment. As it was, invisible rain was spitting in my face, and my gloveless hands were going numb in my pockets.

The one thing I didn't see was ghosts.

Tree. Really, Stephen. For a guy who loved precision and details, this is all the information he gave. *Tree.*

I reached what the map called the Egyptian Avenue, which began with a wide, sculpted archway that wouldn't have looked out of place in a Las Vegas reconstruction of ancient Egypt. It didn't look ancient, it didn't look Egyptian, but it did look like set dressing. Vines climbed all over the walls on either side of the arch, and these ended in a matching pair of obelisks that reminded me of the bookends that my cousin Diane used to prop up her books on auras. The archway led into an open-air corridor with a series of stone doorways on either side, tightly packed. A nice, cozy neighborhood for the dead in what amounted to a tourist attraction.

And then, as I came out of the Egyptian Avenue, I saw what Stephen might have been talking about. There was a tree—but not just a tree—a massive honking tree, considerably larger than anything else around. It was the center of a circle of tombs that had clearly been built around it, marked on the map as the "Circle of Lebanon." Here, the stone doorways were only a few feet apart—a collection of elegant portals to rooms that contained the dead. There was writing carved into the lintel and in the thick doorways—sometimes a line or two, sometimes long screeds. It was all snug, and extremely quiet, maybe the quietest place I'd been outdoors in London. I made my way around the circle once, then again. No one was around.

"Hello?" I called.

Nothing. I tried again.

"I'm looking for the Resurrection Man," I called.

The stones had no reply. The tree was silent.

I walked on, to a row of tombs in a long, covered, curved passage called the Terrace on the map. All of these tombs—the Terrace, the Egyptian Avenue, the circle—these were the expensive ones. All these tiny, private cells for the richest dead people Victorian London had to offer. (So said the commentary on the side of the map.) I trailed around, making what I could of the already declining day. I wandered down path after path, past a statue of a sleeping angel on a tomb and a monument with a sculpture of a loyal dog sleeping by his master. That one made me pause and even tear up a little.

"That's ol' Tom Sayers," said a voice behind me. I turned to find a man leaning against a tree. "Hero of the people. Great fighter he was. I saw him fight once. Beautiful thing to see. That there's his dog, Lion. Lion was the chief mourner when he died. 'Alf of East London turned out for that funeral."

I could see what he was in a moment: that grayness of aspect, the general look of being out of time. People of a certain period—and by that, I mean almost any time but the present—they didn't age like we're used to. They had lots of stuff wrong with them. Every capillary in his face looked like it had burst. His neck had something purple swelling out the side of it. Something had grown on his face that could have been a beard or a kind of mushroom. His clothes were all brown—loose pants with rips in the knee held up by a thick belt, and a shirt that may not have started off brown, with cloudlike sweat formations under the armpits. He had on a heavy, floppy brown hat. He was friendly enough and smiled nicely, showing off a mouth of decaying teeth.

"You called me the Resurrection Man?" he said. "Why's that, now?"

"That's you?" I asked.

"Aye, but it's a old name," he said. "I'm Ol' Jim. Everyone calls me Jim. Why's a young lass like you looking for Ol' Jim?"

Old Jim, as he called himself, was of an indeterminate age.

"You met a friend of mine," I said. "Tall, probably dressed like a policeman. I need . . . information?" It sounded ridiculous when I said it out loud. In fact, Jim laughed out loud and slapped the monument wall in amusement.

"What can a poor ol' man like me tell you?"

"I need to know, when someone becomes a ghost, where do they appear? How do I find someone?"

"That"—he pushed himself forward and rubbed his lips together before finishing the sentence—"depends on who yer looking for."

He stepped toward me, and I backed up.

"Ol' Jim won't hurt ya," he said.

"It's not that. I don't want to hurt *you*."

"How's that, then?" he asked.

"I have . . . I can do something."

There was no easy way of explaining this. I toed a pile of dead, slimy leaves at my feet.

"There's a thing called a terminus," I said.

"A light," he replied.

"You know about it?"

"Aye. There was a lad here once. He had one."

"That was my friend," I said eagerly. "He's the one I'm trying to find."

"He's dead. Oh, that's sad. So sad. An' you think he's . . ."

He pointed to himself.

"Like you," I said. "He is. But I can't find him. I was there with him when he died, and I know he came back, but I don't know where."

"Aye," Jim said, nodding his head. "I see the problem. And yer looking for 'im."

"Right."

"And this thing he had—the ter . . ."

"Terminus," I said.

"You 'ave one?"

"I am one," I said.

He whistled between his teeth.

"Cor . . . Now, *that's* something." He looked me up and down—a full top-to-toe scan. If a living person had done that to me, I would have reached for my pepper spray. I decided this situation got a pass. Neither one of us was really that normal.

"Well, then! Let Ol' Jim show you around. Ol' Jim's the man. Not many of my sort here, but a lovely spot. Best in London. Maybe the best in the world. That's what they used to say. Noplace like this since the 'Gyptians. I'll show you."

"I don't—"

"Come, now, you can't come to a place like this an' not let Ol' Jim show you around."

"I don't have a lot of time," I said.

Old Jim ignored this protest.

"Plenty o' time," he said. "Ol' Jim can explain it all for you. Ol' Jim knows how it works. You can count on Ol' Jim. Not much Ol' Jim hasn't seen. You want to find your frien', Ol' Jim's yer man."

This was a guy who made sure you knew his name, that was for certain.

"Okay," I said. "Sure. I can look around. And you can tell me . . ."

"Oh, lass, you've come to Ol' Jim, and Ol' Jim never let a lass down. An' I knew yer lad. Good lad. Good lad."

"He was," I said.

"And how did you know about me? Did he talk about Ol' Jim?"

"He wrote some notes," I said.

He nodded again, as if this was exactly what he was expecting to hear.

"Well, now. Let Ol' Jim show you the place. Things to see, things to see."

It looked like if I was going to get any information at all, it would only happen if I followed Old Jim around the cemetery. So that's what I did for about an hour. He didn't take me to any of the big monuments or the things on the map. Instead, he told me stories of things he'd seen at funerals—fights, people falling into open gravesites. He told me about the Great Vampire Hunt of 1970, when some people thought they saw a vampire running around the grounds and searched for it with stakes. He seemed to like that one a lot, and told me about all the things he put out for them to find. He led me far back, where there were no paths at all. I remembered the warning from the bottom of the map, about how some parts weren't safe, but Jim assured me he knew where the safe parts were. I decided it was worth risking and I would have to do my best to feel out the ground and not fall into a hole. I was pretty sure I could manage that. I mean, I grew up in a swamp. There's quicksand all around my neighborhood. This was one thing I had covered. I tried to get him back on the topic at every possible opportunity, but Jim was taking his time. He clearly liked having company, and he wasn't going to answer my questions until he'd shown me around for a while.

He was showing me a stone that had grown a bit of tree root that bore a resemblance to a certain part of the male anatomy when I caught some movement out of the corner of my eye, around the back of a tomb that was about the size of a large shed.

"Did you see something just then?" I asked.

Jim looked up and frowned.

"Aye. The beast lives around here."

"The *beast*?"

"Aye."

Given Old Jim's seemingly relentless instinct to point out every single thing of interest, you'd have thought that something called "the beast" might have come up before.

"It won't hurt you if I'm here," he said. "It's scared of Ol' Jim. But it does 'orrible things."

"Like what?"

He shook his head to indicate that such things were not to be described.

"There it is," he said, pointing. "Poking out the back there."

Sure enough, a thing was behind the tomb.

"Come outter there!" Old Jim said. "Show yerself!"

The thing poked out some more.

The first thing I noticed was the filth. That was what confused me for a minute. There was so much dirt that it was hard to make out features. But when I did make out features, there were far, far too many of them. Too many eyes, mostly bloodshot. There were some more shoulders above. And legs—I could count five, but there could have been more on the other side. And arms—seven. There were no heads, just a fusion of skulls into a lumpy dome, with bits of hair here, bits of hair there. Bits of hair all over the place. There was something brown and clothlike weaving in and out of the mess.

Sickeningly, it reminded me of something we make at home at Christmas that we call "very rocky road." You toss handfuls of things into a bowl—marshmallows and nuts, bits of pretzels and smashed M&M's. There is no science to very rocky road. You beat all this crap into a bigger bowl of melted chocolate and drop lumps of it on a tray. I get very absorbed in this process, watching little M&M pieces land side by side, or trying to get lumps with marshmallows on either side. That was what this thing was like. An eye here and there. An arm up high, another down low. It was without human shape—just a glob of people pieces mixed together and permitted to stick together however they were thrown down.

"What is it?" I said.

"Not sure," Old Jim said, disgust in his voice. "Came in the night one night from the *east side*."

By this he meant the east side of the cemetery, which was clearly an abhorrent place to him.

"It's a menace, that thing. This place is a jewel. Jewel in the crown, they says. An' a thing like that, menacing about."

He shook his head some more, and I continued to watch this disgusting thing lurking around. I wasn't sure what to feel. Scared? Probably. I was a bit. But mostly I was disgusted. I couldn't take my eyes off it.

"Now," Jim said. "A minute, 'ere. If yer a . . . what did you call it?"

"A terminus," I said.

"If yer one of them, maybe you can do sumthin' about that thing."

Could I? I had no idea. It was a ghost of *some* kind, clearly. It was many ghosts of some kind that had become one big, terrible ghost.

"I don't know," I said.

"But yer might? Ol' Jim would be grateful. Why, Ol' Jim would be yer frien', and he's a good frien' to have. So much Ol' Jim can tell ya. Ain't much he ain't seen. Do this for Ol' Jim."

"Like, tell me where people end up when they die?"

"Ol' Jim knows all sorts," he said. He smiled a little. There was something in his smile I didn't quite like, but I wasn't here to make friends. I was here for information. If I could get information by ridding the cemetery of a menace, then so much the better. If I could do this.

I stepped toward it, very, very slowly.

"Hey," I said.

It was as good an opening as any, I guess. I mean, how do you address a multieyed, no-faced blob of limbs? A few of the eyes rolled in my direction, and one of the hands made a circular motion. Maybe it was waving. Maybe it was doing jazz hands. It was unclear.

"Look," I said, "I don't know what you are. I don't know if you can understand me."

It must have sensed something bad, because it started to shift away from me. A few of the legs were moving, but not in a recognizable walking motion.

"'Orrible thing," Jim said. "Put it out of its misery."

Something about his tone caught my attention again, but now I was troubled by the more immediate concern of being face-to-face with the thing.

"My name is Rory," I said.

It quivered.

"I'm American. You can probably tell by my accent, and I'm . . . cold. It's cold, right? What is this fog? We don't get fog like this where I'm from. But sometimes? After storms? It rains frogs. Not even a joke."

It quivered again, but it was a gentler quiver.

"Frogs," I went on, stepping closer. "This doesn't *always* happen, but . . ."

I was kind of lying to the blob. My grandma said she saw a frog rain once, but I never had. I didn't have enough frog rain material to spin out this story, so I changed topics.

"What do you think of my coat?" I asked. "It's kind of big, right? I never even owned a winter coat before I moved here. It doesn't get that cold where I'm from."

Once I was within two feet, the thing came into greater focus. It was no longer simply ugly—it was wretched. It was terrible and loose, a dirty bandage of a being. All the eyes, no matter which way they pointed, had cloudy irises. I came a bit closer, at which point it started running once again, and we went after it, catching it again in another tangled corner of tombs and monuments and trees. This was my moment. I put up my hand to do the deed, but something wasn't right about all of this.

"Here you are, girl!" Jim said. "Take care of it."

It occurred to me what my problem was with Jim's tone: it was *eager*. Was it a coincidence that we had wandered the cemetery for forty-five minutes, looking at mostly nothing, only to come upon this thing that he clearly hated and wanted dead?

"What exactly did it do?" I asked.

"'Orrible things."

"Like what?" I said.

"Look at it! 'Orrible."

"I'm going to need you to be a little more specific," I said.

"Look at it! A thing like that . . ."

I turned toward Jim. His smile was a bit strained.

"You can't tell me one thing it's done," I said.

"It killed a man!"

That was a little too quick, especially since this was the third time I'd asked, and only now was this the answer.

"How?" I said.

"Scared 'im to death!"

We'd reached the point in this conversation where it was clear that I wasn't really buying it, and Jim was getting tired of selling. He dropped the smile and leaned against a nearby stone.

"What does it matter?" he said. "It's 'orrible."

"It matters because I'm about to kill it."

"Can't kill what's dead."

"I can," I said. "It hasn't done anything, has it? It ran from me. Why do you want it gone?"

Jim scratched at his beard.

"I wants it gone," he said. "This cemetery is mine."

"How can a cemetery be yours? What's there to have?"

"It's *mine*," he said, an edge developing in his voice. "It was my patch."

The lump cowered and backed itself against the fence. I stepped closer to Jim, hand extended.

"How about you tell me anyway?" I said. "I need to know where the dead turn up. Tell me that, and you won't get your ghost ass blown to the moon, how about that?"

"Dear, oh, dear," Jim said, smiling once more. "Dear, oh, dear. Shame to hurt Ol' Jim when he knows so much."

"I won't if Old Jim tells me something."

"Ah, won't ya, now? Won't ya?"

Behind me, the thing wobbled off into the trees and the gentle fog that had started to fall on the cemetery. I turned for a second to watch it go—a second, I mean it—and when I looked back, Jim was no longer in front of me. I heard something behind me, in the tomb. It was a small sound, like a pebble hitting the stone. The gate of the tomb was hanging open, and, like I said, it wasn't large. I could mostly see inside from where I was standing. There was a stone crypt inside to hold the casket, but nothing else.

As I turned, a small rock hit me on the forehead. This stunned me for a moment—more surprise than physical pain. Another rock, right on my closed eye. Another, on my arm. I stepped quickly into the tomb for protection, tucking myself back against the inside of the doorway, as a hail of rocks, some really big now, were nailing the tomb.

"You have to be kidding me," I said to myself, as one flew in the doorway and cracked into the back wall.

This went on for about two minutes and then it stopped. I was just about to lean around to see if the coast was clear, when—

Slam.

The gate clanked shut. I moved quickly when that happened, but by the time I did, I found that it was solidly closed. I shook it with all my strength, but it wasn't giving. Jim stood in front of me and watched with a smile.

"Dear, oh, dear," he said. "Look what a pretty bird I've caught."

"You've made a big mistake," I said. "When I get out of here . . ."

Jim wandered off, leaving my threat hanging in the air. I felt my pockets for the phone I knew wasn't there, but was worth checking for anyway. I yelled out, but the cemetery was large, and the wind was sharp, and it seemed to shunt my cries into the ground. No one was around. I was locked in a tomb, very alone. I returned to the secure position on the safe side of the doorway wall and sank down to the ground and balanced my head on my knees. There was a thick coating of leaves on the tomb floor, some wet, some dry. Either way, my butt was freezing.

This had been a stupid idea.

Possibly all of my ideas were stupid ideas.

They would find me, though. I mean, I wouldn't be here forever. Someone would come around, eventually. Probably some guard who checked the place before closing, which would be . . . I unfolded my damp map and scanned the information section . . . five in the evening. It probably wasn't even noon yet. So five hours until someone (possibly) found me.

Thorpe, Boo, Callum . . . they would be looking too, but I'd left no indication of where I was.

I would get out. Of that, I was certain. And it didn't particularly bother me that I was in a tomb. The tomb was sturdy and safe, I was out of the rain and wind, and there was plenty of light coming in. I would get out. I would wait until I was sure that the rocks were not being thrown anymore, and then I would resume my campaign of yelling, and I would try to reach over to the lock and see if there was a way of getting it open. I would do this. I was finishing this little pep talk with myself when I heard something outside, a little noise, a *snick*. Then what sounded like a breaking twig.

"Hello?" I called.

No answer.

I peered around carefully. No one was there. Possibly it was an animal. A rat, for instance.

Now I didn't like being in the tomb. I got to my feet, and when I did, I found that Jim was standing by the gate again, just out of reach.

"People come here, leave all sorts," he said. "Lots of these. Lots of them over the years. Ol' Jim's got dozens of 'em."

He held up a plastic lighter.

"Young ones love a fire," he said. "'Orrible thing, fire. Oh, they come here, and they burn things."

He flicked the lighter on and set the flame to the end of a

stick.

"Ever see a bird burn? Sad thing, if they get caught in a fire. Oh, their wings burn when they try to fly. Saddest thing. 'Orrible."

He watched the end of the stick burn. Then he threw it into the gate. I immediately stomped on it, but he was already lighting another. I ducked as this one came through and landed in a pile of wet leaves, which smoldered. I stamped that out as another came, and another. As they came, I stamped.

"Can you light a light?" he said. "Only one way to know."

I continued running around the inside of the tomb, stamping on anything that smoked. Most of the leaves were too wet to catch, but enough dry ones were on top to get something going. I was stamping on flames now, not smoke. The circulating air only spread this around. I jumped with both feet on every square foot of the leaves, bouncing around and around. Still, little snakelike wisps of smoke peeked up here and there, making me run to the other side and jump some more. The inside of the tomb stank of smoke, which clung to me and stung my eyes. It was like I was at an out-of-control barbecue—and I had somehow locked myself in the pit.

Boom. Another rock flew in, and I stepped back.

"What is *wrong* with you?" I yelled.

No reply. I started yelling properly, using every ounce of energy I had in me. I jumped and yelled, even long after the fires were out.

"It's all right!" a voice called. It sounded like the person was running in my direction. I looked out and saw a girl, roughly my height, with a tousled head of curly hair. She had big brown eyes, framed by a large pair of round tortoiseshell glasses. Her face was sporadically freckled and had that rude glow of skin that has never known makeup—a healthy, warm veneer against which a few blemishes stood out proudly. She wore an over-sized chunky knit sweater and jeans that were some kind of hybrid of baggy art student and mom jean.

"It's all right!" she said, in a plummy, full accent. "Oh, dear, is that smoke? We'll have you out of there in no time!"

There was someone behind my mysterious savior, someone I knew well.

It was Jerome.

ST. MARY'S HOSPITAL, WEST LONDON
10:30 A.M.

HOSPITAL MORGUES TEND TO BE QUIET PLACES, FOR A number of reasons. For a start, the patients are silent. Also, not many people are allowed into the morgue. Usually it is located in a remote corner of the hospital, tucked away behind security doors, often with deliberately inaccurate signage to prevent distress to patients and families and mislead curious creepers. (This particular morgue had a sign on the hallway door marked "Lower Level Conference Room C.") It is a steady, dignified place, and patients passing through leave by back entrances in the care of funeral directors or a representative of the coroner's office.

On this morning, a plain black Transit van pulled up in the morgue car park in a small nook behind the hospital. A man and a woman in plain black suits got out of the front. A woman in an equally grave gray suit emerged from the back. Her fuchsia lipstick was the only bright note in the whole group.

The two from the front went ahead to the service doors and requested entry from the guard, who quickly admitted them all after seeing their credentials. The three walked down the corridor, which was eerily lined with empty gurneys.

"I'll do the formalities," the fuchsia-lipped woman said. "Stay here for a moment."

She stepped inside the morgue, into a small office space with a desk and a computer. The attendant, named Oren, was eating a snack bar and idly scrolling through a website.

"Can I help you?" he asked.

"I'm Dr. Felicia Marigold," the woman said. "Someone will have phoned about an hour ago from the Home Office."

"From the Home Office," Oren repeated, setting down his snack bar and dusting his hands. "Yeah. Stephen Dene, was that it?"

"Correct."

"I've got the paperwork here," he said, picking up a clipboard. "Hang on a moment. I'll go and get Dr. Rivers to sign him out."

Dr. Marigold looked at the clock on the wall. She'd been kept in the dark for an entire day. Thorpe was buying time—but for what, she wasn't sure.

Inside the examination room, Dr. Rivers, the pathologist, looked at the clipboard.

"Dene, Stephen," she read. "Motor vehicle accident, head trauma, subdural hematoma. Life support terminated. Signed off at nine ten yesterday morning. All right. Get him out. Unit twenty-one."

Oren positioned a gurney under a drawer of the cold storage unit and pulled back and twisted the handle, releasing the door. The body inside was wrapped in a blue sheet. He rolled out the shelf while Dr. Rivers read and checked boxes.

"Are you doing a coffee run any time soon?" she asked, flipping casually through the pages. "I'd love a latte."

Oren pulled back the sheet to reveal the body. He stopped moving for a moment.

"Hey, Doc . . ."

Oren's tone caused the doctor to look up. The body of the boy was exposed to midtorso. The doctor saw the problem at once and quickly flipped back through several pages.

"This can't be the right one," she said.

"It's Stephen Dene," Oren said. "I checked the bracelet."

"Then someone's put the wrong bracelet on. Stephen Dene was meant to have died yesterday morning."

She grabbed a latex glove from a dispenser on the wall, snapped it on, and lifted the boy's arm gently, flexing it at the elbow, looking at the underside of the arm. Then she placed the arm back down carefully and rolled the boy's whole body slightly to the side, examining the back.

"There's no lividity," Dr. Rivers said. "There's not even any real pallor to speak of. This can't be Stephen Dene."

"I know." Oren's eyes had gone very round. "But this is him. I put him here *myself.* Yesterday. I always remember the young ones."

Dr. Rivers lifted the boy's eyelids and looked into his eyes.

"No clouding of the cornea either. Something's going on here. Get me a crash cart from the corridor. Now. I need to check his heart."

Oren ran for the cart while Dr. Rivers moved the gurney into the middle of the room.

"Get some blankets," she said, over the rumbling sound of the cart being dragged into the examination room. "What in Christ's name is going on here?"

Behind them, the access door opened and Dr. Marigold entered the exam room.

"You can't be in here," the attendant said as he rushed across the room with a pile of sheeting.

"What's going on?"

"We have a problem," the pathologist said. "You need to leave."

"I'm a doctor," Dr. Marigold said. "Tell me what's happening."

"What's happening is this," the doctor said, indicating the body in front of her. "He's been declared dead and has been in the cooling unit for a day, but I'm seeing no signs of death. Look at him yourself."

Dr. Marigold took the boy's chin and turned it from side to side, then got very close and examined a laceration at the hairline while the pathologist attached the electrodes to the boy's chest and switched on the machine. All it produced was a straight line and a dull hum.

"I have absolutely no idea what's happening," Dr. Rivers said. "He's dead but he's not. We need to move him upstairs at once and start warming him properly. This could be some deep narcoleptic state or . . . I have no idea. We need to phone upstairs."

"That won't be necessary," Dr. Marigold said, pulling the sheet back up. "I'll take it from here."

"You most certainly will not. I'm not going to release someone who might not be dead."

"He has no heartbeat."

"Well, tell *him* that," the pathologist snapped. "He also has no clinical signs of death, which means he's going back upstairs, and he's going now. You need to step back outside."

Dr. Marigold took out her phone and sent a quick text as the pathologist detached the leads. A moment later, the two dark-suited people appeared in the exam room.

"All of you," Dr. Rivers said, "out. Now. Or I call security."

"This patient is going with us," Dr. Marigold said calmly. "We are from the Home Office. We outrank hospital security by several orders of magnitude. I will personally take responsibility for this patient."

"I don't care what you . . ."

Oren stood to the side, watching as the two nameless suited people took their places on either side of the gurney. Dr. Marigold opened the bag she had hanging from her shoulder and removed some papers. She passed them to both Dr. Rivers and Oren, along with a pen for each.

"What is this?" the pathologist said. "And get away from—"

"It's a standard copy of the Official Secrets Act, which I'm going to need you to sign."

"I'm not signing anything. I'm not releasing the body."

"I don't need your permission to release the body," Dr. Marigold said. "I told you, he's coming with me. Security will not stop us. The longer it takes for you to sign, the longer the patient goes without monitoring or care. His fate is now resting on how long it takes you to put a pen to a piece of paper."

Dr. Rivers regarded her fellow doctor for a long moment.

"What did you do to him?" she asked. "What exactly is going on here?"

"Nothing that concerns you. It's not dangerous. You haven't been exposed to anything. You're wasting valuable time asking these questions, which I'm not going to answer. If you care at all about the well-being of the patient, you need to sign."

The two suited people remained at attention on either side of the gurney, but something in their demeanor changed. There was a suggestion that this situation was going to end exactly as Dr. Marigold said, and they were prepared to make sure that happened.

Dr. Rivers looked to Oren, who had been steadily backing toward the wall, clutching the document and the pen.

"I want no part of this," he said, taking the pen and scrawling his name.

Dr. Marigold accepted the document. Dr. Rivers looked down at Stephen Dene, who was now obscured by the sheet.

"For his sake," she finally said, before scrawling her name in a disgusted gesture.

Dr. Marigold accepted this as well and tucked it in her bag. Her two companions silently rolled the body away and out the door.

"So you understand," Dr. Marigold said, "everything that has happened here today with this patient is now classified. You do not discuss him or anything you have seen. If you do so, you will be prosecuted."

"This is a travesty. Something is going on with that boy."

"Prosecuted," Dr. Marigold said again, "to the fullest extent of the law."

With that, she turned and followed the path of her associates and the gurney. When they had been gone for a moment or two, Dr. Rivers and Oren looked at each other.

"What the bloody hell was that?" Oren said. "I don't want trouble. I can't have trouble. I've got a daughter."

Dr. Rivers went back into the office, pushed away the abandoned snack bar, and started typing into the computer.

"He's already gone from the records," she said when Oren joined her. "They've already wiped everything about him."

"I don't want trouble," Oren said again. "I can't have trouble."

"You won't have trouble," Dr. Rivers said, pushing back in the chair. "You signed, and I signed. We say nothing. Not that there's anything to say."

"What was wrong with that body? Bodies don't do that. He should have been . . ."

"I don't know," Dr. Rivers said. "I have absolutely no idea."

She eyed the screen blankly for a moment, absorbing the events of the last few minutes. The office door opened again, and a man with pure white hair entered.

"Home Office," he said, producing his identification. "I'm here about a body. You should have had a call this morning. The subject's name is Stephen Dene . . ."

The black van was already snaking its way into London traffic, away from the hospital. Dr. Marigold looked down at Stephen Dene, lying on the gurney. She leaned in close and examined his face again, resting the back of her hand against his cheek, then his forehead.

"Well," she said quietly, "I knew you were stubborn, Dene, but no one is this stubborn."

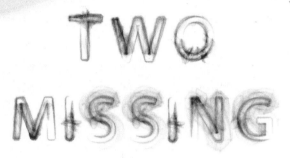

TWO MISSING

I stand amid the roar
Of a surf-tormented shore,
And I hold within my hand
Grains of the golden sand—
How few! yet how they creep
Through my fingers to the deep,
While I weep—while I weep!
O God! can I not grasp
Them with a tighter clasp?
O God! can I not save
One from the pitiless wave?

Edgar Allan Poe,
"A Dream Within a Dream"

8

WHAT JEROME WAS DOING HERE, AT HIGHGATE, I HAD NO idea, but he and the girl were totally consumed in the process of getting the gate open.

"Are you okay?" he asked, leaning into the gate. "Is that smoke?"

"Kind of," I said. "I'll be okay. I just need to get out."

The smoke was dissipating, but it was still pretty strong inside the tomb, and it hurt my throat and eyes. I pressed my face to the gate to breathe the fresh, cold air.

"Hang on a moment," the girl said, pulling off her backpack. "I have something."

She pulled out some kind of white tube about a foot long, and she used it to whack the crap out of the lock until it fell open and I stumbled out into the murk.

"Bike pump," she said, catching her breath as she held it up. "Always handy. Are you all right?"

I leaned over my legs to catch my breath and nodded heavily.

Jerome was at my side, not touching me, but leaning down to look at me.

"Are you?" he said.

"Yeah."

I saw him looking at my hair, then back at the still-smoking tomb.

"Who locked you in there?" he asked.

"It was . . . an accident."

"You locked yourself in a tomb and set a fire?"

"I'm fine."

"You don't seem fine."

"Fine," I said again, standing and trying to smile.

The girl tucked her bike pump back into her bag, which she reapplied to her back. Then she came over and extended her hand.

"You're Rory!" she announced.

Unable to contradict this, I nodded and took her hand. Her grip was firm, serious, and at the conclusion of the gesture, I felt like I may have sealed an important deal on behalf of my client.

"I'm Freddie," she said. "Freddie Sellars. Freddie isn't short for Fredericka. It's my name. But your name is short for Aurora? Very pretty name. Aurora. The Roman goddess of dawn. *But all so soon as the all-cheering sun should in the farthest east begin to draw the shady curtains from Aurora's bed . . .*"

When I stared blankly, she filled in the missing information.

"*Romeo and Juliet*," she said. "I memorized quite a lot of Shakespeare for my A-levels, and now it keeps popping out all over the place."

While she spoke, Jerome stood there, staring at me like I

was a bird that had flown out of the depths of his cereal. The last time I'd seen him, we were on the green at Wexford, and I was impulsively dumping him because I couldn't keep up with the lies anymore. There were, to put it as mildly as possible, a few questions he probably wanted to ask me. This girl knew my name and seemed to be the only person who had any outward appearance of understanding the situation.

"I told you," Freddie said to Jerome. "I did tell you."

"You did," Jerome said, never taking his eyes from me. "But stil—"

"How did you find me?" I asked.

"We heard you," Freddie said.

This wasn't really an answer, but to be fair, my answers weren't answers either. We were three people in a graveyard, and none of us should have been there, and no one was talking first.

"This is probably confusing," Freddie said. "Maybe I should explain. Possibly not here, though. You need to get out of there. We should all sit down, maybe have a cup of tea and—"

"Here's fine," I said.

"Oh. There's a coffee shop and a pub just up Swain's Lane in Highgate Village. I know the place fairly well. It's quiet in the winter—it's mostly there for tourists. Not many people around. I imagine maybe avoiding very crowded places, and . . . well, it's quite a story and it might go down well with some refreshment. And it *is* raining—"

"Here's fine," I said again.

"Oh. Right. Of course. Well, we're here because of the Ripper case. Jerome and I met online, on a discussion board. And . . . well, this is a bit awkward . . . You see, I have a great interest in this case. I have been following it quite closely. I identified a few people working on it, and I found out where they were based. Then Jerome put the news up on the board that you were gone from school—he posted before the BBC—and as he did so, I spotted you going into a flat behind Waterloo station. I had my bicycle, and I took the opportunity."

So much for all of Thorpe's precautions. Busted by a girl and her trusty bicycle. Well played, MI5.

"I was hanging about a bit, and today I saw you come here. I phoned Jerome and told him, and by the time I reached him, I'd lost you. But then he arrived and we were looking around and we heard you, so that's how we . . ."

"Can we have a moment?" Jerome asked.

"Oh! Right! Yes. Right. How about I walk back to the gate? Yes. I'll wait there. And perhaps then maybe we could get out of the rain and have a chat?"

Jerome turned to Freddie, and she flushed red and hopped off down the lane of tombs, leaving us alone.

I'd never been so happy to see someone. Well, almost. It was up there. Jerome was familiar. Jerome was about normal life and Stephen not being dead and awkward things that still made some kind of sense. I found myself warming, wanting to throw my arms around him, to drink in everything that was ordinary about him. I wanted everything to stop being terrible. I wanted a hug.

This was also acutely terrible, because Jerome was now staring at me in a graveyard, and he wanted an explanation.

"What's going on?" he said quietly.

"It's really complicated," I said.

"I gathered that. But you have to tell me something. Where's Charlotte?"

I ran my hand through my hair and was confused when there seemed to be very little hair there to run a hand through. I kept forgetting.

"I don't know," I said. "She's not with me."

"What were you doing in that tomb?"

"I was looking at something, and the gate closed in the wind."

"And then it caught on fire?"

"I was . . . smoking."

"You smoke now," he said. He didn't ask. He didn't believe me.

"It's been stressful."

"I know," he said. "For everyone. Jaz is with your parents right now."

"What? Why?"

"Because you spoke to them, and they're frantic. They thought she might know where you went. And she was worried for them, so she's staying with them at their hotel."

"Hotel?"

"They came to London when you left Wexford. Rory . . . everyone's freaking out. And you're . . ."

As established, in a tomb on fire.

"You need to tell me something," he said. "I'm not leaving until you tell me something. Is the Ripper case still going on? Are you a witness? Are you in hiding?"

"That's . . . kind of it? It's—"

"Don't say complicated. Tell me something."

"I'd tell you if I could," I said.

"Tell me how you ended up in there," he said, pointing at the tomb. "Really. You were screaming."

He looked at me warningly.

"The truth is it was an accident," I said. "I'm a moron. Did you see anyone else around? It was just me, being an idiot. Have you *met* me? This is the kind of thing that happens to me."

Oh, Jerome. I was always lying to him. What choice did I have? I don't think he accepted this entirely, but there was enough of a ring of truth about what I'd said to quiet him for a moment.

"Who's this *girl*?" I asked.

"She is who she said she is. Her name is Freddie Sellars. She's really into the Ripper case, like me. More than me. Way more than me. Apparently she was following the investigators. She's kind of intense, and I thought she might be crazy, but she told me she knew where you were. I went along with her, but I didn't actually think she'd be right."

"But you went anyway?"

"She was right," he said, his voice rising a bit. "She did know where you were."

"So, that's all you know about her?"

"What does it matter?" he asked.

"Everything kind of matters now," I said, tightening my arms around my chest and looking around. Old Jim was nowhere in sight. It was time to go. It was probably best not to go anywhere with them, but my throat was burny from the smoke, I was shivering in the damp and the cold, and I had a feeling that Freddie Sellars—whoever she was—had a lot more to say. Because if she knew about the Waterloo flat, that meant she knew about Stephen, or Callum, or Boo.

"Listen," I said, "I'll come to this pub, and we'll sit and talk. I'll tell you what I can. I can't tell you much."

Jerome took his hands from his coat pockets and for a moment floated them in my direction.

"All right," he said. "Come on."

He offered me his crooked arm like he used to when we dated. I wondered if somehow our breaking up had been canceled out by the overbearing drama of the days that followed. Maybe I could pick up my life again, right now, by walking out arm in arm. I could go to my parents, see Jazza. He was literally offering me a way out of the woods.

I tucked my hands into my coat pockets, and we walked out of the cemetery side by side.

9

REDDIE SELLARS WAS WAITING FOR US OUTSIDE THE GATE. We informed her that we were willing to go for the drink, if the pub was quiet and out of the way, and she assured us it was most quiet and out of the way. As we walked down the lane to the village, there was no dead air. Freddie was bountiful in her knowledge of Highgate Cemetery and spent the whole time pointing out various tombs and talking about how the Victorians invented a culture and industry of death.

Everyone was a tour guide today.

And so on, out the gates and up the road to a pub called the Flask. It was one of those places so picturesque that my American brain assumed fakery and the hand of Disney—except of course it was real. They always were. It was right off the road, with a wide stone patio full of tables and a cheery red sign. Freddie wanted us to go inside, but I said I wanted to stay out. There was an area off to the side with a bit of roofing, a kind of porch unconnected to the building. No one was out there, and it was tucked off in the corner of the courtyard in a place where no one was likely to immediately look.

"I'm kind of dying for a Coke," I said, pulling out some of the money I'd been given.

"I'd love an herbal tea," Freddie said, carefully counting out a few pounds of her own.

Jerome went into the pub, casting a glance over his shoulder as he left. When he was safely inside, I set to work.

"I need to know how you found me," I said.

"I told you! I—"

"Followed people. For how long?"

"For some time," she said.

"Who did you follow?"

"There are three of them," she said. "A tall one, who I think is named Stephen—he wears a police uniform. A very fit person whose name I've never been able to catch. And a gorgeous girl who I believe may be called Boo? But I must have heard that wrong. Unless it's a joke."

"A joke?"

"Because . . ." Freddie drew a sudden breath and shifted in her seat. "Oh, dear. I imagined how this would go if we met, but I didn't . . . Well, boo. Boo. As in . . . well. What says 'boo'?"

I knew what said boo, but I wanted to hear her say it.

"I'm from Cambridge," she said. "My parents are both profs. My mum is associate chair of ancient history at one of the colleges, and my dad is a behavioral psychologist. When I was fifteen, we were off for six weeks one summer when my dad was doing research in Turkey. I was swimming at the beach in Cirali and I was stung by a jellyfish—a whacking great *Rhopilema no-madica,* to be specific. I had a terrible allergic reaction. It almost killed me."

She looked to see how I reacted. Suspicion confirmed.

"What happened to you?" she asked.

There was no point in lying to her. Not about this.

"I choked at dinner," I said.

A creeping flush came up over her jawline and spread across her cheeks as she saw she'd hit home.

"It's true, then," she said. "I was right. You're like me. I wasn't sure. But I was fairly sure. I felt fairly sure, and—"

"What do you know about the Ripper?" I said, glancing toward the pub door. Freddie flushed with excitement when she saw how this conversation looked to be going.

"I had a theory." She was talking faster. "No appearance on CCTV. The culprit turns out to be a random drifter, someone with no known identity, no story. Someone tremendously clever and yet utterly no one at all, who dies very conveniently at the end of a chase. No trial. No more information. I started following the case not because I cared about the Ripper, but because I suspected what he was. I actually didn't think I'd be *right,* but . . . Can I ask, what were you doing in the cemetery?"

"I was there trying to get information from someone called the Resurrection Man."

"The Resurrection Man? You mean a body snatcher?"

"What?"

"A resurrection man," she said, "was what they called people who used to get cadavers for medical students back when there was a shortage. This was only a bit illegal, so it was fairly popular. It was regarded as a problem when some of them started to murder people in order to sell the bodies. Mostly, though, they went after freshly dug graves, which is why so many graveyards had watch houses or bars or gates over the tombs."

A body snatcher—that cemetery was his. It began to make sense.

"Is there a reason you know all this?" I asked.

"There was a very good exhibition in the Museum of London about it recently," she said. "But because of what I am, I've made this sort of thing my field of study. I'm a student at King's, in history, specializing in English folklore and religious history, which covers quite a lot of death customs. And I—"

"Does Jerome know? You didn't tell him any of this. About you, about me?"

"God, no! No. How do you tell someone that the Ripper is a . . . well, a dead person? But he's going to want some explanation."

Yes, he probably would, now that Freddie had brought him here.

"So what do we tell him?" she asked. "I always prefer telling the truth. It's dashed complicated, but if we both tell him—"

"We don't tell him."

"We don't have to," she said quickly, "but he's going to ask questions. None of this makes any sense unless you know the major piece of information here, and I think you'd be surprised how—"

"We don't tell him," I said.

Here I was, being just like Stephen, who hadn't wanted me to know that I was seeing ghosts, even though I was seeing ghosts. It was Boo who'd argued that denying reality was weird and cruel and wrong. But Jerome didn't have the sight. This was different.

"So why did you follow them?" I asked.

"Because . . ." she said, and she got a little shy and flushed. "Because I want to join."

I tried to look like I had no idea what she was talking about, but that didn't really work. I mean, she clearly knew.

"How did you even know they existed?"

"It's been rumored for years that there used to be some part of the police that handled ghosts but that Margaret Thatcher had it shut down because she didn't like ghosts. Which wouldn't surprise me—she didn't even like *beards*. No one in her cabinet could have a beard, so I can't imagine she had much time for ghost police. In any case, I do a lot of research on this topic. No one knew for certain, but there was a rumor that it had started back up. I started to track sites that were known for hauntings, places that had problems. I found a Tube platform that had started to have a lot of issues—you can follow this easily online—and I got there in time to see a woman on the platform. But she was a spirit. And then in came this tall person in a police uniform, and I saw that he could see her too. They closed the platform for a bit, but I watched him speak to her. And when he left, I followed him. That's how I started. Then when the Ripper came along, everything came together. I started following your story too."

She looked a bit bashful.

"They said there was a witness. Plenty of people were visiting your school to look at the crime scene, so I went along as well. I knew you had to be . . . I didn't mean to follow you. I've been looking for them so long. Do you think they'd take me? The tall one, is he in charge? Stephen, is that his name?"

I was glad that Jerome emerged with the drinks, because I wasn't about to answer any questions about Stephen. Freddie stopped talking a little too suddenly. He looked at the two of us, and he was well aware that we had stopped talking because he came over. Jerome was anything but stupid.

"Look," I said, "I'm okay . . . despite how you found me."

His expression suggested that he rejected the idea that I was okay, largely due to the way they had just found me.

"So," he said, "this is all about the Ripper. The case is still going on. So he's not dead?"

"You know," Freddie said, bobbing her tea bag nervously, "possibly you should drink that pint. And then—"

I prepared to cut off whatever she was about to say. This was not the time. There would likely never be a time to rip apart the fabric of Jerome's reality. I debated jumping up and dragging her bodily away from the table. It turned out that was completely unnecessary, because we had company. For the second time today, a familiar face popped up next to me.

"A word," Thorpe said.

10

DON'T HAVE MUCH OF A HISTORY OF TROUBLEMAKING. IT'S
not in my nature. I've always done stupid things, but with
an awareness of the general boundaries. Attempts are always
made to meet the curfew, put the car back where it belongs,
hide the phone down the front of the shirt in class. I observe
the niceties.

Which I guess is another way of saying I'm kind of a low-
grade sneak. I don't try for much. I'm like the Toaster Thief.

The Toaster Thief was a famous figure in Bénouville. He or
she or they made the rounds when I was ten or eleven. There
was a rash of burglaries in town, the first of which, at Miss
Carly's house, was notable because the only thing taken was a
toaster. It seemed unlikely that someone would take a toaster
and leave the television and computers and stuff, but that's
what happened. Miss Carly was telling my parents about it down
at the soccer field—people tell my parents anything even remotely legal, because they are the big lawyers in town. She was

asking if she should file a police report, because it was only a toaster, and my parents said yes, of course, someone has been in your house and taken your toaster. You don't know what they might get up to. And then, in the next few days, someone took Ralph Murchis's old microwave. And then it was Dolly Allen's blender. Just when the town was convinced some thief was slowly building up a not-super-great kitchen somewhere, it was a lamp from Pat Silvo's, some folding chairs, a landline telephone. It got to the point that it was sort of a badge of honor to have had the Toaster Thief come to your house, except it was also creepy. But the point is it was all so low-level that the police, who really had nothing better to do, still thought it was barely worth looking into. Because who cares about a six-year-old blender, really, when people are getting murdered (not in our town, but certainly somewhere else in the world)? Bénouville police like to do one thing only, and that's set speed traps and catch strangers from up North. That's it. So no one bothered to look for the Toaster Thief, and they stopped because I guess they had all the appliances they needed. The Toaster Thief was simply accepted as a facet of our lives.

This was my level of bad. So I'd gone out. I hadn't gone far. I hadn't gotten my face up on a Jumbotron. I'd gone to a cemetery, which was certainly part of my remit. I was in a quiet pub in a quiet corner of London. And, well, yes, I was now sitting here with my former boyfriend and a complete stranger . . .

This was not going to go well. Because Thorpe, unlike the Bénouville police department, seemed to take infractions pretty seriously. There was a kind of low-grade radiation that seemed to come off his back and shoulders in waves. You don't go white-haired when you're that young unless you lead a pretty serious life. Freddie and Jerome regarded our new companion warily.

"Oh," I said. "Hi."

Jerome looked at me, his eyes asking who this was.

"Rory," Thorpe said, "why don't you step over to the car with me for a moment."

Jerome rose out of his seat a little. I think he may have been trying to defend me—from what, he likely didn't know. It made my throat close up.

"Perhaps I can explain—" Freddie said.

"Rory." Thorpe tapped on the underside of my elbow, indicating that I should rise. While I felt cowed and cornered for a moment, I remembered what had gotten me out the door in the first place—Stephen's report, the fact that Thorpe had known that Stephen might do something dangerous. I wasn't inclined to blindly follow him anywhere right now. I held my seat. Thorpe resigned himself and dropped into one next to me.

"I'm Freddie—" Freddie said.

"Sellars," Thorpe said. "Yes, I know exactly who you are."

That stopped Freddie for a moment.

"You do?" she asked.

"I wouldn't be very good at my job if I didn't. And you are Jerome Croft."

A nod to Jerome, who leaned back in his seat a bit on hearing this stranger say his name. Thorpe sniffed a bit, and I knew he was getting a whiff of smoke from my clothes and hair.

"I'll make this very brief," Thorpe said. "Rory is part of an active investigation . . ."

"I just told a bunch of people we found her," Jerome said.

My heart seized.

"No, you didn't," Thorpe said, not missing a beat. "But I understand your impulse to say you did. You're afraid for her safety, and you're generally suspicious of authority. I've seen your work on the Ripper message boards."

Thorpe spread his hands on the table and stretched out his fingers, and the gesture mesmerized us all a bit.

"If you *have* told someone where she is, you've put her at serious risk. She'll be taken into protective custody immediately, and the investigation will be compromised. So is what you said true?"

One thing I always liked about Jerome—he never seemed cowed by authority. Which was weird, because he was a prefect and in charge of making sure rules were followed. But it was in his conspiracy-theory-loving nature to stick it to the Man a little. He looked at Thorpe for a long moment before replying.

"No," he said. "We just found her."

Thorpe accepted this answer with a nod.

"Have you been in a fire?" he asked me.

"Not a *fire*, exactly . . ."

"She was locked inside a tomb," Jerome said. "There was something on fire inside. Your protection isn't great."

"It's easier to protect someone when she cooperates," Thorpe said.

"It wasn't a big fire," Freddie said. "It did look like you had the situation in hand."

"I'll address this in a moment," Thorpe said.

"Who are you?" Jerome asked.

This was another reasonable question, and I was surprised it hadn't come up before. I guess we all kind of knew roughly where we stood except for Jerome.

"My name is Thorpe. And I'm responsible for Aurora. I think you have her best interests at heart, so I hope you comply with what I ask. I can't make you do anything—you can simply choose whether to be a help or a hindrance to this investigation."

"The Ripper investigation?" Jerome asked. "Not just Charlotte."

Also, Jerome still thought we were talking about the Ripper.

"For now," Thorpe said, "I need to establish the rules and ask for your assistance. I realize, Jerome, that the temptation to act on what you've seen or heard today will be strong. I could put you in custody—"

"On what grounds?"

"I would have thought you'd know that I don't need grounds. Something can always be arranged. But I have no desire to do that."

"So my choices are keep quiet or get banged up on some fake charge?"

"It would be more constructive to think of it as—"

"You want to know about Jane Quaint," Freddie blurted out.

This stopped us all. This Freddie was like a can of pop-up snakes.

"Who's Jane Quaint?" Jerome said.

"What do you know about Jane Quaint?" Thorpe said.

"Yeah," I said. "What?"

"I know about something that happened in that house. I know someone you can talk to. He's not going to talk to you," Freddie said. "No offense. He's quite countercultural. He'll talk to us, though. To me, to Rory . . ."

She left that little hint dangling in the air. She tipped her chin up as a kind of challenge, but I could see uncertainty swimming in her eyes. Thorpe never appeared to lose his footing, but it took him a moment to collect his thoughts and compose his reply.

"If you know something and you fail to disclose—"

"What I know isn't something you want me to disclose to anyone else but you. I want to be a part of this. If you know who I am, maybe you know why. You know the kind of information I'm talking about isn't the kind you ring the police with."

Whoever this Freddie was, she had some spine. She was probably bluffing. I'd bluffed my way through similar things, but that was with Stephen, not Thorpe. They were both challenges in their own way, but Thorpe was the one who could probably call in helicopters and people with guns if annoyed. Worse, he could cancel everything. Maybe Freddie had just blown it all. This challenge, the fact that two people now knew I was here— even though it wasn't my fault—maybe this would make Thorpe turn me in. Maybe I would have to run. Maybe I needed to get up right away, claim to need the ladies' room, go into the pub, sneak out a back door, and start running across the fields of north London. Running forever and ever without end.

All these thoughts passed through my mind as Thorpe sat there, silently regarding Freddie.

"Who's Jane Quaint?" Jerome said.

Everyone ignored this question. Thorpe had decided to speak, and when he did, it was not with the voice of someone who was going to call down an air strike.

"Where is this person?" he asked.

"Soho. I'll tell you exactly where in the car. If there's a car. Or Tube. I can certainly show you the way on the—"

"There's a car."

"And we all come," Freddie said eagerly. I had no idea if Jerome wanted to come with us, given the nature of the conversation, but Freddie had attached herself to him and thrown them both overboard.

"Soho," Thorpe said.

"Yes." Freddie sat up straight. "Soho. He's there now. I was going to tell Rory about him when you came in. If you want to talk to him, you take us all."

"If I take you all," Thorpe said, "you both hand me your phones. Now."

Freddie handed hers over pretty quickly, but Jerome held back a moment before passing his over.

"You'll get it back," Thorpe said. "It's a simple precaution."

For Jerome to give his phone to someone who was still unknown to him—someone like Thorpe—it must have gone against his every self-protective instinct. But he did it. Thorpe got up, and we followed him to the black Mercedes, which was parked outside. I sat in the passenger's seat, and Freddie and Jerome were put in the back.

"Soho," Thorpe said, starting the car.

"Soho," Freddie repeated.

"Could you be more specific?"

"I'll tell you as we get closer."

Thorpe sighed quietly as he pulled the car out.

"Perhaps," he said, "someone will explain the tomb and the fire."

"I went to talk to someone," I said. "It didn't work out."

"Later, then," Thorpe said.

Thorpe was tolerating this, but I couldn't tell for how much longer.

This new assortment of friends and strangers was messing with my head something terrible. It was like a dream where people in your life who shouldn't know one another are all in the same place, and you have to put on a show together or something like that.

"How is it that you know who I am?" Freddie asked. She leaned in with polite interest.

"You've been following us for some time. A colleague spotted you hanging about months ago and looked into your background."

"How?"

"He followed you," Thorpe said.

Stephen. Had to be. Boo or Callum would have noticed her and tackled her. Only Stephen would follow and research.

"You followed us for miles on a bicycle yesterday," Thorpe said. "I let you tag along for a bit, but lost you on the Archway Road."

"You didn't lose me," Freddie said. "I went behind a bus and followed the reflection in a car window."

That was pretty impressive. I mean, Freddie seemed a little intense, but that was good going. Thorpe, as usual, registered nothing.

"Have Boo and Callum—" I asked in a low voice.

Thorpe gave me a sharp side look, and I realized too late that using names was probably bad.

"Her name *is* Boo!" Freddie said from the back.

"Boo's a part of this?" Jerome said.

The dawning of a great realization crossed his face. Boo— my chatty roommate—was a cop.

"Let's end this particular conversation," Thorpe said. "How

about you tell me more about whoever it is we're going to meet."

"My friend is someone who knew Jane a long time ago."

"And how do you know about Jane?"

"I saw her," Freddie said. "She used to hang about near Wexford sometimes. It caught my attention, the way she was lurking about. So I made a note of it in my book. I knew I was on the right track if *she* was interested in Rory too."

"What does that mean?" Thorpe asked.

"Jane Quaint is famous to some people. If you're interested in some things—"

"Who's Jane Quaint?" Jerome asked again.

But no one was ever going to answer him. I knew this. I wanted to answer, just to put him out of his misery on this point. What I wanted to do, actually, was crawl into the backseat and bury myself inside his big coat and wrap my arms around him and—

Seriously. What was my brain doing? Nothing was working right. This was nerves. It was fair for me to be freaked out. It had been a bad few days, and the thought of sinking into Jerome's chest and blocking everything out sounded like a good way to spend the rest of the day.

There was no going back to that now.

Though Thorpe had said nothing when I mentioned Callum and Boo, I was sure that the answer was no. He wouldn't be at his parents' house. Again, this knowledge just landed on me. It came from nowhere and was based on nothing. But I was as sure of it as I was sure that this was London—old and weird and perpetually rainy, full of people who didn't die.

11

ONCE WE GOT TO PICCADILLY CIRCUS AND THORPE DROVE
around the statue of Eros, he demanded better directions.
Freddie guided him turn by turn into the increasingly slender
and people-filled streets of Soho. London was weird like this—
one of the world's biggest cities and crammed with people, but
the streets would have passed as driveways where I came from.
It was okay when there were sidewalks, but a lot of these streets
had nothing but wall on either side, and I would never have
driven down them. It looked like we were going to scrape or
get stuck to me, but Thorpe barreled along.

"Here," Freddie said.

We were on a quiet street with a few boutiques and shops
painted bright colors like red and purple, and many more
quiet doorways with small plaques next to them. There was no
one here. Before we got out, Thorpe once again demanded information. He was not the kind of person who walked through
a door without knowing what was behind it.

"Number fifty-six," she said, pointing at a midnight-blue building to the left. "That's Hardwell's. It's the most famous magic bookshop in the country."

Thorpe leaned over the wheel to examine the building.

"Magic bookshop?" Jerome said.

"Very famous," Freddie said.

"To whom?"

"To people who go to magic bookshops," Freddie said.

There was no sign on the front of the building. The only writing was the number *56* painted in gold above the black doorway. The window curtain was of a similarly colored blue-black fabric, which completely hid whatever was inside.

"And who are we going to see?" Thorpe asked.

"His name is Clover."

"Clover?"

"Yes. He's a manager."

"What's his last name?"

"I don't know. It's something . . . something raven?"

"Of course it is," Thorpe said, almost under his breath.

The door to the bookshop was recessed and stuck, and we were admitted with the tiny triple tinkle of some bells suspended on the back. The inside of the bookshop was one of the closest rooms I'd ever been in. Our local bookstore at the mall is so big, people practically stretch out in sleeping bags in the aisles while they sit and read. That's what I was used to—places with coffee bars and floor-to-ceiling windows and six square miles dedicated to blank notebooks and tiny book lights. There literally wasn't enough space to turn around in these aisles.

I'd been watching Jerome since we got out of the car, hoping that I'd somehow be able to reassure him about what was going on. Our new location visibly consternated him. Jerome loved a conspiracy theory, but he didn't strike me as the kind of person who had much time for magic or astrology or any of the related crafts. I didn't either, but at least it was fully familiar to me. My cousin the angel whisperer had a house that was knee-deep in crystals and figurative portraits of star signs. And while I was sure those things would have been welcome here, there was simply no space, and the vibe simply too serious. There was no pan flute music, no burbling table fountains that made you want to pee all the time, no statues of the Buddha that seemed to have no relation to actual Buddhists being present. There wasn't so much breathable air as there was incense and dust, punctuated by the occasional oxygen molecule that must have gotten lost on its way somewhere else.

"I think I may have an asthma attack," Jerome said.

"You have asthma?" I said.

He nodded and pulled an inhaler from his pocket. This revelation left me reeling for a moment. How had I not known my former boyfriend had asthma? Further proof that I was the worst girlfriend in the world. I wanted to reach out now and hold his hand, because the thought of him not breathing right made me panic. Jerome stuck the inhaler in his mouth and took a puff, then breathed slowly for a moment. I relaxed as he took in another breath.

"Stuff like this does it," Jerome said in a low voice, jerking his head up at the offending scents. "Why the hell are we here? Who's Jane Quaint?"

Freddie was at the counter. The counter was a hatch opened up in the back of a bookshelf. This was covered in tarot cards and crystals hanging from colored ribbons. There was a girl behind it in a black woolen hat covered in tiny reflective gold disks, like jazzed-up snake scales. My granny Deveaux had a shirt covered in something similar, but the effect was different. This girl's hat said, "I am reading a magic book." Granny Deveaux's shirt said, "I am going to the casino for dinner tonight."

"Oh, hello, Cressida," Freddie said, in a chipper manner that was already starting to wear on me. "Is Clover about?"

"He's in the back on his tea break."

"We'll just go and see him," Freddie said.

The girl didn't respond except to give Thorpe a dirty look for being alive and in a suit.

We all oozed down the widest of the tiny aisles. The books were a mix of new and used and extremely used, the spines flaked and bent and riddled with tiny white lines. These were not the kind of titles my cousin favored. Hers were things like *Heaven Is for Pets* and *Angels Among Us*. These titles were long and contained words I didn't know, and even the ones I did know, I don't think I really knew. The back wall was all bookcases and one maroon velvet curtain. Freddie pushed this aside and revealed a door, which she knocked on. A gruff voice said to come in.

"You stay right here," Thorpe said to Jerome.

"I'll read a grimoire," Jerome said, before taking a long hit on his inhaler.

I hadn't picked badly with Jerome. I really hadn't. I had to smile at him when he said that—and I hadn't even known it was still possible for me to smile. In fact, once I did it, the guilt came down. I couldn't go around *smiling*, not now.

The three of us went into the room. There was a single

cabinet and a teakettle and a counter-high fridge. The table was a folding TV tray, and the single chair in the room was inappropriately large—a beat-up but luxurious-looking red velvet reading chair that sagged from use. Clover himself was probably sixty or so. He was bald save for a hint of white bristle around his ears. He had a white beard that had been tapered to be thin and long, the end braided and sealed with a silver bead. He wore a black T-shirt with a brown vest over it and several necklaces—the most notable of which was a big animal tooth. In front of him was a clear glass teapot full of leaves and some kind of colorful flower bud things and a lot of stuff that looked like broken twigs, all of it floating sadly around the pot. Garbage tea. The whole room smelled like it. It reminded me of when our septic system backed up after a flood and we had to move into a Holiday Inn for two days.

"Who's this?" Clover said as I appeared behind Freddie and Thorpe appeared behind me.

"Friends," Freddie said.

"Friends?" Clover said as we packed in tighter and Thorpe shut the door most of the way. We leaned awkwardly against the walls.

"I know this is weird," Freddie said. "But it's really quite important. Something has happened."

Clover, like the girl in the spangly hat, disliked Thorpe on sight.

"I don't talk to—"

"Really *quite* important," Freddie said again. "I know how you feel about . . . I wouldn't be here if . . . A girl is missing. We need your help. You know that story you said you had about Jane Quaint?"

This seemed to displease him even more, and he shook his head.

"You need to leave," he said. "I'm not talking about that."

"Our friend is missing," I said. "She was with Jane Quaint at her house, and now they're both gone. Jane took her. She said something about taking her to the country. We're trying to find her, and we don't have a lot of time. She's been missing for two days."

He ran his tongue along his teeth.

"Is this about that missing student, from the news?"

"Yes," I said. "Her name is Charlotte."

"You said there's a story," Freddie prompted. "Please, Clover. She was in that house. She's with Jane. We really need to find her."

"Is this about Sid and Sadie?" I asked. "And what happened in 1973?"

Clover tugged on the big tooth.

"Not with him here," Clover said, pointing at Thorpe.

"He stays," Thorpe replied. "And you talk, or *he* comes and visits your shop all the time."

Now Clover was very unhappy.

"Clover," Freddie said, reaching over and taking his hand, "I wouldn't do this to you, I promise, if it wasn't important. You do good work. You help people. This is helping."

"That was a long time ago," Clover finally said. "I don't like talking about it, but I suppose with a girl missing . . ."

He picked up the teapot and poured the disgusting liquid through a strainer and into a mug. After a moment of considering this terrible drink he'd made, he spoke.

"What you need to understand is that things were *different* then," he said. "The late sixties and early seventies—the whole atmosphere was different. Everyone knows about the drugs and the free love and all that, but there was this air that anything was possible, that society was about to turn, that a new age was coming. For us, in the world of magic, it was a very exciting time. We were really making progress. England was on the verge of coming back to its true magic roots. We were trying to show people how to use magic to bring peace and good health, how to be aware of the world around them and bring balance. But there's always someone in every age of magic, there's always someone who goes into the dark. Someone who focuses on the sex and power and death magic. That was Sid and Sadie. They were the worst kind—Aleister Crowley types, power trippers. They came around to the bookstore sometimes—but never looking for books. They always claimed they had more books and better ones than we could ever carry. They used to laugh at us, say we were lightweights. What they were really looking for was kids to bring into their group. This was their hunting ground."

"Hunting?" I said.

"You're too young to remember any of this—you weren't alive—but back then, there were all kinds of gurus and cults. You had the Manson family murdering people in California because those kids thought Manson was god. There was Jim Jones making his own church, taking his followers to Guyana, and then convincing them all to commit suicide with him. Well, in London, there was Sid and Sadie. But you'll never know what they got up to, because they didn't want it known. They kept their business secret and behind closed doors. There was a whole group of kids—freaks, but nice enough. All these kids worshipped Sid and Sadie. They did whatever Sid and Sadie told them to do. There were ten of them, and I knew all in one way or another. Domino Dexie—no idea what his real name was, but he used to help us do stock sometimes. Nice lad. There was Aileen Emerson. She worked at a macrobiotic restaurant in Soho. Quiet lass. Ruth Clarkson—she used to read tarot in the street. Very good at it too. Michael Rogers. I didn't know him, but lots of other people did. Prudence Malley—she was an art student who came in the shop a lot. Mick Dunstan—he was cock of the walk. Looked a bit like Mick Jagger and had the same name, so he basically lived on that. You could do that then. I think he lived in a squat up in Muswell Hill. Badge— he named himself after a song, no last name. Musician type. Always had a guitar. Johnny Philips was a straight—had a job in a chemist. George Battersby—bit of an early goth type. And Dinah Dewberry, little Dinah Dewberry . . ."

He sipped his tea sadly for a moment.

"I liked Dinah. She had red hair, and she rode an old military bicycle she'd pulled out of a skip and painted blue with little yellow stars. We went out once, but I think we were both too shy. It might have gone somewhere eventually, but then Sid and Sadie came along . . . anyway, there were ten of them. Sid and Sadie gathered them up over the course of a year or two. How Sid and Sadie picked their group, I never knew. And once they went off with Sid and Sadie, that was that. They'd never tell you what they were up to, but they all had an *attitude*. Like they knew something you didn't. Jane—Jane Quaint— she was the head of the pack. Sid and Sadie came in one day and found her reading on the floor. She left with them, and that was that. Next thing any of us heard, she was living in their house with them. She was their right hand. She rode around in their car, bought things with their money, basically took care of business. In the end, Jane was doing the recruiting and no one saw Sid and Sadie at all. This went on for a while. Like you said, it was the end of 1973. On New Year's that year, a lot of us in the community met for a party. We got to talking and realized that none of us had seen any of Sid and Sadie's kids in over a week."

"There's no record of ten teenagers disappearing all at once at that time," Thorpe said.

"There wouldn't be," Clover said, looking at Thorpe as if he were very stupid. "A lot of the kids were runaways, or they were older but their parents had no idea where they were living or what they were doing. You need to understand, it really was a different time. London was full of runaways. They'd join communes, or decide to live in India or California. People went missing. It happened. There was no Internet. No CCTV. You'd hitch a ride and go. And the police were different then as well. These kids were all put down as hippies and freaks, and therefore no one was going to look too hard. We didn't talk to the police. No one cared about those kids but us. And we tried. We put out the word to people in magic communities in other parts of the world. We sent copies of their pictures. No one had seen them. We scryed for them, we held circles. What we got back was strange. Our best seer, Dawn . . ."

"Dawn Somner?" I asked.

"Yeah, that's Dawn. She died a few days past. Good friend of mine."

Thorpe registered this just as I did. Dawn Somner—the psychic who had fallen out of the window a few days before.

That's where I was when Charlotte was being kidnapped. That whole scene had looked set up. Stephen was sure someone had killed Dawn and staged it. This couldn't be a coincidence.

"Dawn truly had the gift—if anyone could find them, it was Dawn." Clover pulled sadly at his tooth necklace. "Dawn read cards for them over and over. Everything she was getting on the kids was bad, and confusing. What she got on Sid and Sadie, that was even stranger. She never got signs of life or death—she saw things like rivers on fire and bleeding stones."

"Did you ever find out what happened to them?"

Clover shook his head.

"A month passed, then six, then a year, then two years. There were all kinds of rumors for a while—that they had all gone to Morocco. Then people said India. Then some people said South America, or they were all in Ireland communing with the fairies."

"Sid and Sadie left a suicide note," I said.

"Suicide note, my arse. Sid and Sadie would never kill themselves."

"Jane could have killed them," I said. "She found the suicide note. She got the house."

"Jane would never have done that," he said, shaking his head. "You don't understand. Sid and Sadie *ruled* her. They were her gods. She would have killed herself in a second if they told her to. The only way—"

He cut himself off.

"The only way what?" I asked.

"It's not likely," he said. "The only way she would have done it was if Sid and Sadie told her to. But like I said, they wouldn't. Sid and Sadie . . . they were *proper* freaks, totally obsessed with themselves and their own magic. They were brother and sister, but the rumor was they were more than that."

"That they were a couple?" Freddie said.

"It's what everyone thought at the time, and it would make sense. No one else would be good enough for them."

"But why would they want their followers to die?" Freddie asked. "Wouldn't that defeat the point of having followers?"

Clover looked down at his necklaces.

"Like I said, this is the darkest stuff, the most forbidden. Stuff we don't keep here. Stuff I don't even believe in. Stuff about death energy. Paranoid, crazy stuff. What do I think? I think Sid and Sadie bought a spell off of some chancer who claimed to know dark magic and saw two fools with money. If you go to Egypt and places like that, people'll sell you all sorts, written on old papyrus. I've seen things like it. I think whatever they did— whatever they ingested or performed—maybe something went wrong. Maybe someone died. Whatever happened, Sid and Sadie probably had to get out. I think they left Jane in charge, and they probably live somewhere—could be anywhere."

"Has Jane been here recently?" Thorpe asked.

"Jane? I haven't seen Jane in forty years. Like I said, it was a long time ago."

"Then I think we're finished here," Thorpe said.

"Whatever happened to your friend," he said, "I can't imagine it has anything to do with Sid and Sadie, or the kids. That was all so long ago. Even if they were alive, any of them, they'd be older now. If any of them had come back, we'd have heard. I'm sure of it. No point in chasing after shadows."

He twisted in his seat a bit. Talking about these people seemed to hurt him physically.

"I'll see what I can do for your friend," Clover said. "Do you have a photograph or anything of hers I can work with?"

I shook my head.

"I think we're finished," Thorpe said again, putting a hand on the middle of my back to guide me out. "We'll be in touch if we need to know more."

12

THORPE AND I STEPPED OUT OF THE TEAROOM, LEAVING Freddie to say good-bye to Clover. Jerome was sitting on the floor, holding a book and clearly not reading it.

"Go outside and wait," Thorpe said to him. "We'll be right out."

Jerome didn't look thrilled to be ordered around like this, but he shut the book and stuck it back on the shelf, then shook his inhaler a few times before leaving. Thorpe guided me over to the farthest aisle. There was little privacy in this shop, and everything you said was pretty easily overheard. He spoke in a very low voice.

"You're a couple," Thorpe said. "Isn't that correct?"

This seemed a bit personal.

"Really? This is your question?"

"Answer it."

"Well, we *were* . . ."

"When did that end?"

"How is that important?"

Thorpe handed me Jerome's phone.

"Give this to him," he said. "And talk to him. Convince him to keep quiet, at least for a few days."

"Me?"

"I could threaten him, but I think it would be much easier and more effective if you asked him to comply. He has feelings for you."

It made me squeamish, hearing Thorpe say something like this, but he said it flatly, as if he were talking about the color of Jerome's shirt or the time.

"Tell him you're fine. Convince him. Tell him you can keep in touch a few times a day by text to reassure him."

"I can?"

"I'll provide the phone, and I'll be checking the messages."

"I don't understand . . ."

"The alternative is having him put on a forty-eight-hour psychiatric hold," Thorpe said.

"But he's not—"

"Of course not. But it's what I would have to do. Stress reaction to the disappearance of his girlfriend, everything he says will be discredited. I don't want to do that. I don't think he's a threat. I think that, given a little information, he'll keep his mouth shut. Do this, Rory."

The girl in the counter hatch eyed me as I left. Jerome was standing outside, huddling in his coat. He was clearly highly charged, but with which emotion, I couldn't immediately tell. I sheepishly handed him the phone.

"What did he do to my phone?" Jerome asked.

"I don't think he did anything to your phone."

"Of course he did," he said, pocketing it. For all I knew, he was right.

"So, what happens now?" he said.

"Look," I said, "I wish I could tell you everything. I wanted to tell you before, when—"

"At school," he said. By that, I assumed he meant "when you broke up with me after I asked you where you'd been."

"Yeah," I said. "At school."

"So all this time, you've been with these people. Who the hell is this guy, anyway?"

"Thorpe."

"Yeah, but who is he? Is he Home Office? MI5?"

"One of those. I don't really know the difference."

He repeated the words *one of those* silently and looked to the sky in desperation.

"Here's the thing," I said. "I need your help. I need you not to tell anyone what you saw."

"I don't *understand* what I've seen. You locked in a tomb, some guy with white hair shows up, some freaky bookshop where some guy tells you about some cult and some people who died in the seventies doing magic?"

So he'd been listening through the door. Of course he had.

"And *who's Jane Quaint?*" he added.

"She's a therapist," I said. "Mine and Charlotte's. Charlotte went to her after the night we were both attacked, and she recommended that I go too. Jane Quaint lured Charlotte in, and she lured me in. She's likely the last person Charlotte was with. She's likely the person who took Charlotte."

"Charlotte was *kidnapped* by her *therapist*? Your therapist? And your therapist does . . . magic?"

"It's a really long story," I said.

"And this has to do with the Ripper?"

At this point, everything had something to do with the Ripper, so I nodded.

"The thing is," I said, "I need to stay here to help. I know stuff, and these people? Jane Quaint and the others? They tried to get me too. I . . . got away. But they're still looking for me. Thorpe is protecting me."

"Not very well," Jerome said.

"He's trying to. I got out."

Jerome shook his head in confusion.

"Freddie mentioned Boo. Boo's a part of this?"

"She was undercover at school. She's a . . . police officer."

"I should have realized that," he said. "The way she just arrived and ended up in your room. Did Charlotte know that?"

"I don't think so. Look . . ." The way we were standing was too awkward to maintain, so I grabbed his hand. I think this shocked him. I know it shocked me. But there we were, holding hands. His hand was warm, and he squeezed, locking the connection. This little throwaway gesture had changed everything, and now that there was touching, his presence was more real.

"This is mad," he said. "I don't even know how this is happening. I didn't think Freddie would be right."

"I promise you, when this is over? I'll explain everything. Every single thing. But now, there's no time. So I need you to not say anything to anyone about where I am. It could get me hurt, and it could hurt the effort to find Charlotte."

"I'm supposed to meet Jaz in three hours," he said.

"You can't tell her," I said, shaking my head. "You can't tell anyone. I know this is a lot to ask. I know it. But I can text you a few times a day and let you know I'm okay. And when it's over, maybe we can talk? Thorpe trusts you. He said I should talk to you because he thinks you'll listen, and he thinks you'll help."

"And do you trust *Thorpe?*"

This was a fair question. It wasn't like I knew Thorpe that well. But everything he had done so far had been designed to help me or . . .

I remembered the intake form that was still in my pocket.

Stephen had trusted Thorpe, though.

"I trust him enough," I said.

"I'm worried about you," he said.

When he looked up at me, I remembered what had attracted me to him in the first place—before my life went crazy. Jerome was this really nice mix of competent and loose. And his face was kind. Everyone talked to Jerome, which was part of the reason he was a popular prefect.

"A few days," Jerome said.

"That's all."

"And you're going to text me?"

"I'll text you."

He balled his hand into a fist and rubbed it on his mouth in thought.

"This freaks me out," he said. "But I'll do it. If I don't hear from you . . ."

"You will."

"What do I say to Jazza?"

"I have no idea," I said. "You say nothing."

"Yeah." He nodded thoughtfully. "I say nothing."

I heard the chime of the door, and the creak as it was forced back open. Thorpe and Freddie rejoined us.

"Are we all set here?" Thorpe asked.

I had the uneasy feeling that he had seen the whole thing. It wasn't that Jerome and I had been doing anything in particular, but I didn't like the thought of being closely observed, especially not with Jerome. Especially when we were meeting again after what had happened between us, in a time when weird and terrible emotions were always following me like a dark cloud.

"All set," I said, looking down.

"I assume you can make your way from here, Jerome?"

Jerome retrieved his Oyster card from his pocket and waggled it at Thorpe.

"Good. Freddie will be coming with us."

Freddie appeared mildly dazed. I took it she and Thorpe had had a conversation inside as well. She went right to the backseat of the car and put herself in it.

"Okay, then," I said, looking from Thorpe to the car and back again.

"Get in," Thorpe said.

There would be no long good-bye, which was probably best. As I got into the car, Jerome came to the door and stopped before I shut it.

"When will you text?"

"Two times a day," Thorpe said, from the driver's side.

"Three."

"Fine. Shut the door."

I shut the door, and then we were driving off, leaving Jerome standing on the street.

. . .

We drove along the river, but Thorpe didn't bother to tell us where we were going. I had a look at Freddie in the side-view mirror and found that she was looking back at me, all apple cheeks and eager eyes.

"Your term ended a week ago," Thorpe said to her. "When are you due home to your family?"

"A few days," she said. "I told them I was staying here to finish up some work."

Having gotten what he wanted, Thorpe didn't feel obligated to add any follow-up. Freddie leaned back. I would occasionally turn my eyes to the mirror to see if we were still watching each other. She had shifted her attention to our route. We stopped in front of what looked one of many London apartment buildings—it could have been Hawthorne, my building at Wexford, just painted white with a black roof. I noticed a sign that read KING'S COLLEGE STUDENT RESIDENCE.

"Get some clothes," he said. "Enough for a day or two. Make it a small bag. Bring your laptop and anything you've collected that's relevant. Be back in ten minutes."

Freddie half fell out of the car in her effort to be quick. Thorpe pulled into an empty space up the street and stopped the car but kept it idling.

"You had one instruction," he said. "Stay indoors."

Here it was. I wanted him to do it. I wanted him to get self-righteous so I could level him with the knowledge that I knew what he had done—or hadn't done—for Stephen. But that was all he said. Thorpe was a bit of a mic-dropper, and he left me no open conversational door to lob my grenade into. All I could say was, "Yeah?"

"So why don't you tell me what caused you to disobey a straightforward instruction."

"Because I read Stephen's report."

No glint of recognition. To be fair, we had several bags of Stephen's reports, so that had really not been specific enough.

"What report?" he asked.

"His intake form."

"His intake form?"

I think he was genuinely confused. My bombshell moment was not having quite the *boom!* effect I had been going for. I dug it out of my pocket and shoved it at him. He accepted it and looked it over. The longer I watched him, the more I realized that he really hadn't seen this document before. Three heavy wrinkles appeared in his forehead as he processed the contents.

"Where did you get this?" he said, looking up.

"Stephen had it," I said. "It was in the box of stuff from his bedroom."

Thorpe considered the paper for a moment more, then leaned back against the headrest. He looked very tired.

"All right, Rory," he said. "I'll speak to you candidly, because I need you to listen and to understand my position on this. We need to come to an understanding. Do you agree?"

"I . . . yes?"

"When I was given the assignment to oversee this group," Thorpe said, "I had absolutely no idea what to make of it. I thought it was a training exercise. Training exercises are quite common, and they can go on for some time. I was given a set of instructions, told that I needed to find a certain kind of person. Young people, highly intelligent and skilled, who had had near-death experiences before eighteen and then reported certain visions. They gave me the termini. They told me about restarting the squad and set me to work. And I did it. I made contacts at a number of hospitals and clinics. And one day, Stephen's name popped up. He was in the hospital following a suicide attempt."

He looked over at me, I think checking to see if I knew this already.

"He told me," I said.

"I thought he might have. He's open about it."

"That's about the only thing," I said.

"That's part of what made him a good candidate. He had a good sense of discretion. Normally, no one would be recruited while still recovering from an incident like that. Working for a secret service is stressful, and it requires silence. And someone recovering from a suicide attempt and a trauma needs less stress and the opportunity to talk about anything and everything. What made his situation unique was that he couldn't talk about what had happened to him because it involved people that others couldn't see. He was also exactly the kind of person you'd want to recruit—top marks, top schools, physically competent."

Some rain pattered on the windscreen, and he hit the wipers for a moment. Then he looked at the paper again.

"I didn't write this report," he said, holding up the paper. "The contents don't shock me, but had I known the contents, I would have proceeded differently. I thought he had done better than this on the risk-assessment tests."

A moment of Thorpey silence. The air in the car became heavy with our thoughts.

"Stephen was very closed off emotionally," Thorpe said. "This is not an uncommon trait amongst people in the security services. But what I came to realize is that he was a very compassionate person who grew up in an atmosphere where compassion wasn't valued. He didn't know what to do with it. So instead of weighing a situation in terms of his own safety, he simply threw himself into it.

"He had been through a system that produces very professional people, very smart people—but sometimes very broken people. Eton's reputation is well earned. Stephen was focused, someone who wanted to devote his life to helping others—and he'd never been put in a position where he could do that. This job gave him meaning and purpose. Whatever happened, whatever risks were taken—he wanted to take them. Stephen was highly intelligent. He made his own choices."

"So . . . that's okay, then?"

"No," Thorpe said sharply. "This is where we need to be clear about my position. It was only after meeting Stephen, actually talking to him, seeing what he was doing—only then did I realize that this was not an exercise at all. It took me some time to come to grips with that, and Stephen was helpful. I regarded him not just as my recruit, but as my friend. If you think I don't care about what's happened on a personal level, then you are much mistaken."

His voice had acquired an edge I'd never heard in it before. It wasn't like it broke, or that he was crying. The words were coming quick and sharp, with a little intake of breath at the end of the sentences. Thorpe was leaning toward me, making sure I took in every word.

"Stephen cared very much about your safety. That was obvious to me from the start. So if you value Stephen, and you value how he felt and what he actually sacrificed himself for, you need to be more careful, and you need to listen to me. Can I get you to agree to that much, for his sake?"

"Yes?" I said.

It was like I'd just been subjected to my own personal thunderstorm, one that passed as quickly as it had come. Thorpe leaned back. He relaxed his expression in what seemed like a very intentional way, cleared his throat, and looked up at Freddie's building and checked his watch. His phone made a noise, and he pulled it from his pocket.

"Nothing at Stephen's parents' house," he said. "Callum and Boo are going back to Highgate to meet us."

"What about his parents?" I said.

"They haven't been informed," Thorpe said.

"Why?"

"For a number of reasons," Thorpe said. "When an officer in a security service dies on duty, certain measures are taken to secure information about that individual. Families are not informed what they actually did for a living. Stephen's parents think that he was a police officer, which he technically was. They stopped speaking to him at that point, I believe. And in this particular case . . ."

Here, Thorpe stopped and took a deep breath. Something had unsettled him.

"His body was removed from the hospital morgue, and all records of his being there were expunged."

"Where is he?"

"He's secure," Thorpe said. But he said it without his normal sharpness. "I believe he was removed for a specialist autopsy. When they need a body for a funeral, we can supply an unclaimed one."

At home, there's a local commercial for an unclaimed freight store where they sell—you may be ahead of me here—unclaimed freight. They just sell *things*. The owner is a small-headed man who screams the words UNCLAIMED, UNCLAIMED, UNCLAIMED FREIGHT! over and over in the commercial, until you are at least 90 percent certain that unclaimed freight is the thing being talked about. This is all that was going through my mind when Thorpe started talking about an UNCLAIMED, UNCLAIMED, UNCLAIMED BODY! Like maybe there was a warehouse of unclaimed bodies somewhere, next to the unclaimed sofas and TVs and tires. And maybe you could buy one and take it home and dress it up and pretend you had a friend. Except it would be an unclaimed body and would keep falling off the unclaimed sofa you had also just purchased, and eventually you would have to store it in the unclaimed freezer or it would rot.

It was possible I was mentally leaving the situation at hand, because I could not process a world in which Stephen was a body that was going to be autopsied.

It was cold in the car, and Thorpe suddenly didn't look so high and mighty. He looked younger than my dad—definitely more built than my dad, though. His white hair was the thing that always threw me off.

"When did your hair turn white?" I asked him. I didn't really care. I just needed to change the subject.

"When I was in my gap year," he said.

"Before college?"

"I was eighteen," he said.

"Why did your hair turn white when you were eighteen? Was it a medical thing, or—"

"Rory," he said again. I had gone too far into personal time with Thorpe. His voice was not unkind, though. "I realize things have not been easy for you, and I'm sorry for that, but things are what they are. And now you understand where I am coming from. From now on, I need you to be more compliant. I'm trusting in what you said you saw. I believe you. If we're to find Stephen, we need to work together. Agreed?"

"Okay," I said.

"Tell me what happened in that graveyard."

My eyes were burning a bit with impending tears, so I gave them a quick rub and cleared my throat.

"Stephen kept notes," I said. "In one of those *A-to-Z* map books. He put notes on all the pages about ghosts they'd found, and on the Highgate Cemetery page, there was one about an informant, someone named the Resurrection Man. So I went over to see what I could find out about where people appear after they die. I found him, and he was really talkative, and he said he wanted to take me on a tour of the place. But really what he wanted, once he found out what I was, was for me to take out some other ghost—some creepy, messed-up thing. He said the cemetery was his, and he wanted this other thing gone. We kind of got in an argument, and . . . then he threw rocks at me. I hid in the tomb for a minute so I wouldn't get hit. He locked me in."

"And attempted to set it on fire?" Thorpe asked.

"I don't know if it would have been that big of a fire," I said. "The gate was open to the air, and there weren't that many leaves. I think he was trying to stop me or scare me because I said I was going to blast the crap out of him—and I am. I'm going to go back and do that."

"Perhaps later," Thorpe said.

"Yeah. Later."

"But he had nothing useful to say."

"Nothing he told me."

He looked into the rearview mirror. "There's Freddie."

"So she's coming with us?"

"She is indeed. She's been working on this case longer than we have. She'll take some training, but Stephen thought highly of her. He planned on recruiting her. She was next on the list and had already been vetted, which is why we can do this now."

Freddie was struggle-running with what looked like a massively heavy duffel bag.

"What did you do to Jerome's phone?" I said.

"I don't need to do anything to access his phone. Mobile phones aren't very secure. He should know that. He seems like the type who would."

Freddie reached the car and breathlessly got inside, dragging the bag in after her.

"Right!" she said brightly. "I have my computer and a few books that might be useful. Where are we off to? What happens now?"

"You'll be meeting the rest of the team," Thorpe said. "Though I gather you have some idea already of who they are."

"Some," she said, leaning forward. "There's Boo. There's

the guy who looks like an athlete of some kind. And the one in charge . . . is his name Stephen?"

I gulped a bit of air and waited to see how Thorpe was going to answer that.

"Officer Dene died in the line of duty," he said plainly.

"What? Oh—oh, I . . . What happened?"

I bit down hard on my lip and hoped Thorpe would be his usual self and offer no long explanation.

"There was an accident," Thorpe said. "We won't be discussing it in detail right now."

"I'm sorry," she said to me. "You seemed close. I didn't mean to . . ."

We seemed close? What the hell had Freddie seen? Stephen and I had never done anything in public. We'd only kissed once, and that was inside, with the curtains shut, in a place she had likely never been. This thundered through my mind. Why did we seem close? Oh, my mind. My broken, frazzled mind. My emotional needle was swinging between "there is a body" to "we seemed close—maybe he liked me all along" from second to second, which made me wonder for another second if feelings were to be trusted at all. Then the needle started wobbling in confusion and my meter cracked in half and I stared out the window.

"This is what happens next," Thorpe said. "We are going to the safe house, which I'm hoping you haven't blown."

"I didn't tell anyone," she said. "Well, Jerome . . . not even Jerome. I had him meet me nearby. I never took him there."

"We meet with the team," Thorpe went on. "We now have something to work with. You'll be with us for several days at least. You may need to make excuses to your family about the holiday. You will not have your phone otherwise. Then we'll talk long-term training. Do you accept these conditions?"

"Absolutely!" Freddie said.

"Fine. Then it's time to meet everyone properly."

And so, we made our way up to Highgate.

13

WHEN WE GOT INSIDE, BOO AND CALLUM WERE SITTING side by side on the sofa, deep in conversation. They stopped the second they saw us, or, more specifically, Freddie. She quivered in the doorway like a spiderweb.

"Freddie," Thorpe said, "come in and shut the door."

"Who's this?" Callum said.

"This is Freddie Sellars," Thorpe said. "She'll be joining us."

"What?" Callum said.

"Freddie, sit," Thorpe said.

Freddie managed to set her bag down and get herself over to one of the chairs. All the confidence she'd been showing had shot off.

"This is Freddie Sellars," Thorpe repeated. "She has been trailing all of you for months. She followed us here on her bicycle yesterday. She's going to be the newest member of this team."

Boo let out a little unamused laugh.

"You must be joking," Callum said.

"Freddie," Thorpe went on, "has made this team an object of study for some time. Stephen caught her at it and found out who she was. He traced her background. Life-threatening accident at age fifteen . . ."

"How did he find that out?" Freddie asked. "That happened in Turkey, and I didn't go to the hospital. They treated me on the beach."

"You spoke to Stephen online, though you didn't know it, on one of your message boards. You mentioned your accident in conversation."

Freddie looked away for a moment and then her face lit up in realization.

"Dreadfulpenny," she said. "Of course."

We all waited for her to explain that one.

"That's what he called himself. Dreadfulpenny was his name online. The reverse of penny dreadful. We used to talk about the Society of Psychical Research. He mentioned one day that he'd almost been hit by a car whilst out on his bike and how scary it was, and I told him about the jellyfish sting. I should have realized, but I didn't think . . . We'd been chatting for weeks by that point."

I felt weirdly jealous at the thought of Freddie getting to talk to Stephen online for weeks. He was probably one of those people who found it easier to talk that way. It had been that way for Jerome and me, when we'd been separated. We actually got closer when we could only be online.

"So she's one of us," Boo said. "It doesn't mean she should be here."

"Stephen was about to bring her in anyway. He had already

vetted her. He would have told you soon enough. Freddie, why don't you give them a quick explanation of your background and expertise?"

"Of course!" Freddie said, perking up. "Well, my parents are profs at Cambridge. My mum is an associate chair of ancient history, and my dad is a behavioral psychologist. I grew up surrounded by academics and researchers. I knew my myths before I knew all the incarnations of the Doctor. My father's work dealt quite a lot with criminal behavior. He's essentially a profiler, though he doesn't work as one. I intended to go into that field myself until I had my accident. Once I started to see things, at first I thought it was purely a neurological event, but then I realized it wasn't. I found out there were people like me—like *us*. I changed my area of interest to history, to folklore and magic. Plus, I read up on the more fringy bits of psychology as it deals with matters like this. My father would be horrified if he knew."

"Freddie has provided us with some information on Jane Quaint," Thorpe said. He removed a device from his pocket and played back a recording of the conversation. Callum and Boo listened, looking over at Freddie on occasion.

"So where does that get us?" Callum said.

"It gets us ten names," Thorpe said. "If those people were in Sid and Sadie's thrall, and if they've been missing since 1973, there might be a property held in one of their names. I already ran them through our database, but there's nothing in there about them, which makes sense. These people were last seen in 1973 and some used aliases. You and Boo need to go to the police archive and see what you can find in the files. See if you can find out who these people were. Given what we've been told about them, some of them will have been picked up for something or other. There will be a lot to look through, but it's all we've got. Maybe we'll get lucky."

"I can help with that," Freddie said eagerly. "I—"

"Will do what you're instructed to do."

"Yes," Freddie said quickly. "Yes, of course."

"Can we talk to Rory for a moment?" Boo asked. "Upstairs?"

"Of course. There are some things I need to run through with Freddie. Don't be long."

I followed Boo upstairs. Callum trailed silently. We went to the front bedroom and shut the door. The room was so empty and echoey that we had to speak in very low voices.

"You ran off," Boo said. "Where did you go?"

"I thought I had an idea," I said. "It didn't really work out, except . . . well, I met her."

"Yeah," Callum said, with an accusatory tone. "You found her."

"She found me," I corrected him. "She could help."

"Help how? She studies *folklore*."

"She knew all about Jane Quaint," I said. "And Stephen thought she was good."

This remark was met by silence and stillness.

"There was nothing at his house?" I asked them.

"We went through the place top to bottom," Boo said. "It was easy enough. His parents are on holiday, and the cleaner left the kitchen door open to let the floor dry. They're on holiday, and their son's . . ."

"They don't know," I said. "Thorpe told me."

"I don't think they would have come home even if they did," Callum said. "That's the kind of people they are."

"So where do we look next?" I said.

Callum and Boo looked at each other, but meaningfully. The kind of look you give when you've already had a long conversation about something.

"I'm going downstairs," Callum said. He left us, shutting the door a little too loudly.

"Is he going to hate me forever?" I asked Boo.

I expected her to say, "He doesn't hate you." Instead, she leaned against the door and shook her head.

"We need to find your friend Charlotte, yeah?" she said. "We have to go."

Downstairs, Freddie was settling on the floor, looking at the bags I'd been going through this morning. I hurried down and took one of his notebooks out of her hands.

"What are you doing?" I snapped. I had no real ownership of Stephen's things. They were, after all, Stephen's.

"He told me to . . ." Freddie said meekly.

Thorpe looked up from his laptop. He was sitting quietly in the corner and typing intently.

"You two will continue going through these," Thorpe said. "Rory, you can show Freddie what you've done so far. She can help. Boo, Callum, get going."

Boo and Callum left without another word. Thorpe took his laptop into the kitchen and closed the door. I sat down on the floor in the middle of the bags and papers. Freddie looked over at me, but kept her eyes low.

"So there's a lot to go through," she said. "You've already started, I see. What exactly are we looking for? Something about Jane?"

"You know about myths?" I said.

"Quite a lot, yes."

"When Jane grabbed me, she told me she was into something about Greek mysteries. Ell—"

"*Eleusinian* Mysteries?" Freddie said.

"I think so. That sounds like it."

"They're also called the Rites of Demeter. It's an ancient Greek ritual, mostly an initiation rite, one that probably involved a lot of drugs and visions. Like a vision quest, except, more . . . well, ancient Greek. I'd have to brush up on it. That's what she was interested in?"

"They said they were going to *defeat death*. Do you know what they could have meant?"

"Defeat death? No. Well, there are certainly traditions that believe death isn't real, not in the way it's normally understood. We're evidence of that. We see the dead all the time. But if they have the sight already, I couldn't tell you what they were hoping to achieve beyond that. I could look into it."

Something in my expression made her sag.

"I'm sorry," she said. "I can be helpful. I promise. I'm very sorry about Stephen. He seemed very . . . well, I never got to meet him except online, and perhaps then he was simply acting a certain way . . ."

"I don't think he knew how to act," I said.

She had nothing to say to that. I looked at the mess of papers around us and wondered if it was information or distraction. Maybe it would lead us somewhere, or maybe Thorpe was just trying to keep me out of the way. Whatever the case, if I had to sit here with Freddie, I would try to get some use out of her.

"We're looking for him," I said.

"Who? Stephen, you mean?"

I nodded.

"He's . . . come back?"

"I think so."

"You saw him?"

"No," I said, shaking my head. "It's a long story, but I'm almost positive he's back. But we can't find him in any of the places we thought he'd be. Do you know anything about where the dead end up after they first come back?"

"Well . . ." Freddie considered for a moment. "I didn't do the kind of fieldwork that all of you have, but I have read a lot of accounts. It's true that most places that are so-called haunted are where someone has died, or where someone has a deep connection."

"We've done everywhere we can think of like that. We did the hospital, the flat, his home. Callum and Boo went back to Eton."

"Perhaps there was somewhere significant he didn't mention to anyone? We all have a place we value, a place we may not mention to anyone else—not out of secrecy, but because we don't even know how much we value it until it's gone or we can't reach it. For me, it's a bit of the back garden at my grandmother's house on a sunny day in June. There's a little stream there where you can see the reflection of the clouds. It's surrounded by wildflowers—a lot of poppies—and you can sit on a little footbridge and dangle your feet in and read a book. It's what I think of when people ask me what my favorite place is, but I don't think I've ever mentioned it to anyone until now. Something like that. There might be a place."

"But if he didn't mention it . . ."

"It doesn't mean I'm right, or that there's no clue. Now, what have you found in here so far?"

"Over here," I said, pointing to the pile of photocopies, "are some research things of his."

She flipped through these and shook her head.

"These are all highly speculative things. Shadow Cabinet and all that."

"What's the Shadow Cabinet?" I asked.

"It's nonsense," she said. "Conspiracy theory. Here, for example, is a copy of some pages from a grimoire written in 1908 by a member of the Order of the Golden Dawn, and one of the original members of the London temple of Isis-Urania."

I'd read that much from the front page of the copy. When I remained silent, she nodded, as if she thought we were in perfect understanding as to what that meant.

"Well, listen. *And so it was that in 1671, Thomas Blood went to the Tower of London and therefrom took the jewels belonging to the King. The theft was completed over several days, taking all manner of goods, including the Crown of St. Edward, and the Orb and the Scepter of the Cross. On being caught, Blood would speak only to the King, who, much to the surprise of all concerned, pardoned him once he returned the hoard. But the great diamond, the Eye of Isis, was not returned. And yet the King pardoned him. It is said that the Eye of Isis was broken into a dozen pieces, and each of these pieces contains the power to dispel spirits in a manner most distasteful.*"

I hadn't gotten that far in my reading. That sounded like research about the terminus.

"It's all about the connections between magic and the government," she said, shaking her head. "I read this sort of thing too, but no one takes it seriously. You've heard of people who believe in ancient aliens building the pyramids? This is similar stuff."

I let that go. Freddie didn't seem to know that the terminus was real. She would probably find out about that soon enough. In any case, it had nothing to do with where Stephen might be hiding.

"There's also this," I said, pulling the black notebook from under a stack of forms.

She opened the book and flipped through. From the way her eyes widened, I could tell this was exactly the kind of thing she had been hoping for.

"Oh, yes," she said. "I love a cipher. I can work on this."

I looked at the pile of papers. There had to be something in here, but my brain was so weary, so stretched out and stressed. What I wanted to do was sleep, or walk every street in London looking for Stephen, or both at the same time. What I had to do was figure out a job for myself that somehow involved these papers.

"Did you find anything else useful?" Freddie said.

"The way I got to the cemetery was this," I said, pulling the A–Z out of another pile. "It looks like Stephen was tracking activity at different locations."

"This could be very useful," Freddie said. "We could plot it on a map. It might give us a geographical distribution. That might tell us something. Is there a large map in here?"

"There has to be," I said. "Stephen loves maps. There's usually one on the wall of the flat. I think Boo took it. It should be in here."

We both dug through until Freddie found it, still in one of

the bags. It was a well-worn map of London. We spread it open on the floor. It had old pinholes in it from where he'd marked information before.

"If you mark an *x* anywhere there was an encounter, we'll be able to get a large-scale picture," Freddie said.

This was something I could do. It made sense. It was a task when I needed a task. I found a pen in the middle of the mess and climbed onto the map, pulling the *A–Z* with me. Each page of it covered a small zone of London. The book was a few hundred pages long and far more detailed than the big map. I would have to work zone by zone, moving slowly across the city with my pen, finding streets or guessing where they should be if the big map didn't have them in detail. Freddie tucked herself up on the sofa with the notebook and a pad of paper. The time started to slip by very quickly. I worked through page after page, crawling around the map of London. There were a few little pools of activity, a few large blank spaces. Nothing I could see that seemed important. I'm not sure how much time went by. The curtains were closed, and it had gotten dark a long time before.

"All right," Freddie said, breaking the silence. "I'm fairly certain it's not a standard substitution code. It looks like it needs a key. Did you find any single pages that seemed to be completely in gibberish? Charts of letters . . ."

"I would have noticed that," I said.

"Of course. Well, all right. Why would Stephen code his own book? What would he want to use it for? That might tell us something about how he keyed it."

"He was careful about everything," I said.

"But was anything else written in this code?"

"No," I said. "Everything else is pretty normal."

"Then this book is different. This book contains some different information. You only record things you need to remember, so why would he—"

The kitchen door opened, and Thorpe hurried into the room.

"They've got a hit," Thorpe said. "Get your coats."

14

THORPE DROVE QUICKLY NOW, MUCH MORE QUICKLY THAN I think you're allowed to drive in London. He was dipping into bus lanes and swerving around other cars. No one stopped him. There must have been something about his car that signaled to the police that he was to be left alone. He did stop at red lights when we hit them, which would send us bucking forward.

"The house was under the name Mick Dunstan," he said. "Real name Michael Phillip Dunstan, born 1952, arrested six times between 1968 and 1973 for possession and selling of cannabis. No records of any kind at all for nine years, until he bought a house in 1982. It's in East Acton, near Wormwood Scrubs, which explains quite a lot."

"What's Wormwood Scrubs?" I said to Freddie.

"I believe it's a prison," Freddie said.

"It's also a nature preserve," Thorpe said. "It's one of the largest green spaces in London. It's the country in the city."

The country.

"She's there," I said.

"I think it's likely."

"So going to see Clover was useful," Freddie said eagerly.

"Yes, Freddie," Thorpe said. He reached into his jacket pocket and produced a phone, which he tossed onto my lap.

"Write a text message to Jerome. Tell him you're fine. Don't hit Send. Pass it back to me."

This was kind of an intense moment to be writing text messages to Jerome, so after a minute or two of thinking, I came up with: **I'm fine.**

I passed it to Thorpe, who eyed it before hitting Send. The reply came quickly.

How do I know this is you?

I considered this, then typed another reply and showed it to Thorpe for approval as we stopped at a red light. Approval was given with a terse nod.

I'm fine dumbass

For much of our ill-fated romance, Jerome and I had traded insults with our affections.

That's more like it was the reply.

"That's enough," Thorpe said, taking the phone back.

A little under an hour later, we arrived in a residential area, somewhere I'd never been before in London. There was a British Gas van sitting in front of the house and a few people in uniforms going in and out. One of them came over to the car and rapped on the window, and Thorpe lowered it.

"It's clean," he said to Thorpe in a low voice. "No one in there. Recently vacated, though. Food out in the kitchen. Fresh rubbish. Shall we process it?"

Thorpe looked at the house for a moment.

"Move your team out for an hour or so. I want a look first. Maintain a perimeter. If you see any of them in the area, you move in."

"Right."

The man looked at me and Freddie but said nothing. He returned to the group and made a quick hand signal, and everyone returned to the van. We waited for a while, until they pulled away, and until Callum and Boo came running up to the car.

"Tube bollocksed up today," Callum said. "Took forever."

Thorpe reached across me, opened the glove compartment, and removed some latex gloves.

"Everybody puts these on," he said.

"Are we going *inside*?" Freddie said.

"We are. We need to be the first in there before the scene is processed. Don't touch or move anything unnecessarily."

I had to admit I felt very *CSI* snapping on the gloves.

From the outside, this was about as ordinary a house as you could imagine. I had come to be suspicious of ordinary-looking houses. Inside, the first thing we were hit with was a faceful of incense—not quite as strong as the bookshop, but similar in scent. It definitely looked like people had recently been there—gross people. There were food wrappers and trash all around. Candles had been burning all over the place, stuck into wine bottles and beer bottles, cemented to whatever surfaces they sat on in their own wax drippings. There was a fine grit over the floor, and the remnants of a rubbed-out chalk circle.

"They doing some kind of rituals in here?" Callum said. "Like witchcraft?"

"They could be doing anything," Freddie said. "From the sound of it, they're into all sorts."

"What they're into is Monster Munch," Boo said, flicking a pink snack bag with the end of her nail. There really were a lot of bags around.

"I think they use a lot of pot," I said. "Maybe they have the munchies?"

"That does make sense," Freddie said. "Many of the ancient Greek rituals were dependent on the ingestion of psychotropic substances, most likely ergot. It's basically nature's version of LSD."

"So they get stoned and eat snacks," Callum said. "That describes half the people I went to school with."

Thorpe was looking up. I looked up too. There was a little device in the ceiling.

"There's a sprinkler system," I said, pointing. "At least they're careful stoners."

"That's a bit odd," Freddie said, "a sprinkler system in a house like this."

We moved on to the kitchen, where Boo felt the side of the kettle.

"Still warm," she said. "Someone was here not that long ago. Must have just cleared out."

"Funny, that," Callum said. "Them clearing out right before we got here. It was almost like they knew we were coming."

They both looked to Freddie, who was backing ever so slowly up against the table.

"She didn't," Thorpe said.

"How do you know?" Boo asked. "Didn't she know all those freaks? Didn't she just take you right to some people who knew

Jane? She comes in, and all of a sudden we find this place? Even if Stephen did vet her . . ."

"I didn't!" Freddie said. "I promise you."

"But you did meet Jane, didn't you?" Thorpe said. "You said she was well known, but that wasn't it, was it?"

Freddie's skin turned faintly purple.

"When I first got the sight, I tried to find other people who had it as well. I met someone at the bookshop who introduced me to Jane. He took me over to her house for dinner once. Just once. They were very nice to me, and it was the first and only place I could really talk about what had happened to me. It was just so good to have someone to talk to. They made me feel normal."

I knew that feeling.

"They talked to me about having the sight, but they didn't tell me any of the things they told Rory. After that night, I never saw them again."

"Why not?" Boo said. "If you liked them so much."

"I didn't like them," Freddie said sharply. "I liked how they made me feel like there was nothing wrong with me, but there was something else in their manner that I didn't like at all. Something I couldn't place. They were too welcoming, too interested in me. I excused myself at one point and had a quick sneak around the upstairs and looked at some of the books. Once I saw some of the titles on the spines, I had some idea that I was dealing with very strange people indeed. I went down and finished my dinner and thanked them, and I never went back. They never did anything to me, but I always felt very uncomfortable about them. When I saw Jane at your school, Rory, I asked around a bit more, and Clover finally told me a few things. That's the truth."

Boo and Callum exchanged a look. I kept my eye on Freddie, who was grasping fearfully at the edge of the table.

"I think she's telling the truth," I said.

"As do I," Thorpe added. "In fact, I know she didn't contact anyone. I put a trace on her mobile and her computer, and I had someone go to her room at her house at the college and go through her things. That same person kept an eye on her as she was packing."

"The cleaner?" she said, her eyes widening. "The one who told me to keep my door open because they'd sprayed for insects?"

"So you were never alone," Thorpe said. "I had Rory sit with you in the house. She was never going to allow you to be alone with Stephen's papers."

"You let her look at Stephen's things if you thought she was a risk?" Boo said.

"I didn't believe she was," Thorpe said. "I believe she is an asset."

"So who told them someone was coming?"

"Perhaps no one," Thorpe said. "It could be a coincidence. But I don't really put much stock in those. I imagine it was someone who saw us go into the bookshop."

"Not Clover," Freddie said. She was slowly releasing her grip on the table. "He hates Jane."

"Anyone around that bookshop could have alerted them," Thorpe said. "I imagine we made an impression going in. Whoever it was, I know it wasn't you. So let's keep going. Upstairs."

Boo and Callum still regarded Freddie with some uncertainty. She put her head down. We headed upstairs, which was only slightly less gross than downstairs. There were three bedrooms.

Two of them had no beds, just some mattresses and blankets on the floor. The one bathroom was dirty, with a pile of wet towels in the corner and an unpleasant, scrummy ring around the inside of the tub. There were a few toothbrushes lying bristles down in a small pool of something thick and filmy—most likely congealed toothbrush drippings. This bothered me most of all.

"Looks like about five or six people have been staying here," Thorpe said.

"Six disgusting people," Boo said.

The main bedroom did have a bed in it, as well as a white area rug. It had an en suite bathroom, which was cleaner than the other one. In this bathroom, the towels were hung and the toothbrush stored upright.

"Jane probably stayed in here," I said. I went to the wardrobe and opened it, revealing a few outfits. They were more conservative than Jane's usual getups, but they looked about her size.

"Take the toothbrushes," Thorpe said to Callum and Boo, passing them some plastic bags he had in his pockets. "Take hairbrushes. Look for anything with any identification."

"This floor is very poorly laid," Freddie said, looking down. I guess she was right—there were gaps between the boards, like someone hadn't bothered to make sure they all lined up correctly.

"Who cares?" Callum replied.

"It's not that I care, but . . . don't those windows look lower than the windows downstairs?"

She went over and pulled back the long drapes. She was right—these windows were definitely lower to the floor.

"Again," Callum said, "who . . ."

In answer to that half-asked question, Thorpe got down on one knee and felt the floor. He poked his nail into the spaces between the boards. Then he looked at the windows again.

"This floor is raised. Something's under here, and this is ventilation. Lift up that bed. Lean it against the wall. Get the rug up."

Callum and Boo lifted the bed and tipped it against the wall, and Thorpe and I dragged back the rug. Freddie was now flat on the floor, her face against it, looking into one of the cracks.

"I think it's open space below here," she said.

As soon as we pulled back the rug, there was a clear outline of a hatch. Thorpe got down and worked on prying it open, and when he did, a crawl space about two feet deep was revealed.

Charlotte was resting on her back, her red hair spread out, her hands peacefully folded on her chest. Thorpe stepped down into the space and felt Charlotte's neck and cheek.

"She's breathing," he said. "Charlotte, can you hear me?"

No response. Callum knelt and helped Thorpe lift Charlotte out of the crawl space. They set her gently on the floor, where Thorpe continued to check her over, lifting her eyelids, listening to her chest. There were no cuts or bruises, no signs of injury. She was simply asleep, lying in a hatch in a floor under a rug and a bed in some random house in London.

"I'll call 999," Boo said.

"No," Thorpe replied. "Bring the car around. Now."

"She's okay?" I asked, getting down on the floor next to her.

"We need to get her to a doctor," Thorpe said, sitting back on his knees. "I know someone. Wrap her in a blanket and get her to the car. Put her in the back. Be as low-key as you can about it."

He pulled out his phone and sent a text as Callum lifted Charlotte up. Her head rolled back.

"Freddie, Rory, you're in the car with me," Thorpe said. "Rory, you stay in the back with Charlotte. Callum, Boo, you keep eyes on this place."

I got into the back, and Charlotte was carefully shifted in, her head resting on my lap. This was perhaps the strangest moment of all, looking down and seeing Charlotte's face, her red hair against my legs. A few minutes into the drive, I felt her head turn.

"I think she's waking up!" I said. "Charlotte?"

Her eyelashes moved. Her eyelids wrinkled, and she opened and closed her mouth silently. Then both eyes fluttered open, ever so slowly, and Charlotte was looking up at me.

"Rory?"

"Hey," I said. "You're okay."

"Where am I?"

"We're going to get you help. We're on our way to a doctor now. You're going to be fine."

"I feel fine," she said dreamily.

"Good," I said.

"Keep her talking," Thorpe said. "We'll be there soon."

I've had some awkward conversations in my life, but this was a new one for me. I had my hand in Charlotte's hair and her head in my lap, and she was gazing up at me with the gentle trust of a puppy. It was deeply unnerving.

"So," I said, "you feel okay? You're okay?"

"I'm very tired. I feel like I've . . . I've been sleeping for ages."

Charlotte's focus turned to a point above my eyes.

"Your hair," she said, "did you cut it?"

By the way she asked, it was clear that she was wondering why I'd committed such an act on my own scalp. Charlotte was still in the building.

"Am I late?" she asked.

"You're not late for anything."

"I must be late. I must be . . ." She twisted her head around, looking left to right. "Are we going somewhere?"

"To a doctor," I said again.

"Oh, that seems silly. I'm just sleepy. Who are you?"

This was to Freddie, who was leaning back between the front seats.

"Freddie Sellars."

"You don't go to Wexford," Charlotte said, squinting in concentration.

"No, I'm—"

"Freddie," Thorpe said, in a warning tone.

"A . . . friend of Rory's?"

Charlotte stirred, and I helped her sit up. She was heavy and uncoordinated, like she was drunk. She lolled back against the seat.

"Where are we going?" she asked again. "Whose car is this?"

"It's mine," Thorpe said. "I'm with the security services, and you're being taken to a doctor."

"The security services?"

She looked out the car window, as if the explanation she was seeking was in the view.

"You were abducted several days ago," Thorpe said. "I believe you've been drugged."

Charlotte considered this information for a moment.

"I've been with Jane," she said. "I was in the house—I was at Jane's. And then I was in a different house. But I can't remember why."

"I'm going to ask you some questions," Thorpe said. "Is that all right?"

"Oh, it's fine."

"Were you hurt?"

"I don't think so," she said. "I'm just quite tired."

"Can you tell me about the people who were at that house? Can you tell me who they were? How many of them there were?"

Charlotte considered this for a moment.

"Jane was there. And Devina. And a blond boy. I don't know . . ."

"That's good," Thorpe said. "That's fine. What else can you tell me?"

"They were always nice to me," she said. "No one hurt me. We ate a lot of soup and bread. And sometimes I watched television. I saw myself on television, on the news."

Which was creepy. But not nearly as creepy as the next thing she said.

"They gave me a bath. Everything after the bath . . ."

"What do you mean, they gave you a bath?" Thorpe asked.

"They put me in the bath—with my clothes on, not naked— and something happened, I can't remember, and I woke up and I was soaked all over, my head and all. I must have been under the water. Then they gave me lots of towels and a dry robe, and we had tea. And they . . . oh, yes, they let me come into the garden for a moment. It was night. There were a lot of stars out. Now I remember. They said, 'Now you can see.' And then, the next day, I met a man who wasn't there . . . Is that a poem? I met a man who wasn't there . . ."

Freddie looked at me.

"Charlotte," I said, "you had this bath, and then you saw someone who wasn't there?"

"In the garden. I know how it sounds. I can't explain it. It was mad. But it was wonderful. It was like he was made of air, but he was real. Jane and the others talked a lot, but I never understood what they were talking about. They said that it was time."

"Time for what?" Thorpe asked.

"Let me think." Even half drugged, Prefect Charlotte was in there, ready to give her answers carefully. "One morning they were very excited because they were close to finding out where it was."

"Where what was?" Thorpe prompted.

"The stone." There was a touch of impatience, as if Thorpe hadn't quite been following along. "They needed the stone to start. I don't know exactly what was happening, but they seemed to have figured something out, and they said they were close to getting it. That's the last I remember hearing. Are we going to the British Museum?"

We were passing a large building, and I supposed that she was correct and that was what it was.

"We're going to a house," Thorpe said. "A doctor I know lives there. She knows you're coming."

When we pulled up, the door to a nearby house opened, and a woman came out to meet us. She was tall and sharply featured, with dark black skin and bright lipstick. She was dressed as conservatively as Thorpe, but with a bit more style—her blouse was creamy white and silky and tied near the neck, and her pencil skirt had a leather stripe up the side. Conservative, but probably designer. It had the look of quality and expense. She came right to the back door and opened it and took Charlotte's wrist.

"Charlotte?" she asked.

"Hello," Charlotte said. She had gone childlike again.

"I'm Dr. Marigold. You'll be going inside now. Do you think you can walk, or do you need to be carried?"

"I think I can walk."

"I'll help you."

The doctor gave Thorpe a deadly look as she assisted Charlotte from the back of the car. She also had a look at me in a way that suggested she knew who I was. Then she escorted Charlotte to the door.

"Who is this?" I asked.

"Someone I work with. Say as little as possible in the house. Repeat nothing you've heard in the car, do you understand? If she asks you anything, keep your answers short."

I guessed they weren't really good friends, the doctor and Thorpe.

Where Thorpe's flat had been stark and Jane's had been some kind of retro fever dream, this woman's house spoke of refinement and tradition. There was no television, but plenty of bookshelves carefully filled with medical and science textbooks and novels. There was an assortment of medical supplies and equipment on the table—a stethoscope, a few vials of things, a needle, rubbing alcohol, and bandages. Charlotte was placed on the sofa, and the doctor listened to Charlotte's chest with the stethoscope, took her pulse, and looked into her eyes with a flashlight. She examined her legs and arms, turning her wrists around several times.

"How do you feel?" she asked.

"A bit tired, but all right."

The woman checked Charlotte's pupils again.

"It looks to me like she's been given a light sedative," the woman said to Thorpe. "I should examine her for injuries. Everyone step out of the room, please. Into the kitchen. Straight back."

I don't think Thorpe wanted to leave the room, but he nodded at us. Whatever silent drama was going on between him and the doctor, we weren't to know. After a few minutes, the woman joined us in the kitchen.

"No evidence of any physical trauma," she said, washing her hands at the sink. "No bruising. No lacerations. She's been fed and hydrated. Her demeanor suggests minor sedation. She's staying here with me. You're leaving."

"We need to discuss the other matter."

"Not now we aren't. Take them and go."

"I don't feel comfortable—"

"Then I'll call for an ambulance and have her transferred to hospital. Would that make you more comfortable? Or you could always . . ."

She looked at me for a moment, and I felt a chill.

Thorpe folded his arms over his chest. There was a silent confrontation. Thorpe pushed off the counter he'd been leaning against.

"Time to leave," he said to us. "We'll be in touch."

Back in the car, I felt safe to speak again.

"We're leaving her there?" I said.

"She's safe. She'll be cared for."

"But who is that?"

Thorpe didn't answer.

"Look," I said, "what about her family? Or the police? I mean, now that we found her—"

"That won't be reported yet," he said.

"Why not?"

"Because we need to find out what happened to her. I think you heard exactly what I did."

"They gave her the sight," Freddie said.

"Precisely. And she's describing something I don't like the sound of. Until we know what's going on, until we have someone in custody, Charlotte stays undiscovered. That means you tell no one."

15

IT WAS LATE, AND WE WERE GATHERED IN THE KITCHEN OF the Highgate house. Callum and Boo had waited at the house in East Acton for a while, but there was no sign of Jane or the others, so Thorpe recalled them. There weren't enough chairs for all of us, so we stood around the table eating some fish and chips. It was the first hot food I'd had in some time.

"So they took her," Boo said. "And they didn't hurt her. But they gave her the sight?"

"If we're understanding her correctly," Thorpe said.

"That's certainly how it sounded to me," Freddie said. "They appear to have put her in a bath and held her underwater."

Callum and Boo didn't look any happier that Freddie was there, but she had proved to be useful, so there was a grudging acceptance.

"But not everyone gets the sight, even if something happens to them," I said. "Right?"

"That's the understanding," Thorpe said. "Otherwise every

hospital in the country would be full of people seeing the dead, and that's not happening. It seems to be a fairly rare trait, hence the exclusivity of your team."

"But why," Callum said. "Why would they want to do that?"

"Perhaps just as an experiment," Freddie said. "But who knows if it's even possible to *confer* the sight to someone?"

"If the power of a terminus can be conferred to Rory," Thorpe replied, "presumably other things are possible."

"A terminus?" Freddie asked.

"What we use to take out the ghosts," Callum said.

"I still don't understand. You're saying you have devices that can destroy ghosts?"

I was right. She had no idea.

"They were diamonds," Boo said. "They're gone now."

"You have *diamonds* that can do this?" Freddie said. "Diamonds?"

"We used to," Callum said. "We lost ours. Now we just have . . ."

"You have what?" Freddie said, turning to me for an explanation.

"Me," I said. "Something happened when I was stabbed. Whatever was in the terminus is in me now. So if I touch a ghost . . ."

"The ghost goes boom," Callum said.

Freddie was struck into a gaping-mouth silence.

"It's a lot to get your head round," Boo said, casually picking up a fry.

"It's more than that," Freddie said. "If those exist, then . . . it could all be true. Amongst people who are interested in the paranormal, there's a story that in some prehistoric time,

England was a gateway for the dead—London was the place of the many rivers the dead had to cross. There were pathways—ley lines. There were points of entry, like Stonehenge. All the anoraky sort of things people speculate on. I was telling Rory a little bit about this before. Stephen had some bits and pieces on the subject, but I thought it was just general interest. This theory holds that London became one of the world's major cities because it's on a point of massive power, but the power needs to be carefully controlled and maintained. At some point in the distant past, a series of powerful stones was placed around the city at certain key locations. The stones are said to possess powers to control the openings between the world of the living and the world of the dead. They're keys, I suppose. But Charlotte mentioned a stone, and if you're saying you had diamonds . . ."

She set her packet of fish down excitedly.

"Freddie," Thorpe said, "breathe. Explain."

In response, Freddie hurried out of the room and returned a moment later with a fistful of the photocopies from Stephen's flat.

"Stephen had this. It's a bit of academic text concerning the stealing of the crown jewels in 1671 by Thomas Blood." She read them the passage she'd read to me earlier. "He was pardoned. That's actually true."

"A diamond," Boo said. "In pieces."

"A dozen pieces," Callum added.

"There's something else on the Eye of Isis here." She flipped through until she found the document she wanted. "This is from a book from 1867, called *Magic of London*. Generic enough title and written by Anonymous—*A stone quite ancient, and beloved of pharaohs. It was placed in the eye of a great statue of the goddess at Heliopolis. It was said to be a brilliant blue and seemed to burn from within. Its size was said to be quite like that of a man's fist. When removed from the statue, it lost its blue color. A great battle was fought for the stone, but it was lost to time, until it reappeared in England in the time of John Dee. By then, it had decreased in size, but he regarded it as most precious and kept it secure in his rooms, saying that it was most vital to the well-being of Her Majesty. After his death, it was moved to the Tower, from whence it was stolen by Thomas Blood, most fiendish and most vile of men. The Eye of Isis was but one of eight stones. We know of one other, called the Oswulf, which is now safe from man's interference. It is to these stones that we owe our happiness. May we never know more of them, for the future of London rests with them, and they must rest forevermore, safe within the bounds of the Shadow Cabinet."*

"The Shadow Cabinet?" Thorpe said.

"Not the government body," Freddie said. "Same name, very different group. The Shadow Cabinet is the group that's supposed to look after these stones. They call them the Shadow Cabinet because it's a group in the shadows. It's who's really in control. That sort of thing. They're supposed to make sure they never get taken or moved. They failed once, when the Eye of Isis was taken, and that's why London is supposed to be so haunted. It was like part of the wall that protects the city came down. I always thought it was some nonsense made up by some Victorian revivalist Druids, based on nothing—a conspiracy theory amongst occultists. These are the same people who believe in the Illuminati and mind control and auras. I thought it was a story based on fact, not reflecting fact. For instance, the Oswulf Stone is a real thing. Charlotte said they needed a stone . . ."

Thorpe had set his fish down and was listening intently.

"What about this Oswulf Stone? What is it?"

"Well, I can look up the details . . ." She pulled out her phone and typed for a moment. "According to the Internet, it was a pre-Roman monolith, and it used to be by Marble Arch. It was speculated that it was a boundary marker of some kind, but no one really knows why it was there. It was just your standard mysterious bit of rock. For hundreds of years, the stone stood there, even lending its name to the area. Then the story does get a bit odd. In 1819, the stone was simply covered over in earth. Then, three years later, in 1822, they dug it back up again. It remained there for forty-seven years, leaning against Marble Arch, until 1869, at which point, it vanished. Presumably the Shadow Cabinet put it somewhere where no one could get at it."

"So you're saying that Jane and them know where this is?" Boo said.

"It sounded like they were close to finding it," Freddie said. "And if it's all true, this stone can open some sort of channel between the living and the dead."

"It sounds like bollocks," Callum said.

"I agree," Freddie said, nodding. "Or I would have agreed just five minutes ago. But if you're telling me even *one* of these stones is real, that you have this power . . . then it could all be real. And clearly Stephen was looking into it."

"They said they were going to destroy death," I chimed in. "It sounded nuts before, but if there's something out there that somehow divides life and death . . ."

"Not just divides," Freddie said. "Protects. Guards. The story goes that if the eight stones were removed, well, a gap would appear. London would become a void, the dead coming back, the living sucked in . . . who even knows? It would be very bad. The stories claim that the fact that just *one* stone was broken has resulted in London being unstable, full of the dead. And it is a quite haunted place, isn't it?"

The truth of this wasn't lost on any of us.

"If Stephen thought it was serious . . ." Boo said. "We should look into this."

Even Callum was looking a bit more concerned.

"It does seem to be worth looking into," Thorpe said. "Especially since Charlotte has been located. Whatever this thing is, we want to get there first."

This ended up taking the next hour. Thorpe had his people on it, and he also looked on his own. Freddie and Boo were on computers. Callum was in charge of watching footage from a CCTV camera pointed at the house in Acton and reviewing anything that was coming in from the people who had gone through the site. None of this, however, proved to be very useful. There was very little about the Oswulf Stone, aside from what Freddie had already said—at least, nothing useful. It was just another rock in a city full of rocks. It was old, maybe about a meter high, probably used as a boundary marker. Nothing much else came up. By one in the morning, we were all so broken that Thorpe called it a night and ordered that we needed to get some sleep. Boo went home to do this and to change her clothes. Callum crashed on the living room floor on some cushions. Thorpe settled in a chair. I was sent up to the bedroom, which was arguably the most comfortable and the loneliest place in the house. I had nothing to change into for bed, so I kicked off the sneakers and climbed in in my clothes. A minute after I crawled under the stiff sheets, there was a knock on the door and Freddie poked her head inside. She was carrying the small black notebook.

"I was told we're supposed to share, but I've had plenty of sleep," she said. "I'll crack on with this. I'll sit up here, if it's all right. I feel a bit . . ."

"It's fine," I said.

Freddie sat against the bed with the book and her pad of paper.

"This cipher," she said. "It likely has a key somewhere. It could be a key he's written out, but many times people use books. Did he have any favorite books?"

I thought about the hundreds of books that were piled up along the walls of Stephen's bedroom back in the flat, and then I thought of the few books in the box. I got up without a word and returned downstairs. Callum was out like a light and didn't move. Thorpe lifted his head and watched me retrieve the box. I went back up to the room and opened it up, pulling out the books inside.

"This was a box of personal stuff I found in his closet," I said. "They must have been important."

"Right," she said, looking through the pile of books and examining them. "He clearly likes space opera. There could be something in here. Is there anything else that Stephen would have considered really important?"

"His sister," I said. "She died a few years ago. I think he cared about her more than anything."

"Right," she said.

I rested back once again and stared up at the ceiling light.

"In the car," I said, "you said Stephen and I seemed close. What made you say that?"

"Oh . . . I . . ."

"Seriously."

"Well . . . when I saw you together, the way you interacted gave me that impression. Whenever you walked away, he always watched to make sure you were inside. He seemed to care. But I know you were with Jerome. He told me."

"Jerome and I broke up," I said.

"He told me that too. I know these things can be . . . well. Difficult. I mean, my last girlfriend and I—she thought I was a bit intense. A bit obsessive. I suppose she had a point. I didn't even notice that she'd met a girl with a lot of anchor and mermaid tattoos who wore her hair in a beehive on weekends. Then she went off to university in Scotland with that girl, and I haven't heard from her since."

"Sorry," I said.

"No, I mean . . . I only mean to say that it seems like I'm coming in at the middle of everything, and I know things can get so complicated. I couldn't tell her what I was obsessing about. I couldn't tell her what I saw. I imagine you and Jerome had sort of the same problem, perhaps."

"Something like that," I said.

"And you and Stephen didn't."

She was right, but it was more than that. I liked Jerome. I felt nice things about Jerome. But Stephen was something very different, something on another level.

"You seem very sure he's . . . I don't want to imply otherwise, but you seem sure that Stephen has returned? How do you know?"

"It was because of something I did in the hospital," I said. I was too tired to explain it all. Freddie was clearly disappointed, but I was already falling asleep. I felt like Charlotte, her head lolling back. We'd found Charlotte. I'd seen Jerome. Had all of this happened today?

There was rain pattering against the window. I let my eyes close and sank into the sound of that and Freddie turning pages.

16

I BECAME AWARE AT SOME POINT THAT SOMEONE WAS standing over me. It was possibly morning—these things were hard to tell in London. There was a head of curls and a face of freckles and a pair of bloodshot but excited eyes.

"Sonnet seventy-one," Freddie said.

My head was full of webs and slowness. I was dehydrated from sleep. My mouth felt like a stretch of roadway in the Louisiana sun. And, when first uttered, these were not words that made any sense to me.

"Sonnet seventy-one," Freddie said, holding up the black notebook. "Stephen's code."

Those words made more sense. I pulled myself upright.

"I spent half the night going through the novels, but then I thought about it again," Freddie said. She had that shaky energy that you get from not sleeping at all. "What you said about his sister. Her death. It was obvious. The first letters of the code are LXXI. That's a number. Seventy-one. He had a book of Shakespeare's sonnets. Sonnet seventy-one begins with the line *No longer mourn for me when I am dead.* Fairly apropos for what we do. I broke down the cipher against the poem. I've translated the first three pages. And it gets better."

Freddie sat on the edge of the bed.

"This book is about a series of meetings," she said. "He never names the person he's meeting with. Here are the first entries. *Went to Chanceford to discuss six. Confirmed location. Currently secure but should discuss relocation.* The next one: *Met E at Athenaeum Club regarding relocation. E against moving. Look into local building works.* And then it goes on a bit about planning permissions and the common rates at which concrete and stone floors need replacing. I looked up Chanceford. It's the family seat of the Williamson family. I looked back and found one particular Williamson. The fifth Lord Williamson, who died in 1896. According to the *Burke's Peerage* and a few other sources, a standing member of the House of Lords, an officer in the first King's Dragoon Guards, a member of the Athenaeum Club, and an early, possibly a founding, member of the Society for Psychical Research, the first society to scientifically investigate paranormal phenomena."

This was all too much, too early, but I forced myself to be more alert.

"So this means . . ."

"I think Stephen read the same websites I did but took them more seriously. I think he was trying to find out about the Oswulf Stone. I think he found someone who knew something about it—and he got information about it at Lord Williamson's house, Chanceford. He discusses it with someone else, some-one called E, who doesn't seem to want to hear it."

This was enough to get me to swing my legs out of bed. I was already dressed. My new hair was clearly sticking up—I could feel it. I put on my shoes and hurried downstairs. I found Boo and Callum on the sofa, hunched over cups of tea.

"Thorpe's out," Boo said, her voice groggy. "He went over to check on Charlotte. Kettle's boiled if you want tea."

I left Freddie to explain what she had discovered. I heard her talking while I was in the kitchen, stuffing tea bags into mugs. According to the clock on the wall, it was eight in the morning, but the sun really hadn't come out yet. The sky out-side was a pale purple, and I think some stars were still out. I stepped into the back garden while the tea steeped and took a breath of the cold, heavy air. Day three since Stephen. That's what days were. Since Stephen.

"Rory."

It was Boo, standing behind me in the kitchen doorway.

"Just getting air."

She nodded and stepped out. Boo was taller than me by several inches, and she never seemed to get cold. She was only wearing an artfully shredded T-shirt and some jeans.

"Freddie told you about Stephen's book," I said.

"Yeah. Thorpe will want to know."

"If Stephen thought it was important . . ."

She nodded wearily and folded her arms over her chest.

"What do you think of Freddie?" I asked.

"I think she seems to know a lot of stuff. I don't know how she'll do when she's in some Tube tunnel in the dark with the rats, looking for some mental ghost."

There was clearly something else she wanted to say, but she wasn't saying it. She leaned against the doorway and looked up at the sky, not at me.

"What?" I asked.

"We did the hospital, the flats, Eton, and his house. We did his dad's flat. We looked all along the route to the hospital. Callum's not going to look any more, and if Stephen is—"

"If? You don't think he's out there now either?"

"I don't know why we can't find him," she said.

"He could be anywhere."

"He could be anywhere, but he probably would have been where we looked. And he could find us, or . . ."

"You know what you saw," I said.

Boo closed her eyes and shook her head. This couldn't happen. Boo couldn't be giving up. Boo giving up made it all more real. It stripped away everything I thought I was sure of. Her eyes welled up, and she dabbed them dry, which was a terrifying thing to watch, considering how long her nails were.

"I'm not going to stop looking," she said. "I'm just saying I don't understand. And I miss him. He feels gone right now. He never said bloody much except about maps and things like that, but he was always there. He was the one thing that always held it all together. I dunno . . ."

"We are going to find him," I said to Boo.

"You need to talk to Callum today," she replied.

"He doesn't want to talk to *me*."

"Which is why you need to talk to him. You're good at talking. Make him talk to you. We need to stick together or it will all fall apart. Stephen would hate that."

"I'll try," I said.

. . .

We waited for Thorpe and drank the tooth-stainingly strong tea I'd made. He arrived wearing a fresh suit, so he must have returned home at some upsettingly early hour. Once again, he carried a small bucket of coffee.

"Charlotte hasn't remembered anything else," he said.

"New girl has something," Callum said.

Freddie gave her speech for the third time that morning, and Thorpe took it in as he drained his coffee.

"Do you know what Stephen was up to?" Thorpe asked me. He seemed even more displeased now. As I watched them all, I realized why this was stranger for them than it was for me. I wasn't part of the team, but they were, and Stephen had been doing something in secret. He'd shut them out.

"I have no idea," I said.

"It makes sense," Freddie said. "He doesn't mention the stone, but he's talking about where the stone was. He's talking about—"

"I understand," Thorpe snapped. The exhaustion was hitting us all. "Where is this Chanceford?"

"Amesbury. By Stonehenge."

"It's not overly far. We could be there in an hour or two, depending on the traffic. All right. I'll phone some contacts and see if we can get access to any of Lord Williamson's papers kept in the house."

"But Charlotte's okay?" I asked.

"She seems to be recovering well. Extremely well, for someone who spent a few days in captivity."

He seemed uneasy.

"That's just Charlotte," I said. "She's very prefecty."

"There's something wrong with the picture," Thorpe said. "They take her. They treat her well. They give her the sight. Then they leave her under the floor in the house."

"They were probably coming back," Boo said. "Right?"

"Possibly. But it's not good practice to kidnap someone and leave her alone."

"But where they had her . . ." Callum said. "No way she was getting out of there. And maybe they never kidnapped anyone before."

"Yes, I've thought of that," Thorpe said. "However, the first part of the plan was extremely well executed. She was removed with care. A car was obtained. A house was prepared. That floor was custom work. Houses don't come with ventilated crawl spaces perfectly designed for storing people under the floorboards. That work couldn't have been easy to arrange— builders don't usually install crawl spaces like that. They might have had to do it themselves. And the house had sprinklers, so whatever they were storing in there, it could be damaged by fire."

"Stones are usually okay in fires," Boo said.

"Nor do they need ventilation. So we're talking about a long-term plan. A house purchased in 1982. Given all of that, there are a lot of questions here. Let me see that."

He reached out for Freddie's pad and the notebook and glanced through them for a moment.

"There's a lot here that doesn't make sense," he said. "Stephen meeting with someone. This house. All of it. If these two things intersect, we're going to find out about this stone."

"You don't think Stephen was working with—" Freddie cut herself off, which was a smart move. None of us would have responded well if she'd finished that sentence. Suggesting Stephen was doing something wrong was just dumb. But Thorpe wasn't as reactive.

"No," he said. "Stephen was not working with Jane. But I'm uncomfortable with the fact that he was keeping secret notes, and that I have no idea what they mean or who he was meeting with. Get yourselves ready. We'll leave in a few minutes. I'll arrange it."

There was a pall over the room now, as gloomy as the London sky. Something had entered the conversation that had managed to make things worse—which I hadn't thought was possible. There was something about Stephen that none of us could understand, that he'd been trying to hide. The room felt airless, and I couldn't help but feel that we were on the verge of something bad.

But then again, that was a good assumption by this point.

17

ENGLAND IS STRANGE IN MANY WAYS, AND ONE OF THOSE ways is that they leave things like Stonehenge sitting at the side of the road. I think I expected something more like Disneyland, with all kinds of buildings nearby, and maybe a waterslide called Druid Dunk! or something. Maybe I thought it would be larger, or behind a wall. No. It was just there, in the field. It wasn't as big as I thought it would be. Several of the stones had fallen over, so really, it was just a pile of rocks. Important rocks, to be sure. England loves important rocks. Everyone loves important rocks.

Chanceford was outside of a town called Amesbury. The grounds were on the River Avon. The entire place was surrounded by a high brick wall and there was a wrought-iron gate we had to pass through to get inside. What we found waiting for us was a tiny stone castle—turrets and portcullis and the whole works. But really small, like a castle that had been put in the dryer and shrunk.

"It's a re-creation of a castle from the fourteenth century," Freddie said. "Lord Williamson was an unusual man."

This became very clear as we got closer, and I noticed that many of the stones were carved into the form of faces or goats' heads. There were pillars by the main doorway that had clawed feet. There was a gothic spire on top of one of the turrets, and a spinning golden globe as some kind of weathervane. That was also the only thing Freddie said in the car, because I think she had gotten the message that casting aspersions about Stephen had been a bad move, even off-the-cuff ones. She slept for most of the ride, snoring softly with her head against the window.

The plan was laid out in the car. Thorpe was to go inside with Freddie. Freddie, after all, had the best working knowledge of the weird stuff and had translated the code in the book. Callum, Boo, and I were to stay together. Thorpe felt that Lady Williamson wouldn't want four young people coming into her house under the auspices of doing some research work. She apparently hadn't been that happy about letting anyone in at all on such short notice. We were to stay on the drive and remain mostly out of sight, keeping an eye on the house. It was always possible that if Jane and her people knew where the stone was, as Charlotte said, then they knew about this place.

We watched as Thorpe and Freddie went to the door, where they were greeted by Lady Williamson herself. I expected a lot from a Lady, but she was just a woman in her fifties who wore a purple cardigan and a pair of khakis. She didn't look thrilled.

"Thank you for allowing us to come, Lady Williamson," Thorpe said.

"I'm not happy about this. What can be so important that you need to be here now? This bloody . . ."

We could hear her muffled complaints after the door was shut.

"Right," Callum said, looking around. "Once around the house. It's open. Nothing to hide behind. If any of Jane's crew are still around here, if they were here at all, we'll see them."

We walked the path around the building, to the supposedly famous garden out the back, which was a proper "physic garden," as Freddie had informed us in the car, full of strange herbs and medicinal plants. Famous or not, it was really just a small plot of plants, with curving walkways between them, and yet more stone figures of goats and sphinxes.

"I'm going around the house the other way," Boo said, taking a few steps backward. "Cover it faster. Rory's with you."

It wasn't the most subtle exit, but it was still effective. Callum and I were stuck together.

"I'm supposed to talk to you," I said to Callum.

"Yeah, I figured that."

"So should we talk?"

"No," he said.

We stepped quietly across the spongy lawn for a few minutes.

"I'm going to talk anyway," I said.

A long sigh from Callum.

"Let me explain," I said. "You don't have to do anything. Okay?"

I guess it was okay, because he didn't respond. He continued to cast his eyes over the horizon.

"What happened . . . neither of us like it. We both think it's the worst thing that has ever happened. Which is why I'm here instead of home. I left my family. I left my friends. I don't even know what happens to my life now. I'm a runaway. I don't know where I live, even. All I want is for him to be okay."

Callum stopped for a moment and looked up at the quickly moving clouds.

"It shouldn't have happened," he said. "He shouldn't have crashed that car. He was so . . ."

I watched him search for the words he wanted, but I could have filled in a few of my own.

". . . He was smart, but stupid at the same time. I never met anyone more clever than him, but when it came to some things . . ."

Some things, I interpreted from his look, meant me.

"I wish he hadn't followed me," I said. "He should have just let them take me."

"He wasn't going to do that. None of us would have done that. But we could have taken care of it some other way. We would have got you back. He didn't need to do it all himself."

When Callum said that none of them would have let me be taken, I started to tear up a little. I turned and pretended to be interested in the view to give myself a chance to clear my eyes.

"He liked you," he said. "But you knew that. I mean, considering how I found you two back at his dad's flat. You were good for him. You got him to loosen up a little. I'm glad that happened. I'm glad he was happy."

"Me too," I said. My throat had dried out, and the words had a crack to them. Things were softening now. At least I knew Callum cared. Or that he cared at some point. I didn't know how far we had gotten on the forgiveness front, but when we started walking again, he didn't keep a stride ahead of me. We walked together. It was a start.

"So, what happens now?" I asked. "Boo said you're going to leave."

"No point in staying. No terminus. No Stephen."

"What about Boo?"

"What about her?" he asked.

"You know."

"You mean that Boo likes me. Yeah, I know that. But that's not going to happen. It's a bad idea."

"Why?" I said. "You like her, right?"

"That doesn't matter," he said, walking again. "This stuff, when I leave it? I've got to leave it all, yeah? Normal life."

"But Boo . . ."

"Just leave it," he said.

It was probably best to drop that. It was a miracle we were talking at all.

"So," I said. "We talked. So are we . . ."

He said nothing. We continued walking around, staring at the dark forms of the low plants and the grass and the specter of Stonehenge in the distance. But a minute later, he reached over and put an arm over my shoulders. Callum had a heavy arm, and a reassuring one.

When we reached the back and met up with Boo, he pulled back. I thought she would be pleased at what she had undoubtedly seen, but she was distracted, looking off at something that resembled a tiny Greek temple—at least, the front of a tiny Greek temple. It was what (I had learned, again, thanks, Art History) was called a folly, I guess because it was a ridiculous and largely pointless bit of architecture.

"There's someone over there," she said. "You see him?"

We both turned to the little temple. At first, I saw nothing, but then a head peered out from around a column. The figure had a white beard. He stepped back behind the column when he saw us looking in that direction.

"Is he hiding?" Boo asked.

"Looks it," Callum said. "Or he's trying to."

In order to get to the folly, we had to pass over the widest and most open part of the lawn. Boo scanned the windows to see if anyone was looking out, and Callum checked around. They moved quickly, and I did the same. As we approached, the man did his best to stay behind the column. But once we were inside, there was nowhere for him to hide. He was old, with white hair. He wore a gray suit, definitely not of this century. His outline was firm—there was no translucence to him, but he still had that telltale faded aspect.

"What do you want?" he said. There was a tremor in his voice. "Go away. I'm an old man. Go away."

"Are you Lord Williamson?" I asked the ghost.

"Bloody stupid question. Go away. Leave me alone."

Sounded like a yes to me. The pleasant attitude must have run in the family.

"We need to talk to you about a stone," I said.

Lord Williamson shook his head sharply.

"I should never have talked to that other one. Now you're here. I want to be left alone. I can't help you."

"Other one," Boo said. "So someone else has been here? Was his name Stephen? Tall? Dark hair?"

"Go," he said again. "I'll tell you nothing."

"You need to talk to us," Boo said. "It's important. We need to know about this stone? The Oswulf."

He shook his head as if he didn't even want to hear the word.

"Someone's after it," Callum said.

"You're after it."

"We're trying to help," Callum replied.

"Look around you," Lord Williamson said, indicating the view of Stonehenge in the distance. "Look at them, standing strong for thousands of years. I built my house here to be close to them. Someone has always had to protect them. So many times they've almost been carted off or knocked over. Some-one must always stand for the stones. You don't know how to *help*."

Callum raised his eyebrows.

"We can help more than you think," Boo said.

"You know nothing of the old ways. If you did, you wouldn't come here like this."

He was yelling, but of course, we were the only ones who could hear him. When we didn't move, he tottered around the folly in annoyance.

"Someone wants the Oswulf Stone," I said. "Someone bad. She says she knows where it is."

"If someone had taken the Oswulf Stone, you would know," he said.

"She could be going for it now. You told our friend where it was, but he's gone. Please. What did you tell him? What was he doing here?"

"Who are you?" he asked.

"Friends of his."

"*Friends?*"

The word sounded like an accusation. He paused and put his hands together in prayer formation and touched them to his chin.

"You know what the Eye of Isis is?" I asked.

"Of course I know what the Eye of Isis is. Why do you ask stupid questions?"

"The Eye of Isis, it's in pieces. And one of the pieces . . . is in me."

This got his attention. He tottered back over and came up to me, forcing me back. Suddenly he didn't seem as fuddled.

"What's the matter with you?" he snapped.

"I just told you."

"You're talking nonsense."

"I'm telling you the truth. Whatever was in that piece of the Eye of Isis is in me, and if you touch me, you'll be gone."

"She's not kidding, yeah?" Boo said. "You can't touch her. She's got the power in her."

His eyes were a bit rheumy, and his white eyebrows were shaggy and animated. This had them doing a little dance. He reached out a hand, and I moved back even more. Callum caught my arm to keep me from toppling down a step.

"It wouldn't do for me to talk about the Oswulf Stone," he said.

"If you can't tell us where it is," Callum said, "can you tell us how to protect it? You have to tell us something."

"The stones," Lord Williamson said, "can only be moved with the utmost care. They must always be placed correctly. It took me three years to calculate where to place the Oswulf Stone.

It was the one work of importance I completed in my life. If I give away the location, I could undo that. Perhaps what you are telling me is true. Perhaps you want to protect the stone. Perhaps not."

"You believed Stephen," Boo said. "Why him and not us?"

He regarded her for a long moment.

"I was born of the sight," he said. "I spent my life trying to understand it. I studied the old ways and the old knowledge. I made a mistake by recording some of what I knew. I should have known all would follow the road here. I said things that were not for the living to know, or for the dead, for that matter. But when we live, we believe we have a right to everything in the universe—that everything is ours to touch. And it was the time when we appeared to own all we could see. The world was ours, why not what was beyond this world? I was a fool, but . . ."

"You were the one who moved it?" I asked.

"I was the one who ordered it moved. It is my belief that I remain because I touched the stone while I lived. And you say you have the Eye of Isis in you? How is that possible?"

So I told him the story of the last night with the Ripper, my attack, the explosion. As I spoke, he seemed to grow tired and sat down on a bit of marble. He was silent for some time after I finished.

"There are elements to your story which have a ring of truth," he said. "I have gone on too long, and I have carried a heavy weight. Knowledge is the heaviest weight of all. It's not something I wish to bear anymore. Your friend spoke of two others with the sight, two that he trusted. He said you were young. He told me many things. He spoke to me of the Eye of Isis, but he did not refer to it as that. He called it a terminus.

I am inclined to believe you. I will tell you, and you will release me. I cannot bear being questioned. I cannot bear what I know. You must agree."

I'd done this before, but this time, it felt different. Somehow, it had been all right when the power to do this, to make this decision and carry it out, was spread over the group. Now it was me, and it would always just be me. I was no longer so willing.

"Maybe you should just . . ."

"You will do this," he said, "or I won't tell you. Here is what you must understand, though—everything in London depends on the stones and the water. The rivers border the lands of the dead and help convey them to where they must go. If the stone is disturbed, if it is lost, the consequences will be grave."

"The river*s*?" Boo asked. "There's just the one. The Thames."

"Oh, no, my dear. London is a city of many rivers, rivers which have been cut up and diverted and covered over. It's part of the problem. When we disturbed the rivers, we disturbed the passages. We threw off the whole system. But you speak of Oswulf's Stone. That stone originally sat in the waters of what became known as the River Westbourne. It was moved hundreds of years ago to a spot not far away from that location, at a corner of what we know as Hyde Park. It was at this location that the Tyburn Tree was built. This was the great hanging spot of London. Many thousands died there. That land became death's property, so the stone was placed there to help keep the energy of the dead flowing in the correct direction. There it stood, this strange stone. Very few knew why it was there or what it meant. And for hundreds of years, this was fine. Tyburn was a remote edge of the city. But my time was an age of expansion. London was growing by the day. Tunnels were being cut under the ground. The dead were being disturbed. It was only a matter of time before someone would remove the stone from its location. So I made a plan to secure it.

"Marble Arch was originally built for Buckingham Palace, but it was soon clear that it was not appropriate there and needed to be moved. I suggested the spot where the Oswulf Stone stood. My idea was that the stone would be imbedded inside the arch itself. Once a part of that monument, it would be very difficult to move it. However, I soon became concerned that the arch may be the target of antimonarchists, bombers, that sort of thing. London has a history of disorder. Guy Fawkes, for example, wanting to destroy the Houses of Parliament. It had to be moved, but the question was where to put it. One doesn't simply move the great stones of London. The person who had moved the stone to Tyburn was obviously versed in the sacred geometry. The work was very carefully done, though, I think, not entirely effective. There were still many spiritual disturbances in the park. As Tyburn was no longer an active hanging spot, I felt it was safe to move it back to its true location. But where was that, precisely? I only knew the stone had been in the River Westbourne. The River Westbourne crosses Hyde Park. It was what originally formed the Serpentine. They bottled the poor girl up and made her a sewer. The blessed river, now a sewer. In the process, they also changed her course. I did the calculations as best I could, using what information I had. I found that there was an inn that still stood from the time when the river was still wild. It was called the Boatman. It used to sit on the banks. I had the stone interred there, in the northeast corner of the cellar floor. It can be distinguished by a small X I had etched, very carefully, into the surface. Now you have the knowledge, and my work is finished. I must go to Albion's ancient Druid rocky shore. You will do as I have asked. If you are what you say you are. If you are a part of the Eye of Isis come to me, then you must do as I ask. Come now."

He crooked his hand at me, beckoning me closer.

"Come now, Isis. Come to your son."

Now it was really creepy. Now I was Isis. Now an old man—an old *dead* man—was calling himself my son.

"You don't have to," Boo said, looking over at me. Boo always understood this, that the terminus wasn't something to be taken lightly.

"You think I don't know what I'm asking for," he said. "No, my dear. The thing that should concern you is that I do understand. Two people have come for the stone now. This has meaning. The stone is stirring. London is stirring. The gates will open. I wish to pass through before that happens."

This man, who'd been doddering around the folly a few moments before, now moved like a ball rolling across ice and was in front of me, his hand on my face. Even as I opened my mouth to try to speak, I felt everything falling away. The marble of the folly looked like it was electrified, glowing. The sky went white. Unlike before, though, this time I felt unable to breathe. I was being flattened, my lungs pressed. Then there was no ground under me. Everything was reduced to a single point.

Then I was on my knees, Boo hunched over me, telling me to breathe, telling me I was fine. Lord Williamson was gone.

"Bloody hell," she said. "Are you all right?"

Callum too was crouched in front of me. I tried to speak,

but my throat was burning. I shook my head. They helped me to my feet. It took me a few minutes to recover.

"It was worse than before," I said when I could talk. "It hurt."

"It didn't hurt before?"

"Not like that. It's getting harder each time."

"Right, come on. Let's walk a bit. Take it slow."

They supported me back to the car. Boo texted Thorpe, and he and Freddie came out a few minutes later, trailed by Lady Williamson, who was still complaining about the intrusion and how she was "going to speak to Philip."

"And who are these people?" she said when she saw us. "What are you playing at?"

"Thank you for your help," Thorpe said, getting in the car.

She was still talking as we pulled off.

"You found it?" he said. "Rory, what's happened to you?"

I let Boo and Callum explain. I needed to rest.

18

I SLEPT IN THE CAR. WHEN WE GOT BACK TO HIGHGATE, I returned to bed and slept some more. When I woke, it appeared to be the middle of the night, but it was only six, or so said the clock on the wall. I made my way downstairs and found everyone in the living room talking.

"You all right?" Boo said.

"I'm okay," I said. "Just hit me hard."

"Is it difficult?" Freddie asked.

"Not like this. Not usually."

"We need to be careful with it," Boo said. "Every time, you're looking worse. We don't know what it's doing to you."

She had a point, but it wasn't a point I felt like reflecting on at the moment.

"I'm starving," I said. "Is there anything to eat?"

There were some cookies. I ate half the pack while they told me what had been going on. While I slept, Thorpe had a team sent over to the Boatman under the auspices of being from a brewery. They'd found the stone marked with the X in the basement, exactly where Lord Williamson said it would be.

"So it's fine," Callum said. "They don't have it yet, but if they know where it is, we'll have to move it."

"I think we need to speak to Charlotte again," Thorpe replied. "I want a better idea of what she heard. I've phoned Dr. Marigold. We can go over and speak to her. Charlotte wants you to come along, Rory. She knows you. She's more comfortable with you there. Are you up to it?"

I brushed some cookie crumbs from my front. I'd now been in these clothes for two days. I'd slept in them twice. I was feeling sweaty and gross and grimy. What I wanted was a shower and something new to wear, and maybe something more substantial than cookies, and maybe a few hours in front of the TV.

"Sure," I said. "Are there any other clothes I could wear?"

"Freddie, do you have anything that would fit Rory?"

"I might," Freddie said, digging into her bag.

I was given a pair of Freddie's jeans, which were loose and comfortable. They kept falling down around my waist a bit. She also lent me a sweater, which was long enough to cover the fact that the jeans were halfway down my butt. I gave myself a quick wash in the sink and stared at myself in the mirror for a bit. My hair was looking coppery and crisp, like a sweet potato fry. I didn't really know my own reflection anymore. I was some strange girl with short hair and someone else's clothes. This feeling was oddly pleasant. For a moment, I was content in a way I didn't really understand. I had simply become someone else. This life was direct. There was no screwing around with makeup or wondering what I looked like. There was no phone in my pocket. There were things that needed doing, and I would do them.

While the incident in the folly had tired me out, it reassured me as well that what I could do was real—that what happened in the hospital still counted. We'd found Charlotte, and now I could concentrate on Stephen.

Every time I even thought his name, I had the inclination to look around. This was especially true in the bathroom. He might be there. It was always possible. Given my luck, he would turn up when I was in there.

But once again, it was me alone with myself, looking around at the tiles and the empty tub.

Thorpe was waiting for me at the foot of the stairs, phone in hand.

"Text your friend," Thorpe said, passing me the phone. "He's been texting for the last two hours and wants to know where you are. *Don't* mention Charlotte. Do it in the car."

As we headed to see Charlotte, I tried to think of something simple to say to Jerome so he would know it was me. I settled for: **It's me, stupid. Everything ok.**

It took longer for him to reply.

I'm with Jazza.

I stared at the phone for a moment, unsure what to do next. I envisioned them together, Jerome and Jaz, my friends, being normal. Maybe going to the pub.

Is she ok? I asked.

A quicker reply.

Not really.

What's wrong? I said.

"That's enough," Thorpe said, taking the phone. And, of course, it was pretty obvious what was wrong. There was no point in asking stupid questions. What was wrong was me.

Charlotte met us at the door, opening it before we could even knock. She looked more alert than she had the other day, more like her old self. Her head was held higher, her gaze more steady, her red hair back piled high and neat on her head.

"Oh, hello," she said. "Come inside."

This was delivered in the crisp tone of a prefect. She was extremely calm. I remembered the days after my first attack. I slept a lot; I was disheveled. Charlotte had pinned her hair up and was neatly dressed in a black sweater and jeans. I passed her on the way in and she smiled. I had to wonder how she was handling this so well. I understood that Charlotte was made Head Girl for a reason, but there are limits to everything. We all break down a little.

"You look well," Thorpe said, eyeing her.

"I feel well," she replied, shutting the door behind us. "I know I should probably be traumatized, but I honestly don't remember much about it at all."

"You certainly don't have to feel traumatized," Thorpe said. From his expression, I could tell he was as puzzled as I was about Charlotte's steady demeanor. Maybe it was shock. Maybe Charlotte was made of something resolutely English, something that was going to *get on with it* no matter what *it* was. Or maybe . . . and this was more likely . . . maybe it was medication. She was staying with a doctor.

"Where's Dr. Marigold?" Thorpe asked.

"Upstairs. I think she's speaking to someone on the phone. She's in her office. It's upstairs. Straight ahead at the landing."

Thorpe started up the stairs. The television was on. Charlotte had been watching a talk show.

"I'll just turn this off," Charlotte said.

When she picked up the remote to turn off the television, she accidentally turned the volume all the way up.

"Oh! Sorry! Sorry, sorry!" She fumbled with the remote for a moment before getting the volume down. She left it on.

"Maybe I'm not quite as well as I think," she said, with an embarrassed smile. "If it's okay, maybe I'll leave the television on. It makes me feel better for some reason. I suppose it keeps me distracted. It's too quiet otherwise. She's busy all day, and she doesn't say much."

This I understood.

"TV was my best friend when I was stabbed," I said. "I didn't even care what was on as long as it was on."

"Then you know," she said. "Come to the kitchen with me. Have some tea."

I followed her back to the kitchen, where she put on the kettle. This was reassuringly normal.

"I'm allowed to treat this house like it's home—as long as I don't go anywhere except this room and the spare room," she said wryly. "I've been told it's important I stay here, for safety's sake. I wish I could see my parents, but . . . well, things are complicated, aren't they? Things have changed for me. Dr. Marigold has been explaining some of it to me. She calls it the sight. I know you have it too. I know that's how you saw the Ripper. So many things make sense now. Now when I look back, I think you were very brave. I couldn't have done what you did."

They were kind words, but they were delivered in a strange, distant tone, like she was reading the weather report for a foreign country.

"Once you get the sight, so many things about the world just make sense suddenly," she said. "You know?"

My experience had been largely the opposite, but I didn't want to say that.

"How are you?" she asked. "I don't know much about what's happening with you, but I know your situation is complicated as well. Whatever's happening, we're both in it together."

"I'm okay," I said. Of course, I wasn't really okay, and I definitely didn't sound okay.

"You seem unhappy," she said.

"I'm . . ." I stopped myself from saying *fine*. There was no point in lying to Charlotte. "I'm treading water."

"You don't like having it, do you? The sight."

"I don't know," I said.

"It's funny, you know. At school, I used to think you were . . . well, I didn't understand. *I* was the one being stupid. I was ignorant. You were always living your life. You were dealing with things that were real. I admire you."

Rory-positive Charlotte was nice enough, but she also made me uneasy. I didn't want to be her role model of how to live with the sight, especially considering she seemed way more into it than I was. She reminded me of this friend I had who went away on a camping weekend and came back really into

211

religion. It wasn't that she became very religious that bothered me—it was the speed of it. I get that life is full of *aha!* moments where everything can turn—my life was now full of those. There was just something about the fact that my friend went away with this group of people to a campsite and came back different. Charlotte had done the same thing, except no one had asked her. They just took her.

She made me a tea and passed it to me, but I found I didn't want it. I wished Thorpe would come back down. I'd never wished for that.

"I have something to show you," Charlotte said. She was smiling quietly, like a saint on a Sunday morning. "It's upstairs. Come on."

"Maybe we should . . ."

"Trust me. You'll want to see this. While they're still talking. She's a bit of a tyrant, to be honest. She probably wouldn't let me take you upstairs if she knew. Come on."

She seemed so eager, I felt like I had to follow her. We went upstairs, passing the doorway where Thorpe and Dr. Marigold were talking, and then up one more floor above that. The noise of the TV blared up in the space between the landings. It was really loud, so loud that Charlotte had to raise her voice to be heard.

"It's this one here," Charlotte said, opening a door at the end of the hall. "See for yourself."

I stepped to the open doorway of what appeared to be the master bedroom, a wide room with three windows overlooking the trees of the square. There was a king-sized sleigh bed against the window wall.

"Go look," Charlotte said, smiling.

There was something about her smile I didn't like. It was reminiscent of the one she'd used in the dining hall at Wexford on the night I'd decided I didn't like her. I still took a few steps into the room. It took me a few moments to process what I was looking at. I had to concentrate very hard in order to put the facts together in my mind and accept the reality.

Stephen was in the bed.

19

THE MOMENT I SAW HIM, THE WORLD REARRANGED ITSELF, but not into a recognizable pattern.

He looked very much like he had on the hospital bed. Peaceful. His hair had been combed. The cut on his head hadn't healed or changed in any way. The only thing different, aside from his location, was that he was wearing a plain white T-shirt instead of a hospital gown.

"Go on," said a voice behind me. "Go to him."

It wasn't Charlotte's voice. Somehow, this was not a shock to me. Maybe you can't be shocked from two directions at once. My brain was processing too much information. I had seen him die, and yet, he was on this bed and somehow not dead. We hadn't been able to find Stephen because he was here all along.

"What did you do to him?" I asked.

Jane crossed around and walked past me, stepping over to

Stephen's side. Charlotte stood there, beaming smugly, the prefect once again. Jane's prefect.

"Nothing," Jane said. "I believe it's more likely that this is something you did to him, and that's no bad thing."

"I saw him die," I said. "What's happened to him? He looks . . ."

"Asleep? Yes, he is, after a fashion."

I wasn't going to think about Charlotte right now, or how she'd gotten this way. But Thorpe and Marigold—I did have to think about them. Thorpe had gone upstairs and Charlotte had turned up the television, drowning out all noise, probably so I wouldn't hear what happened. The doctor I didn't know, but I had a surge of affection and concern for Thorpe.

"What did you do to *them*?" I asked.

"They won't be joining us."

"Did you hurt them?"

"They're quiet now," she said. "What happens next depends in all ways on you. You have nothing to fear. You can leave if you like. No one will stop you. Go right ahead! Or you can stay and hear what we have to tell you. Such good news, Rory."

"You need to listen to her, Rory," Charlotte said. "She can help. She can help so many people."

I was deeply torn between wanting to understand how Charlotte had gotten to this point where she was shadowing Jane with such clear devotion and wanting to grab her by the hair and shake her until her eyes fell out. I wanted to hold Stephen, but I wasn't going to go anywhere near him. Just seeing his face, though, I was dizzy. My knees were going out from under me.

"Charlotte," Jane said, seeing this, "tell Jack to bring up water. Now, hold on. Come here."

She came over to me and mothered me into a chair, where she put my head down between my legs and had me breathe deeply. A glass of water appeared in front of me, but I didn't take it.

"It's just water," she said. "I assure you."

"Get the hell away from me."

"If you don't want the water, then continue the breathing. Nice, slow, and steady. Deep breath in. Hold. Relax. And out, nice and slow. It's a lot to take in."

Charlotte brought in a chair from another room and put it next to me so Jane could sit with me. I picked up my head. The world was slightly less wobbly, and Stephen was still in the bed.

"Is he alive?" I asked, nodding at Stephen.

"Not precisely," she said. "But more important, dear, he's not exactly dead either. And it is my belief that he can be restored."

"*Restored?*"

"You see, you and I have the same problem. We both have people we care about who are deeply asleep, and you, my dear, could be the one who wakes them. But I realize that you most likely don't quite believe or trust me at the moment. I will tell you the truth. You deserve the truth, and the people around you haven't given it to you."

"How do I wake him up?" I said.

"I have always been honest with you, Rory. You may not like what I have done, but I have always told the truth. I told you that when I was a girl, I was attacked in a field and left for dead. I told you that after that experience, and when I gained my sight, I went to London and met the people who would forever

216

change my life. Their names were Sid and Sadie, and they were the greatest seekers of their time."

"Yeah, I heard about them," I said. "I heard that ten people who followed them disappeared in 1973."

"There were ten of them, yes." Jane's tone was infuriatingly reasonable. "They were my friends. I was there that night, and I will tell you what happened to them. You see, Sid and Sadie are extremely special people. They came from a very wealthy family. When they were in their teens, the entire family was in a car accident. Sid and Sadie survived, and their parents did not. They gained their sight that day. But with Sid and Sadie, something was different, most likely because they were twins. Something in them was magnified. They were very powerful, and very wise. They inherited their parents' fortune when they were quite young and instead of going to university, they spent their time and money traveling the world, learning. They accumulated a great amount of esoteric knowledge. They understood that people who have the sight stand in the doorway between worlds. And doorways—well, they go both ways, in and out. Doorways are just passages. What would happen, they asked themselves, if someone simply removed the door? They looked back, to the time of the Greeks, when it was understood that the underworld was a place that humans could pass in and out of. They looked to the old rituals. They looked to the goddess Hecate, she who guarded the doorways and the liminal spaces. They looked to Demeter and her battle to reclaim her daughter Persephone from Hades. They realized these were not just old stories, but actual facts, lost to time. They sought to reclaim that knowledge. What they discovered was that there was a ritual to break down that door. But it was not a simple affair. Are you sure you won't have some water? You're still quite ashen."

I waved the glass away.

"In any case," she said, "something went wrong. I have spent the last forty years trying to figure out what, but it's not been easy. Sid and Sadie retained most of the information themselves. True mystical teachings are often not written down—they're simply too powerful. The ceremony we performed that night in 1973 was called the Blood of the Light. It required a very potent exchange of energies. Namely, we needed to open a channel between worlds. This required a certain sacrifice. Ten followers gathered in the house. We gave them a drink laced with poison. When those ten people left their bodies, a certain amount of energy was released."

"*Left their bodies,*" I repeated. "When you *killed* them."

"We do not believe in death. But that night, once they had left their bodies, we took a small amount of blood from each. Sid and Sadie then completed the ritual by consuming that blood, along with a dose of the same poison. They also wore these."

She opened her large necklace and revealed that inside, behind a bit of glass, were two dirty-looking clear gemstones.

"I believe you call this a terminus? It's what you are. It's actually two pieces of a diamond called the Eye of Isis. It was broken into many pieces. Sid and Sadie managed to get two."

She closed the locket again and patted it against her chest.

"My job was to watch and wait. What should have happened was that the energy exchange should have blown open a passage between the two worlds which all of us in the room could perceive quite easily. What actually happened was that Sid and Sadie seemed to fall asleep. And they have been asleep since that night. I have taken care of them since that time, guarding them, moving them as necessary. I acquired a house for them to rest in and modified it. You saw the house and the space under the floor. That is where they have been for some time now. They are exactly as they were. Nothing has changed."

"What happened to the ten people you poisoned?"

"Had it all gone to plan, we would have brought them right back again. I believe I can still reach them. At the time, all I could do was deal with the remains. It was not the most pleasant task I have ever had to undertake, but I knew it was for the greater good. I have always tried to do the greatest good, Rory. I know this may be hard for you to believe, but it is true. The world lives in blindness! Most of the people you see—they don't know what reality is. They can't perceive what's really around them. We can. Fear drives people to do terrible things. Fear causes war. Fear causes violence. Remove the fear of death, and the world could be cured of so many ills. What if we didn't need to fear death at all? What if we could exist in more than one state? It would be the greatest achievement of all mankind."

Charlotte was nodding, eyes half closed, enraptured.

"As I said, I've been working on this problem for quite a long time. I found the answer some time ago, but it required things I could not get—things I wasn't sure even existed. But when you came along, I realized what had gone wrong. You've probably heard the expression 'like getting blood from a stone.' It means, of course, an impossible task. Stones do not bleed. You, Rory, you are the stone, but you are also the blood. You are the stone made live. I believe there were more like you in the past. I believe someone like you is the key to this ritual—you, and a stronger stone. With you and the Oswulf Stone together, wonderful things will happen. Our friends will wake again. He will wake again."

"So why did you need Charlotte?"

"Charlotte played a role. She helped push you to find the stone. From what we understand of the historical record, the stone was moved by someone in the government many years ago, which means that there was likely a record within the government of what had happened to it. We had faith that the powers that be could muster themselves enough to determine the location of a stone. We need to know where it is, Rory. If it has been found, and I suspect it has from the look on your face . . ."

My face. My stupid face doing things I didn't know about.

". . . then we must know. The information is important enough that we will endeavor to get it from one of you, either you or the man with you. But, Rory, Stephen needs it. Without it, he will be like this forever. All you have to do is tell us, and I can help. I want to help more than anything."

"How do I know this will even work?" I said.

"My magic work is solid, Rory. I've been doing this for quite a long time. I'm not a crank working in a bookshop."

"Stephen had a head wound," I said. "His brain had been injured."

"This ceremony undoes the process of death. In recorded histories, people with far greater injuries are returned. The *person* is restored. The body and soul reunited. It is my belief, truly, that Stephen as you knew him will return. Your blood, my knowledge, and all we have lost will be restored. He will come back."

I felt the urge to throw up, but fought it.

"Let me see Thorpe," I said. "I need to make sure he's okay."

Jane turned around and nodded to Charlotte. Charlotte moved instantly. I heard her speaking to someone in the hall. A minute later, Thorpe was carried in and set on the floor like a sack of potatoes in a suit.

"What did you do to him?" I said.

"He's unconscious," Jane said. "But perfectly safe. Now, stand up. Come here."

When I wouldn't stand on my own, someone hoisted me up. It was Jack, the weird blond guy from her house, the one dressed like some kind of romantic space cowboy with slicked-back platinum hair. The last time I'd seen him, he'd tackled me in Jane's foyer and held me down in the backseat of her car. He was gentler now, as if he was really trying to help. They moved me over to Stephen's bedside. When I kicked and dug in my heels a few feet away, they stopped.

"That's close enough," Jane said. "She doesn't want to go closer. You think you can destroy him, don't you?"

"I don't know," I said. "And I'm not taking the chance."

"You're quite safe. Watch."

She took the necklace from around her neck and dropped it onto his chest. I coughed out a scream. But it bounced and slid off, apparently harmlessly.

"He's not a spirit," she said. "He's flesh and blood. The terminus has no destructive power on him. Go ahead. Go to him. It's perfectly safe."

I put my hands on the bed first, then I crept them ever so slowly closer to Stephen until they were both flat on his unmoving chest. No breath. No movement. But it was him. This was the same chest I'd pressed against that night. I put my hand on his cheek. He was cool to the touch, but not cold. Jane laid her hand on mine, pressing it down into his face.

"He needs you," she said. "You are the only person who can help him. You can help everyone. All you need to do is tell me."

"And I'm supposed to believe you?"

"What I propose can *only* help us both. If my friends wake, Stephen wakes. I promise to you, on all I hold sacred—I promise on blessed Demeter herself—"

"Blessed Demeter," Jack said.

"Blessed Demeter," Charlotte echoed.

"I promise to her and her daughter that I will keep my word to you. We will wake him. We will wake my friends. We will serve the greater good. May my soul be locked away forever if I lie, down in the depths of Hades."

There was little question in my mind that she meant this. A reverential silence had blanketed the room. Charlotte even put her head down, like she was praying.

All I had to do was tell her where to find a rock. That was it. I didn't really know anything about this rock except that if it brought back Stephen, it was a rock worth having.

"Please, Rory," Jane said. "If you delay, we'll be forced to be aggressive. We will find out where it is. Jack, show her."

Jack pulled something from his pocket that I thought was a harmonica at first—because of course Jack would have a harmonica. Of course, Rory. But it was that shape and size, and it had some pearled inlay on the surface. He flicked his wrist, and a blade came out. He stood over Thorpe's body on the floor, one leg on either side. He leaned down and put the blade at Thorpe's eye.

"Stop it," I said.

"Rory, that's up to you. I don't want that to happen. I don't want to hurt Stephen here either. Or the doctor. But we must know. This is bigger than all of us."

Thorpe, Stephen, Dr. Marigold . . . even Charlotte, whatever had happened to her. All of these people needed me *now*. We could work something out later. We always did. I needed to do something now.

"Rory, Jack's impatient," Jane said quietly.

Jack moved, and I put up my hand.

"It's under a pub," I said, "called the Boatman. It's somewhere near Marble Arch. The stone's in the basement, in the floor."

Jane grasped both my hands.

"That's good, Rory," she said. "That's very good. It pains me you don't know the good you do."

Charlotte came around and clapped her hands on my shoulders, like I'd done something in field hockey aside from get hit in the faceguard with the ball.

"I want to stay here with him," I said. "Let me stay here with him."

"That's fine," Jane said. "There's time now. You stay with your friend. We will prepare. You have done a great thing today, Rory."

I looked down at Stephen's sleeping face and wondered what he would make of all of this, then I decided not to think about that again.

THE BOATMAN PUB
LANCASTER GATE, LONDON

Allie Langly needed to work on her "no." Such a simple word. *No.* "No, I don't want to come to your Christmas party, Gertie. I'd rather dip my hair in the shredder." "No, Gert. The last time I went out with you, you came back to my flat and vomited on my cat." "Actually, Gert, I'm going to have myself put into a medically induced coma that day. Sorry."

That's all it would have taken.

Gertie worked with the worst people in the entire world. They'd only left uni last year and they weren't even good friends while they were there, so why did Allie feel so *obligated* all the time? If she'd said no, she would have been at home. Her roommates were out at their own party, so she would have had the flat to herself. She would have gotten a nice Indian takeaway, which she would have spread out on the coffee table. She could watch telly on her own, then take a nice long bath with no interruptions—a proper bath, with music on and a book and a cup of tea. It would have been heaven.

But Allie couldn't say no. It was like she was physically unable to do it. And now here she was, at some pub in the middle of London, surrounded by people she didn't know and didn't want to know. They were all pissed. The normal Christmas party things were all present and correct—Christmas crackers, paper crowns, Bing Crosby and Slade playing in the background. There was awkward, drunken dancing and toffee vodka shots. There was a lot of talk of branding. And then, to top it all off, someone knocked over an entire tray of pints, which went crashing to the ground. Allie jumped out of the way, but everyone around was soaked to the knee. Allie turned when this happened and saw a slip of a girl duck under the bar and pass through a door marked EMPLOYEES ONLY. Maybe she was going for a mop.

Instead of looking sorry about the accident, the people Gert worked with laughed. Sure. That's funny, Allie thought. Make the people from the pub clear all that out of the carpet, a dozen glasses broken. That's hilarious.

The mess and broken glass were cleared away, and Allie was pulled around the room to stand there while Gertie talked about things and people Allie knew nothing about. She had to do something. She had to stand up for herself. If she went right now, she could catch the bus, she could still be home by seven, she could still get the curry and get a full night's telly in. All she had to do was make a move.

"Gert," she said, "I think I'm going to—"

Gert turned toward her and grinned, like she'd just remembered Allie was there.

"I need a ciggie," Gert said, pulling on Allie's arm. "Come on, come on."

Another thing Allie hated was smoking, and standing outside in the drizzle so people could smoke. Again, no. If she could only say *no*. What was wrong with her? They went outside, where London traffic pulsed around them. The pavements were crowded with people pushing their way to and from Oxford Street. This was the worst possible place to be—the middle of the shopping district right before Christmas. Getting home would be a nightmare. And it was cold. They moved around to the side of the pub. There was a white van parked there. Two doors set into the pavement were flapped open. These kinds of doors—the ones actually set in the ground where people walked—always made her nervous. But this was not a delivery. She watched as a bit of paving stone was pulled out of the doors on a rope.

Gertie was drunk and kept fumbling with her lighter in the rain.

"Gert," Allie said, "I'm just going to . . ."

There was something a bit odd about the young men in the coveralls. She wasn't sure what. Maybe it was that they looked so young. Maybe it was the extreme blondness of the hair on the tall lad, and how he wore his hair slicked over to the side with a flat-top cap.

"Oh!" Gert yelped. "I need to show you the *most hilarious text . . .*"

Allie moved just in time as Gertie flailed around with her lit cigarette while she dug around in her bag. That would have been her hair on fire or a hole burned in her new jacket. Stupid Gertie and her stupid cigarettes. Why did she agree to come outside with smokers?

Also, these people with the van, they were definitely strange.

The girl she'd seen slip under the bar popped out of the opening and got in the back of the van. The blond boy shut the delivery bay doors. He looked up and saw Allie watching and smiled in a way that made Allie very uneasy, then he doffed the cap before hopping into the van. It almost hit Gert as they pulled out.

"Did you see that?" Gert said, wheeling around. "Did you see . . . I should get the registration number . . ."

Allie watched in some amusement as Gert tried to type the numbers into her phone, but the van was already gone, slipping into the mad traffic.

"Forget it," Gertie said. "I don't even want to smoke now. Let's go back."

"Actually? I'm just going to—"

"Oh, you can't leave."

This was her moment. This was the test. *Say you are going home.*

"Actually, Gert, I really need to . . ."

"Did you feel that?"

Allie had felt it—a rumble under the pavement. It lasted for about twenty seconds.

"Probably the Tube," Allie said, pointing at the Tube sign across the road.

"I come here all the time. I've never felt that. That wasn't the Tube."

Truth be told, it was a pretty strong vibration. Then it hit again—another pulse. Then a distant, muffled sound of people yelling. Allie and Gert both watched as people began spilling out of the Tube at the entrance of the park. And as they did so, something began to change in the air itself. The rainy night air felt like it was thickening. A fog began to take over, developing around them. Within a minute, it was so thick that Allie didn't see the cracks that were beginning to form in the pavement under their feet.

London fog is like fish and chips, salt and vinegar, crown and jewels, tea and biscuits. Jack the Ripper hid in it. Sherlock Holmes hurried through it. Every character in Dickens stood in a clump of it. Poets rhapsodized about it. Painters tried to snare it and stick it to a canvas. It mostly vanished fifty or sixty years ago, when the coal fires stopped and people got more serious about the environment. You couldn't burn just *anything* anymore and send orphans up the chimney to deal with the mess. Modern London is a responsible place, and its air is relatively clean and clear.

So people forgot that the fog wasn't always such a nice thing. It was the city's dark shadow, echoing between the rivers and the chimneys and the sky. It came in various colors—not just gray, but brown, black, yellow, or green. It didn't always stay outside. It crept into homes. It lingered in corners. Occasionally, the fog would kill. People wandered in front of carriages and into rivers; some simply choked from the sheer weight of it. The fog could turn day to night and breathable air into poison. Water could combine with pollutants and turn into hydrochloric acid and burn out your eyes. In four days in December of 1952, the London fog killed twelve thousand people.

Still, the fog returned from time to time, squatting over the city like a long-absent dragon guarding the precious things below. This fog was greater than all those fogs together. It poured out of the Tube entrance like milk, and the voices of the people in it were silenced instantly. It took the Tube entrance and it took the pub and it took Allie and Gert too. It stopped spreading at that point and stayed precisely where it was, a formation of white, made of quiet.

Around that end of Hyde Park, the people outside the fog looked on. They pulled out phones and took pictures. Then, very quietly, like a frost, the windows of the buildings and every car window along the street began to show spider cracks. The cracking started from the ground-floor windows in single cracks that grew up and up like the branches of a tree. The cracks inexplicably skipped from pane to pane, not minding the frames. Then they spread to the next story, oblivious to the bricks and mortar, then the next story, until each reached the top story of its respective house. There, the branches grew so dense that every pane went white with breaking.

And then, like an orchestra moving in unison to one great, final note, every window on the street exploded at once.

THREE
FOUND

From Golgonooza the spiritual Four-fold
   London eternal
In immense labours & sorrows, ever building,
   ever falling,
Thro' Albion's four Forests which overspread
   all the Earth
From London Stone to Blackheath east:
   to Hounslow west:
To Finchley north: to Norwood south. . . .
All things begin & end in Albion's ancient
   Druid rocky shore. . . .

               William Blake,
               from Milton: A Poem

20

THERE WAS A HOME N' DECK NEAR MY TOWN (WE DON'T get a Home Depot; we're not that fancy). One night, a few years ago, it burned down. It was a huge fire—you could see it for miles. Everyone was pretty interested in this fire, so a few friends of mine and I drove over to look at it, because this is what you do for fun in Bénouville—you look at the burned-down remains of a building supply store and then you get some soft serve. When we arrived, there was a ring of cars around the place. The building had collapsed upon itself. There were charred riding lawn mowers out front and burned-out and half-melted racks where plants had been. The place was sunken and stinking. And in the middle, as if nothing had happened at all, a big pile of paving stones. They were the only thing still standing that looked totally unaffected. There was something about them that seemed to be saying, "What? Is that all you got?"

By this I mean: stones, they're tough. I guess this is an

understood concept. Also, stones are stones, and maybe something in my mind was saying, "It's okay, you only told them about a stone. Who cares about a stone?"

Stephen would care. Of that, I was sure. And if this stone was what we'd been told it was, then moving it would be bad. Very bad. The kind of bad that Stephen would be extremely agitated by, if he hadn't been completely motionless and unable to do anything about it.

I sat on the bed, cradling his head on my lap, my hand over the injury on his brow. He had his glasses on this time, obviously the ones he'd been wearing at the time of the accident, because they were crooked and one of the lenses had a bit of a crack in the corner. The light shadow of hair that had grown around his chin on the morning he had slipped away was still there. I liked this slightly disheveled, morning-after look. It softened him.

Everything would be all right now. I would stay with him. Nothing would move me. Somehow, this would all work out.

I'm not sure how much time went by. Stephen and I were alone in the relative quiet. I could hear people coming and going below. There was music coming through the floor, but I didn't know the songs. Story of my life.

The afternoon ebbed away, bleeding out its light and falling into dark. Someone was in the room with me at all times—various weirdos I'd never seen before. Later in the day, I was watched over by Jack. It was easy to recognize Jack with his anachronistic clothes and his hair that looked like plastic. Given his size and the nature of our previous encounter, I knew he would take me down in a second if I tried to go anywhere or do anything. Not that I could. Jane understood completely—as long as Stephen was there, I was there. They might as well have set me in concrete.

I tried to work out how this scene had come to pass. Marigold was a doctor, and someone who worked with Thorpe. Thorpe had mentioned that someone had taken Stephen's body. Clearly, she'd been keeping him here for a reason—she'd realized that something was going on. She'd kept him in bed. There was some medical stuff in the room. She'd been trying to do something.

So Charlotte had come here. Charlotte, who was now playing for Team Jane. I would work out how that happened later. Charlotte told Jane where to come, what was going on. Then they'd set the trap and waited for us to spring it.

These people were crazy—of this, I was reasonably certain. Still, they had managed to give Charlotte the sight. They obviously knew some tricks we didn't, or at least that *I* didn't. And I was sitting here holding Stephen, who somehow had not exactly died, and now we were all waiting around for a magic stone. This would have seemed more stupid, was I not also a magic stone myself.

There was no road map for where I was. I realized something about that moment, now an hour or two past, when I had told Jane where the stone was. I did it because I was afraid for these three people who were now depending on me. But what was more disturbing was that in that moment, something in my brain—some tiny, tiny version of me made a tiny, tiny leap because she wanted to believe. Get the magic stone, wake the sleeping Stephen. Of course, these same people who wanted to help me out with this were also talking about defeating death and kept friends of mine under floorboards.

On some level I'd been expecting Boo or Callum or even Freddie to come sailing through the window. They had to realize we'd been gone too long. Except that "too long" was impossible to judge with Thorpe. Thorpe came and Thorpe went, and no one questioned the ways of Thorpe. It was unlikely they'd come here if no one got in touch with them. I was going to have to get a message out. That was going to be very hard. I couldn't leave. I had no phone. I was locked in a room.

There *was* one person who would notice if I didn't get in touch. Jerome.

If I could let him know something was wrong, then . . . well, I wasn't sure what happened then. It wasn't like I could tell him where I was, or that he should call the police. But Jerome was smart. Maybe he could work something out. As to how I would text him, well, that would require telling Jane the truth. Just tell her what happened. She knew enough about my life. She knew about Jerome.

"I need to speak to Jane," I said.

Jack rolled his eyes and leaned against the door.

"I mean it," I said.

"She's busy."

"I need to talk to her," I said. "Because if I don't, this whole thing is going to get screwed up, and then she'll beat you to death with her shoe. Get her."

I sounded like I meant it. I was using the lawyer voice I copied from my parents, the one they used when they had to put the frighteners on people. I had never done it so well.

Jack cracked the door open and yelled down for Jane. I heard a creak on the stair. He spoke to her by the door in a low voice, and then she came in, pushing past him.

"What is it?" she said. There was a note of impatience in her voice, but she was still doing the "I'm a therapist, I never get annoyed" thing. We were both doing voices.

"Remember, in therapy, I told you about Jerome?"

"I do," she said.

"And I told you how he's into conspiracies?"

She nodded.

"He found me yesterday. And Thorpe talked him into not saying anything. Well, Thorpe had me do it. The deal was, I have to text him a few times a day. If I don't, he'll go to the police. He knows where I'm staying. They would trace where I've gone. Did Thorpe have a phone in his pocket? Check it. Check the text messages. Call the number if you want. The only number in the phone is Jerome."

"I want to believe you're telling me this for the right reasons, Rory, but given your situation, I'm not sure it's what I would do."

After watching me for a moment, Jane called out for someone to bring Thorpe's phone up. She examined it.

"See?" I said.

"And how did he find you?"

"A Ripper conspiracy site," I said. "There was someone watching the school. They saw me. Some Internet freak followed me and mentioned where I was. The Internet, huh?"

Jane read through the messages again.

"Look," I said. "It's not going to help Stephen if the cops come here. He's dead. They'll take him. They'll . . . they'll do an autopsy. They'll cut him apart. I can't let that happen."

My grief had the right ring to it because it was real.

"That's true," she said.

"If you think I can wake him up, then I'm going to try it. And if they come here, that gets screwed up. Also, it's just *Jerome*."

Jane gave me the once-over.

"Tell me what you want to say," she said. "I will type."

"Tell him: 'I'm good. Have fun with Freddie. Love you.'"

"'Love you'?" she said, raising an eyebrow. "This is the boy you broke up with. And at the moment, it's very clear that your feelings lie elsewhere. There was something in your demeanor that told me you were in love, but obviously not with Jerome. It all made sense once I saw this one. The way you reacted to seeing him only confirmed it. This is the boy you love."

"That's true," I said, wiping my face with the back of my hand. "But I also realized that Jerome was the one who got me through a lot. He found me, even though the government was hiding me. He's my friend. I don't have to be weird about it anymore. I do love him, like a friend love, and he gets that. Or don't type that. I don't care."

"And who is Freddie?"

"Friend from school. Jerome's visiting him over the holiday. Some prefect thing. You can add, 'even though he's an asshole.' That's better than 'love you.'"

"That sounds a bit more like you, I think," she said.

Jane typed. They clearly knew things about the squad, but they didn't know about Freddie. They didn't know she was a girl, and not from my school.

All I could do was set the dominoes falling and hope they made a pretty pattern on the floor. I held on to Stephen's hand, squeezed it. *I will get you out of here* is what I thought. Maybe he would know. Maybe he knew I was there.

What I felt like was a plastic bag, blowing in the wind.

More time passed. I was brought soup, which I first refused to eat. But Jane ate a spoonful herself to show me there was nothing wrong with it, and I was told it would be in my best interests to keep my strength up for the journey ahead. They seemed really concerned about this, so eventually I got some of it down. It settled heavily in my stomach, but I probably had needed it. I felt a bit clearer with something in my stomach. I tried to figure out how many people I was hearing down-stairs, to tease apart their voices and count them. There were, I thought, maybe eight people in the house. Things were be-ing moved around. Then there was a car out front, the door opened again, and new voices came into the mix. These voices were excited, out of breath. Jack looked out the door a lot, and then he was swapped out with Charlotte. She came in, all smiles.

"It's almost time," she said. "Rory, I'm so excited for you. It's all going to happen now. It's going to be so amazing."

I said nothing.

"I know what you're thinking," she said. "It's new. It must seem so odd. But, Rory . . ."

She crossed the room. She still had that prefect walk—erect, head up, alert.

"My mother died," she said. "Five years ago. I've tried since then to be good, to do all the right things. But I always knew, somewhere, in me, that she couldn't be gone. Those things I was doing, they were for some life I thought she would want me to have. But it's a life based on fear of something we don't need to fear. It's a life based on buying things and collecting things like someone's keeping score. She's not gone. My fear is gone.

I find it tremendously empowering. I think that . . . despite all that's happened . . . I feel like I've come out of this stronger. I'm not afraid anymore. How can I be, knowing what I know now? No reason to be scared of death. Death, the thing that defines us all. It makes everything I did before feel so unimportant. All that worrying I used to do at school. All the panics I got into over Latin and history and getting into Oxford. I thought all of that mattered. I thought that was the most important thing in the world. Seems silly now. Jane was trying to tell me all along, during therapy, but I needed the sight to understand."

Jane had drugged Charlotte throughout her therapy, but this was maybe not the moment to bring it up. When I thought about it, Jane had been working on Charlotte for a while. I hadn't known about Charlotte's mom. It turned out you might do just about anything if you thought you could see someone again. Here I was, sitting on the bed with Stephen, living proof.

"So this ceremony . . ." I said.

"The Eleusinian Mysteries. They were also known as the Rites of Demeter. They were central to life in ancient Greece. Many of the greatest thinkers participated in them—Socrates, Plato, Cicero. Those who were initiated lost their fear of death, but they could never speak of what they had experienced. It was a sacred secret, and one that vanished for thousands of years. Do you know the story of Persephone? In Greek myth, Persephone was the daughter of Demeter. She was kidnapped by Hades, god of the underworld. Demeter went to the underworld to try to rescue her daughter. Hades said she could return to the world above as long as she hadn't consumed anything from the underworld, but Persephone had eaten four pomegranate seeds, so she was forever tied to Hades. You, my dear, are our

Demeter. You must go to Hades to reclaim what we have lost. But when our work is complete, no one will be bound."

She had definitely memorized the script. She also might have known some of that. She studied classics.

The door opened, and Jane entered. She had changed her clothes and was now wearing a pure white dress, a lot of fabric that seemed to corkscrew around her body. She was still wearing the necklace.

"It's time," she said to both of us. "You need to prepare for the next steps. It's all going to be fine. Come now."

Charlotte nodded eagerly and held out her hand to help me. I didn't want to leave Stephen, for a number of reasons, including the fact that it appeared as though I was going to have to go through whatever it was they had planned. I had been expecting something to happen by now, but maybe Jerome didn't get the message. Maybe . . .

"He'll be all right," Charlotte said. "He'll be better. Come on."

The two of them guided me to the bathroom, where the door was open and the lights on. The bathtub was full of lightly brownish water. Charlotte stepped outside, but Jane stayed.

"This water is from the Thames," she said. "It is our sacred river. You must bathe in it. Please remove your clothing. I will witness."

With Jane standing there watching, I took off all my clothes. This wasn't great, but it wasn't the worst thing I'd ever had to do.

"Into the bath."

"Are you going to do to me what you did to Charlotte? Hold me under?"

"No, dear. You've already turned. This is to wash and purify you. It is a critical part of the ritual. You need to clean yourself in the water."

The water was cold and smelled like metal. I splashed it over myself. Jane didn't quite look satisfied, so I splashed some more and rubbed some of it in my hair.

"This ceremony," I said. "Before, you killed those people."

"This is not a repeat of that ceremony."

"So what happens?"

"You do not need to worry," Jane said. "Everyone here has practiced. Everyone is ready. We will show you what to do. Your part is very simple. There is no need to worry about knowing your part."

"That's not what I was worried about," I said. "Before, you had to kill people. You need my blood."

"We need very little of it," she said. "A few drops. And that's enough."

"And then what?"

"You can get out now," she said gently. I would not be getting any more answers.

I stood, dripping, cold. I dried myself and was handed a plain white gown, which I put on. I think I had detached from the situation enough to be able to function. I had to do this. Jane lit a stick of incense and began to mutter under her breath, half closing her eyes. She moved the incense around me, tracing my body from the floor, around the sides, over my head, and down to the floor again. She handed the incense to Charlotte, who was waiting outside.

"Carry this downstairs and give it to Devina, dear."

Charlotte went off, a finger of smoke trailing in her footsteps.

"It's time for you to meet my friends," Jane said.

She led me out into the hall, which felt very cold now that I was damp with Thames water and wearing nothing but a sheet. All the lights had been turned off, but there was a glow at the end of the stairs and the sweet smoke of the incense. Marigold's living room had been transformed. Everything had been cleared from the middle of the room, including the carpet. There were candles all around. There were nine people in the room, some I'd seen before, some I hadn't. All were young. They sat in the shadows between the candles, talking amongst each other in low, gleeful voices. What I was really focused on, however, were three figures on the floor. One was Stephen. The other two I had seen once before in a picture. They were instantly recognizable—long, pale, nearly identical. The female was wearing a white diaphanous dress, the male in a white suit. Both their faces had been made up with a silvery powder. They didn't look like they had eyebrows. All three had been placed like spokes on a wheel with their bare feet toward the center of the room, where they rested on a large, flat rock.

It didn't look like anything special, this Oswulf Stone. It could have been part of a patio.

"I can't wait for you to meet them," Jane said, looking down at the twins on the floor. "They'll be so glad to see you."

A murmur of happiness from around the room.

"It is nearly time for us to begin," Jane said. "Have you all washed in the water upstairs?"

Jane checked to make sure every single person had nodded. This was when I realized I'd taken a bath in Thames water that had probably been used by ten people before me. This was hardly the worst news of the day.

"Gather around," Jane said. "We begin the work."

Everyone in the room formed a circle, with Jane and me standing on the inside with Stephen, Sid, and Sadie.

"Mags, bring forth the kykeon."

Mags, a tall black girl with short dreadlocks, brought forward a gold-colored bowl, which she held up reverentially.

"And now," Jane said, "Rory, please go and stand on the stone and hold out one of your arms."

With everyone watching, Jane assisted me as I stepped over and took my place on the uneven surface of the stone and held out one arm. I was looking around to figure out why, when there was a sudden flash and a pinching feeling. Jane had cut my arm, very quickly. It wasn't that painful, but it was a shock. The cut was a surface one, half between my elbow and hand. It bled quickly, and Jane turned my arm so that a few drops of the blood dripped down, falling to the stone.

"Blessed Demeter," Jane said.

"Blessed Demeter," said the others. This included Charlotte, who was looking at me with glossy-eyed wonder. How had it happened? I thought. How had they done this to her? How did we all get here? Hadn't we just been sitting around the refectory, eating sausage and talking about exams?

"I charge you," Jane said to me, in a low, chanting tone, "to find these three lost souls. We ask blessed Demeter to grant your passage, that you may go down and bring forth these sleepers."

Jane motioned to Mags, who passed her the bowl.

"The kykeon," Jane said, holding it up. "The sacred drink of the mysteries."

She gave it to me. It smelled like the shavings from a freshly cut lawn.

"This is a sacred mix of barley, mint, and honey," Jane said. "Drink from it, Rory. Drink deeply."

It seemed unlikely to me that whatever was in this cup was simply barley and mint and honey. Barley and mint and honey sounded like some half-assed herbal remedy for a cough, not something that would open the door between life and death. This was the real end. Whatever came next—I wouldn't be able to prepare for it. I couldn't guess what it was, or what it would be like, if it was like anything at all. Perhaps I drank this and died and everything stopped. The thought didn't scare me like it probably should have. It was so wide a thought that it filled my vision. It was sky, it was air. It was simply there. Because in the end, we aren't supposed to survive life.

Or maybe this went somewhere else entirely.

I thought of Stephen behind the wheel of that car, only seconds to make his decision—possibly less than that. *Do I drive in front of this car?* he must have thought. *Do I stop it? Do I put myself in the way?* That's what he had done for me, and he'd done it not knowing the outcome.

I had no desire to die. So, I decided, I wouldn't. Somehow, I would avoid it. I would not leave this world of weirdos and accidents and sunshine and rain.

I drank.

21

I WAS WALKING DOWN A LONDON STREET. NO ONE WAS around. The air was so sweet, like a night on the edge of summer, on the first day the grass has to be cut. This was Louisiana air—late April, early May, something like that, before things got swampy. It was the smell and feel I liked best in the world. It was evening, maybe, or almost evening. The sky was vivid and strange—a deeply supersaturated blue. There were no cars, which made it easier to walk in the street.

I wasn't dreaming. I was reasonably sure of this. In dreams, there was always that faint degree of knowing that something wasn't really there—that you were doing something impossible, with all the wrong people. This wasn't like before either, when I imagined talking to Uncle Bick. This was solid reality. I could smell the sweet air and feel it on my face. I reached over and touched the front of a building and felt the smooth white stone, the cool of a glass door. I was aware that things about this were odd—the emptiness, the quiet, the colors. So there was Louisiana air over London. Somehow, this was all right. It was like Uncle Bick said—or like I said to myself in the guise of Uncle Bick—home was the sky. Home was the air. There was something immensely comforting about quiet London as it glowed around me. It was waiting for me to do something. I needed to go somewhere, and somewhere would feel like home.

It occurred to me that I had arrived in this place midwalk, so I stopped to get my bearings. There looked to be some kind of intersection down ahead of me, and when I got to it, I found I was at Piccadilly Circus, by the statue of Eros. Several streets radiated off this circle, with no particular indication of which one to take. I decided to walk down the one we had driven the other day, on the way to the bookshop. It felt right. I would go to Soho.

There were lots of stores here, stores, restaurants, pubs. They were all quiet, waiting. I walked until the street turned to cobbles and became a bit narrower. Funny, I had no idea where I was going, but no anxiety about getting lost. The moon was very large, very low in the sky, and colored a bright yellowy-white. Everything was sharp and clear. Even gray stone buildings seemed to be etched sharply from the fabric of the air around them.

There was a diner at the end of this particular block. It was called Frank's Diner, and it had a big red neon sign with a neon drawing of a waitress in a pink dress with a white cap. The lights on the sign and in the windows were a bit brighter than anywhere else. It was clearly supposed to be an American-style place, but like all the American-style places I'd seen in London so far, it bore no resemblance to anything I knew.

It was someone's dream of America, snatched from television and old pictures. I could have gone in anywhere, but for some reason, this diner appealed to me. Even before I opened the door, I think I knew what would be there—a long counter with silver trim with a row of round stools running along it, a revolving case of pies, glossy red vinyl booths and kitschy signs with pictures of old-timey waitresses holding up hamburgers. The whole place was empty except for one table.

I think I knew what I would find there too.

Stephen was sitting in his police uniform sweater, the dark material matching his hair. He was facing the back of the restaurant and was watchful, like he was waiting for something or someone to emerge from a door in the back.

"Stephen?" I said, but I didn't say it very loudly. The quiet of the place was too overwhelming. It felt like if I called out, the walls might come down. He didn't look over.

I stepped very carefully across the black-and-white-tiled floor, assuring myself that every step was real. I could feel the floor, hard beneath my cheap, no-name sneakers. There was even a gentle squeak as the rubber met the tile. I was perfectly in his range of vision, but still he didn't see me. The closer I got to him, the more the diner came alive. I could smell food—the heady mix of fries and burgers, all that animal fat thickening up the air. I got all the way to the table before he noticed me. He took off his glasses, blinked, and then replaced them.

"We're fine for now," he said. "I'm waiting for my sister to come back."

"I'm not a waitress," I said. "It's me."

"I'm sorry?"

I made my way into the other side of the booth. The seat was heavily stuffed and mildly buoyant, and it lifted me so my feet didn't quite touch the ground anymore. I was sitting directly in the line of his focus. He looked confused. Stephen rarely looked confused. I'm sure he felt that way all the time—we all feel confusion—but he always masked it behind something else. He'd turn his face a bit or look at his phone or read something. Now there was no mask and nothing to hide. I always thought of Stephen's face as being angular and sharp, but now I saw how wrong that was. Yes, he had a strong bony line around the nose and a firmness around the chin, but so much of what I'd taken to be hard and sharp was just the way he must have been holding himself—tense the jaw, squint the eyes to see. He wasn't trying now, and the openness of his face moved something inside of me—I mean, I really felt like something around my heart was pushed open.

There was no mark on his head that I could see, no sign of the blow that had killed him, but that mark had been small. The damage had happened when the brain bounced inside the cranium. The hurt was all on the inside, as was typical with Stephen.

I let him study me, and the intensity of his thoughts was nearly palpable.

"Rory?" he finally said.

I went through a thousand messages and words and feelings and impulses, and somehow what I came out with was:

"You're wearing your glasses."

He touched his glasses.

"You'd think at least your eyes would get fixed," I said, trying to smile.

"I . . . don't know what you mean? Rory?"

"It's me," I said. "I know my hair is different, but it's me."

I put my hand on the table. I didn't know if I could touch him wherever we were. The rules of this—whatever this was—they were unknown. He looked at my hand and shifted in his seat before tentatively putting the fingers of his right hand on the edge of the table, as if trying to reciprocate.

"I . . . I feel like you're not supposed to be here," he said. He was speaking mostly to himself, his brow furrowed with concentration. "I'm not sure why. Rory, I—"

"It's okay," I said. "It's okay. I swear it's okay. I came to get you."

"Get me? Why did you come to get me?"

I thought about his body on the cold floor, the feet up on the stone, my blood dripping down. I remembered the liquid burning my throat, the rising impulse to be sick, then a cottony darkness. I had been charged to bring him back and I had landed here, wherever here was.

"I'm waiting for Regina," he said. "She went to the toilet with her friend. She'll be right back. You can meet her."

I think he realized there was something not right about that. Talking seemed to bring him back to the moment, so I would make him talk. I looked around the empty diner. I'd never actually seen the place before, but it felt real enough. The fact that I'd been drawn to it, that I'd found Stephen in it—it had to mean something.

"Stephen," I said, "where are we? What is this place?"

"It's a restaurant," he said plainly. "I came here with Regina."

"When did you go here with Regina?"

"What do you mean? We've only just gotten here." On saying that, confusion clouded his expression again. "I believe we

253

did. Though I've been waiting for some time. Something must be keeping her."

"Where did you come from?" I asked. "Where were you before this?"

He concentrated on the question. It took him a moment to find the answer, and he perked up when he did. "My parents forgot me," he said. "They left me at school at the end of term. They went to Barbados. They forgot me. So I called Regina."

"Your parents forgot you and left you at school," I said.

I really hated those people.

"I phoned Regina," he said again, in that tone of light pleasure you get when you've just found something you've misplaced. "She helped me get home, and we went to London. She said it was my weekend. I could do whatever I wanted."

"That was a long time ago, Stephen. You were younger then. You were a kid. You're older now. Look at what you're wearing. You're in a uniform."

Stephen blinked and studied his hands. He looked down at his chest and examined the sweater with the police insignia. He looked around at the diner again, but this time he stopped on different objects. The counter. The display case. The menu. Then he looked back at the bathrooms, where he thought his sister was.

"She's taking drugs," he said calmly. "That's what they're doing. That's what her friend brought. That's what she was waiting for."

This piece of information must have kicked off a chain reaction, because I saw him coming back more and more.

"You can't be here," he said, and this time, there was more certainty in his voice. "Rory, you can't be here."

"Well, guess what," I said. "I'm here. And we're going to leave. Together."

"I need to wait for Regina."

"She's not here," I said. Whether she was or not, I didn't know for sure, but I was pretty sure she wasn't. This place was like a spiderweb—if something moved in another part of it, I was sure I'd feel the shake, the tiny vibrations. This was like being in my own mind—I knew I was the only person in there, even though I had no actual proof of that fact.

"Come on," I said, gesturing toward the door. Stephen did not move. This news about Regina had silenced him again, and he frowned at the back wall. I had to get him talking once more and convince him that he should come with me.

"I need you to think," I said. "You're good at thinking. Come on. You know who I am. I'm Rory. What's the last thing you remember?"

He struggled with this one. His breathing—here, he was breathing—quickened. He took his glasses off and shut his eyes and covered his face with his hands.

"Stephen, look at me."

I reached over and took his hands from his face.

No boom. Just my hands on his.

I held them from across the table, and he looked down. He wasn't crying, but he was struggling—a confusion so deep it had become fear. I'd never seen him like this.

"You were so pissed at me because I got kicked out of Wexford. You told me to go back to school. Do you remember?"

This got a slight nod.

"Good. That's good. You remember I was kicked out. You put a phone in my coat. You followed me. And some people

took me. They kidnapped me. You came after me. Do you remember that?"

"Vaguely." His voice was uncertain.

"Jane took me. Her name was Jane. She took me, and you
followed. And there was an accident. You pulled the car you
were driving in front of Jane's car."

"I did?"

"You did," I said, fighting to keep my voice steady. "Callum
and Boo came. You guys got me out of Jane's car. You took us
back to your father's flat."

A glint of recognition at that.

"Regina destroyed the flat."

"Regina isn't here. I'm here."

"She tore the curtains."

He took his hand from mine and reached up and felt along
his hairline, where he'd been injured. I'm not sure he even
knew why he was doing it. There was no cut there now. I saw
him trying to piece it together. I think he knew, but it was a
vague knowledge, like something he'd heard once, a long time
ago.

"Stephen, listen to me. We were in the flat together."

"She said I couldn't go to Eton."

"It was us in the flat. You. Me. Callum and Boo."

"I told her I had to go. I had to."

Words weren't going to do it. I got up and joined him on
his side of the booth. I had no idea if this was possible, but I
was doing it anyway. It was the only thing to do. I took his face
in my hands and for a moment he looked utterly lost, utterly
hopeless.

I kissed him.

This was not like any other experience I ever had. This was not a moment in time. I'm not sure the diner was there anymore, but he was. He was warm. He was unsure at first, but he was kissing me back. His body eased, his shoulders slumped. His heart was going strong.

Wherever I was, right now, I had no desire to leave. If this was it, I would stay.

He stopped the kiss, but not abruptly. Our lips remained together for a half a minute, closed, barely touching. It was like this bit of contact was holding all of reality together. He leaned back and looked at me, and this time, he saw me. The lights were on.

"We were in the flat. There was an accident. We went to the flat. And then we . . ."

"We kissed," I said. "Like that."

"We did," he said. "Callum came in."

"And said he lost a bet."

"And said he lost a bet. And I went into the living room to sleep . . ."

And that, I guess, was where the memory ended for him.

"I don't think you're supposed to be here," he said. He was less fearful now, but he definitely didn't sound sure of anything. This must have been some kind of rising hunch.

"Well, I'm here," I said, taking his hand. "And we're leaving."

"Why are we leaving?"

"Because you're not supposed to be here either," I said.

"Where am I supposed to be, Rory?"

That last word, when he said my name—it was said like a question. A pure question asking for reassurance, asking for some kind of proof or explanation. At that moment I understood the impulse that led him to drive a car into another car. It was so simple. I wasn't going to let anything hurt him. This was on me. I would get him out of wherever we were. How we did that was less clear. But it started with getting up.

"Come on," I said, guiding him out. He followed, but stopped at the door and looked toward the bathroom again.

"She's not in there," I said.

The furrowing stopped, and he blinked quickly and adjusted his glasses.

"No," he said. "I think you may be right."

We stepped out on the street.

22

THE AIR WAS DIFFERENT NOW—IT HAD REGAINED THAT particular London quality. A little bit like seawater, a faintly metallic tang, a bit of pollution and old smoke. The moon had become intensely bright, washing the streets with a bald white light. This moon was going overboard, glowing like the sun. The change of air seemed to affect Stephen. He stood up straighter and lifted his chin to look around.

"I'm a little confused," he said as we stood on the empty street together. "I can't remember much."

"I'll remember for you for now," I said. "Let's go back the way I came."

Except that street was no longer there. When we turned the corner, Piccadilly Circus was gone and we were in a neighborhood of houses—quiet, stately ones in tidy rows. It was vaguely familiar to me in the sense that it looked like so many neighborhoods in London I'd passed through.

"Okay," I said, "I take that back. I might need you to remember more. Does this place look familiar to you?"

Stephen stood in the middle of the street and slowly took in the entire scene.

"I'm not sure," he said. "West London, most like. But there are no landmarks, and . . ." He walked to the corner and examined the view up and down. "No street signs. Where the hell are the street signs?"

The old Stephen was coming back more and more with every second as he realized how little sense all of this made. He stood at the end of the street and looked at the moon, looked at the emptiness of it all.

"What exactly happened?" he said. "I remember going after you. And I remember getting you out of the car, and we went back to the flat. I know we . . . I know what we did, you and I. I think I went to bed then, maybe, but I can't remember anything after that."

He had to be told. I suppose here, and now, wherever we were, in whatever London this was. This was not something I wanted to do, but clearly it needed to be done. The goal now was to get out, and it looked like the more Stephen could put the picture together, the more awake he got. So he would need the truth, even if the truth scorched my throat as I tried to make the words.

"You died," I said. "Sort of."

I guess this hadn't quite occurred to him yet.

"I . . . *died*? Of what? I only cut my head. I had a little headache . . ."

"You were bleeding inside, on your brain."

"When did I die?"

"We couldn't wake you up in the morning. We called an ambulance. You were in the hospital. They said they couldn't save you . . ."

Stephen had died. He died. And now I was telling him all about it, the one person I'd needed to talk to all this time. I had to tell him he *died*.

"There was a machine . . ."

I tried to get some of it out, but I gagged on the words. I physically couldn't do it. I coughed, and then I started crying. Stephen got blurry in my vision, but I was aware that he was moving closer, and I rushed to him. The next thing I was aware of was being held by Stephen in the middle of the street and sobbing into the front of his sweater and holding on to him like he was the only thing in the world. Which, I guess, he was. His embrace was the most solid thing I'd ever felt. His hand was on the back of my head and I heard his heartbeat in my ear.

The rest of it went away for a while. It didn't matter.

I eventually stopped crying, but we stayed as we were, in the road.

"I remember now," he said.

I stepped back to look at him. He probably should have been the one freaking out, but he wasn't. I checked his expression to make sure he was okay, and he seemed to be. The information was now in place, and with Stephen, information was something that could be worked with.

"I remember you were there," he said. "I don't know where. I remember you talking to me and telling me not to go, and you were holding my hand. You said not to go, and so . . . I didn't. I suppose. Because I'm here. Am I here? Is this real?"

"Pretty sure," I said.

"This could be residual brain activity."

"Okay," I said. I coughed out the last of the throaty tears and cleared my face. "I'll tell you something you couldn't make up."

I scoured the yard sale of my mind, looking for something to hand him. Something stupid. Something pointless. Something that I hadn't told him before because there would be no reason.

"I used to work in an ice cream place called Grunt's . . ."

"Grunt's?"

"That's the guy's name. It's this place out by the bayou, off the highway. It looks like a big smiling ice cream cone, but it hasn't been painted in about twenty years, so it looks like a smiling ice cream cone whose face is falling off. And one time the soft-serve machine failed and started dumping out soft serve for, like, an hour. And there was nothing I could do. So I started catching it in a bucket, and I took it out back to dump it. And this woman in our town, Miss Allouette, who is pretty much the worst person in town? She saw me and, I don't know if she thought I was stealing or something, but she pulled over her car? She'd just come from the hairdresser because she had her *do*—I mean, tight curls, big hair—and she said she was going to call the cops and tell them I was stealing. I was trying to hold the door open, but when she was yelling at me, I got locked out, and I got so pissed off at everything because I hated this job anyway that I dumped the entire bucket of soft-serve crap on her trunk. Which I thought was funny but she said that it ate at the paint or something and she made my parents give her three hundred dollars and I got fired and then I started working at the burrito place. There. Does that sound like something your brain would make up?"

After a moment, he said, "No."

"I can tell you more stuff. I can tell you gross stuff."

"No, I . . . I think I believe you. I think that wherever we are, we're there together. I mean, it's all possible, I suppose. Considering what we see all the time. Multiple dimensions or . . . I don't know. But if I'm here, and you say I'm dead, and you're here . . ."

I saw something move. It was a yellow car, and it was driving slowly toward us. We both watched it turn onto a road a street up. I recognized the car right away, because you didn't see many like it—colored like butter, classic, long and curvy. There were two figures in the front seat. I could only see their very similar outlines, but that was enough.

"I think that's them," I said.

"Who are they?"

"Sid and Sadie."

I looked around again, and suddenly things started to make sense. I had been here before. This was Jane's neighborhood.

"Sid and Sadie?" he said. "The names sound familiar."

"They're friends of Jane's," I said. "I don't think we want them to see us."

"I think it's a bit late for that," he said.

The car was heading for us, driving slowly down the middle of the road. We walked faster. The moon that had been so full was now only half, and it had suddenly gotten cold. By the time we hit the corner, it was snowing. I turned to look for the car, and it was gone.

"They're gone," I said.

"No they aren't. Look where we are."

A single street sign appeared at the end of the tiny road where Jane lived. Hyssop Close. We took the few steps down to the house. The car was parked in front, there was music playing, and their house was the only one with any lights on. We stood on the pavement, looking down the walk, up the steps, at the door hanging open in the cold like an unfinished thought.

"Are we planning on going inside?" Stephen asked. "I don't think we can stay out here."

The snow was falling crazily. There was already an inch or two on the ground, despite the fact that it had only been going for a few moments. I shivered violently as the wind kicked up. Stephen's sweater was going white from the accumulation. The outdoors was turning on us, and we had exactly one place to go. It felt inevitable.

"Before we do," Stephen said, "I need to understand. You said I died. So if I died and I'm here, did you . . ."

"It's complicated," I said, brushing snow from my lashes.

"Try me. You said you came to get me. What exactly does that mean? What did you do?"

"I did what I had to. And now we just have to find the way back. Which I guess starts here."

"What do you mean, you did what you had to do?" He sounded angry. "Rory, what exactly did you *do*?"

"*You* drove in front of a car. So we're even, okay?"

"I need to know," he said. He was very loud, possibly to be

heard over the shriek of the wind, or maybe just because he was mad. The worsening weather filled me with urgency.

"I did a ceremony," I said.

"What sort of ceremony?"

"A weird one! Does it even matter?"

"Yes!"

"Look," I said, "Jane said there was a way you could come back. She would show me. The deal was, I'd come for you but I had to find them for her. And now we're in front of their house and we can't stay out here. So I guess I have to deal with them. We just have to be careful. They kind of murdered ten people."

Stephen stared at me.

"You're joking."

"The point is, there's a way back." I pointed at the dark doorway. "I think they're kind of crazy, but they may know where it is. They did the ceremony too, and it didn't work, and they ended up frozen and asleep, like you. Except they've been that way since 1973. I'm not saying we have to take them back with us, but they are literally the only other people here. I think we have to go inside at least."

He shook some of the snow from his arms and looked again at the house, then reached around on his belt and produced a small flashlight, which, to our surprise, actually worked.

"Murdered ten people?" he said.

"Probably."

He pointed the beam at the doorway as he stepped forward.

"Let's not bring them with us, then," he said. "Agreed?"

We stepped forward together, the snow crunching under our feet. I had a sudden sweeping recollection of home. Every year in my town, the fire station puts on a haunted house to raise money. They do it in the firehouse reception room, which is this big linoleum rectangle that you can rent for weddings and fried oyster nights or whatever you want. It's a blank space with an industrial kitchen, ready to be filled. The haunted house is the biggest event of the year. All the volunteer firefighters and their families spend about two weeks getting it ready. They turn the room into a maze using room dividers and cardboard. Considering that and all the fake cobwebs, you'd think it would be a fire hazard. We always sort of assume it's not, because it's in the firehouse. Or if it is (which, given our town, it probably is), at least the fire can get put out really quickly.

Going to this haunted house is a rite of passage in Bénouville. You have to do it. There's a lot of discussion as to when kids should be allowed to go. The minimum age is eight, and that's the age I insisted I should go. My parents are the kind that like to encourage self-reliance. They are also some of the least superstitious people I know, and they have always been eager to show me that things that my neighbors think are going bump in the night are rabid possums and alligators and other neighbors. They were fine with me going when I was eight, and I was so proud of this fact, I wore it like a badge for a full week. "I'm going," I said to everyone, while coolly eating my organic dried fruit jerky. This was a Very Big Deal on the playground, and for that week I felt like a pioneer, someone brave, someone with her eye on the horizon. I had a ticket for Friday night. Uncle Bick was going to take me through, because he was friends with a lot of people in the fire department. It never occurred to me once that entire week that this might *actually be scary*. And it's not that I was brave—it's more that I didn't think ahead. I was in the moment, living it up on the monkey bars. It wasn't until we pulled up to the actual firehouse and I saw this girl who was two grades ahead of me sitting on a concrete parking bumper crying uncontrollably that I realized that maybe there was something to this haunted house thing. That was the moment I remembered the details of the stories—how people would reach out for you in the dark. How they'd follow you. How you'd put your hands into jars, and they would be full of spiders and millipedes and brains . . . and how one year a kid went in and *actually went insane.*

I considered backing out, but then I saw one of the only other kids in my class who was going. He was heading to the door, looking green. His parents were asking him if he was sure, and he was nodding, but it looked like he was going to barf. He lifted his head and turned in my direction. I'd been spotted. I had to go now. I kept telling myself, "It's not real." Which was true to a point—the firehouse was not full of monsters. But it was real enough in that it was full of unknowns. People would follow me around. People would jump out. Maybe I could talk myself into not being scared of this . . .

Stephen had stepped ahead, and I saw that while light came from some of the windows, the doorway itself was entirely dark. It was exactly like the haunted house—they made it pitch-black, and they turned the air-conditioning all the way down, and they also had a fog machine, so frosty air puffed out near the door where the two atmospheres met. You knew then you were going *somewhere else.*

I was already somewhere else, and I was with Stephen. But this house was different. I knew this somehow. Once we got inside, things would change. There was a world of unknowns. And as to whether or not any of this was real, that had yet to be determined. Inside, I was eight years old, staring at the dark, knowing what I was about to do and having no idea what the outcome would be.

This was not a haunted house in a Louisiana firehouse.

I was the one leading this, even though Stephen had physically walked ahead with his flashlight.

"Rory?" he asked, turning around.

I took a last look at the sky. The moon had never been so low. I felt like I could touch it if I wanted, but you're probably not supposed to reach up and touch the moon. This was not a place anyone was supposed to be.

"Coming," I said.

23

NOTHING JUMPED OUT AT US AS WE CROSSED THE THRESH-old. That was the first and clearest difference between this and the Bénouville haunted house. Back there, someone in a mask, rubber monster gloves, and surgical scrubs had snatched at me in seconds, and I started running through that maze, screaming one unbroken scream until I emerged in the parking lot about a minute later. It was just the one room, after all, and you can only put up so many cardboard dividers.

This was quiet. Settled. It was the house I knew. There was the stupid ceramic leopard by the door. There was the silvery wallpaper. It was warm, at least. My hands had gone purple from the cold. I rubbed them together and shook the snow from my clothes. Stephen dusted himself off as well and used his flashlight beam to probe around past the vestibule. The hall was straight ahead, leading to the kitchen. The coat pegs where I'd found Charlotte's blazer were not there. The stairway itself was so dark, it couldn't be clearly seen.

If I'd been coming to visit Jane, I would have gone into the room on the right, but that door was closed now. The other door, the one on the left, was partway open, and there was light from this room. I'd only been in this one once or twice before. I'd always gotten the impression that Jane used the room on the right for work, the room on the left for her personal living space. I pushed this door open very slowly, inch by inch, revealing a room entirely, almost blindingly, illuminated by candlelight. It took me a second to realize it wasn't the candles alone that made it so bright, it was the fact that there were so many mirrored surfaces—actual mirrors, the mirrored table, and a mirrored cabinet. There was a chandelier, also full of candles. It rained wax drops.

I'd seen this room, and it looked mostly correct, but some things were different. There was a thick white shag rug on the floor and a large cabinet along the one wall that hadn't been there before. There was a weird little silver globe thing in the corner that had a screen and may have been a television. The mirrored table didn't have the usual selection of coffee table books about decorating. Instead, there were a bunch of red glasses—goblety ones, like you might get at the ren faire, but better quality. Heavy glass. There was also an open black box and three curved knives. Stephen examined one of these, then went over to the long cabinet and looked inside.

"There's a turntable in here," he said. "And albums. Old vinyl ones. Rolling Stones, David Bowie . . ."

"This is definitely Jane's house," I said.

"I don't think it's so much a question of where we are as *when* we are," he said, picking up a pile of magazines and looking through them. "The dates on all of these say 1973."

It was pretty clear once he said it where and when we had to be. I counted the glasses on the table. Thirteen. Ten people, Sid and Sadie, and Jane. There was a decanter with a bit of liquid inside. I gave it a delicate sniff. It seemed to be the same disgusting stuff that Jane had given me, though there was a strange sweetness to the scent that hadn't been in the batch I'd had.

"1973," I said. "This is where it happened. The kids died down here. And Sid and Sadie . . ."

Before I could finish, there was a female voice—a cheerful one.

"Upstairs, darlings!"

It was a voice you might hear across an English garden offering you more lemonade or cake or a game of tennis.

I looked over at Stephen.

"I think we go," I said. "I don't think they can hurt us here."

"Who knows what happens here," he said.

"Do come up," the voice said. "Straight up."

He switched the flashlight back on and moved toward the door. He led the way up the stairs, guiding us with the beam of the flashlight. The darkness on the stairs was absolute. We turned along the corridor of the second floor and looked up the next story. There was light at the top of these stairs, and standing in it was a woman in a filmy white gown. She was tall and blond, her fine hair landing in gentle, feathery bursts at her shoulders. She was also completely backlit, so we could see the entire outline of her body.

"This way," she said. She turned and vanished into the room. I was almost knocked over by the smell—a cloyingly sweet incense burning, undercut with musk and the skunky smell of pot. This was about ten times stronger than the bookshop.

We reached the top and were standing in a room that took up the entire floor. I had been in this room before, and it looked very much the same as I remembered. Overlapping carpets on the floor in a variety of patterns and colors, books filling the walls, the tiny inlaid tables. But something was different—a round table in the middle of the room. The woman stood by this. She didn't look like any person I'd ever seen, and I grew up going to New Orleans on Mardi Gras. Her gown swept the floor, and I could see her bare toes peeking out under the hem. Her face was faintly silver, and she had streaks of duck-egg blue and stark white on her eyes. She was part nature goddess, part elf.

"I don't think we've met," she said. "My name is Sadie."

She put her hand to her décolletage. The arms of her gown were like bat wings, making every gesture a grand sweep.

"This is my brother, Sid."

I finally took my eyes from her and saw a figure elegantly slouched on a low chair in the corner of the room. He wore a white suit with wide lapels, with a white shirt and a silver tie. He even wore a hat, a fedora style, tipped a bit over one eye. His one leg was crossed widely over his knee.

"Enchanted," Sid said, smiling and raising a hand. "I love what you're wearing."

"It's been so long since we've had guests," she said. "We've been waiting."

"It's been an absolute drag," Sid said. "Tell us, how long has it been?"

"About forty years," I said. "More than that."

"Well, that explains it," Sid said. "I'm famished. I'm going to have five fry-ups. I absolutely am."

"Have six," Sadie said.

"I will. I'll have six."

"Might we know your names?" Sadie asked.

"We love names," Sid said. "Otherwise we'll have to call you This One and That One, and you deserve better."

"We give better names than that," Sadie said to him reproachfully.

Sid tipped his head in concession of this fact.

"I'm Rory," I said.

Stephen did not offer his name, and I didn't offer it for him.

"So you're Rory," Sid said, "and . . . well, he's handsome but not chatty. *Very* stone-faced. Like the white cliffs of Dover."

"Those are chalk," Sadie replied. "He's more solid than that. Like the Misty Mountains."

"Over the hills where the spirits fly . . ."

"With Rivendell in the foothills."

"And Orcs in every pass," Sid concluded. "So perhaps he's . . ."

"Stephen," Stephen said, bringing an end to that.

"Stephen it is." Sid finally made an effort to stand, unfolding like origami. He joined his sister at the table, and the moment he did, she wandered off to a basket chair by the window. All their movements were fluid, like they were doing some kind of ballet.

"And tell us," Sadie said as she draped herself over the wicker, "how did you get here?"

I hadn't actually told Stephen this yet, and he looked over at me curiously. I had to choose my words carefully here. I wanted to tell them something—I mean, if they were going to help us leave. But I couldn't tell them everything. That just seemed like a bad move. "You killed ten people" probably wasn't a good opener, so I went with:

"I know Jane."

"You know Jane!" Sid said merrily. "Our Jane? Darling Jane."

"Sweet Jane," Sadie said. "Forty years. And Jane's waited for us all that time? She *is* a dear."

"She's getting a Christmas bonus," Sid said. "A fat goose for our Jane and a half day off work. So, if you're here, I suppose Jane must be up to something."

Sadie got restless in her seat and got up. I was mostly amazed that in this reality, a gown that filmy and delicate didn't catch on the wicker. If that had been me, I would have been dragging that chair around on my hem. Sadie rose, like she was mostly made of air and birdsong, and glided over to Stephen. She gave him a once-over that made me very uncomfortable. She raised a curious finger to his chest and drew an invisible line under the word POLICE on his sweater.

"You aren't really," she said, smiling coyly.

Stephen didn't reply, which was enough for her.

"Oh, Sid. He's actual police!"

"Is he?" Sid said. "Things *have* improved, dear sister. Come to bust us? Feel free. Come over. Search me. Make it thorough."

He leaned backward over the table in a dramatic stretch. His hat tumbled off his head and turned upside down. While Sid was joking around, Sadie seemed more intent on working us out.

"There's something different about you," Sadie said. "You're different. You see it, Sid, don't you?"

Sid straightened up to look at me.

"I do, now that you mention it," he said, replacing his hat on his head. "Quite different."

"What is it, I wonder?" Sadie circled me curiously.

"I'm not sure. I like her hair quite a lot. It's very Angie Bowie. But that's not it. That's not it at all."

"No," Sadie said. She reached out and touched my hair. "No, she's . . . I can't place it."

She rejoined her brother at the table. Side by side, they looked far stranger than when they were even a few feet apart. Side by side, the eeriness of their resemblance came through, the strangeness of their dress, the odd highlights of their makeup.

"She's very interesting," Sadie said.

"She is," Sid replied. "What is it? It's going to drive me crazy, Sadie."

Stephen, during this time, had been taking in the contents of the room with a long sweeping look. We had our own dance. I would keep them talking—that was my strong suit. I was buying him time to think. When Stephen thought, he was like one of those dogs that froze in position when they heard a rattle in the bushes.

"So," Sid said, "tell us how you got here. We're *ever* so curious."

"We really are," Sadie said. "What did our sweet Jane do?"

"She's a clever girl," Sid said.

If we were going to get any information, I was going to have to say something.

"There was a ritual," I said. "The mysteries."

"I assumed as much," Sid said, with a dismissive hand wave. "But she did something different. Something about you."

Stephen stepped a bit closer to me, partially in a protective move and partially because he'd become transfixed by the window wall in front of us. Maybe in this world Stephen was really into staring at walls.

"I came here to get him, and now I have to get back. And I thought you'd know how."

"Us?" Sid laughed. "We've been here for forty years, if what you say is true. If we knew, we'd have done it by now."

"It's very boring," Sadie said.

"It is, it is. And we hate being bored. However, perhaps we can work this out together. Or we'll all be stuck here together. Either way! But I don't think you want that. So why don't you tell us your secret? You have one. I can see it in your eyes. We're very good at ferreting out secrets."

I followed the line of Stephen's gaze. The window wall had the least on it of any wall in this room. Just a few tapestries, the curtains, a long mirror on one side. But above the windows, there were some painted things—symbols. Some astrological ones. But in the space between the windows, up where wall met ceiling, I saw what he was focusing on. It was a series of Roman numerals: I II III IV V VI VII VII IX X XI XII. From what I could remember from fourth grade, that was just a sequence of numbers, one to twelve. Why Sid and Sadie had painted the numbers one to twelve along their wall in Roman numerals was anyone's guess, and really no weirder than, say, murdering ten people in your living room because you thought Greek gods were real.

Actually, no. There was something wrong with those numbers. One was incorrect.

"So what was different?" Sadie said, pulling me back to the conversation. There was something so soothing about her voice. It wasn't strange or cloying or evil. It was soft and nice, like Jazza's. And it was rich and full, like the English people in period pieces on TV. I had to give them a little something more.

"She used a stronger stone," I said.

On this, Stephen's head whipped in my direction. His eyes were utterly clear. He knew what I was talking about, about the stone. I was sure of it.

"We should go," he said. "Now."

I saw Sid and Sadie both seize on this, and Sadie turned, ever so slowly, and looked at the numbers on the wall.

"Oh," she said. "That does explain it to some degree."

Sid glanced over his shoulder and then smirked and nodded, as if he'd been very stupid.

"Of course," he said. "Honestly, Sadie, we're a bit thick."

"It's been some time," Sadie said. "We can't blame ourselves."

Stephen had taken hold of my arm.

"Rory," he said quietly, "come with me. Now."

"Are you one of them?" Sadie asked politely. "Did they actually put you in a police uniform? That seems a bit on the nose."

"Always hide in plain sight, Sadie."

Stephen was pulling now, and I was actively resisting.

"What?" I said. "What is it?"

"Darling," she said, "he's in the Shadow Cabinet."

I looked over to Stephen. He really did look like a rocky cliff face. They had a point.

"Please, Rory," he said. "Now."

"What's the Shadow Cabinet?" I asked Sid and Sadie.

Somehow, this was important. I was sure of it. This was a key to getting out. Maybe this was Stephen's mind resisting my knowing something, or . . . I had no idea how this worked.

"The Shadow Cabinet," Sid said, "is what makes London go 'round."

"And shackles it," Sadie added.

"When it could be free. And your friend Stephen is a part of it. Aren't you?"

Stephen's grip didn't lessen, but he no longer pulled. I got the sense we'd moved into a conversation that he knew had to happen.

"What is it you think you know about me?" Stephen said.

"It speaks!" Sid said. "The stone speaks! Maybe there's a reason he looks like a stone. Maybe that's how they're chosen."

"I'll ask again," Stephen said.

"Why tell you what you already know?" Sadie said coyly. She retreated to the window and closed the curtain.

"Tell *me*," I said. "I want to know."

"You're still a puzzle," Sid said. "It's going to drive me mad. Sadie, you're better at this. What is it about her?"

Stephen cut in before she could answer.

"As I thought," he said. He released my arm, and his voice got as crisp as theirs. I think he went full Eton, proper I-know-better-than-you English. "You don't know anything. You're a couple of chancers with some magic books."

"That's us!" Sid said merrily, throwing up his hands. "A couple of chancers with some magic books. You caught us. And yet, somehow you two ended up here after performing the Rites of Demeter. And you . . ."

That was to Stephen.

"*You* didn't perform them. *She* did. She was the object. And she wound up here. Which tells us something. I mean, we don't know much, do we? But even we might guess that she has the gift."

"More than that," Sadie said, "or she never would have made it. You're the host of this party, Rory. Not us. We're simply providing the venue."

I felt something on my arm, something warm running down it toward my wrist. I pulled back the sleeve a bit and found that I was bleeding. It happened just like that—there was a cut in my arm, maybe three or four inches, nothing serious. But I had a bad relationship with things like this—slashes that came from nowhere. I became profoundly aware of the scar that ran along my abdomen. It had stopped hurting some time ago, but now I felt every inch of it. It was hot. It itched. I remembered feeling the cut going in that day on the bathroom floor. I reached for it, putting my arm against it. It wasn't bleeding—it was fine. The only injury was my suddenly bleeding arm.

I'd been cut. I was remembering too. Jane had cut my arm.

I looked to Stephen. His wound had not reappeared. I was the only one. He saw the blood.

"It's fine," I said, yanking down the sleeve. But I was also now coming to the conclusion that maybe we needed to leave here. This was how I had left Jane's house the last time—I had a sudden knowledge that something was wrong, and I knew to run. I wasn't actually sure what they could do to us, but the feeling was overwhelming, pure instinct. This house was dangerous. This house would trap us forever.

"I think," I said, "maybe . . ."

"Go."

We tore down the stairs, me in front and Stephen behind. The stairs were now completely dark, and I kept stumbling and grabbing on to the rail for support. Again, this was far too much like meeting Newman when I'd gone down into the King William Street station, descending into the dark, Stephen just behind me. It was all happening again, just in a different place, somewhere—a funhouse mirror version of realities I'd already known.

When we passed the sitting room by the front door, I gave one final look inside, which was probably a mistake, because it made me pause. This time, the room was not empty. There were ten bodies strewn around.

"Oh, God," I said.

There was a lot of long hair, and a lot of colorful clothes. A girl in a red shirtdress with vibrant orange circles, a boy in head-to-toe leaf green. There was a tiny girl covered in freckles in a bright purple minidress and striped purple tights. But what got me was their positions. All of them were contorted. Many were on the floor, facedown in the carpet. Some were slumping from the sofas. A few had grabbed others and were clinging in one last, desperate embrace—a tangle of death. One was by the door—a boy with shaggy black hair and faint traces of eye makeup. His head was to the side, his arm extended as if trying to swim across the floor to safety. Their skin was blue and purple and washed out. Everything about their bodies suggested agony and shock. There was a bitter, sick smell in the air.

Stephen caught up behind me and saw what I was looking at.

"Don't," he said. "Keep going."

He gave me a bit of a push, and then we were outside, in a night with no moon, in a furiously falling snow.

24

WE RAN DOWN THE STEPS AND OUT OF HYSSOP CLOSE, into the neighborhood of no signs. We were at a crossroads, no indication of where to go next. The sky was rosy, giving us at least some light to navigate by, should we ever figure out where to go. The snow fell harder. This was like the whiteness that appeared behind my eyes when I terminated a ghost—this was the whiteness I'd seen when I'd reached out to Stephen on the hospital bed. I closed my eyes again and commanded myself to *figure this shit out.*

"What's the Shadow Cabinet?" I said to Stephen.

He brushed snow from his face.

"This isn't the time."

"This is exactly the time. What is the Shadow Cabinet?"

"More important, what did they do to you? You said that Jane used a stronger stone. What did you mean?"

"She said there was a stone called the Oswulf Stone. We had

to find it, and if we did, we could use that and me, and I could wake you up."

"How?"

"I had to drink something," I said. "They said they needed some of my blood. They said I had the blood of the stone. We found the Oswulf Stone. Freddie—"

"Freddie *Sellars?*"

"Yeah. She helped us."

"How long was I gone?"

"About two days."

"All of this happened in *two days?*"

"Thorpe said you vetted Freddie! He said you were going to bring her into the group!"

"I was," he said, sounding angry. "She's very smart. This isn't about Freddie Sellars. Rory, what happened to the Oswulf Stone?"

"They took it," I said. "They brought it to the house."

He grabbed the back of his head in both hands and paced away from me.

"Stephen, *talk to me,*" I said. "Explain this."

There was a black London cab behind him all of a sudden, parked, but clearly running, lights on. It was simply there where previously there had been nothing.

"There!" I said. "Behind you!"

We rushed to the cab. There was no one in the driver's seat, so he got in it and I got in the seat next to him. He switched on the wipers to clear the snow from the windscreen.

"What is the Shadow Cabinet?" I asked again.

He shifted the car into gear and started to drive. He hit

the gas pretty hard, considering the fact that it was snowing—except it was tapering off a lot, and every time we turned a corner, the sky and road were clearer.

"Where are we going?" I said.

"Marble Arch," he said. "If this has something to do with the Oswulf Stone, that's where we have to go."

As we sped along, London unrolled around us, but it wasn't the real London. It was like a series of pictures of London, often repeated, that someone shuffled in front of me. I didn't know if we could go to Marble Arch—if we could drive anywhere at all. For all I knew, we were driving down the same street over and over.

Something popped into my peripheral vision, and I looked in the side-view mirror to see the yellow car following along behind us. It seemed to be driving at a leisurely pace, but it kept up with us the entire time. Stephen saw it too and went faster.

There was a break in the view in front of us—a park. Stephen drove right into it. Why not? I guessed. There was no one to stop us. He drove down some wide gravel walkways, through open expanses of green, around a lake of some kind.

The snow stopped as we passed through some trees. It was day again, bright and sunny. The trees were green. Then there were a lot of trees, more and more, until we reached a point where the car simply couldn't pass. Stephen started working the gears quickly. When it became clear we weren't going to avoid the trees, he pulled the handbrake and turned the wheel hard. We went into a wide curve of a skid, narrowly missing a direct impact. The cab's engine sputtered and stopped.

"Are you all right?" he asked me. He was breathing fast and swallowing hard, his hands gripping the wheel.

I was shaking all over. No more car accidents for Stephen.

"Don't ever do that again," I said.

"I didn't have much choice," he said. "They came from no-where. I'm not even sure where we are now. I think we go on foot from here."

We got out of the car. Something smelled familiar to me, something I definitely hadn't smelled in England. It was floral, herbal. We walked through the tree covering, the light drip-ping through, spotting us with dots of sun and shade. I don't know what tipped me off first—it may have been something as simple as how the ground sloped and dipped. The slight incline. The hole I knew to avoid. And just as I realized it, we walked out of the opening and into my backyard.

My house, well, the back of it. The sliding doors were open. I could hear a radio on inside. NPR. One of my parents was at home. Bucky, our neighbor's dog, was barking. The hammock I'd gotten for my fourteenth birthday slumped invitingly on the back patio.

"What is this?" Stephen said.

"It's home," I replied.

The sun rained down on us. I'd missed the sun so much. This abrupt change slowed us both. Sid and Sadie weren't right behind us anymore.

"This is where you're from," Stephen said.

"Yep."

"It's hot," he said.

"I told you it was."

I approached the house, and he followed, and we both stopped on the patio. I reached out and felt the nylon of the hammock and then stretched it out to make somewhere to sit—such a familiar gesture. My feet came an inch off the ground when I sat like this, and when I rocked, the soles of my feet would brush the cement at regular intervals. I'd done this a hundred, maybe a thousand times? So much of my life had been spent in this hammock. Homework. Talking to friends. Working on my computer. Reading and sleeping. Planning for my trip to England. That's what I had been doing in it last. I sat here, my computer on my lap, rocking back and forth slowly, watching English TV shows and reading about how the school worked. I'd felt so ready, like I had some idea what it would really be like. I remembered explaining it all to my friends.

It was laughable now, really.

Stephen stretched out the netting to make a seat for himself. He was taller, so his feet stayed on the ground, plus his added weight sank us. We stopped rocking.

"I can't really imagine growing up somewhere this warm all the time," he said. "I think it explains something."

"What's that?"

"I think you get a certain kind of personality when you live somewhere where it rains all the time. Here, it seems like you might be more optimistic. I think it explains you."

"You think I'm optimistic?"

"I think you're almost pathologically so." He didn't smile, but there was a smile in the way he said it.

As we had settled to a stop, everything seemed to settle around us. When it gets this hot on a Louisiana summer day, nothing moves. There's a total stillness. Even the bugs go quiet.

"Should we go inside?" he asked.

"I'm not sure. I guess we could."

The house looked shady and inviting. There was no feeling

quite like coming in from the bright sun into the cool of the house, stretching out on the sofa or the bed, taking a nap. I got up and slid open the screen door. It hiccupped and bowed a bit because it always popped out of the track and had to be knocked back in.

"This really is my house," I said.

Though the radio was on, I couldn't hear anyone. I called to my parents, but no one replied. I walked from room to room. Our house is one of those McMansiony places, big and hollow feeling, but in a pleasant way, with high ceilings and lots of ceiling fans. Stephen looked up a lot as he went around, which is why I noticed this.

"It's not what I expected," he said.

"What did you expect?"

"Some kind of Gothic place," he said. "Given your stories."

"We're the normals around here, I guess," I said.

We got to the steps, and I went up, still looking for anyone who might be at home. With every room we went to, I became very conscious that Stephen was in my house now, something I had never envisioned happening. And while there wasn't anything to particularly reveal me—it wasn't like my underwear was stapled to the walls or something—it was all information. It was all truth.

I stopped by my bedroom door. This was the only one that was closed. If this was my subconscious talking, it was kind of a dick.

"Hello?" I called.

No reply from inside. I cracked the door open just a bit. I opened it farther, and then all the way. The blinds were drawn, and a gentle sun came through.

Even though there was no one there, it felt unnatural to step inside. It felt a bit dangerous. I tentatively put my foot forward, feeling the cushion of the carpet. My room was kind of big. This is because I'm an only child, and these McMansions only do big. Compared to my English room, it was hilariously huge. It was embarrassing—a waste of space. But it was mine, so deliciously familiar. For example, it was a mess. The bed was unmade, the comforter half on the floor, like it was drunk. There was a pile of cables for devices next to my bed, like a weird little nest for electronic animals. There were about six mugs on my nightstand, a pile of half-read books by the side of the bed. I had folded my clothes, at least some of them, and dropped them in piles on the floor. Stephen seemed very interested in the inflatable alligator I had suspended above the bed, its neck draped in beads. This gave me time to have a quick look around for underwear.

I found I was disappointed that I hadn't left any around. How was this the one time I hadn't left a bra out?

Was I trying to make out with Stephen again? Here? Is that what was happening? My brain said, "This is not the time," but the stirring feeling somewhere else said, "There has never been a better time, because who even knows what counts here?"

Suddenly, nothing felt urgent. I sat on the edge of the bed and pretended to be deep in thought. If I looked like I was thinking, Stephen would want to think too, and he would sit with me. We'd made out on a bed before. It could happen again. We had just done it in the diner, technically, but that was very different. My mind had been on something else, and his mind kind of wasn't there at all. That was a necessity.

But he was still looking around, taking it all in, frame by frame.

"This is more what I expected," he said.

I *mmmm*-ed like I was still thinking.

"Do you think we should go?"

"I'm thinking," I said. After a moment, and I guess seeing that I was not getting up, he moved a bit closer. I don't think he knew what to do, so I said, "Sit down."

And he did. The moment I said it. Very professionally.

"So why are we here?" I asked, stretching myself out a bit and leaning back toward the pillows. I hated myself for doing this even as I cheered myself on. And he noticed too, because he was looking at me—all of me, and then he looked away quickly and pinched the bridge of his nose and looked at my lamp.

"It could be a number of reasons," he said.

Everything was very heady. I really didn't care about getting out right now. All I could think about was the way Stephen was sitting there, the outline of his shoulders against the white of the blinds. His shoulders were broad and strong.

"Rory," he said, "I don't think . . ."

"We kissed the other night," I said.

"I know we did."

He couldn't meet my eye.

"Do you regret it or something?" I said.

"I . . ." He shook his head and looked very confused. "I think that—"

"Stop thinking and tell me. Do you regret it? Because I don't. I really wanted to."

So much furrowed brow. I sat up in alarm. Maybe Stephen

had never liked me at all. Maybe this was all something in my head that had gone very wrong. Maybe it was the head wound that had made him do it.

"No," he said, still not looking at me. "I wanted to. Very much so. For a while. I—"

"So do it again," I said. I didn't like how urgent I sounded. I got closer, and he got very still. Then he stood up.

"Something's not right," he said. "Something about this place isn't right."

There was no way I was leaving this bed. I hadn't lost him yet. He wanted to—I was sure of it. He was scared. Something was preying on his mind. I was never leaving this bed, or home. Everything could be perfect here. Me and Stephen.

He went to the window and adjusted the blinds, and the sun came streaming in. I had to put up my hand and shield my eyes. Stephen was talking, but for some reason, the fact that it was so bright made it impossible to hear him.

"Stephen?" I said. I started to come out of my haze. I still wished we had kissed, but I didn't feel as dopey. There was so much sun by the window that I couldn't see him at all.

"Stephen?" I called. "Stephen!"

It was all just light blindness. Home—it throbbed. It was taking me over. I couldn't stay here. Stephen couldn't be here with me. These things didn't go together. I heard him calling for me, and his voice sounded like he was at the other end of a long, empty hallway, not in a small, quiet room. I pulled myself from my bed and stumbled out into the hallway and down the stairs, the sunspots crowding my eyes. I continued calling for him as I made my half-blind way down to the living room. The screen doors were wide-open, but the view outside was blurry—like an out-of-focus picture of a yard. I went out anyway and found myself in a very different day from the hot and sunny one. The sky was restored to a slate gray, and the house was gone. The air was cool, and we stood in a London park, with Marble Arch maybe a hundred feet away. Stephen was a few yards away.

"Are you all right?" he asked.

"What the hell was that?" I asked, pointing at the spot where the house had been.

"I'm not sure that can actually be known," he said. "It seems to be a place that presents to us things that are familiar, things that compel us to stay. It gets inside of us. I suppose it knows what we want."

If that was the case, Stephen had just seen all too clearly what was inside of me. I turned away in embarrassment and looked at the expanse of park that had reappeared all around. The only difference this time was that the park had been denuded of trees, making the gentle roll of the green lawns clearly visible. There was nothing beyond the park—no London to see. It was just green field. Sid and Sadie's car was nowhere in sight.

"Something about this place washes out your mind and makes you forget a lot of things," he went on. "It takes away everything except what you most want. I wanted to see my sister. You want to go home."

I couldn't figure out if he was lying to make the awkwardness go away, or if that's what he had actually taken from what had just transpired. I also couldn't figure out if I should be relieved or disappointed.

I found myself leaning toward disappointed.

"So what now?" I said.

"I believe that's the way out," he said.

I turned around to see him pointing at Marble Arch, which had appeared at the edge of the park.

25

I HADN'T ACTUALLY SEEN MARBLE ARCH BEFORE, BUT IT WAS easy enough to identify. It was, as the name implied, a massive arch made of white stone that must have been marble. It was the obvious destination, and so we walked toward it. It seemed close, but we walked for five minutes, and then ten, and we were no closer. It was like the grass was rolling under us, treadmill style. We still couldn't go.

"What's the Shadow Cabinet?" I said again.

"Rory . . ."

"When it came up, things got weird."

Stephen looked at his hands. He put them in his pockets and took them out again.

"We're here because of all the things we didn't tell each other," I said. "I didn't tell you about Jane. I didn't tell you I got kicked out. I didn't tell you where I was really going. If I'd told you, you wouldn't have had to chase me. I might not even have gone. Then this wouldn't have happened. But it did, and

I came here for you. And you—you don't tell people things all the time. And I know it's your job, I know all that, but, a lot of it? Is because you don't tell people things. What's the Shadow Cabinet?"

"I can't—"

"*Look at where we are,*" I yelled.

"I know!"

I'd never heard Stephen yell. It was a rumbling, distressing noise. He turned on his heel and walked away a few paces, then turned back.

"All of these problems started because you came here." His voice was cold—artificially so. I knew what he was doing. It was pretty obvious. He was trying to say something to make me go. Stephen was many things, but a good liar wasn't one of them. Not for things like this.

"So you don't care about me," I said. "And you wish you'd never met me? Is that it?"

"You cause problems. I—"

"Stephen," I said. "Stop."

He pulled his glasses off and angrily rubbed his hair.

"I don't know where I am," he said, his breath coming quick. "But I know it's real, and I know you came here for me, and I don't know how to process that. I know I can't let this happen to you."

"No one's asking you," I said. "I came here myself."

"*Why?*"

There was the question. He genuinely didn't get it. The blankness on his face was real.

"I haven't actually *met* your family," I said, "but if I do? I think I'm going to do a lot of punching."

"This isn't a joke."

"I'm not laughing," I said. "Somehow, you ended up this way where you think you can sacrifice yourself for everyone and no one can do it for you. I know. I read your file."

This didn't help. In fact, as I said it, a hollowness came over his expression, and I knew I had inadvertently screwed up. I think Stephen was prepared for a certain amount of personal information getting out, but me reading that file was somehow wrong.

"Your things," I said, "we had to take them. All the file said was that you were really good but that you didn't take care of yourself—"

"What it said," he cut in, with real anger, "was that I was unstable."

"It didn't say that at all."

He made a noise of disgust and walked off in the direction of the ever-elusive arch. I followed. It eluded us some more. He sat on the ground, and I sat next to him, our legs side by side.

"We don't get out until I talk, is that it?" he said wearily.

"Unless you have a better idea."

He flicked some remains of the grass from his knee.

"What I say now," he said, "it doesn't go back with us. It stays here. This is critical, Rory."

I wanted to press into his side. I wanted to hold him, to do everything we'd done before and more—but this was serious. I held my body rigidly in position, in listening mode.

"They recruited me after I joined the squad," he said. "It's an organization. They aren't government. They're . . . they're beyond that. It's the living and the dead. Its entire function is to keep London secure, and it does that by being secret. Once you join, you're in. That's it. You don't quit. It's always your top priority. They first came to me when I joined the squad. They followed me, watched me. They started to explain how it all worked. At least, the parts I'm allowed to know."

He concentrated, looking at his knees, then at me.

"The boundaries between the living and the dead, they used to be better understood. As we're evidence of, they're permeable. London is what you might think of as a place of passage—a port city, places where the water meets the land. There are several like it: Paris, Giza, Rome, Shanghai, Baghdad, New York, Santiago, New Delhi, São Paulo, Alexandria, a few others. New Orleans is one, actually. When I saw that's where you were from, when I first met you, I thought you might be one of us. I figured out pretty soon you weren't, but I don't think it's a coincidence you come from there. It's a powerful place."

He glanced over at me for a moment.

"These places of passage tend to be in cities because humans instinctively gather at them, often because of the rivers. The rivers are key. A long time ago, protections were put down to try to strengthen these unstable places. That's the thing about all of this—we always think of humans as gaining knowledge as we go on, but we used to know a lot more, about this at least. The system of protection was extremely complex, with some of it being visible and some of it being hidden. In some places, it didn't hold very well. Those places tend to have problems. Still, as long as there's some kind of barrier, things generally work as they should. In London, a series of eight powerful stones were placed in key locations. The seventh stone was designed to move and was traditionally put in the crown of the king, but it was stolen, and it was smashed."

"The Eye of Isis," I said.

"The Eye of Isis. The terminus. How do you know about that?"

"Freddie."

"Freddie. Of course. It doesn't surprise me that she knows something about it."

"She'd heard of the Shadow Cabinet, but she didn't think it was a real thing. She didn't think termini were real either."

"Well, it sounds absurd. It's meant to. The Shadow Cabinet generates some of the more implausible stories about itself. They even adopted the name just so people would be confused by the fact that there's a government body with the same title. But the name fits. We work in the shadows and deal with the shadows. Some real information about the group and its work is out there, but not much. The Eye of Isis and the Oswulf Stone are the two stones that are generally known to those who look around enough."

"What about the others?"

He shook his head.

"You can't say," I said.

"No," he said. "Nor do I know the full picture. It's safer that way. Our job is to protect those stones. Telling people we exist means telling people about what really protects London."

"And what happens if they're moved? What's so bad about it?"

He looked up and blinked into the sunny day that stretched above us.

"Things fall apart," he said. "I think it depends on what you believe. Do you remember when Newman was quoting Revelation during the Ripper scare?"

"'The name of the star is Wormwood,'" I said. I knew my

Revelation because our local seafood place put a quote from it up every week on their sign. This is why we called it Scary Seafood. I could instantly recall images of seals breaking and lions and lambs and blood, all mixed in my memory with the smell of fried shrimp.

"So," I said, "not good."

"No."

We fell silent for a few moments.

"Are Callum and Boo in the Shadow Cabinet?"

He shook his head no.

"Thorpe?"

"Has no idea it exists. At least one member of this squad has always been in the Shadow Cabinet. I was recruited because of the three terminus stones. They're part of the Eye of Isis. The Eye of Isis was broken into a dozen pieces. We had three, just three. Now we have one."

He looked at me again, but this time his gaze was steady, and sad.

"Me," I said. "Your job is to protect me."

"It became my job the moment the power of the stone went into you."

I couldn't understand why this made him look so sad.

"So what?" I said. "We know what I am."

"I'm saying . . ." He inhaled deeply. "I'm saying I have a job I have to do that's much bigger than me and how I feel. I'm supposed to keep you safe. I'm supposed to keep you in London. It's very, very complicated."

"It's not that complicated. I'm still me."

"Believe me. I know. But I'm alone in thinking that way. To the Shadow Cabinet, you're a stone. You're a thing to be watched and kept. It matters. You don't understand. It's all that matters."

There was such finality to it that the conversation seemed to fall to the ground. It was quiet in the park, with all of London's noise put away. No birds. No wind. Just us. Stephen had told me his secret, and yet, we were still here, still staring at Marble Arch in the distance.

"Jane has two terminus stones," I said, almost as an after-thought. "They were Sid and Sadie's. She has them in a locket around her neck."

"Jane? Has two terminus stones?"

"Like the ones you had."

That would have been such critical information before. Now it felt like a minor detail. I continued to turn what Stephen had said over in my mind.

"Did you come after me because I'm a stone?" I asked. "Is that the only reason you're interested in me?"

"I would have done that no matter what," he said.

"But is that why you—you know. What we did. Did you just pretend to like me?"

"Rory, I don't think you understand—"

I didn't get to hear what it was I didn't understand, because there was one noise. A car, purring along. It wasn't so much that it was a loud sound as much as it was the only other sound in that moment. Everything else went on mute and the atmosphere was filled with the gentle rumble of the car.

"They're here," he said. "I think we need to go."

When we stood, I saw the yellow car slowly making its way around the edge of the park. We started walking again. This time, however, we made progress. In fact, we seemed to be in front of the arch in a moment. Directly at the center, there was a Tube entrance—the familiar red-and-blue circular sign, an opening, and a set of stairs leading down.

"That's not where the Marble Arch Tube entrance is located," Stephen said. "It's across the street."

"This isn't the Tube," I said.

"No."

The car was at the curb. I heard the doors open but didn't turn around to look. This was the end. I knew it because when I looked down the steps, I saw nothing at all. It wasn't just that it was dark or shadowy—it was nothing.

"Come on," I said.

"You go. I'll follow."

Like I said, Stephen was a bad liar.

"Together," I said.

"Rory—"

"Together."

"Rory, they can't come back with us. I can't let it happen."

He sounded sad, but it was nothing compared to how I felt.

"Okay," I said. "Then I guess we both stay here."

"Rory—"

"Stop saying my name," I said to Stephen. "Here's what *you* need to understand. What happened the other night? It was kind of important. It was kind of *the most important thing*. You matter to me. I had to watch you die, and I am not doing that again. So either you come with me, or we're both staying."

"Darlings!" Sid called.

They were walking toward us calmly, like we were meeting for a picnic in the park. Sid raised a hand in greeting and smiled.

"There's nothing you can do," I said.

"There's always something. This is my duty. This isn't a discussion."

"You're right," I said. "It's not."

I pushed him down the steps. I guess he was in no way expecting this. I saw the surprise. I saw that his body didn't lock and guard like it does if you know you're going to fall. He stumbled against the wall, then rolled down a few steps, and I saw him knock his head, and then I couldn't see him at all.

His head . . . his head? Again?

Sid and Sadie were still a bit in the distance, but coming closer. Now I understood—I had been charged with getting all three of them out. If I wanted Stephen, Sid and Sadie were coming too. They would pass through, or none of us would pass through.

It was time for me to go. I rushed down the steps, into the void, and then I—

26

OPENED MY EYES.

I think I did, anyway. Maybe they were already open. Everything was moving in a wide circle, like a carousel. Then everything decided to move in smaller and smaller circles until it stayed still—not that this helped much. I was in a dark place, with little tongues of dancing light around. It smelled very strongly of something smoky. There were voices.

"She's moving."

"Did she open her eyes?"

"Move back."

"Get her water."

Then there was a glass of water hovering over me, clasped in a hand. Someone was helping me sit up by pulling me up under the armpits. The water was put to my lips, and I drank some, but I had trouble swallowing, and it ran down my chin.

"Rory?"

That voice I knew. I turned to see Jane next to me. I was on a sofa, covered in a blanket. It was Jane who was giving me the water.

"You'll need this," she said, wiping my chin with her hand. "Try to drink."

Something thrummed in the back of my mind—a kind of ticking clock. I had to hurry. But hurry to do what? No, something had to happen now. Something should have happened? Was I late for class?

I drank again, and it ran out of my mouth again. A third try was more successful, and the water going down my throat turned out to be one of the most welcome feelings I could imagine. I gulped more and more, until I choked on the water and Jane took the glass away.

There were other people in this dark room. I'd seen them before, but couldn't place them at the moment. A boy with blond hair and a girl with dark brown hair. The boy reminded me very strongly of someone. His clothes were weird—like a costume. He was trying to dress like someone I knew.

"We weren't sure if you were coming back for a moment," Jane said. Her voice was affectionate. I knew I shouldn't be with Jane, but she was taking care of me. Why? And these three people on the floor—two looked strange but familiar. And Stephen? Why was he sleeping on the floor? I knew the answer to this question, but I couldn't place it.

"What . . ."

"It's all right," Jane said. "Now you are returned, by the blessing of Demeter, you are returned."

Jane stood and addressed the group.

"It is time," she said. "The vigil is over. If it is to happen, it will happen now. For this, I must be alone with them, and you must do your part. Blessed Demeter."

Everyone in the room said, "Blessed Demeter." Then there were hugs, like this was a big day. The group trailed out, and it was just Jane and me and Stephen and the two strangers on the floor.

"You have been very brave, Rory," she said.

How did I know these people? I had definitely seen them before. If only I could *think*. I should have been more concerned about Stephen, but it felt like we'd just been talking? In his father's room. No. Somewhere else. Another room. I'd been with Stephen in another room.

All my thoughts were like balloons. I'd reach for them, but they'd float off if I didn't catch the string just right. All I knew was that I had to get off this sofa and to Stephen. This was maybe a distance of eight feet, but at the moment it felt like it might as well have been eight miles. When I tried to move, all my limbs were heavy. They got the message from my brain that they were supposed to do something, but they didn't seem to have a clear idea of what. Instead of standing, I fell from the sofa. My legs were two dumb sacks of meat. I dragged myself along the floor. I could only think of a picture I must have seen in art history—maybe other places—a famous painting of a girl dragging herself across a field toward a house that seems so vital and far away. Of all the things my brain was offering me now, only this was clear. I was the girl in the field, and I had to move myself across this room. The physical effort this took cleared my mind a bit more. Stephen . . . Stephen was . . .

I was getting some motion in my knees now, which meant

I could crawl the last two paces. Jane paid me no mind. She was intent on the two strangers. They looked so much alike, blond and weird and dressed in white. I knew these people. I knew I didn't want to be in the same room with them. By the time I got to Stephen, I was exhausted. I fell against his chest. It wasn't moving.

"It will be soon," Jane said to me.

I wanted to ask her what this meant. I wanted the fog in my mind to clear. I *had* to clear it. I knew something very, very important.

"Stephen," I said, shaking his arm.

Then Jane let out a tiny, high-pitched noise. The female stranger had moved. I saw her foot twitch.

"Blessed Demeter," Jane whispered. "Blessed Demeter . . . Sadie? Sadie?"

Then the other one moved. Jane covered her mouth with her hands.

Stephen was not moving. Now I felt panic. He was supposed to be moving. Everything was wrong. His chest didn't rise and fall, and I felt like I was supposed to know why. The other two gained movement bit by bit. The process took several minutes. Their movements were tiny. There'd be a violent jerk of a knee or an arch of the back. The male figure sat up on his elbows and, with what seemed to be great effort, opened his eyes fully.

"My word," he said. "I'm not doing that again."

He looked right at me and broke out into a long, snaky grin.

"Hello, you," he said.

He turned on one side to examine the woman next to him. He took her face gently in his hand.

"Sadie. Wakey, wakey."

"Oh . . ." Her voice was like a songbird's. "Oh, Sid."

"I know. But it gets better when you sit up."

He didn't seem that strong himself, but he managed to help prop her up. She was like a rag doll. Then, as soon as she was upright, she seemed more alert. Her eyes snapped open.

"Sid?"

"I don't think we're in Kansas anymore," he said. He managed to get to his knees, and then, with effort, to stand. He extended a hand and helped his sister from the floor. They relished their movement for a moment, flexing their hands, bending their elbows, moving their heads from side to side. This was when they noticed Jane, who was kneeling behind them.

"Jane?" Sadie said.

"It's been so long," Jane said. She had been sitting there, like a brook waiting to burble. Now that they had spoken to her, it all came out in a loud, wailing kind of cry. She scrambled to her feet.

"There, there," Sid said, putting his arms around her and tucking her head to his shoulder. "It's all right. We're all here now."

"Hello, you," Sadie said, looking down at me. "Do you remember us? We've met. You're Rory."

"You know me?"

Sadie smiled lightly and extended her arms, offering to help me from the ground. I stayed where I was.

"She's looking a bit rocky," Sid said while guiding Jane to the sofa. "I don't think she was quite as prepared for the journey as we were. Our trip took a bit longer, but we seem to have arrived in better condition. It does pay to go first class, doesn't it?"

"It does," Sadie said, looking down at me. "We prepared for months. But you'll be all right in time. Don't worry."

Sadie crouched down by me and took my left arm, flipping it over and examining it. It appeared I'd been cut. Someone had bandaged the wound. This was familiar. I looked over at the rock on the floor and saw some dark red drops on it. That was my blood.

"She's been cut," Sadie said. "There's blood on the stone. Is it hers?"

"I told you there was something about this one," Sid said.

"There is," Sadie said. She tilted my chin up so I was looking at her face. "What is it about you?"

Jane managed to pull herself together for a moment. She coughed a bit and wiped at her face and straightened up.

"She's got part of the Eye of Isis in her," she said, her voice thick.

"No!" Sadie said. "You are joking. That's marvelous. Oh, Sid. Isn't it?"

"It is," Sid said, giving Jane a shoulder-squeeze. "Jane, you rotten old cleverclogs. You found a living stone. No wonder that one there on the floor was so protective of her."

"And the stone," Sadie said, pointing her heavily sleeved arm at the rock. "The Oswulf, I believe. Darling Jane. However did you find it?"

"It took a long time. There's so much to tell you."

"I'll imagine there is," Sid said. "It looks like you've re-created our work, gotten some of the knowledge."

"I had to get to you."

"And you did. That's why you're our Jane."

Sadie peeled my bandage back carefully. When I winced, she slowed.

"I'll be careful," she said. Her voice was so soft.

The cut was dark and ugly, still seeping blood. But it wasn't deep. I had been standing in the middle of the floor when I got it, I remembered. I had been standing on the stone. I drank something. This house belonged to someone I'd just met. A doctor. There had been a doctor, and Stephen had been asleep upstairs. It had something to do with Charlotte, but I couldn't remember what.

"What made this wound?" she asked.

"Right there," Jane said. "Under the cloth."

There was a low table in front of the sofa, with a number of strange items on it—a golden bowl and a white cloth stained red. Sid picked this up with his free hand and revealed a curved knife, like a crescent moon.

"This looks familiar," he said.

"It's one of yours. It was blessed with water from the river, thrice blessed."

"That's quite correct," Sid said. "You've learned the ritual well. You've done so much, Jane."

"I did it," she said. "I watched. All this time. I never stopped. I've kept you safe. I've worked so hard. I had to learn so much."

"It certainly seems that way," Sid said.

"I'm almost as advanced as you now. I've conferred the sight to a non-seer . . ."

"*Did* you?" Sadie said, cocking her head to the side and looking at her brother.

"Yes. And as you can see, I've worked the mysteries. I'm ready. I've been waiting all this time. I want to ascend. I want to be with you. We'll be together, always. We will defeat death once and for all."

"Jane." Sid pulled her close once again, kissing the top of her head as he did so. "Oh, Jane."

"Sweet Jane," Sadie said.

It happened so fast. Sid's arm swung up and the blade went right to the exposed side of Jane's neck. He pulled it straight along the side and hooked it out at the end. I saw something fly out of Jane, and it took me a moment to realize it was her blood. Sid set the knife down and embraced her again, holding her to his chest as she convulsed. I watched his white suit turning red.

"Don't fight it," he said, clasping Jane's head down on his shoulder. "Now, now, Jane. Let go. Almost there. Come now. Almost there. I've got you."

After a minute or so, she stopped moving. Her hand, which had been clawing at Sid's thigh, went limp. Her entire body sagged, and she dropped in his arms. What was funny was that I was very calm watching Jane die like that. I'd been drugged. I was thankful for it now. It was clouding my thoughts, but it also made the scene bearable. It also helped me remember. I'd come here to rescue Stephen. I'd been in a ritual. He was supposed to wake because of what I'd done. It all rolled back into my mind like some footage from a movie I didn't remember being in, but clearly had been.

"Oh, Sid," Sadie said, her voice a sad sigh. "It had to be."

"I know," he said. He adjusted himself to let Jane's body fall across his lap. "But I feel guilty. She's done such a good job."

"Don't tear yourself up about it," Sadie said. "I'm sure she had a good life."

"Very true. You see . . ." Sid bent down over Jane's body to address me as if I were a small child. "This is all quite powerful magic that's been happening here. Jane's done a good enough job, I suppose, but it's not very elegant, and there are far too many loose ends. It must seem beastly, but you have to be a bit ruthless with these things. Magic is not for the weak. She was useful, and we cared for her deeply . . ."

"Deeply," Sadie said.

"You need to be special. I can tell you these things, because you're special, aren't you? My sister and I are special too. We knew we could ascend, become more than people who live and die. You need assistance in these things. You need staff. We needed Jane's help, and poor old thing, she always thought we were going to help her ascend once we'd done it. But you don't bring the help with you on a journey like that. You don't share the magic and wisdom of the ages with just anyone. No. The power lies in keeping the information to yourself. You can't go around giving people the sight and re-creating the mysteries so haphazardly. We did it neatly. We took our little group along with us. But this lot . . ."

"They'll all have to go," Sadie said, sounding a bit bored by the idea of another mass murder.

"I know, I know. It's tiresome. But if Jane touched that stone, then we still have work to do right now. Wait for it . . ."

A shape was taking form by the sofa—something like smoke coming off of Jane. It came together in a rush, as if filling an invisible mold just on top of her.

"Now," Sadie said.

Sid rolled Jane off his lap violently. She landed hard on the floor. Sadie dragged her by the arms and dropped her on top of the stone. The smoke disappeared at once, and all was quiet. Jane was limp, draped over the stone.

"There," Sid said, looking down at his hands and then rubbing them on his blood-soaked jacket. He peeled this off and checked the damage on the shirt and pants. "This is my favorite suit. It might be hoping for too much that I can still buy a replacement."

He went over to the stairs and hung the coat on the banister.

"We'll have to deal with the rest of them," Sadie said. "They'll be back soon."

"Oh, I know."

Something in the room had changed. My hand was on the floor, next to Stephen, but he wasn't as close to my hand as he had been. He had moved several inches over, toward the table. Just as I realized this, his arm shot out for the knife. In the next moment, he had rolled up on his knees and had Sadie caught in the crook of his arm. His face was pale, and he looked a bit shaken by the sudden movement. He was alive.

"Well, now," Sid said. "Someone's awake."

"Rory," Stephen said, slowly and evenly, "back away."

"He's quite a pistol, isn't he?" Sid said. "I like these two, don't you, Sadie?"

"They're fab," she said. She smiled gently, like Stephen was showing her a baby rabbit.

"Now, here's the dilemma," Sid said, leaning against the railings. "You have my sister, and I'm very fond of her. I have to ask myself—is this handsome young policeman prepared to kill her? However, given what you are, I suspect your only interest is that stone. Take it. It's of no interest to us. We want to go and explore this wonderful new world."

"That's not up to you," Stephen said.

"Isn't it? In a moment, this house will be full of people, and they're all going to be upset to find poor Jane here like this. They'll attack you, and you'll be outnumbered, and they'll win. Can't imagine it will be long now. We can both wait and see what happens."

"Do you want to test that theory?" Stephen said.

"We *love* testing theories," Sid replied. "Don't we, Sadie?"

"We adore it," Sadie said. "Boredom is the enemy."

She reached up to the knife Stephen was holding at her throat, letting her fingers sink into the blade. Without any visible effort, she pulled it away from her neck. Stephen struggled against her, but he was helpless. It was like he was a small child being pushed aside by an adult. She stood up, and the knife came with her, as it was imbedded in the pads of her fingers. She removed it calmly and watched in interest as the blood ran down her arm. Stephen fell back a bit, and I stumbled over to him. He was shaking all over, and I could barely stand. He wrapped his arm around me, and the two of us supported each other to keep from falling down.

"Are you all right?" he asked me quietly.

I nodded. I was in no state to ask him the same. I could only hold on to him. I grabbed his hand and felt it becoming warmer even as I held it. Sid was completely focused on his sister.

"Sis! You impress me. Does that hurt?"

"Not very much. Look. The blood is flowing very slowly now."

She held the hand up for Sid to see. The wound seemed to be healing even as we looked at it.

"'Struth! That's very clever of you. And look! I like these two. The stone and the guardian. Can we keep them?"

"You're not good with pets," Sadie said.

"I'm not good with parrots. Or cats. This is different."

"What are you?" Stephen asked.

"You need to understand," Sadie said to us, her voice full of patience, "we are a bit special, my brother and I."

"You'll spoil the surprise!" Sid said.

Somewhere in the room, a phone rang. Sid trailed the sound, producing what looked like the cell phone that I had used earlier to text Jerome. They'd brought it downstairs and set it on one of the tables.

"What's this?" Sid said. "Annoying noise."

"It's a phone," I said. "Why don't you answer it?"

Sid held the phone in a pinched grip at arm's length.

"Strange telephone," he said. "I suppose we have lots of surprises too. How do you answer this thing?"

I walked over and took it from him and hit Accept. Sid watched in amusement, leaning back and folding his arms over his chest. I put the phone to my ear.

"I'm outside," Jerome said. "I've called 999. The police will be there any minute. Tell them."

"Oh," I said, looking to Sid and Sadie. "The police are coming."

"Are they?" Sid said. "Well, I—"

And then something looped around his neck and pulled him back against the railings so hard that I heard a crack. Thorpe had removed his tie and was strangling Sid. I got teary seeing him. He was all right. Sid was gasping and laughing at the same time. Sadie went to swing the knife at him, and I threw the phone in her face, hard. This surprised her enough to make her drop the knife. Stephen lurched forward and threw himself at her, pinning her to the ground. I looked around for something heavy. Sid was still struggling and kicking and going blue, but smiling all the while. Thorpe pulled back with all his might. Sid's head went straight back through the railings.

Sadie had thrown Stephen off and was picking up the knife again when the door opened.

"Oh, my God," Jerome said. "Oh, my *God.*"

I'd found a bookend made of marble. I brought it down on the back of Sadie's head with all the strength I had. This caused her to fall forward a bit, and I fell right with her, carried by the momentum of my swing. Stephen pinned her down again, and I got the bowl from the table. It was still full of the disgusting barley drink.

"Get her head up," I said. I forced the bowl to her mouth and poured. Stephen held her mouth open. She gagged a bit, but I got most of it into her mouth. Her eyes fluttered, and she looked dozy. Above us, there was a very bad sound on the stairs, where Sid had gotten himself free and had his hands around Thorpe's neck. Jerome ran up the stairs and tried to get him loose, but Sid punched him right in the face and knocked him back against the wall. Stephen pulled on Sid's lower body, forcing him back through the hole in the railing. Thorpe collapsed, coughing and heaving against the splintered banister. Jerome was picking himself off the stairs and pulling his inhaler from his pocket. Sid got down next to his sister, turning her head in either direction.

"Oh, dear," he said. "Someone is going to have a hangover."

He scooped her up and stood in one fluid motion.

"It's been fab," he said. "It really has. But we must be going. Things to do, things to see. I suppose you'll have your hands full if that's been moved."

He nodded at the Oswulf Stone.

"That'll be very bad indeed, I think. That's been holding back some very naughty energy—how many thousands of dead criminals, or worse yet, dead innocents? I couldn't even guess what might come out of Tyburn. I'd hurry if I were you. I'll tell you this, though—I wouldn't put that back where you found it. It looks like simply *anyone* could take it. What you want to do is get it into the river, in the sewer, ideally. No one wants to go looking for rocks in the sewer."

He swept past us, passing only a moment to look down at me and smile.

"I'll see you later, little diamond. We'll have a wonderful moment."

With that, he nudged the door open with his foot and carried his sister out of the house, into the fading day. The rest of us were broken and scattered around the room. Stephen fell to his knees right where he was, and I fell too.

"We need to go," he said. "The stone. We need to get it back into position."

Thorpe's face was discolored, and his eyes were bloodshot, but he managed to speak.

"Marigold?"

"I don't know," I said. "Somewhere in the house."

"Need to find her. Shut that door. Need to find her."

"We need to leave," Stephen said to him. "We need to take this stone and go."

Jerome was now standing, looking at Jane's body on the stone. "This woman is dead," he said.

"Don't look," I said to him. "She's . . ."

"Something's happening," Jerome said. His voice sounded very far away. "There was some trouble. Freddie said there was trouble. She told me the address."

"Trouble where?" Stephen said.

"Marble Arch."

Stephen got to his feet, using my shoulders to help push himself up. He helped me after that. The two of us were walking like we were drunk. Stephen had just woken from the dead, so this seemed fair enough, but I had no idea what was wrong with me.

"Callum? Boo?"

"They're all at Marble Arch," Jerome said. "Freddie said everyone went to Marble Arch."

"How did you get here? Do you have a car?"

"Tube."

"We need to leave before the police come," Stephen said.

"You go," Thorpe said. "Take the stone. I'll find her. My car—keys." He patted his pockets, but his keys were not in them. "Look for the keys."

"Clothes," Stephen said to me. "You need clothes."

I found my clothes folded and sitting on the piano. I pulled the pants on under the sheet, then quickly turned my back to get the shirt on. It did cross my mind that I was doing this in the presence of two guys who were already somewhat familiar with this part of me, but it was habit. Stephen walked right past me and into the kitchen, where I heard lots of banging and the rattle of cutlery as drawers were quickly opened. I pulled the plastic sneakers on without any socks. I didn't bother to look for the coat. I happened to look up on the piano, where there was a low bowl with a few things in it, including some keys.

"Keys!" I shouted.

Thorpe was gone. I could hear him moving around upstairs, looking for Marigold. But Stephen returned from the kitchen and took the keys from my hand.

"Good," he said. He looked them over for a moment. "These aren't for Thorpe's car. Probably hers. Doesn't matter. We're taking it. Come on."

Jerome was still frozen in the middle of the room, arms wrapped around himself, looking at the scene. Stephen pushed Jane's body off the stone.

"Get that cloth from the table," he said.

I pulled the dark cloth that had been covering the coffee table, and we used it to wrap the bloody stone.

"We're going to need your help," he said to Jerome. "I don't expect you to understand, but this is important. It's the most important thing you'll ever do. You're Jerome, correct?"

"Yeah . . ."

"You've seen me before. I'm with the police. I was at the Ripper scene. I'm telling you the truth. I know this is . . ."

"I'll do it," Jerome said. He blinked a few times, which is something he often did right before we kissed, at least when we first met. It meant he was nervous. He was blinking like mad.

"There's a back door," Stephen said. "Come on."

Right as we were about to go, I remembered something very important. I went to Jane's body. Her neck was—barely a neck at this point. It was a thickening mess of dark blood and hair. I steadied myself as best I could, thanking whatever was still in my system numbing me, and felt around until I came upon her locket.

"She's got two of them around her neck," I said. "Two termini."

I couldn't get it unhooked, so I snapped the chain with my hands. I was covered in blood now. I wiped my hands on the carpet, but it barely helped. I thought about using her dress. I could already hear the sirens. It seemed like there were a lot of sirens. All this blood—on my skin, under my nails.

It was Jerome who handed me the white cloth from the table and helped me get some of it off. He held my hand and pulled the cloth along, finger by finger. He looked nauseous all the while.

"Thanks," I said.

He nodded, lips pursed against the smell and the sight.

"We need to move," Stephen said.

27

THERE WAS A SMALL WALLED GARDEN AT THE BACK OF Marigold's house. I would never have known it, but there was a door in the back of it, almost entirely covered in creeping vines. These were clearly tended to do this. There were nails around the door frame where they'd been wrapped and tamed. We pushed through into a small alley between the houses and other walled gardens, holding the wrapped stone between us. Stephen walked a bit unsteadily, occasionally touching his free hand against one of the walls as he walked. He pressed the Unlock button on the key fob, and there was a friendly toot somewhere on the street.

"That dark green Jaguar," he said. "That's hers. Come on."

"Hang on," Jerome said. "Are you all right to drive? I have no idea what happened to you, but you look high."

Stephen wavered a bit.

"You drive?" he asked Jerome.

"Yes."

"Do you drive fast?"

"Fast enough."

"Right. Set the stone down. Careful."

We all lowered the stone to the ground as one.

"Get the car," Stephen said, wiping his brow. He was sweating, and when I noticed that he was, I realized I was too. "Bring it here."

Jerome took the keys, looked at me, then jogged toward the car. Stephen leaned against one of the walls and closed his eyes.

"Does he drive well?" he asked.

"I don't know."

"Maybe I should drive."

"You should *not* drive," I said.

We didn't need to go over what happened the last time Stephen drove.

"We can't risk getting pulled over," he said, rubbing his eyes with the heels of his hands before opening them. "All right. He drives."

"Are you okay?"

"I have no idea what I am," he said. "Except here."

He touched his hairline, pulling the bandage off. There was no mark underneath. This made me well up at once, but it was no time for crying. He clearly noticed this.

"What's happening at Marble Arch?" I asked. "How bad is this?"

"Very bad," Stephen said. "Far worse than anything we've ever seen."

"That could mean anything. What's happening?"

"I don't know," he said. "I'm not sure it's ever happened before. Imagine this stone is a dam, holding back a flood. Well, there's no dam now. Anything could come through. It's a question of what's under there. But I think we can reasonably assume that whatever it is, it's not going to be good."

"Okay," I said, blinking and trying to take this in. "And what about them, Sid and Sadie. What the hell are *they*?"

"That," he said, "I have no idea. There are no instructions for anything that's happening right now. We just have to get this stone back to where it belongs."

"Why did he tell us not to put it back where it had been?"

"Rory, I don't know." He sounded exhausted. "But he was telling the truth about the sewer. That's where the River Westbourne was diverted. If we can get it into there, close enough to the point of the breach . . ."

Jerome pulled the car up to the opening of the alley, and we loaded the stone in the back. I sat with it, and Stephen took the front seat.

"We need to get to Marble Arch," he said. "I'll tell you the route. Drive slow and steady through here. Avoid Oxford Street. Use New Cavendish."

I heard the sound of sirens—many sirens, possibly all the sirens—caterwauling in the near distance.

"The police are going to be at the house," Jerome said. "We're going to be—"

"The police aren't going to get into that house. It's owned by someone in the security service, and she will never allow them in. Those sirens are coming from somewhere else."

What became clear pretty quickly was that we were not going

to be able to get to Marble Arch. Traffic was at a standstill. Cars were practically parked. Stephen kept directing Jerome to turn down smaller streets, looping around, cutting through all kinds of passages, but everything was blocked up.

"Are you some kind of human sat nav?" Jerome finally asked him.

"I did the Knowledge."

"Right," Jerome said. He eyed me through the rearview mirror. "Of course you did."

Stephen put his head against the car window. I wanted to sleep as well. It was taking everything I had in me to keep my eyes open. I stretched out over the cloth-covered stone. It was surprisingly soothing. I could rest here, maybe just for a minute.

"What the hell is that?" Jerome asked.

Both Stephen and I sat back upright. Ahead of us, maybe a half mile down the road, was a solid wall of white—like a cloud sitting on top of part of the city. It was like over there was its own place with its own weather, and its own weather was a solid white mass. Every car was stopping.

"Turn around," Stephen said, craning around in his seat. "Now. Right here. Turn."

"I can't—"

Stephen made to grab for the wheel, and Jerome elbowed him off.

"Fine!"

Jerome made a frustrated grunt and ground through the gears, turning the car in the middle of the street and heading the opposite direction. Stephen turned on the radio and scanned through the stations quickly until he got to the news.

. . . unconfirmed reports of a possible explosion at Lancaster Gate Tube station. The area has been cordoned off and . . .

"Lancaster Gate," Stephen said. "Right next to Marble Arch. This is not good. We won't get into Marble Arch this way."

Stephen continued giving directions, leading Jerome down an endless sequence of smaller roads and paths. Every time the traffic was blocked, we turned again. After ten minutes of this, Stephen let out a weird half yell of frustration. I'd never heard anything quite like this come from him.

"What the *hell* is going on?" Jerome yelled.

"You just need to drive."

"I need to know."

"Jerome," I said, "please. I promise. We'll tell you. Please."

I reached up and put my hand on Jerome's shoulder. I felt his muscles tensing as he drove. His expression was grim, and he looked a bit terrified, but I think he got the message. Stephen pulled off his glasses and pinched the space between his eyes. This was maybe too much for him. The news report droned on, and the story only got worse. Reports of smoke, people being evacuated from the area, the Tube being shut down.

"Pull over," Stephen said to Jerome.

Jerome did this, but from the way he was holding his head and the stiffening of his shoulders, I knew he didn't like being ordered around like this.

"We're going to need to get in some other way," Stephen said.

"We're not getting in if the whole area is blocked off," Jerome said.

"We don't have a choice." Stephen put his glasses back on and exhaled loudly. "Right. This is what we do. We go to the Athenaeum Club on Pall Mall. We'll cut north and go around."

"Why there?" Jerome said.

"Because that's the way in."

We got there eventually, though it took much longer than it should have. The fog wasn't quite as bad in Pall Mall, which was a wide stretch of what were clearly critically important buildings, all white, all large, all stinking of Queen and Empire and that kind of thing. The road ended pretty much at the club, where it butted up against a set of steps that led down to a park. Jerome pulled up where Stephen directed. Stephen had already unclicked his belt and was halfway out of the car before it was in park.

"You need to stay here with the stone," he said to Jerome. "Rory, with me."

"We'll be back," I said to Jerome. "Promise. It's . . ."

I hurried after to Stephen. The building was large, with a cream-white façade. Some kind of classical scene cut into marble ran along the roofline. A statue of some kind of goddess sat on the top like a proud pigeon. I guessed this was Athena, judging from the name—and it made me uneasy. I didn't really want to see any Greek gods or goddesses right now.

Stephen went into the foyer, which was quiet and cold and marble. A man in a perfect gray suit stood by a desk and took one look at us, dressed in our scrappy clothes, no coats.

"I'm sorry—"

"I need to leave a message for the timekeeper," he said. "Give me a piece of paper."

The suited man looked a bit surprised, but immediately produced a piece of letterhead and a pen. Stephen began to write something. When he'd said "timekeeper," I'd happened to look up and notice a large clock in the middle of the landing straight ahead of us. The clock was weird. It took me a moment to work out what was so strange about it: it had two number sevens and no number eight.

"That clock," I said. "It has two sevens."

Stephen glanced over at it, and something very uncomfortable passed over his expression.

"I'm already here," said a voice. "Step outside."

A woman had appeared behind us. She looked to be about fifty, maybe sixty. She was sizable and wore very practical-looking high-waisted pants and a stiff white blouse. Her hair was buzzed neatly and utterly flat on top.

"A moment, sir," the porter said.

"No," Stephen replied, folding the paper and shoving it in his pocket. "It's fine. It's fine."

The porter hadn't seen her, and judging from her aspect, it was obvious what she was—though she looked so firm and clear. She grabbed Stephen's arm and gave it a shake.

"The reports of your death seem premature," she said. "We'll discuss that later. Do you know what's transpired?"

"I have the stone," he said. "It's in the car."

"How did you get the stone? Never mind. We'll discuss that later as well. The important thing is getting it back in place. And you've brought her. I suppose that might be useful."

The woman gave me a curious, yet dismissive look.

"Neither of us is very strong right now."

"Well, you'll need to buck up, dear boy. It's started. We've mustered everyone we could to try to hold it back, but we won't be able to contain it much longer."

Jerome was leaning over the wheel, staring at Stephen talking to the air. This was bad. So bad. I angled around so he couldn't see me speaking.

"What is it?" I asked her.

The woman regarded me with arched eyebrows.

"My dear girl," she said, "it is the breach. It will envelop and extinguish life. It is the end of order. You must assist. The stone must be replaced. You can't go over the land. They've shut down everything all around, especially around the palace. But you can go under. I will open the doors. You must get it through."

Stephen started walking to the car and waved me over to do the same. He opened the back door of the car to get the stone. Jerome opened the driver's door and stepped out.

"Who the hell were you talking to?" he asked.

"I was on the phone," Stephen said. "Headset."

"Then why did you take *my* phone?"

Poor Jerome was clearly getting nervous about all these strange people taking his phone. Stephen was carefully pulling the stone from the backseat, but he was having a hard time.

"We're going to need your help," he said to Jerome. "Rory and I are weak. Too weak to get it that far. We need to get this into Hyde Park, and we need to carry it. Will you help us?"

"Will you tell me what's going on?"

"When it's over," Stephen said.

Jerome looked to Stephen, then to me.

"Can I talk to you a minute?" he said.

Stephen closed his eyes, probably in a kind of agony that

this was taking so long. The woman had come over to us and was looking at Jerome.

"Why are you all playing sillybuggers?" she asked. "This is no time—"

"*Let me talk to Jerome a second,*" I said, for everyone's benefit.

Jerome and I walked far enough away not to be heard.

"This is insane," he said. "I can see there's something going on. I saw someone dead, on the floor. I think we just ran from the police? You're being guarded by some security services people who don't seem to be doing a good job. And now we've got some kind of *rock* that can make the explosion stop?"

"Trust me," I said, holding out my hands. "I know how bad this is, how weird."

He shook his head and looked up at the sky. And in that moment, I'd kind of had it. It was time to release anything and everything inside.

"You think I'm not sick of it?" I said. "It's been weird for me since I got here. Jerome, it's been one unending river of weird shit."

Jerome looked back at me and seemed to be about to say something, but I held up my hands.

"No," I said. "No, I'm not looking for that. I don't want you to say you know how bad it's been. I know how bad it's been. All this stuff I couldn't say, well, it's all coming out. There won't be any secrets. And it's not all bad—there's stuff that actually makes sense too. There's good stuff too. But you know what? We need to do that later. People need us now. I know you don't like being in the dark—no one likes that. Sometimes you have to go with it. This is one of those times. I need you to trust me.

I know that's kind of crazy to ask, considering, but you just have to do it, because—look around."

The street was really, really quiet. Everyone could hear me.

Jerome was still standing there, bobbing the car key nervously. It was time for something more decisive. I was going to have to do this, even though I wasn't sure what it meant, even with Stephen behind me. I walked right up to Jerome, got right up against his chest, and took the lapels of his coat. Our faces were inches apart.

"Us breaking up," I said. "It was all this stuff. You think I didn't want to say?"

He swallowed hard. I was close enough to smell his breath. Jerome had very sweet breath. And I was lying to him—well, I wasn't being entirely truthful. But I was doing this for a very good reason. I leaned in more, so we were almost mouth to mouth. He tipped his head down to look at me.

We weren't going to kiss, but I think we were exchanging a promise. I was telling him to put his faith in me.

Also, Jerome was not an idiot.

"Jerome," I said, "I'm really scared, and I almost died tonight. Please help us."

That was true.

Jerome breathed in a few times, his nostrils actually flaring from the force of his breath. Then, in a sudden, decisive move, he walked over to Stephen. Stephen, I noticed, had been watching us closely and he turned away, focusing his attention on the stone and decidedly away from me. I followed, my stomach queasy, with strange prickling feelings in my palms. Stephen had seen it all and I could tell from his expression that something had just changed. There was something coming off of him that suggested I shouldn't get too close. I had no time to worry, no time to mourn. Emergencies bind as many wounds as they open.

Jerome picked the stone up by himself.

"Right," Stephen said gruffly. "Good."

"The entrance is down here," the woman said. "At the foot of the steps."

The staircase down to the park was as wide as the street itself and had solid stone walls, and there was a large column in the middle—some piece of statuary in a place that was built for statuary. Built into the wall on the left side was a doorway—a discreet one that I otherwise would have walked by.

"I can get through this and open it from the other side," the woman said. "Though it may take a minute. From there, the paths are marked on the walls. There's an exit at the east end of the Serpentine. That is as far as this passage goes. You'll need to get to the river from there by separate access."

With that, she turned to the door and forced herself through it. I'd seen this happen once before. Jo had done it to rescue me. It was like watching someone get hit by a car, taking the impact slowly, second by second. The woman let out a low groan that became more of a cry as she pushed through, her body sinking into the metal of the door, inch by inch.

"What are we waiting for?" Jerome said, shifting under the weight of the stone.

I watched her face vanish, her cries muffled—one leg, then another.

"I need your phone again," Stephen said.

Jerome turned and indicated the right pocket of his jeans. I reached over and removed the phone sticking out of it. Stephen rattled off a number for me to dial.

"It's probably best if you speak," he said. "They might not believe it's me. Tell them we have the stone and to meet us at the east end of the Serpentine."

Someone had already answered. I could barely hear the person on the other end for all the yelling in the background, but I eventually made out that it was Boo.

"We're coming!" I said. "Meet us at? The east end? Of the Serpentine?"

I could just pick out from the jumble and the somewhat broken connection that they were there, in Hyde Park, but that Hyde Park and all the roads around were being closed off. I repeated this out loud so Stephen could hear. Then the call was cut off.

The woman had now vanished completely into the door. There was a long moment, then it opened. We were admitted to a concrete passageway, maybe six feet wide, lit along the top by a single, bright line of industrial bulbs. The woman was down on the ground, holding herself around the middle.

"Go," she groaned. "Go quickly."

Jerome stepped in, unaware of the suffering by his feet. I think he stepped on her.

"Which way?" he asked.

Stephen gave the woman a final look before nodding.

"We're going under the park toward the palace," he said. "Toward Hyde Park."

28

FIRST, WE HAD TO GO DOWN. THIS WAS A THEME IN MY LIFE these days. There was a set of steps that took us down what felt like maybe two stories. Unlike the terrifying entrance to King William Street, this staircase was well maintained and lit. When we reached the bottom, the passageway turned almost at once, making a sharp right. From here, the tunnel stretched long and got wider, wide enough that a car could have easily driven along. It was pristine, the kind of smooth, unblemished concrete and empty space that made my inner ten-year-old miss my bike. There was very little to see along the path, except the occasional bright yellow box on the wall—some kind of fuse or something. A fire extinguisher here and there. Some blue lightbulbs, unilluminated, under black mesh cages.

Jerome was fine at first, but after ten or so minutes of walking, he struggled a bit under the weight of the stone. Stephen and I helped at points, but I knew it was taking all I had to keep going, and Stephen didn't look much better.

"So what is this tunnel?" Jerome said. "Must be important, considering where it is."

"I expect it's a safe route for ministers," Stephen said. "Possibly the royal family. We should be passing under the palace in a few minutes."

Sure enough, as the corridor turned slightly and branched, there was a spray-painted sign on the wall and a door marked PALACE. Next to that door was an ominous-looking blue door with several safety signs and warnings on it.

"These were built during the war," Stephen said.

"It looks new," I said.

"This is the tunnel you use when things are very bad, not when the queen doesn't want to get wet. Things can stay in good shape for a long time without use, protected from the elements. They make sure everything is sound."

"I need to stop for a minute," Jerome said, setting the stone down.

"We can't," Stephen said.

"I'm asthmatic. Give me a minute."

Stephen let out an exasperated sigh, but nodded. "Of course," he said. "I'm going to go ahead. Follow when you can."

Jerome pulled the inhaler out again and took a hit, then leaned over with his hands on his thighs.

"How come I never knew about your asthma?" I said.

"It never came up. And it's only triggered by strong smoke, or stress, or a lot of exercise. Like everything that's happened."

He shook his head, sending his curls flopping from side to side.

"Who the hell is he?" Jerome said. "Is he MI5?"

"Not exactly."

"Well, he did the Knowledge, but I don't think he's a cabdriver."

"I have no idea what that means," I said.

"The Knowledge is what London cabdrivers have to do. They memorize the entire map of London—all the streets, all the hotels and main buildings and train stations, all the routes. It's famously hard, and it makes your brain get bigger, literally. Like, they scan people's heads after they do it."

This sounded like something Stephen would spend his free time doing.

"But we have to keep going. If you can. Are you okay?"

"I should be," he said.

"I'll help."

"You look like you're going to pass out."

"At least I can breathe, dumbass."

It was just a little gesture, an attempt at normality, at the way we used to joke with each other—and it was maybe not quite the moment. That was from before, when Jerome and I were together, and not from whatever and wherever we were now. His lack of reply told me that. But he was moving again. I got on one side, and Jerome got on the other. Together we shuffled on down the corridor until we caught up with Stephen, who had stopped where the tunnel branched.

"This way," Stephen said. "Are you all right to keep carrying?"

"I'll do it," Jerome said, which wasn't exactly an answer.

Our footsteps got more lonely and developed more of an echo as we progressed. Aside from the occasional pause for breath, we continued on, following the signage on the wall. Finally we saw one that pointed toward a pump room. There was a muffled sound of water above us.

"This should be it," Stephen said, looking up the dark stairwell. "I've been trying to gauge our distance. We should be into the park now."

This set of steps was very narrow, barely wide enough for one person to walk at a time. The stone scraped along the concrete walls, so Jerome had to go sideways, with one of us in front of and one behind him to make sure he remained steady. We emerged in a very small, very dark building, just one room. It was almost entirely filled with pipes and one very loud machine in the middle of the room that was clearly designed to pump water. Jerome made it just to the top of the steps, where he edged the stone onto the floor and then sat. He pulled out his inhaler and gave it one violent shake, then took a hit.

"It's almost empty," he said, shaking it again. There was a touch of fear in his voice.

"Then this is as far as you go," Stephen said. "Rest here until you can breathe again and then go the way we came, back to Pall Mall. Take the car, drive it back to the house. Leave it on the street. Just stay here until you're stable. I wouldn't linger."

Stephen stepped over the stone and went to open the door, carefully avoiding me and Jerome and anything that might pass between us.

"Are you all right?" I said, getting down to look Jerome in the face. He hung his head and took several long, slow breaths before replying.

"I will be. I just need to sit."

Stephen pushed open the door. The outside air came in. There was a strange smell—not smoke, but some cousin of smoke. Something more watery. Something I'd never encountered before.

"We have to go," I said. "But you're really okay, right?"

"There's nothing you can do anyway, unless you have an inhaler."

Jerome's look said, *You're really going out there? This is happening?*

"Be careful," he said. "Or something. I don't even know what to say. I don't think you should go out there. But I have no idea what's going on."

"I'm going out there. I have to. And you can't."

"I know my limits," he said. He gripped the handrail and lifted himself slowly. "You're sure?"

"Go," I said. "I'll see you. I promise."

I made sure he got down the stairs safely before turning to Stephen, who was still standing in the open doorway, his back to me.

"When I go out there," he said, not turning around, "when they see me . . . I don't know how they'll react. For some reason, this part is hard."

"It's going to be a surprise," I said. "But a good one. They're going to be happy."

"Will they?"

"Of course they will."

He turned around. I couldn't see his face in the shadow.

"You said I died, Rory. I shouldn't be here. People don't come back."

"We see people come back all the time," I said.

"No. We see people who didn't leave. There's a big difference. But . . ."

He dismissed the conversation and stepped over to where I stood, next to the stone.

"We're both going to have to do this," he said. "I can't manage on my own."

We bent at the same moment, catching the stone from underneath. The closest we got was when the tops of our heads almost brushed together. Together, separated by the width of the stone, we stepped into the dark.

The Serpentine is a large lake in the middle of Hyde Park, and from what I knew, it was usually a very busy place. We'd come out at an area where the rental boats were tied together and stored. Aside from a few ducks bobbing in the water, we were alone. The one thing we could clearly make out, though, just ahead of us, was a pillar of white, about two stories high and maybe a block wide. The top wasn't flat, but seemed to reach for the sky with foggy fingers, as if pointing in accusation. Unlike fog, which you can usually see through to some extent, this looked solid and white and impenetrable and unmoving. It was a structure made of cloud, as solid in appearance as marble.

"What's it made of?" I said.

"The dead," he said. "Merged energy. It looks like thousands."

I thought of the thing I'd seen in Highgate Cemetery, the formless, monstrous mass. That had been maybe a few people. This was probably thousands—many thousands.

"Over there," Stephen said, jerking his head in the direction of a few dark silhouettes a short distance off. I could just about make out the shapes of Boo, Callum, and Freddie. They saw us right away. I think it was good that there was some space between us for a minute as we made our way over. It gave them a few moments to process the sight. When we got there, we both set the stone gently on the ground. It was very cold. My breath was making huge plumes in front of me as we stood in our silent circle.

Of course, Freddie spoke first.

"You're Stephen," she said.

"Yes," Stephen replied.

Nothing from Boo and Callum. Boo put her hands over her mouth. Callum remained where he was, tense, unmoving, uncertain.

"It's me," Stephen said.

"Is this a trick?" Callum said.

"No."

"But we saw it happen," Callum said.

"Oh, bollocks." Boo ran for Stephen, grabbing him around the middle. It was part embrace, part examination. She clapped her hands on his back, then stepped back to run them down the outside of his arms. She reached up to the side of his neck, and it took me a moment to realize she was taking his pulse.

"It's true," she said, turning to Callum. "Callum, it's true."

She turned back to Stephen and regarded him with wonder.

"You're here," she said. "It didn't happen. Somehow it didn't happen."

There was a hush around that even the chaos couldn't penetrate. Freddie stepped forward and, taking a deep breath, extended her hand.

"Good to meet you at last," she said.

Stephen extended his hand as well, looking as dazed as Callum and Boo.

"Yes," he said. "Look, I know this is . . . I don't know what this is. I only know we have to take care of what's happening here first, and then we can talk about everything else. But I'm here. I'm not incredibly strong at the moment, and neither is Rory . . ."

Only then did anyone notice I was standing behind, with a large lump at my feet.

"Where's Thorpe?" Boo managed to ask.

"He'll be all right, but he's not coming. We need to move this—"

Freddie came over and pulled back the cloth to reveal the stone.

"The Oswulf Stone?" she asked.

"I take it you have a certain amount of information already," Stephen said.

"I know what stone this is, and we know where it came from. We know it was removed from under the pub and that this happened." She pointed to the great mass of white.

"There's a barrier all the way around," Callum said. "We were able to get clearance to come this far, but no one without a protective suit is allowed near that barrier. They don't think it's breathable. Do you know what it is?"

"It's where the barrier between life and death is blurred," Stephen said plainly. "It's something we haven't seen before. It's something we're not supposed to see. It's still something we need to deal with. We're the only ones who can. But I need to be honest with you—I don't know what happens to us if we get near it. I don't know how far away is safe. I don't know what happens inside. None of this is good. I only know we have a job to do, and it's up to you if you want to come along. I'm going. We'll have to go under. We need to get to the river. If you don't want to come, you should walk away now."

A long moment passed.

"You think we're going now?" Boo said. "After you've just appeared? With that thing happening? You're daft."

"Are you all in agreement?" Stephen asked.

I heard someone breathe in sharply. I think it was Freddie. Still, no one walked away. Callum laughed a little—a nervous, weird laugh.

"Good," Stephen said. "The Westbourne used to run through here, but it was dammed at the upper end of the park, at what's now Lancaster Gate. It should run east from there, close to the point of the breach. The river is carried in the sewers, so that's what we'll be going into. I don't know how far we'll make it, but we have to try to get to the north of the park. I think that's our best hope."

"The Ranelagh Sewer," Freddie said.

Freddie and Stephen really did share the same weird interests. Even though this was useful, I didn't like the feeling that rose in me when she said it. She seemed to have more connections to him than I did.

"We need to find an access point," Stephen said. "I need one of your phones."

"No point in that," Boo said, handing hers over. "Emergency services is swamped. Calls aren't getting through."

"I'm not calling anyone. I'm looking up urban exploring sites. They always know the access points to things like old sewers. There should be one quite close."

He scanned for a moment.

"Right," he said, looking up. "It looks to be a few meters away in that direction, toward Rotten Row. Look for a dip in the ground. That's a sign of where the river was. Someone will have to carry the stone."

Boo hoisted the stone with no trouble at all. We walked away from the fountain, toward the trees. There were lights in the fountain area, but where we were going was pure dark. Boo and Callum had flashlights, but they couldn't do much but illuminate a step or two ahead.

"Just try to feel your steps," Stephen said. "The ground may also get more marshy."

"Here!" Freddie called after a moment. "It goes down a bit here."

It was squishier underfoot.

"Look for a plate, probably metal," Stephen said.

This was located—a small, square opening made of thick metal. Boo and Callum pried it open, revealing a black hole and a metal ladder going down about ten feet.

"So we're going down here?" Callum said. "With nothing."

"Wait," I said. I pulled the bloody locket from my pocket and held it out. "Jane had these. Two termini."

"You're joking," Callum said, taking the locket and opening it. "What's on this? Is this blood?"

"I ran our previous ones through the phone and the batteries to give them a range," Stephen said, not answering that last question. "We don't have time to rig them now. If you want to use these, you'll need to make direct contact. And they're untested. I don't know how strong they are, or even if they're real or if they work."

"Only one way to find out." Callum closed the locket and put it in his pocket.

A harness was quickly rigged together by turning Callum's coat backward and putting the stone in the front, like a giant baby. Boo climbed down first to make sure the going was safe and shined a flashlight up to guide Callum down.

"Freddie, you should stay here," Stephen said. "I can't imagine you've been trained in the last few days, and we'll need someone topside in case . . ."

He didn't need to finish that statement.

"Keep your eyes open," Stephen continued. "If you're in trouble, get out. Don't try to do anything on your own. And, Rory . . ."

But I was already on the ground, the wet grass under my hands, lowering myself into the dark.

29

WE WERE UNDERGROUND, MOVING ALONG A PASSAGE much narrower and shorter than the one we had previously walked down. This tunnel was circular, so we were walking on a curved surface, in about a foot of water. The walls were made of dirty golden brick. Unlike the well-lit passage from before, in front of us was a circle of pure black. We did have flashlights, but they illuminated only a small section of the path in front of us. We could barely hear each other over the sound of water moving down the passage. This fact, and the darkness and lack of rails or anything to guide us—it reminded me that this was a *sewer* I'd lowered myself into.

One good thing—it didn't smell the way you'd expect a sewer to smell. This smelled like seawater and a little bit like soap. The bad things were many. The fact that we were walking through water was one of the biggest. It came up to just below my knee and rushed against us, making every single step a massive effort, pushing against the flow. I wasn't wearing a coat, and though the temperature in the tunnel was warmer than above, the cold water still ran up my legs, making me shake. There were some marks along the walls that indicated how high water levels might go. I was unhappy to see one that went well over my head.

Our progress was slow and steady, as we had very little sense of what was ahead aside from more round tunnel and dark. Stephen was leading the way, because presumably he was the only one who had the best idea which way led to the north entrance of the park, by Lancaster Gate. His walking was steadier than before, not quite as sideways and drunk, but he didn't move as quickly as he might have normally. Callum kept right with him, stone and all, and Boo stuck by my side. They were flanking us, of course, making sure we didn't pass out facedown in the water. Boo kept giving me sideways looks.

"I'm okay," I said.

She didn't respond.

We slogged on, pushing against the water, unable to see where we were really stepping. At some points, the water was a bit lower, but a few seconds later, there would be a dip and my knees would go under and I'd stumble, Boo catching me. The tunnel narrowed. Stephen, Callum, and Boo all had to bend a lot. I had a slight advantage, being a few inches shorter, but not much. The tunnel narrowed a bit, then narrowed some more. The bricks changed color—some red, some brown. It was then that the tunnel really seemed to close all around me— darkness behind and darkness ahead, water rushing everywhere. My breath caught and my heart started to pump wildly and I stopped and put my hands against the curve of the wall, which was covered with a dirty slime. I couldn't breathe. I couldn't even see. The walls of the tunnel were shrinking to a single point in my head—the point at which the universe winked out of existence. Boo was at my side telling me to take deep breaths, but there was no point. I closed my eyes for a moment and saw . . .

People on a floor. Bodies on a floor.

"Rory?"

I don't even know who said it, but I could tell all three of them were around me now. I had to pull myself together. Had to. I didn't know how—my brain was driving itself to Feartown. I had to get the wheel. Get the wheel, get the wheel. My brain. I was in control. I could decide not to let this happen, not to let my body go weak. I could breathe. Clearly, I was breathing. I had to be breathing. I was breathing quickly. That was the problem. Slow, slow, slow.

They were all talking to me, but I heard only water.

I could still see the mental images of bodies on a floor—an unknown floor. My brain was giving me a weird slideshow.

Someone's hand was on my back.

"It's just panic," Stephen said. He was close to my ear. "It passes. Panic can't hurt you."

Bodies. I saw a mental image of bodies. This terrible tangle of bodies on something white. A dark room flooded with candles. When I'd panicked before, back in the hospital, my mind conjured images of Uncle Bick and home. I had no idea what it was doing now. My brain was a collection of broken pieces rattling around in a useless skull.

"Listen to me," he said. "Try to focus on my voice. You can hear me, right? Nod if you can."

I nodded.

"We're both broken right now. Something's happened to us. But we can do this. We have to. I'm with you. Whatever is going on in your mind right now, I'm with you."

In my mind, I was now sitting at a restaurant table listening to Stephen talk. This was at least a calmer, more pleasant mental setting.

"I've been in the dark," Stephen said. "I know what this feels like. But, Rory, I can't do this without you right now. I'm not strong enough. I need you to take my hand. Take my hand."

He put his hand on mine, and I had a strong flash of reaching across a white table—Formica—flecked with silvery bits. I opened my eyes and I saw my hand was on the wall. I turned it awkwardly to embrace his. I commanded myself to focus in front of me, to take in the sight of the wall with its varicolored brick flickering in the beam of the flashlight, to take in the water. I would breathe, and I would go. The air down here was full of watery mist, but it was still air. I could breathe.

"Good," he said. "Deep breath. Deep one."

My hands slid down the wall.

"I can walk," I said.

Once more, we moved on, Stephen and I linked together, pushing through the water. The tunnel was still dark, but at least I could make out the walls again. If I was thinking—and I *was* thinking—I was in control. I would make it another step. And the one after. And again. I would make a little song in my head.

Step, step, step
It's just a little wet
Dark, dark, dark
Under Hyde Park

Not the greatest I'd ever done, but it kept my mind occupied, and I let it play on constant repeat. I gave all my attention to it. Stephen was gripping my hand tightly as we all bent to fit through the passage. We crouch-walked, the water now completely over my knees. Stephen and I had to separate, and we all used the sides of the tunnel for balance to get through. Stephen stumbled on something, and Boo and I helped pull him up. Callum had to do all of this while holding the stone at his front.

When it seemed we would almost not be able to get through, there was a sudden widening and we could stand. The water went back to shin height, and we were in a larger chamber with two passages in front of us.

"That looks like overflow to me," Stephen said, raising his arm with some difficulty and pointing to the slightly higher and narrower of the two openings. It also had a steady and fairly strong flow of water gushing out of it. "I think we want this one."

This one was wider and drier, so I approved of the choice. There was only a bit of water in this one. We could walk down it with little problem, side by side once again. There was even a lightness about this tunnel as we went on—a pinkness to the dark ahead. I think the calm and ease of this part of the passage unnerved me more than the tightness and dark before. The lightness was unnatural to the tunnel. The lightness didn't belong. Then, finally, we were at a wall of white, as solid as any brick. We stopped a few feet away from it. The surface was not completely smooth—it had wisps, like frosting, like clouds, little fingers that snapped out at us and were sucked back into the mass behind. It also was moving within itself, like a hurricane twisting along, wrapping around itself.

An old memory from the file cabinet in my mind drifted to the front of my consciousness—the town haunted house again, the smoke machine by the door that puffed chemical smoke into the night air. I had been to this place before. Not back then, not in Louisiana, but more recently. I knew what was in this mist. I understood it in a way I couldn't quite place. Stephen had turned to me and was regarding me.

Like he knew what I was thinking.

"The part we need to get to is through there," Stephen said.

"So we go in," Callum said. "To that."

There was a flatness to his tone that unnerved me. We were all afraid of the thing in front of us, and the reality of who we were fell on me all at once. None of us were fearless—we were four people too young to be doing this, under London. If Freddie went away, no one would even know we were here under the ground.

"We have this," Callum said, indicating the Oswulf Stone. "Doesn't it do something? Is it a terminus?"

"Not precisely," Stephen said, his voice edged with exhaustion. "As I understand it, there are charges. Our stones are a negative charge—they repel. This stone is neutral. It has a function, but not a charge."

"We still have the termini."

"They won't be enough. Not against this. I don't know what happens if we go in there."

Something was forming in the mist by Callum's shoulder. There was a parting in the air, a hole of dark here and there, and then a face was peeling itself between the bars—a face stretched in pain. Then there was another a moment later, and bit of a body pulling out of the fog, made of the fog. It was suddenly all hands and eyes. It was like the thing I had encountered in Highgate, except this thing was not wretched and dirty and scared—this was air incarnate, bending itself, filling the tunnel opening with faces and limbs and screaming mouths. The faces extended toward us, the necks growing long. Then arms. Then hands were reaching out. We backed up, but they extended for us with every step.

It was Boo who made the first blow. She pulled the locket from Callum's pocket and swung out her arm, the locket clasped in her fist. She made contact with part of a face. The result was a vibrating crack that shook us all and a blinding flash. The tiny bit of fog snapped back, and Boo fell to the ground. Then a new hand formed and reached again for Boo. A face floated in front of mine—a face that stretched and changed and turned into a hundred faces within a minute. Then a hundred more and a hundred more.

"I can do it," Stephen said after a moment. "Give me the stone."

"Bollocks you can do it," Callum replied. "You're not going in there. We just got you back."

"Callum, this is—"

"Shut it, Stephen. That's not happening again, you understand?" Callum put his arms around the burden at his chest. "I'm going. I have this stone, I have a terminus. Tell me what to do."

"I'm going as well," Boo said. "And Callum's right. Stephen, look at yourself."

I looked as well. We were all wet, bedraggled, uncertain. Stephen's face was an ashen color, and his eyes were shaded in exhaustion. He closed his eyes and the last reserves of whatever was keeping him upright appeared to be on the brink of leaving him.

The fog still danced in front of us. A parade of Londoners long gone appeared and disappeared in front of me, all looking me in the eye, all challenging me, but none venturing to touch me. A hand came out of the mist and formed a crooked finger, beckoning us on.

"And me," I said. "If any of us even has a chance . . ."

"Then we all go," Stephen said. "We stand a better chance together. Agreed?"

Stephen pushed himself off the wall. Callum reinforced his grip on the stone, and Boo pressed herself against him to take some of the weight. I saw a look go between them, acknowledging something. Stephen took my hand. I took the front.

As a group, we stepped forward. The hand vanished back into the sea of the fog, and faces appeared once again as we got closer. Then we were against it. When we used the terminus before, there was a smell of burning, like a flower—this smelled of all the flowers burning, great fields of them, smoke and life going up together into the air.

I saw nothing as we passed inside. But I could feel, and I could hear. There was still the warmth of the others around me and Stephen's hand in mine. In front of me, the fog parted inch by inch, giving me the tiniest view. I put my feet down one in front of the other, though I had no idea where the ground was. I heard Callum and Boo crying out, but their voices dissipated, and I started to forget why I had come . . .

The hand in mine. The feel of the others.

Faces swam around me like clouds of fish underwater, except these faces came and went and multiplied, and they all looked at me as if I *knew* something. And on some level, I felt like maybe I did know something. Something old, something so far back maybe it was from when I was born. I had a sudden remembrance of the nurse in the hall of the hospital, the one who told me to get out. I hadn't belonged there. The dead did not want me around. Lord Williamson had given up when he met me. The Resurrection Man had tried to burn me up. I was outnumbered here, but I still had strength. I had life.

I stepped again. I was almost pulling Stephen's hand, the hand that was not visible. The faces kept coming up in front of me, but I decided I could not be afraid of them.

"Move aside," I said.

To my amazement, the inch or so in front of my eyes turned into a sliver of dark that widened second by second. But I still couldn't see the others.

"Let us through," I said.

Stephen's grip on my hand was loosening.

"I said, *let us through.*"

And then, there were four of us, alone in a sea of white. Boo was weeping, and Callum had fallen against my back. I had no idea how any of this had happened, but the fog was now against the wall, and there was a clear path ahead of us.

I turned and found Stephen clutching my hand firmly again. He was half draped over Boo.

"What . . ." Boo looked up and saw Stephen slumped against her. "Why am I crying? What happened?"

Callum too was pulling himself back up. The wall of fog was encircling us, leaving only this small space for us to stand.

"There," Stephen said. "Ahead of you."

A few feet in front of me, the tunnel was blocked by a half wall topped with metal bars, like an old-time jail cell. This marked off some other channel we couldn't access, one that went perpendicular to where we were. I could hear water flowing. There were some loose pipes on the floor by the wall, but that was it. Nothing to get us through.

"I believe that's the river," Stephen said. "It's diverted at this juncture."

"We need to get the stone up there?" Callum asked, looking at the bars. They were about a hand's width apart—much too narrow for the stone.

We had come this far, through whatever it was we'd just walked through, only to be defeated by a few metal bars. Stephen shook his head.

"They diverted the river," he said. "We can do the same."

He grabbed the bars and pulled himself up to look through the opening.

"Give me a pipe," he said.

Boo handed him one, which he shoved between the bars. He dropped down, falling almost to his knees. He would have gone down completely if Boo hadn't caught him. Stephen moved the pipe around a bit until a trickle of water started to come out of the end on our side.

"The stone!" he said to Callum. "Put it there."

Callum put the stone down under the flow. We watched the stone become damp, water gently pooling on and around it.

It was nothing much to look at, but the fog around us began to pull in on itself, sucking back into a more concentrated form. The path behind us was clear, but the force of its movement was like being in a wind tunnel. The four of us struggled against the pulling force behind us, which was now wailing and screaming through the tunnel. Then there was one final blast, which sent us all pitching forward into the filthy water.

And then the fog was gone.

30

IT WAS ONE OF THOSE JUMBLED DREAMS—ONE WHERE THE scenes switch abruptly, like pieces of a movie cut together all wrong. Stephen was there sometimes, and sometimes he wasn't. Sid and Sadie were there, and then I saw Jane again, right before the knife went into her neck. Then I was in a tunnel, somewhere dark, and the Ripper—Newman—he was behind me, following me, telling me that all of these people I thought I knew were lying to me and that he was the only one who wasn't. Then he stabbed me again, but this time, I didn't collapse, and he didn't vanish. I staggered after him, telling him off, telling him he didn't know my friends. And he laughed at me. Then there was a fire, and I was gasping in the smoke.

I woke up, and there was suddenly a bottle of water within my reach. I grabbed it and guzzled about half the contents in one go, squeezing it and waking myself up with the earsplitting crinkle of the plastic. I was on a sofa, and everyone was sitting around me. Boo sat on the floor next to me—she had given me the water. Thorpe was in the chair across, looking up from his computer. Freddie was sitting in the middle of the paperwork we had been sorting. Callum was setting down a few shopping bags on the floor.

Boo got up on her knees to face me.

"Morning. How do you feel?"

"Okay. Just thirsty. Really thirsty. What time is it?"

"It's tomorrow. You've been asleep for almost twenty-four hours."

"I have?"

I sat up. My head was cottony, but in the way you'd expect after sleeping for an entire day. I was still in my clothes. I didn't have to sniff myself to know I smelled. I hadn't showered for days.

"We have some new clothes for you," Boo said. "And soap, a brush, things like that. We thought you might need that first."

"Where's Stephen?"

"He's upstairs," Thorpe said. "Asleep."

"Asleep?"

"He's fine."

"And the doctor?"

Thorpe nodded.

"We're all fine, Rory. Why don't you get yourself together? Callum brought some food. You need to eat something. Then we'll all talk."

I took the shopping bags Boo handed me and went upstairs. As soon as I was gone, I could hear the others talking in low voices. I moved quietly to the bedroom and pushed open the door—softly, softly . . .

I'd just done this. My life was looping around on me.

Stephen was there, stretched out on his side, his back facing me. The blankets were twisted around him and half falling off the bed. I couldn't see his face, just the back of his hair against the pillow. His glasses were the only object on the bedside table. What I wanted to do was climb into the bed with him and hold him tight. What I actually did was get close enough that I could see his chest rise and fall at least three times before I backed out of the room and gently shut the door.

There was one hall window, and it revealed a pinkish sky, much lighter than normal. I went to the bathroom, where the light was harsh and brought some realities into sharp focus. The person I saw in the mirror was a wreck. My chopped-up hair was in all directions. My eyes were bloodshot. When I went to get undressed, I found that there was some brown, dried blood under my fingernails and encrusted on the nails themselves. I rubbed this off under the running water, then I took a shower that never got very hot and tried to wash everything away. I washed my stiff, short hair, which smelled like cat food when I got it wet. When I brushed it after the shower, it made scraping noises against the brush. I would need to cut more of it off—not just a bob. Cut it short. Let this terrible dye job grow out.

Boo had clearly been doing the shopping again, and this time, the clothes had more of her personality—a black sweater with plasticky-leather bits on the shoulders, slightly better-fitting jeans, some red flats. There was even a little bag of makeup in there, which I didn't use. It was nice that she'd thought of me.

I returned downstairs, where a small feast of prepared convenience foods was spread out on the coffee table. Thorpe was right—I needed to eat. I worked my way through two ham and pickle sandwiches, a banana, some kind of date and nut cookie, a bag of cheddar and onion crisps, and a piece of ginger cake. I washed it all down with two bottles of apple and elderflower drink and a Coke.

"It's going to snow tonight," Freddie said. The remark met no reply—it just floated into the room, and we all looked at the window for a second.

"I've never been in snow," I said. "We don't get it where I live."

As I said it, I had some memory of snow, but I couldn't place it. We didn't get snow at home, so where had I been? Somewhere. It would come to me.

"Are people okay?" I said. "The people in the fog?"

"Only a few people were harmed, mostly by debris and glass," Thorpe said. "What's more disturbing is that they have no recollection of what happened to them. The news is saying it was a nerve agent."

There was a creak on the floorboards upstairs. Then footsteps, the sound of someone walking toward the bathroom. Water running.

"He's awake," Boo said.

Callum could sit no longer and hopped out of his seat, pacing by the foot of the stairs. Thorpe closed his computer and rested his head on his chin and stared at the floor, deep in thought. Freddie looked like she wanted to say something but had no idea what, so she tidied the piles of paperwork around her.

"Maybe we can be normal," I said.

Sometimes I say stupid things.

Stephen came down about fifteen minutes later. He had

changed his clothes as well, but was wearing his own—a familiar black sweater and pair of jeans, and a pair of sneakers. Someone must have gone back to the flat and gotten more of his things. He was unshaven, and there was a surprising amount of dark stubble along his chin, which stirred something in me. He came into the room quietly and tucked his hands into his pockets. He looked at the spread on the coffee table.

"May I?" he asked. "I'm famished."

We watched him take two egg and cress sandwiches and sit on the arm of the sofa to eat them. Some things are so big, you can't even react to them. You almost have to act like they never even happened, because they don't fit in any kind of reality you know.

So we watched Stephen eat, and Stephen watched us watching him eat.

"Someone should probably say something," he finally said, "because I'm going to be eating for a few more minutes."

"How do you feel?" Callum said. "You seem all right. Do you feel all right?"

He chewed for a moment and nodded before answering. "I feel fine. Which is fairly remarkable, considering."

"Oh, God," Boo said. She went right for him and grabbed him, holding him in a long, somewhat awkward crouching hug. He held his sandwich at arm's length to keep egg salad off of her and looked at the opposite wall a bit bashfully.

"All right," Boo said. "Callum, now you. Come on."

Callum did the same, but a bit shorter.

"Since we're all doing it!" Freddie gave him a quick embrace. Thorpe settled on a nod.

I was too nervous to move. I had no idea what I'd do. So I

smiled a weird, sloppy smile and shoved another cookie in my mouth.

"Do you have any recollection of what happened to you?" Thorpe asked.

"Very little. I remember the car accident, and I remember going to the flat and going to sleep in the chair. I think Rory might know more."

"Not a lot," I said. "They had me do some kind of ceremony, and I drank something, but I don't remember anything after that."

"Nothing?" he said.

"Nope."

He watched me curiously for a moment.

"It's possible we'll never really know the mechanics of it," he said. "But why was I at Marigold's house?"

"She got to the hospital morgue before I did," Thorpe said. "She was there to get your body, and what she found was that you hadn't exactly died. You were removed, and all records of your being there were wiped clean. I did meet a very agitated pathologist who had been forced to sign the Official Secrets Act."

"You're an Official Secret," Boo said to Stephen.

"Congratulations," I said, trying the smile again, and again it came out super weird. No smiling. Smiling not working right now.

"So who is Marigold?" I asked.

"We got this explanation when you were out cold," Boo said. "She works with Thorpe."

"To a limited extent," Thorpe said. "She's a medical officer who works on very sensitive matters. She was instrumental in initial recruitment and in trying to determine what it is about you that makes you different."

"So she wanted to do my autopsy," Stephen said.

"I believe that was her hope."

"Glad she checked, then." He reached for a bag of chips. "That could have been awkward."

This tiny joke lightened the mood in the room, and Callum broke into a smile.

"Mate . . ." he said. "Mate."

"We're all here," Boo said. "We survived. We're back."

I felt a moment dawning, a moment when we were all taking this in—that we were together and happy. This is when Freddie, who had clearly been looking for a chance to chime in, accidentally brought us back to the matter at hand.

"But one thing," she said. "You had this information about the Oswulf Stone and writing in cipher code. How did you know so much, and why were you keeping it secret? Not that . . ."

Stephen shrugged. "I was looking at the same sites and sources you were. I knew we had stones that could dispel the energy of the dead, and they seemed to match the description of the Eye of Isis. I looked into the Oswulf Stone, and there did seem to be evidence indicating that it existed and it might have some actual power. I wrote the notes in code because I like cryptology and I was bored of the crossword I'd been working on. I went to Chanceford, as I'm assuming you did. I assume you broke the code. It wasn't very complex, I'm afraid."

"But this means the Shadow Cabinet—" Freddie said.

"Is ridiculous," Stephen replied. "You know as well as I do that it's a conspiracy theory."

"But they're right about these two stones," she said.

"A lot of these fantasies are based on some actual fact," Stephen said. "Given the amount of research these people do, someone would have turned up something on the other stones. No one ever has."

"So you don't think they exist?"

"I think it's highly unlikely. I chased up a few leads, but they were all nutters. There's no cabal protecting magic stones in London. But we do have two new termini."

Callum smiled broadly at that.

"Oh, it's a sweet day," Callum said. "We are back. For reals. Back."

"So what happens next?" I said. "What about Charlotte? How did she turn like that? And where is she?"

"Stockholm syndrome, possibly," Freddie said. "It happens quicker than you might think. The original Stockholm case only took a few days. But more likely she was conditioned over time. You said Jane used drugs. Drugs, isolation . . . and they gave her the sight."

"We don't know where they went," Thorpe said. "We don't have identification on most of the people in the group. We couldn't find Charlotte on CCTV. She's gone, but this time of her own accord. As are Sid and Sadie."

"Listen to you lot," Callum said, coming to the middle of the room. "We should celebrate better than this. We need to. Come on. Come *on*."

Thorpe considered for a moment.

"I expect a drink or two isn't out of order," he said. "There's a pub at the end of the road. We won't be using this house anymore, so I think we can go. Not for long. But one round."

As we went out, the first flakes started to fall. They were

much bigger than I expected, and faster. I reached out and grabbed one, only to watch it vanish in my hand the second it landed.

"That's disappointing," I said. "I thought it would last longer than that."

We walked slowly, and Stephen and I fell to the back of the group. He tucked his hands deep into his coat pockets. This had been restored, as had his scarf.

"What do you remember?" he asked me. "About the last day? About what happened to you?"

"Not much," I said. "Like I said, I drank something, then I woke up."

"Do you know how long you were unconscious?"

"No."

"So you don't remember anything?" he asked again.

"About which part? You mean Sid and Sadie, and Jane?"

I heard him sigh quietly. I looked up, but he was keeping his gaze ahead, on the others.

"What are they?" I asked. "Sid and Sadie."

"Something new," he said. "Or something very old. I don't know. But they worry me. Very much. And I think . . ."

He stopped and pushed his hands deeper into his pockets.

"You think what?" I said.

Stephen turned to me, finally. His chest rose and fell quickly, and I think he was holding himself in place, forcing his hands down. He examined my face, leaning in, just a bit. He was trying to read me. He was close enough to kiss, if I could get to my toes in time. If I could find the courage. But something told me I shouldn't . . . something in the way he was examining me. Something in his face was both sad and satisfied.

So I looked up, past him, as if that was what I meant to do all along. I stared into the falling snow. It was weird—looking up into snow made me feel like I was falling.

"You've *never* been in snow?" he asked.

"I don't know," I said, keeping my head tipped up. "Maybe? When I was little?"

"You two!" Callum said, turning around. "Keep up. Snogging later. Drinks now."

As I moved my gaze back down, I caught Stephen looking into my face again.

"We should . . . keep up. I suppose," he said. "No telling what Callum's likely to do. We do deserve one night off, you would think."

He reached out and touched my arm, then clasped it, then, after an agonizing moment of hesitation, put his hand back in his pocket again.

31

THERE WAS ONE MORE PIECE OF BUSINESS TO TAKE CARE OF, and we did it the next morning. Thorpe took me. I picked the place, and the place I picked was the Wexford Library. He balked at this at first, but I insisted. It was important. There was someone there I needed. I wished I could have gone with Stephen, but he was being worked up by Marigold—a full test, hooked up to machines, blood taken, the works. Once you die and come back, it makes people ask questions.

"You're sure about this?" Thorpe said.

"I promised. And Jerome's already seen so much."

"There are decisions to be made after this—serious ones."

"As opposed to all these casual decisions I've been making," I said.

"Fair point. But now it's time to talk next steps. Next steps involve making things more official. New identities. Training. And perhaps most important, what we tell your family."

"Let's talk about that later," I said. "I have to do this now."

"One hour," Thorpe said.

He handed me a plastic card with a magnetized strip and a key. The card had been coded to override the external locks. The key was a copy of our housemistress Claudia's skeleton key that could open any room in Hawthorne. I pocketed the two of these and got out of the car.

Boo was already there, sitting on a bench in front of the building, keeping watch. She ate an apple and pretended to talk on the phone. The expensive new CCTV system was down for an hour of "maintenance," so there would be no record of my coming or going. Claudia was known to have gone off to Truro to see her family for the holiday. All the other staff members were gone—teachers, librarians, dining hall, administration. Just for safety, the teachers had been told all the offices were shut for heating repairs, in case they might have wanted to cut short their holidays to do any work. The only person who would be on the grounds was the security person, and he had also been dispatched through a "glitch" in the schedule.

A tiny hole had been opened for me to come see my old life. But there were still rules: scarf over face, gloves on hands, all of that.

I walked quickly, as I'd been instructed, to the library. I went down the recessed stairwell to the basement service entrance—the very entrance that had caused so much trouble earlier. Today, there would be no problems. When I pressed the card against the reader, the door clicked open readily. The library basement was unfamiliar to me. It was full of boxes placed to ensure maximum shin-banging as you made your way to the steps.

These were uncomfortably dark but, in the end, just steps. You go up until there's nothing to take you any farther. I exited in the gloom of the second floor, by the history section. It took me a moment to get my bearings and wend my way around. I gave myself a bit of a fright by triggering the stack lights along the way. History, foreign languages, literature . . .

Alistair was there, as Alistair was always there. Hair ever spiked. Jeans ever slouched. Doc Martens ever . . . Martening. He was reading. Alistair was always reading. He'd read every book in the literature section.

"Hey, stranger," I said.

As was typical with Alistair, he took a good, long moment, finishing the page or paragraph or poem before looking up.

"Merry Christmas."

"Is it?" he asked.

"Close enough."

"Well, then."

As usual, Alistair was full of conversation.

"Things have been weird," I said, coming a little closer. "I can't really explain it, and I don't have a lot of time. But I wanted to tell you to be . . . careful, I guess."

"Careful about what?"

"If you need help, or if something weird happens, grab someone's phone and text this number . . ." I pulled a slip of paper from my pocket and set it on a nearby shelf. "You know what texting is, right?"

"I'm not an idiot."

"Do you think you could do that, though? Could you press the buttons and send a text?"

"I could do it."

"Okay. This number?" I tapped the paper with my gloved finger. "It belongs to a spare cell phone that Boo carries. Just send the word *help,* or *come here,* or whatever. If you need to."

"Why would I need help?"

"Keep the number, okay?" I said.

He nodded and returned to his book, and I turned to go back the way I had come.

"I'm glad you're okay," he called after me. "Alive, I mean. It's better for you that way."

"Thanks," I said.

But he was already ignoring me again.

I emerged on the blind side of the library and turned back onto the Wexford square. It was a quick thirty-pace walk to the same recessed entrance to Hawthorne. All of these buildings had been built along the same model, back when they were workhouses. This basement was largely disused as well, full of broken furniture and crates of old books. Near the steps, things got tidier. There were four laundry machines and several storage cabinets. I climbed up and went into the lobby.

The only reason I was being permitted to go inside of Hawthorne was that I had told Thorpe there was another ghost in there I needed to speak to. There wasn't, of course. Not a real one. A ghost of my life, possibly.

The building was frigid. This was no surprise. It had never been toasty warm, except for a few freak surges. I remembered how I used to sit right up against the flat radiators, trying to suck out every precious drop of heat, store it in my bones. I'd had many conversations that way. The handful of times I'd actually attempted homework, I often did it sitting on the floor, glued to the heater.

Now, with no one here but Claudia, all the main heating had been shut off, and the building was like a cold storage unit. You could easily have stored cheese anywhere. I didn't really feel the cold today. Maybe that's how English people dealt with it—they noticed it, pulled their sweaters down over their hands, and moved on. I did the same.

The only thing illuminating the hallways was a bit of milky light coming from the window at the end. They'd made a shrine of Charlotte's door. Hers was a single room, and from top to bottom, the door was covered in little notes and paper flowers. I plucked off one that said WELCOME HOME! I didn't recognize the handwriting, but whoever it was was deeply optimistic.

I'd never gotten the sense that Charlotte was well loved. She wasn't a warm person, but she was, now that I thought about it, a respected one. She was someone who got the job done. I suspected a lot of the first-years had left the notes. Charlotte was *their* head girl. *Their* prefect. *Their* leader with the big red head.

I put the note back where I found it and continued down the hall.

The door to my old room was not a shrine. Jazza still lived here. The message board on the door was full of scrawled notes letting Jazza know that they were leaving, wishing her a happy holiday. There were a few still-sealed Christmas cards shoved behind the board.

I used the skeleton key and opened up the room. The emptiness of the place made everything very loud. My empty furniture and stripped bed. They were waiting for me on Jazza's side. Jerome was prepared, at least to some extent. But Jaz gasped. She almost fell from the bed.

"Easy," Jerome said, steading her.

"Hey," I said.

She had righted herself and got up to stand. She walked over to me, very carefully, very deliberately. I thought she was coming in to hug me, but instead she landed her fist into my shoulder—not hard enough to hurt me, but hard enough to make a point.

"Where were you?" she said, choking a bit. "Where were you? All this time?"

She pulled back her hand, looking ashamed, and hugged me.

"I wanted to get in touch," I said, over her shoulder. "I promise."

I looked at Jerome across the room. He had folded his arms over his chest, but there was an acceptance in his face. I had to explain it all—the Ripper, the ghosts. I was not to talk about the squad, but simply to say I was under official protection. I was about to destroy the fabric of their reality, and I didn't want to do it. This may have been how Stephen felt when this happened to me, except they couldn't see what I saw. Jerome had seen the fog and the stone and the murder. He was already in deep.

"We need to talk," I said, shutting the door. "Sit down . . ."

DECEMBER 21
HARDWELL'S BOOKSTORE, SOHO

THE DAY WAS FREEZING COLD—THE SHOP'S INEFFECTUAL heaters couldn't keep up. Cressida peered out of the hatch in the shelves that served as the counter. It was too cold to read, so she pulled the sleeves of one of her two jumpers down over her hands as impromptu mittens. The quiet of the shop was too much for some. People were used to more ambient noise, more music, people talking on mobiles. Hardwell's owned its quiet, and Cressida had grown accustomed to it. She could sit and look out at the shelves and be content. Good magic practice required concentration and appreciation of silence.

The tiny tinkle of the bell announced the arrival of visitors. Cressida leaned her head out far enough to see two tall figures enter. Despite the deep freeze outside, they wore no coats. The figures were close to identical. There was a man, young and shaggily blond, dressed in a light, silvery suit with a wide lapel. There was a woman who stepped in after him, her hair just a finger longer. She wore a long, deep green dress with a pattern of climbing red flowers. Neither outfit was enough protection in this weather, but they showed no signs of being cold.

The man approached the opening and unrolled a long smile. His companion, who had to be related—the resemblance was too strong—stood behind, casually running a finger down the spine of a book. He wore a little eye makeup, and she wore none at all.

"Happy Yule," he said.

"Happy Yule," Cressida replied.

"Nice to see some things haven't changed." He leaned an elbow on the counter and had a look around. "One fixed point in a strange new world."

Cressida had no idea what this meant, but working in a shop like this, you got used to people saying strange things.

"Is Clover here?" the woman asked. Her voice was gentle and quite high.

"In the back, sorting books."

"Dearie me, working on a holiday?" The man shook his head, and his grin became more rakish. "We'll have a word with him. We're old friends. Lovely hat, by the way."

He pointed at Cressida's woolen hat with the tiny metal disks she had so carefully knitted into the weave. The woman was already passing through down the aisle toward the back door. Her feet were obscured by her long dress, and her gait was so smooth she almost seemed to float. The man gave Cressida a mock salute before following along. In a moment, they had passed through the curtain that hid the door to the back, and Cressida continued her silent watch over the cold and silent cash register, wondering to herself why it was that Clover attracted so many freaks and outsiders.

In the back of the shop, Clover was alone, earbuds in, making himself a cup of tea. He didn't even notice the door open, though the room was small.

"Well, well," the strange man said, "and blessed be."

When Clover didn't turn, the woman slipped into the room and tapped him on the shoulder. He turned around and regarded the strangers. His jaw dropped open, and he pulled the buds from his ears with one jerk. A trickle of chanting music spilled out and dripped on to the floor.

"A hello would be appropriate," the man said. "Or hi, if you must."

Clover's mouth moved, but no sound came out.

"A wave. A wink. We'll take anything, really . . ."

"Oh, Sid." The woman walked up to Clover and draped her arm over his shoulders. "We've given him a fright."

"We can be a lot to take in at once," Sid said, dropping into a beaten-up chair and throwing his legs onto a wobbly tea table. "It's a fair cop. Drink it in, fair Clover. Absorb the sight."

Clover became unsteady, and the woman helped him into a chair. She pulled his phone from his pocket and examined the device for a moment. She pulled up the earbuds and tucked one into her ear for a moment, then smiled with pleasure.

"It plays music, Sid."

"Does it? Honestly, everything I've seen so far has been fab. I think we came back at the right time."

Sadie handed the phone back to Clover, who accepted it and shut the music off with shaking hands.

"He's wobbling, bless him," she said. "I'll get him his tea."

"You are a ministering angel, Sadie."

Sadie completed the tea making, spooning out the tea bag and adding the sugar and milk.

"A nice sweet tea," she said, setting it down in front of Clover. "Just what you need. Drink it."

Clover reached for it with a shaking hand while Sadie leaned by his side. He managed two large sips, and she took the cup from him and set it back down.

"Sadie?" he said, in a small voice. "Sid?"

"Present," Sid said.

"And accounted for," Sadie added, standing up and brushing her fingers gently through the remains of Clover's thinning hair.

"I like the beard," Sid said, pointing. "It's very Gandalf. What do you think, Sadie?"

"It's lovely," Sadie said, extending her arm to reach for the beard. She ran her hand down it like it was a delicate silk rope.

"You're . . ." Clover trembled a bit more and sipped some more tea. "You're . . ."

"It might save us some time if we skipped over that part," Sid said. "Let's just say 'here.' That covers the matter. And now that we are, who do you think we wanted to see first?"

"Out of everyone," Sadie said, leaning into the side of the chair and half draping herself over Clover.

"Everyone," Sid said. "At least, of the people who are still alive. We're still sorting that one out. Over forty years . . . all these people dropping dead. I don't want to take it personally, but it *feels* sort of personal. Whatever the case, you have, so politely, remained alive!"

"We're very happy," Sadie said.

"We're delighted. So we came right around."

Clover began to weep silently.

"Oh, Sid," she said, stroking Clover's head some more. "I think we've upset him."

"Should we have rung first?"

"Possibly. Turning up like this may be a bit much to take in."

"You're right, Sadie. You're right." Sid leaned back and put up his hands in admission. "A faux pas on our part."

"I never . . ." Clover staggered on his own words. "I didn't . . ."

"Didn't what?" Sadie's voice was a gentle coo.

"I didn't think I'd see you again," Clover said, breaking into a heaving cry.

"I wonder if they're all going to do this?" Sid asked his sister. "We seem to have this effect."

They let Clover work this out for a moment. When he was finished, he dried his face and stood.

"I never knew if it would happen," he said, "but I was ready. I prepared. I thought—I thought the time might have come. There was that event at Marble Arch, and some kids came asking about you and Jane, and they had a pig with them."

"We met them," Sid said. "A wonderful bunch."

"But did you do what we needed you to?" Sadie said.

"I did. I did, Sadie. I have them. I brought them here in case . . . in case you came. And you came. I thought Jane would say, but I haven't been able to reach her. But I was ready."

"Oh, Clover!"

"One thing I'll say about us, Sadie," Sid said, "is that we chose well. Our family is the best family."

"It's true," Sadie said.

Clover looked down and smiled with pleasure.

"I never gave up hope," he said. "Even though it was so long. You surprised me. I'm so glad to see you. I'm still . . ." He rubbed his eyes for a moment. "I'm taking it in. Forgive me."

"There's nothing to forgive," Sadie said.

"I keep them up front, behind the counter. I'll go and get them."

"We'll come," Sadie said.

"The girl doesn't know. She'll—"

"It's quite all right," Sid said.

The three passed back into the main room of the shop, where Cressida was still staring blankly down the empty aisles. Clover hurried to the counter hatch, ushering her aside and ducking under to get to the back. There was a moment of scrabbling before he popped back under—no mean feat for such a tall man—carrying a red vinyl zippered bag with large handles.

"We should go back and . . ."

But Sadie had already taken the bag from his hands and unzipped it.

"Any joy?" Sid said.

"Boundless," she replied. "Clover, you've a wonder."

"An absolute star!" Sid added.

"It took a few years," Clover said, putting his head down modestly. "I had to find them, find the money. Some of them were . . . we should maybe talk in the back."

"No need," Sid said. "We have no secrets."

Cressida watched all this in silent confusion. She was completely unprepared when Sid reached over and grabbed her by the top of the head, turning it once with a quick flick, like he was twisting open a bottle. Cressida made no noise except for a slight gurgle, then she fell like a stone against the counter. Her head bounced once, and then she dropped behind the counter, vanishing from sight.

Clover jerked in reaction to this. Before he could speak, Sadie took him lightly by the arm and threw him the length of the bookstore aisle. He hit the back wall with such force that the door cracked and the curtains half fell. She glided down the aisle to examine him while Sid had a look inside of the bag.

"He's done extremely well," he said. "I thought we might need more time to get the rest, but he appears to have gotten them all."

Sadie bent over Clover and finished him in much the same way that Sid had done with Cressida. She came back down the aisle slowly, stopping for a moment to examine the spine of a book before plucking it from the shelf.

"Good read?" Sid asked.

"It looks like a new book."

"I think they're mostly new books. To us, anyway."

Sadie nodded in consideration of this fact.

"This shop was always so naff," Sid said, looking around. "Terrible selection."

"Very good staff, though," Sadie said.

"Absolutely. You could never fault the staff. It's unfortunate, really. Our children grew up. They grew old. They learned a little too much."

"This is the problem with growing old," Sadie said.

"I'm more glad than ever that we avoided it. But Clover's hard work will not be in vain. This contains everything we need. We won't have to wait to start the party."

"I think we've waited long enough as it is," Sadie said, stretching out her arms. "It's time to rise. Time for everyone to rise. Oh, Sid. It's actually going to happen. It's all happening."

"It's barely started, dear sister. The fun is yet to come." Sid shouldered the bag. "Shall we? It's freezing in here, and I'm dying for a drink."

The two of them left the shop, closing the door behind them politely and quietly. Once outside, they got into a buttery yellow Jaguar parked out front and drove off into the declining day.

ACKNOWLEDGMENTS

I HAVE MANY THANKS TO DISTRIBUTE—FAR MORE THAN ARE LISTED HERE. But here goes.

Thanks to:

My agent, Kate Schafer Testerman, a woman who can do more or less anything and without whom nothing is possible.

My editor, Jennifer Besser, who has been the champion of the Shades gang from the start.

Robin Wasserman, Holly Black, Sarah Rees Brennan, and Cassie Claire, for their constant support and brilliant advice. I am so lucky to know you all.

Libba Bray and Barry Goldblatt, who sheltered us when a hurricane hit in the middle of writing this book.

Felicity Disco (Kate Welsh), my assistant, who has made sure I do not catch on fire.

Kiersten White, for her motivational technique.

Medical advisers Elka Cloake, MD, and Marianne Hamel, MD, as well as Mary Johnson, RN (or, as she is better known to me, my mom).

Everyone at Penguin who has provided so much support: Elyse Marshall, Lisa Kelly, Anna Jarzab, and everyone else on Hudson Street.

The folks at Hot Key Books, who publish my work in the UK: Sara O'Connor, Sarah Odedina, Sanne Vliegenthart, Rosi Crawley, and everyone else at Hot Key HQ.

My Leaky/Geeky family, presided by Melissa Anelli and Stephanie Dornhelm (but I am thanking you all—there are dozens of us. Possibly hundreds?).

Night Vale creators Joseph Fink and Jeffrey Cranor, for the internship at their radio station.

Hamish Young, for everything.

And to my readers, to the booksellers and librarians and teachers. I don't get to do this without you. Thank you from the bottom of my heart.